UNCLE TOM'S CABIN

SELECTIONS

UNCLE TOM'S CABIN

SELECTIONS

Harriet Beecher Stowe

a *Broadview Anthology of American Literature* edition

General Editors, *The Broadview Anthology of American Literature*:

Derrick R. Spires, Cornell University
Rachel Greenwald Smith, Saint Louis University
Christina Roberts, Seattle University
Joseph Rezek, Boston University
Justine S. Murison, University of Illinois, Urbana-Champaign
Laura L. Mielke, University of Kansas
Christopher Looby, University of California, Los Angeles
Rodrigo Lazo, University of California, Irvine
Alisha Knight, Washington College
Hsuan L. Hsu, University of California, Davis
Michael Everton, Simon Fraser University
Christine Bold, University of Guelph

broadview press

BROADVIEW PRESS – www.broadviewpress.com
Peterborough, Ontario, Canada

Founded in 1985, Broadview Press remains a wholly independent publishing house. Broadview's focus is on academic publishing: our titles are accessible to university and college students as well as scholars and general readers. With over 800 titles in print, Broadview has become a leading international publisher in the humanities, with world-wide distribution. Broadview is committed to environmentally responsible publishing and fair business practices.

© 2023 Broadview Press

Library and Archives Canada Cataloguing in Publication

Title: Uncle Tom's cabin : selections / Harriet Beecher Stowe.
Other titles: Uncle Tom's cabin. Selections (Broadview Press)
Names: Stowe, Harriet Beecher, 1811-1896, author.
Description: Series statement: A Broadview anthology of American literature edition. | Includes
   bibliographical references.
Identifiers: Canadiana (print) 20230141595 | Canadiana (ebook) 20230141668 | ISBN
   9781554816309 (softcover) | ISBN 9781770488939 (PDF) | ISBN 9781460408254 (EPUB)
Subjects: LCSH: Stowe, Harriet Beecher, 1811-1896—Criticism and interpretation. | LCSH:
   American fiction—19th century—History and criticism. | LCGFT: Fiction.
Classification: LCC PS2954 .U5 2023 | DDC 813/.3—dc23

Broadview Press handles its own distribution in North America:
PO Box 1243, Peterborough, Ontario K9J 7H5, Canada
555 Riverwalk Parkway, Tonawanda, NY 14150, USA
Tel: (705) 743-8990; Fax: (705) 743-8353
email: customerservice@broadviewpress.com

For all territories outside of North America, distribution is handled by Eurospan Group.

Broadview Press acknowledges the financial
support of the Government of Canada
for our publishing activities.

Developmental Editor: Helena Snopek
Cover Designer: Lisa Brawn
Typesetter: Alexandria Stuart

PRINTED IN CANADA

Contents

Introduction

Harriet Beecher Stowe
1811 – 1896

Harriet Beecher Stowe's first novel, *Uncle Tom's Cabin* (1852), may well have excited more controversy than any other work of fiction in American history. In the 1850s it was welcomed by abolitionists for the impetus it gave to their movement—and met with furious indignation by white Southerners. Its characters and dramatic scenes were absorbed into the nation's consciousness, and the novel spawned—largely without Stowe's approval—a veritable industry of crude "Tom shows" whose characters hardened into racist cultural artefacts, at once wildly popular and routinely mocked. By the mid-twentieth century, *Uncle Tom's Cabin* was widely dismissed as irrelevant politically, a failure artistically, and—in what would have struck readers of the 1850s as an extraordinary irony—pervasively racist in its portrayal of black people. In our own century, its estimation as literature and as a political work engaged with the most serious political and moral questions of its era has continued to fluctuate wildly, although no one can deny its significance or popularity.

Harriet Beecher was born in Litchfield, Connecticut in 1811, the seventh child of Lyman Beecher, a Congregational minister, and Roxana Foote Beecher. Roxana died in 1816; her death (and subsequent idolization in the family's collective memory) had a lasting psychological impact upon Stowe. Lyman (who promptly remarried, and had four more children) was a strong shaping force in her life in large part through his passionate Calvinist religious convictions.

Stowe attended the Litchfield Female Academy and later her elder sister Catharine's Hartford Female Seminary, an influential and progressive institution that, in addition to teaching the "domestic arts," offered a level of academic instruction rarely available to young women in the early nineteenth century. Stowe proved an enthusiastic student with a particular talent for writing, especially on moral, philosophical, and religious themes. By 1827 her formal education was considered complete and she took on a teaching position at the Seminary, where she remained for five more years.

In 1832 the Beecher family moved to Cincinnati, Ohio, a rapidly growing city then considered the westernmost outpost of "civilized" America. The following year Harriet and Catharine together wrote and published a geography textbook, *Primary Geography for Children*, which sold well; they also helped form the Semi-Colon Club, an informal literary association where Stowe received encouragement to start writing sketches (some of which were published in the local *Western Monthly Magazine*). In 1836 she met and married Calvin Stowe, a teacher at the Lane Seminary where her father taught; they had their first children, twin daughters, later that year. The couple had a companionate, intellectually fulfilling relationship, though differences in their temperaments and Calvin's frequent trips away from home in the early years of their marriage led to recurring tensions.

In the mid-1830s, Cincinnati, just across the border from the slave state of Kentucky, saw an explosion in public debate over slavery, with radical abolitionists increasingly unwilling to tolerate the passive antislavery sentiments of respected community leaders such as Lyman Beecher. Several anti- and proslavery riots shook the city; in their aftermath, many of the Beecher children, including Stowe, began to distance themselves from their father's careful tolerance of slavery and to interest themselves in the movement for immediate abolition.

To supplement the income for her growing family, Stowe began in the late 1830s to write short fiction for commercial magazines, including the new and increasingly popular *Godey's Lady's Book*; she experimented with various genres including brief domestic sketches, tales of the frontier, and religious and morally instructive stories. Her stories were in sufficient demand that in 1843 a selection was published in Boston in book form as *The Mayflower*. Throughout much of the 1840s, however, Stowe wrote little fiction; tensions in her marriage were recurrent, and household duties were utterly exhausting (by the end of the 1840s she would have six children, five of them living; her seventh child was born in 1850).

At the end of the decade, two dramatic events combined to provide Stowe with the impetus to begin writing *Uncle Tom's Cabin*. The first was the death of her infant son, Charley, during a cholera epidemic in 1849; Stowe's grief and devastation would inform much of her depiction of the sufferings of enslaved women and mothers in the novel. The second was the passage of the Fugitive Slave Act in September 1850. Part of the Compromise of 1850—a package of federal legislation meant to diffuse the increasing political tensions between the North and the South—the Act protected the right of slaveowners to pursue individuals who had fled North and re-enslave them; more than that, it required Northerners to assist in the pursuit, and threatened substantial fines or jail time for those found to be assisting fugitives. The Act was widely hated in the North, and made the injustices of slavery impossible to ignore. Stowe, who was already a supporter of immediate abolition, was enraged by the Fugitive Slave Act—"I have felt almost choked sometimes with pent-up wrath that does no good," she wrote to her sister. But her rage was transformative. She turned toward what was arguably the most effective means for American women to have their say in moral and political affairs—the pen.

The first installment of *Uncle Tom's Cabin* was published in the Washington, D.C., abolitionist paper *The National Era* on 5 June 1851, the last on 1 April 1852. The novel follows the interrelated stories of several enslaved characters: George Harris, a mixed-race man who defies his cruel enslaver and escapes to Canada; his wife Eliza, who flees her otherwise "kind" enslaver when she discovers he intends to sell both her and her young son; and the titular Uncle Tom, a deeply pious middle-aged man who is sold onto a Louisiana plantation and defies slavery not through violence or escape but through Christian forbearance. The serialized novel was moderately successful, eliciting many passionate responses from readers who wrote Stowe to share their feelings. However, it was the novel's publication in book format on 20 March 1852 that turned *Uncle Tom's Cabin* into a phenomenon. "Reader, buy *Uncle Tom's Cabin*," commanded an 1852 review in the New Hampshire *Morning Star*; "By all means do not go out of this world without having read 'the Story of the Age.'" The two-volume book became a bestseller almost overnight, selling over ten thousand copies in its first few days and over 300,000 within the year in the United States alone. In Britain (which had abolished slavery in the 1830s), it sold over one million copies in its first year.

As influential literary figure Edwin Percy Whipple observed in an 1876 essay in *Harper's Monthly Magazine*, the publication of *Uncle Tom's Cabin* turned out to be "an important political event. It was one of the most powerful agencies in building up the Republican party, in electing Abraham Lincoln to the Presidency,[1] and in raising earnest volunteers for the great crusade against slavery." The novel was widely praised for its effective combination of political suasion, religious feeling, and sentiment. And, as one letter-writer put it, the story was "peculiarly calculated to enlist the moral and religious sympathies, and call to action the latent energies of the female heart." But while the novel's sentimental rhetoric in many ways sought to appeal to women particularly, male readers were clearly affected too: the story of prominent newspaper editor Horace Greeley, who was said to have sobbed his way through the book in a hotel room in Ohio, is far from unique. The narrative inspired writers such as William Wells Brown and Mary Hayden Green Pike to write abolitionist novels of their own, and it inspired poets as well—including Quaker abolitionist John Greenleaf Whittier and activist Frances Ellen Watkins Harper (whose 1854 "Eliza Harris" is directly based on the novel).

In the other direction, countless proslavery apologists characterized Stowe's novel as an "infamous book of lies," and some questioned the propriety of Stowe's delving into the subject at all—as a Northerner, and as a woman. As one reviewer for *The Southern Literary Messenger* put it, "It is a horrible thought that a woman should write or a lady should read such productions as those by which [Stowe's] celebrity has been acquired." Proslavery authors began writing "anti-Tom" novels—novels portraying a romanticized view of the South and of master-slave relations; Virginia author Mary Henderson Eastman's

---

1   The most frequently recounted Stowe anecdote concerns Lincoln, who is said to have greeted her in 1862 with these words: "So you're the little woman who wrote the book that made this great war." But the anecdote, which originated decades after the fact in family lore, cannot be said to have any basis in fact. Stowe and Lincoln did meet in November of 1862, but there is no reliable record of their conversation.

Aunt Phillis's Cabin; or Southern Life as It Is (1852) enjoyed considerable popularity in the North as well as in the South.

Though most abolitionists welcomed Stowe's success in awakening "the strongest compassion for the oppressed and the utmost abhorrence of the system which grinds them to the dust" (as William Lloyd Garrison put in *The Liberator*), Garrison and others were deeply uncomfortable with the degree to which Stowe portrayed passivity in the face of oppression to be appropriate for the enslaved; they found the portrayal of the titular Uncle Tom particularly troubling in this respect. The novel's conclusion—which appears to endorse the controversial, primarily white-led movement to transport free African Americans to the colony of Liberia—was also deeply troubling to many. (Stowe would renounce the colonizationist movement in later years, partly as a result of her correspondence with the black abolitionist and anti-colonizationist Frederick Douglass.)

In 1853, Stowe responded to charges that she was ill-qualified to tackle the subject of slavery with *A Key to Uncle Tom's Cabin*, in which she provided exhaustive documentation of the facts on which she had based her novel (and also revealed that the character of Uncle Tom had been heavily based on that of the formerly enslaved minister Josiah Henson). The Stowes subsequently embarked on a tour of England and continental Europe, where her novel's egalitarian themes resonated with many who had supported the various democratic revolutions of 1848.

Stowe's next book was a second novel, *Dred: A Tale of the Great Dismal Swamp* (1856), which offered a more radical view of the struggle against slavery; her detailed appendix of research sources made it clear that her title character was a composite of the early nineteenth-century slave revolt leaders Nat Turner and Denmark Vesey. *Dred* sold modestly well, but had far less impact on America than had *Uncle Tom's Cabin*. Stowe's fame nevertheless continued unabated; she wrote several more novels over the next decade, including *The Minister's Wooing* (1859), a work set in eighteenth-century New England that turned a critical eye on the legacy of Calvinism, and *A Pearl of Orr's Island: A Story of the Coast of Maine* (1862).

Stowe's career was sufficiently lucrative that Calvin decided to retire in early 1864. Stowe courted controversy again in 1869 with "The True Story of Lady Byron's Life," which discussed English poet

Lord Byron's incestuous affair with his half sister; though rumors of the affair had been widespread for years, the article was nevertheless explosive, nearly ruining both the prestigious *Atlantic Monthly* magazine in which it had been published and Stowe's own reputation. For decades scholars and biographers puzzled over this turn in Stowe's literary career; in recent years some scholars have read "The True Story" and the subsequent *Lady Byron Vindicated* (1870) as proto-feminist explorations of nineteenth-century gender roles and of the subjugation of women in sexual relationships.

Stowe's final novel was the 1878 *Poganuc People*, a regional novel that evoked the New England of her childhood. Her physical and mental health deteriorated rapidly over the next few years, especially after Calvin's death in 1886; Stowe herself died in July 1896.

The legacy of *Uncle Tom's Cabin* in American culture far outlived Stowe herself. The first stage adaptation had been written shortly after the novel's publication by George Aiken, a white playwright who also starred in the production as the novel's mixed-race hero George Harris. The novel was adapted countless additional times over the following decades, with many productions substantially altering the plot and exaggerating the racial stereotypes that had underlain the original narrative. These stage plays came to be known as "Tom Shows," and though their popularity was waning by the 1930s, they were still occasionally encountered even in the North as late as the 1940s. Some Tom Shows were wildly melodramatic, while others added song-and-dance numbers and comic scenes, adopting racist tropes from the minstrel show genre.

The "Tom Shows" were disdained by the literary establishment, but the novel itself continued to have broad appeal through the late-nineteenth century and into the twentieth. It was admired by respected European novelists such as George Eliot, George Sand, and Leo Tolstoy, who in 1897 declared it as an example "of the highest art flowing from love of God and man." By the 1920s, however, the novel had begun to be dismissed by the literary establishment as a hackneyed work of sentimentalism, with little in the way of aesthetic or intellectual value, and by mid century it was being attacked as downright pernicious. In his famous 1955 essay "Everybody's Protest Novel," James Baldwin dismissed the novel's "self-righteous, virtuous sentimentality" and condemned its two-dimensional characters.

Baldwin treated *Uncle Tom's Cabin* as the paradigmatical protest novel, and condemned all such novels for their sentimentality— "sentimentality is the mark of dishonesty, the inability to feel," he proclaimed—and for the way in which, as he saw it, they simplified and distorted complex psychological and cultural truths; in his view, Stowe's "self-righteous sentimentality" and "catalog of violence" left "unanswered and unnoticed the only question that actually matters: what it was, after all, that moved her [i.e., white] people to such deeds." In another famous essay published a year later, J.C. Furnas focused more narrowly on Stowe's portrayal of black people, crediting her work for contributing significantly to "the wrongheadedness, distortions and wishful thinkings about Negroes in general and American Negroes in particular that still plague us today."

The reception history of *Uncle Tom's Cabin* has continued to take new turns in the twenty-first century. The literature of sentiment and the literature of protest are being read more sympathetically than they were for much of the twentieth century. Since the 1970s, critics have come to take the works of many nineteenth-century female writers much more seriously—and to question the gendered biases that often underlaid twentieth-century dismissals of popular and sentimental fiction as unworthy of study. Increasingly, twenty-first-century critics are interested in examining *Uncle Tom's Cabin*'s strategies in the context of the 1850s and 1860s as well as its legacy for race relations in subsequent periods; some critics also use Stowe's novel as a springboard for discussions about the role of emotion in literature more generally. The novel continues to entrance, infuriate, and, most of all, intrigue readers and scholars into our own day.

Note on the Text

The excerpts presented in this edition are based on the 1852 first edition of *Uncle Tom's Cabin; or, Life Among the Lowly*. Spelling and punctuation have been modernized in accordance with the practices of *The Broadview Anthology of American Literature*. The editors would like to express our gratitude to Faye Halpern (University of Calgary) for her assistance and expertise in preparing the material in this edition.

அ

from *Uncle's Tom's Cabin; or, Life Among the Lowly*

Chapter i
In which the Reader Is Introduced to a Man of Humanity

L ate in the afternoon of a chilly day in February, two gentlemen were sitting alone over their wine, in a well-furnished dining parlor, in the town of P——, in Kentucky. There were no servants present, and the gentlemen, with chairs closely approaching, seemed to be discussing some subject with great earnestness.

For convenience sake, we have said, hitherto, two *gentlemen*. One of the parties, however, when critically examined, did not seem, strictly speaking, to come under the species. He was a short, thick-set man, with coarse, commonplace features, and that swaggering air of pretension which marks a low man who is trying to elbow his way upward in the world. He was much over-dressed, in a gaudy vest of many colors, a blue neckerchief, bedropped gayly with yellow spots, and arranged with a flaunting tie, quite in keeping with the general air of the man. His hands, large and coarse, were plentifully bedecked with rings; and he wore a heavy gold watch-chain, with a bundle of seals of portentous size, and a great variety of colors, attached to it—which, in the ardor of conversation, he was in the habit of flourishing and jingling with evident satisfaction. His conversation was in free and easy defiance of Murray's Grammar,[1] and was garnished at convenient intervals with various profane expressions, which not even the desire to be graphic in our account shall induce us to transcribe.

His companion, Mr. Shelby, had the appearance of a gentleman; and the arrangements of the house, and the general air of the house-keeping, indicated easy and even opulent circumstances. As we before stated, the two were in the midst of an earnest conversation.

"That is the way I should arrange the matter," said Mr. Shelby.

---

1 *Murray's Grammar* American scholar Lindley Murray's widely used textbook *English Grammar* (1795), which dictated proper grammar usage.

"I can't make trade that way—I positively can't, Mr. Shelby," said the other, holding up a glass of wine between his eye and the light.

"Why, the fact is, Haley, Tom is an uncommon fellow; he is certainly worth that sum anywhere—steady, honest, capable, manages my whole farm like a clock."

"You mean honest, as niggers[1] go," said Haley, helping himself to a glass of brandy.

"No; I mean, really, Tom is a good, steady, sensible, pious fellow. He got religion at a camp meeting,[2] four years ago; and I believe he really *did* get it. I've trusted him, since then, with everything I have—money, house, horses—and let him come and go round the country; and I always found him true and square in everything."

"Some folks don't believe there is pious niggers, Shelby," said Haley, with a candid flourish of his hand, "but *I do*. I had a fellow, now, in this yer last lot I took to Orleans—'t was as good as a meetin, now, really, to hear that critter pray; and he was quite gentle and quiet like. He fetched me a good sum, too; for I bought him cheap of a man that was 'bliged to sell out; so I realized six hundred on him. Yes, I consider religion a valeyable thing in a nigger, when it's the genuine article, and no mistake."

"Well, Tom's got the real article, if ever a fellow had," rejoined the other. "Why, last fall, I let him go to Cincinnati alone, to do business for me, and bring home five hundred dollars. 'Tom,' says I to him, 'I trust you, because I think you're a Christian—I know you wouldn't cheat.' Tom comes back, sure enough; I knew he would. Some low fellows, they say, said to him—'Tom, why don't you make tracks for Canada?'[3] 'Ah, master trusted me, and I couldn't,'—they told me about it. I am sorry to part with Tom, I must say. You ought

---

1   *nigger*   By the mid-nineteenth century, this word, when used by white speakers, had acquired the extremely derogatory connotations it carries today, though it was sometimes used by African Americans without any derogatory intention; "negro" was, by contrast, considered a polite term by both black and white Americans.

2   *camp meeting*   Outdoor religious gathering; camp meetings were associated particularly with evangelical Christian denominations, and provided a form of worship that was more accessible to the enslaved communities of the South.

3   *why don't ... for Canada?*   Due to its location along the border between Kentucky and the free state of Ohio, Cincinnati was an important center of the Underground Railroad, a secret network that aided enslaved people escaping to freedom in Canada.

to let him cover the whole balance of the debt; and you would, Haley, if you had any conscience."

"Well, I've got just as much conscience as any man in business can afford to keep—just a little, you know, to swear by, as 't were," said the trader, jocularly; "and, then, I'm ready to do anything in reason to 'blige friends; but this yer, you see, is a leetle too hard on a fellow—a leetle too hard." The trader sighed contemplatively, and poured out some more brandy.

"Well, then, Haley, how will you trade?" said Mr. Shelby, after an uneasy interval of silence.

"Well, haven't you a boy or gal that you could throw in with Tom?"

"Hum! none that I could well spare; to tell the truth, it's only hard necessity makes me willing to sell at all. I don't like parting with any of my hands, that's a fact."

Here the door opened, and a small quadroon[1] boy, between four and five years of age, entered the room. There was something in his appearance remarkably beautiful and engaging. His black hair, fine as floss silk, hung in glossy curls about his round, dimpled face, while a pair of large dark eyes, full of fire and softness, looked out from beneath the rich, long lashes, as he peered curiously into the apartment. A gay robe of scarlet and yellow plaid, carefully made and neatly fitted, set off to advantage the dark and rich style of his beauty; and a certain comic air of assurance, blended with bashfulness, showed that he had been not unused to being petted and noticed by his master.

"Hulloa, Jim Crow!"[2] said Mr. Shelby, whistling, and snapping a bunch of raisins towards him, "pick that up, now!"

The child scampered, with all his little strength, after the prize, while his master laughed.

"Come here, Jim Crow," said he. The child came up, and the master patted the curly head, and chucked him under the chin.

"Now, Jim, show this gentleman how you can dance and sing." The boy commenced one of those wild, grotesque songs common

---

1   *quadroon*   Term commonly used in the nineteenth century to classify a person of mixed racial ancestry, generally with one black and three white grandparents.

2   *Jim Crow*   While the origins of this pejorative term for an enslaved African American are unclear, its widespread usage by whites in the mid-nineteenth century stems from the popular 1828 song and dance "Jump Jim Crow" by Thomas Dartmouth Rice, a white performer of blackface minstrelsy.

among the negroes, in a rich, clear voice, accompanying his singing with many comic evolutions of the hands, feet, and whole body, all in perfect time to the music.

"Bravo!" said Haley, throwing him a quarter of an orange.

"Now, Jim, walk like old Uncle Cudjoe, when he has the rheumatism," said his master.

Instantly the flexible limbs of the child assumed the appearance of deformity and distortion, as, with his back humped up, and his master's stick in his hand, he hobbled about the room, his childish face drawn into a doleful pucker, and spitting from right to left, in imitation of an old man.

Both gentlemen laughed uproariously.

"Now, Jim," said his master, "show us how old Elder Robbins leads the psalm." The boy drew his chubby face down to a formidable length, and commenced toning a psalm tune through his nose, with imperturbable gravity.

"Hurrah! bravo! what a young 'un!" said Haley; "that chap's a case, I'll promise. Tell you what," said he, suddenly clapping his hand on Mr. Shelby's shoulder, "fling in that chap, and I'll settle the business— I will. Come, now, if that ain't doing the thing up about the rightest!"

At this moment, the door was pushed gently open, and a young quadroon woman, apparently about twenty-five, entered the room.

There needed only a glance from the child to her, to identify her as its mother. There was the same rich, full, dark eye, with its long lashes; the same ripples of silky black hair. The brown of her complexion gave way on the cheek to a perceptible flush, which deepened as she saw the gaze of the strange man fixed upon her in bold and undisguised admiration. Her dress was of the neatest possible fit, and set off to advantage her finely moulded shape; a delicately formed hand and a trim foot and ankle were items of appearance that did not escape the quick eye of the trader, well used to run up at a glance the points of a fine female article.

"Well, Eliza?" said her master, as she stopped and looked hesitatingly at him.

"I was looking for Harry, please, sir"; and the boy bounded toward her, showing his spoils, which he had gathered in the skirt of his robe.

"Well, take him away, then," said Mr. Shelby; and hastily she withdrew, carrying the child on her arm.

"By Jupiter," said the trader, turning to him in admiration, "there's an article, now! You might make your fortune on that ar gal in Orleans, any day. I've seen over a thousand, in my day, paid down for gals not a bit handsomer."

"I don't want to make my fortune on her," said Mr. Shelby, dryly; and, seeking to turn the conversation, he uncorked a bottle of fresh wine, and asked his companion's opinion of it.

"Capital, sir—first chop!" said the trader; then turning, and slapping his hand familiarly on Shelby's shoulder, he added—

"Come, how will you trade about the gal? What shall I say for her—what'll you take?"

"Mr. Haley, she is not to be sold," said Shelby. "My wife would not part with her for her weight in gold."

"Ay, ay! women always say such things, cause they ha'nt no sort of calculation. Just show 'em how many watches, feathers, and trinkets, one's weight in gold would buy, and that alters the case, *I* reckon."

"I tell you, Haley, this must not be spoken of; I say no, and I mean no," said Shelby, decidedly.

"Well, you'll let me have the boy, though," said the trader; "you must own I've come down pretty handsomely for him."

"What on earth can you want with the child?" said Shelby.

"Why, I've got a friend that's going into this yer branch of the business—wants to buy up handsome boys to raise for the market. Fancy articles entirely—sell for waiters,[1] and so on, to rich 'uns, that can pay for handsome 'uns. It sets off one of yer great places—a real handsome boy to open door, wait, and tend. They fetch a good sum; and this little devil is such a comical, musical concern, he's just the article."

"I would rather not sell him," said Mr. Shelby, thoughtfully; "the fact is, sir, I'm a humane man, and I hate to take the boy from his mother, sir."

"O, you do? La! yes—something of that ar natur. I understand, perfectly. It is mighty onpleasant getting on with women, sometimes. I al'ays hates these yer screachin', screamin' times. They are *mighty* onpleasant; but, as I manages business, I generally avoids 'em, sir. Now, what if you get the girl off for a day, or a week, or so; then

---

1 *waiters* Personal servants.

the thing's done quietly—all over before she comes home. Your wife might get her some earrings, or a new gown, or some such truck, to make up with her."

"I'm afraid not."

"Lor bless ye, yes! These critters an't like white folks, you know; they gets over things, only manage right. Now, they say," said Haley, assuming a candid and confidential air, "that this kind o' trade is hardening to the feelings; but I never found it so. Fact is, I never could do things up the way some fellers manage the business. I've seen 'em as would pull a woman's child out of her arms, and set him up to sell, and she screechin' like mad all the time; very bad policy—damages the article—makes 'em quite unfit for service sometimes. I knew a real handsome gal once, in Orleans, as was entirely ruined by this sort o' handling. The fellow that was trading for her didn't want her baby; and she was one of your real high sort, when her blood was up. I tell you, she squeezed up her child in her arms, and talked, and went on real awful. It kinder makes my blood run cold to think on't; and when they carried off the child, and locked her up, she jest went ravin' mad, and died in a week. Clear waste, sir, of a thousand dollars, just for want of management—there's where 't is. It's always best to do the humane thing, sir; that's been *my* experience." And the trader leaned back in his chair, and folded his arm, with an air of virtuous decision, apparently considering himself a second Wilberforce.[1]

The subject appeared to interest the gentleman deeply; for while Mr. Shelby was thoughtfully peeling an orange, Haley broke out afresh, with becoming diffidence, but as if actually driven by the force of truth to say a few words more.

"It don't look well, now, for a feller to be praisin' himself; but I say it jest because it's the truth. I believe I'm reckoned to bring in about the finest droves of niggers that is brought in—at least, I've been told so; if I have once, I reckon I have a hundred times—all in good case—fat and likely, and I lose as few as any man in the business. And I lays it all to my management, sir; and humanity, sir, I may say, is the great pillar of *my* management."

---

1 *Wilberforce* English politician and abolitionist William Wilberforce (1759–1833), a leading figure in the movement to end British involvement in slavery and the slave trade; the Slavery Abolition Act of 1833 (which took effect in August, 1834) ended slavery in most of the British colonies.

Mr. Shelby did not know what to say, and so he said, "Indeed!"

"Now, I've been laughed at for my notions, sir, and I've been talked to. They an't pop'lar, and they an't common; but I stuck to 'em, sir; I've stuck to 'em, and realized well on 'em; yes, sir, they have paid their passage, I may say," and the trader laughed at his joke.

There was something so piquant and original in these elucidations of humanity, that Mr. Shelby could not help laughing in company. Perhaps you laugh too, dear reader; but you know humanity comes out in a variety of strange forms now-a-days, and there is no end to the odd things that humane people will say and do.

Mr. Shelby's laugh encouraged the trader to proceed.

"It's strange, now, but I never could beat this into people's heads. Now, there was Tom Loker, my old partner, down in Natchez;[1] he was a clever fellow, Tom was, only the very devil with niggers—on principle 't was, you see, for a better hearted feller never broke bread; 't was his *system*, sir. I used to talk to Tom. 'Why, Tom,' I used to say, 'when your gals takes on and cry, what's the use o' crackin on 'em over the head, and knockin' on 'em round? It's ridiculous,' says I, 'and don't do no sort o' good. Why, I don't see no harm in their cryin',' says I; 'it's natur,' says I, 'and if natur can't blow off one way, it will another. Besides, Tom,' says I, 'it jest spiles[2] your gals; they get sickly, and down in the mouth; and sometimes they gets ugly—particular yellow[3] gals do—and it's the devil and all gettin' on 'em broke in. Now,' says I, 'why can't you kinder coax 'em up, and speak 'em fair? Depend on it, Tom, a little humanity, thrown in along, goes a heap further than all your jawin' and crackin'; and it pays better,' says I, 'depend on't.' But Tom couldn't get the hang on 't; and he spiled so many for me, that I had to break off with him, though he was a good-hearted fellow, and as fair a business hand as is goin'."

"And do you find your ways of managing do the business better than Tom's?" said Mr. Shelby.

"Why, yes, sir, I may say so. You see, when I any ways can, I takes a leetle care about the onpleasant parts, like selling young uns and that—get the gals out of the way—out of sight, out of mind, you

---

1   *Natchez*   City in Mississippi, an important center of plantation agriculture.
2   *spiles*   Spoils.
3   *yellow*   Racial descriptor designating individuals of mixed racial ancestry with light brown skin.

know—and when it's clean done, and can't be helped, they naturally gets used to it. 'Tan't, you know, as if it was white folks, that's brought up in the way of 'spectin' to keep their children and wives, and all that. Niggers, you know, that's fetched up properly, ha'n't no kind of 'spectations of no kind; so all these things comes easier."

"I'm afraid mine are not properly brought up, then," said Mr. Shelby.

"S'pose not; you Kentucky folks spile your niggers. You mean well by 'em, but 'tan't no real kindness, arter all. Now, a nigger, you see, what's got to be hacked and tumbled round the world, and sold to Tom, and Dick, and the Lord knows who, 'tan't no kindness to be givin' on him notions and expectations, and bringin' on him up too well, for the rough and tumble comes all the harder on him arter. Now, I venture to say, your niggers would be quite chop-fallen in a place where some of your plantation niggers would be singing and whooping like all possessed. Every man, you know, Mr. Shelby, naturally thinks well of his own ways; and I think I treat niggers just about as well as it's ever worthwhile to treat 'em."

"It's a happy thing to be satisfied," said Mr. Shelby, with a slight shrug, and some perceptible feelings of a disagreeable nature.

"Well," said Haley, after they had both silently picked their nuts for a season, "what do you say?"

"I'll think the matter over, and talk with my wife," said Mr. Shelby. "Meantime, Haley, if you want the matter carried on in the quiet way you speak of, you'd best not let your business in this neighborhood be known. It will get out among my boys, and it will not be a particularly quiet business getting away any of my fellows, if they know it, I'll promise you."

"O! certainly, by all means, mum! of course. But I'll tell you, I'm in a devil of a hurry, and shall want to know, as soon as possible, what I may depend on," said he, rising and putting on his overcoat.

"Well, call up this evening, between six and seven, and you shall have my answer," said Mr. Shelby, and the trader bowed himself out of the apartment.

"I'd like to have been able to kick the fellow down the steps," said he to himself, as he saw the door fairly closed, "with his impudent assurance; but he knows how much he has me at advantage. If anybody had ever said to me that I should sell Tom down south to one of those rascally traders, I should have said, 'Is thy servant a dog, that he should do this thing?'[1] And now it must come, for aught I see. And Eliza's child, too! I know that I shall have some fuss with wife about that; and, for that matter, about Tom, too. So much for being in debt—heigho! The fellow sees his advantage, and means to push it."

Perhaps the mildest form of the system of slavery is to be seen in the State of Kentucky. The general prevalence of agricultural pursuits of a quiet and gradual nature, not requiring those periodic seasons of hurry and pressure that are called for in the business of more southern districts, makes the task of the negro a more healthful and reasonable one; while the master, content with a more gradual style of acquisition, has not those temptations to hardheartedness which always overcome frail human nature when the prospect of sudden and rapid gain is weighed in the balance, with no heavier counterpoise than the interests of the helpless and unprotected.

Whoever visits some estates there, and witnesses the good-humored indulgence of some masters and mistresses, and the affectionate loyalty of some slaves, might be tempted to dream the oft-fabled poetic legend of a patriarchal institution,[2] and all that; but over and above the scene there broods a portentous shadow—the shadow of *law*. So long the law considers all these human beings, with beating hearts and living affections, only as so many *things* belonging to a master—so long as the failure, or misfortune, or imprudence, or death of the kindest owner, may cause them any day to exchange a life of kind protection and indulgence for one of hopeless misery and toil—so long it is impossible to make anything beautiful or desirable in the best regulated administration of slavery.

Mr. Shelby was a fair average kind of man, good-natured and kindly, and disposed to easy indulgence of those around him, and there had never been a lack of anything which might contribute to the physical comfort of the negroes on his estate. He had, however, speculated largely and quite loosely; had involved himself deeply, and his notes[3] to a large amount had come into the hands of Haley; and

---

1   *Is ... thing?* See 2 Kings 8.13: "But what, is thy servant a dog, that he should do this great thing?"

2   *patriarchal institution* I.e., an institution in which slaveowners are perceived as benevolent, fatherly figures.

3   *notes* Documents outlining debt and repayment terms.

this small piece of information is the key to the preceding conversation.

Now, it had so happened that, in approaching the door, Eliza had caught enough of the conversation to know that a trader was making offers to her master for somebody.

She would gladly have stopped at the door to listen, as she came out; but her mistress just then calling, she was obliged to hasten away.

Still she thought she heard the trader make an offer for her boy—could she be mistaken? Her heart swelled and throbbed, and she involuntarily strained him so tight that the little fellow looked up into her face in astonishment.

"Eliza, girl, what ails you today?" said her mistress, when Eliza had upset the wash-pitcher, knocked down the work-stand, and finally was abstractedly offering her mistress a long night-gown in place of the silk dress she had ordered her to bring from the wardrobe.

Eliza started. "O, missis!" she said, raising her eyes; then, bursting into tears, she sat down in a chair, and began sobbing.

"Why, Eliza, child! what ails you?" said her mistress.

"O! missis, missis," said Eliza, "there's been a trader talking with master in the parlor! I heard him."

"Well, silly child, suppose there has."

"O, missis, *do* you suppose mas'r would sell my Harry?" And the poor creature threw herself into a chair, and sobbed convulsively.

"Sell him! No, you foolish girl! You know your master never deals with those southern traders, and never means to sell any of his servants, as long as they behave well. Why, you silly child, who do you think would want to buy your Harry? Do you think all the world are set on him as you are, you goosie? Come, cheer up, and hook my dress. There now, put my back hair up in that pretty braid you learnt the other day, and don't go listening at doors anymore."

"Well, but, missis, *you* never would give your consent—to—to—"

"Nonsense, child! to be sure, I shouldn't. What do you talk so for? I would as soon have one of my own children sold. But really, Eliza, you are getting altogether too proud of that little fellow. A man can't put his nose into the door, but you think he must be coming to buy him."

Reassured by her mistress' confident tone, Eliza proceeded nimbly and adroitly with her toilet,[1] laughing at her own fears, as she proceeded.

Mrs. Shelby was a woman of a high class, both intellectually and morally. To that natural magnanimity and generosity of mind which one often marks as characteristic of the women of Kentucky, she added high moral and religious sensibility and principle, carried out with great energy and ability into practical results. Her husband, who made no professions to any particular religious character, nevertheless reverenced and respected the consistency of hers, and stood, perhaps, a little in awe of her opinion. Certain it was that he gave her unlimited scope in all her benevolent efforts for the comfort, instruction, and improvement of her servants, though he never took any decided part in them himself. In fact, if not exactly a believer in the doctrine of the efficiency of the extra good works of saints,[2] he really seemed somehow or other to fancy that his wife had piety and benevolence enough for two—to indulge a shadowy expectation of getting into heaven through her superabundance of qualities to which he made no particular pretension.

The heaviest load on his mind, after his conversation with the trader, lay in the foreseen necessity of breaking to his wife the arrangement contemplated—meeting the importunities and opposition which he knew he should have reason to encounter.

Mrs. Shelby, being entirely ignorant of her husband's embarrassments,[3] and knowing only the general kindliness of his temper, had been quite sincere in the entire incredulity with which she had met Eliza's suspicions. In fact, she dismissed the matter from her mind, without a second thought; and being occupied in preparations for an evening visit, it passed out of her thoughts entirely.

---

1   *toilet* Dressing and personal grooming.

2   *the doctrine ... of saints* Reference to the belief held by Catholics and some other Christians that the good works of the saints have direct benefits for the souls of the living (the importance of earthly "good works" was generally held in low esteem by nineteenth-century Calvinists in comparison with the inner quality of grace).

3   *embarrassments* Financial difficulties.

Chapter 3
The Husband and Father

Mrs. Shelby had gone on her visit, and Eliza stood in the verandah, rather dejectedly looking after the retreating carriage, when a hand was laid on her shoulder. She turned, and a bright smile lighted up her fine eyes.

"George,[1] is it you? How you frightened me! Well; I am so glad you's come! Missis is gone to spend the afternoon; so come into my little room, and we'll have the time all to ourselves."

Saying this, she drew him into a neat little apartment opening on the verandah, where she generally sat at her sewing, within call of her mistress.

"How glad I am! why don't you smile? And look at Harry—how he grows." The boy stood shyly regarding his father through his curls, holding close to the skirts of his mother's dress. "Isn't he beautiful?" said Eliza, lifting his long curls and kissing him.

"I wish he'd never been born!" said George, bitterly. "I wish I'd never been born myself!"

Surprised and frightened, Eliza sat down, leaned her head on her husband's shoulder, and burst into tears.

"There now, Eliza, it's too bad for me to make you feel so, poor girl!" said he, fondly; "it's too bad. O, how I wish you never had seen me—you might have been happy!"

"George! George! how can you talk so? What dreadful thing has happened, or is going to happen? I'm sure we've been very happy, till lately."

"So we have, dear," said George. Then drawing his child on his knee, he gazed intently on his glorious dark eyes, and passed his hands through his long curls.

"Just like you, Eliza; and you are the handsomest woman I ever saw, and the best one I ever wish to see; but, oh, I wish I'd never seen you, nor you me!"

1　*George*　Eliza's husband George Harris, a mixed-race man enslaved on a neighboring estate under a cruel master. In Chapter 2, it is explained that George had been hired out by his enslaver to a bagging factory, where he had invented a machine for the efficient cleaning of hemp; resentful of the esteem this invention had earned George from his supervisor and fellow laborers, his enslaver had him removed from the factory and set to field labor instead.

"O, George, how can you!"

"Yes, Eliza, it's all misery, misery, misery! My life is bitter as wormwood; the very life is burning out of me. I'm a poor, miserable, forlorn drudge; I shall only drag you down with me, that's all. What's the use of our trying to do anything, trying to know anything, trying to be anything? What's the use of living? I wish I was dead!"

"O, now, dear George, that is really wicked! I know how you feel about losing your place in the factory, and you have a hard master; but pray be patient, and perhaps something—"

"Patient!" said he, interrupting her; "haven't I been patient? Did I say a word when he came and took me away, for no earthly reason, from the place where everybody was kind to me? I'd paid him truly every cent of my earnings—and they all say I worked well."

"Well, it *is* dreadful," said Eliza, "but, after all, he is your master, you know."

"My master! and who made him my master? That's what I think of—what right has he to me? I'm a man as much as he is. I'm a better man than he is. I know more about business than he does; I am a better manager than he is; I can read better than he can;[1] I can write a better hand—and I've learned it all myself, and no thanks to him—I've learned it in spite of him; and now what right has he to make a dray-horse[2] of me? to take me from things I can do, and do better than he can, and put me to work that any horse can do? He tries to do it; he says he'll bring me down and humble me, and he puts me to just the hardest, meanest and dirtiest work, on purpose!"

"O, George! George! you frighten me! Why, I never heard you talk so; I'm afraid you'll do something dreadful. I don't wonder at your feelings, at all; but oh, do be careful—do, do—for my sake—for Harry's!"

"I have been careful, and I have been patient, but it's growing worse and worse; flesh and blood can't bear it any longer; every chance he can get to insult and torment me, he takes. I thought I could do my work well, and keep on quiet, and have some time to read and learn out of work hours; but the more he sees I can do, the more he loads on. He says that though I don't say anything, he sees I've got the devil

---

1 *I can ... he can* Unlike most slave states, Kentucky never passed legislation banning enslaved people from learning to read and write.

2 *dray-horse* Work horse.

in me, and he means to bring it out; and one of these days it will come out in a way that he won't like, or I'm mistaken!"

"O dear! what shall we do?" said Eliza, mournfully.

"It was only yesterday," said George, "as I was busy loading stones into a cart, that young Mas'r Thom stood there, slashing his whip so near the horse that the creature was frightened. I asked him to stop, as pleasant as I could—he just kept right on. I begged him again, and then he turned on me, and began striking me. I held his hand, and then he screamed and kicked and ran to his father, and told him that I was fighting him. He came in a rage, and said he'd teach me who was my master; and he tied me to a tree, and cut switches for young master, and told him that he might whip me till he was tired—and he did it! If I don't make him remember it, some time!" and the brow of the young man grew dark, and his eyes burned with an expression that made his young wife tremble. "Who made this man my master? That's what I want to know!" he said.

"Well," said Eliza, mournfully, "I always thought that I must obey my master and mistress, or I couldn't be a Christian."

"There is some sense in it, in your case; they have brought you up like a child, fed you, clothed you, indulged you, and taught you, so that you have a good education; that is some reason why they should claim you. But I have been kicked and cuffed and sworn at, and at the best only let alone; and what do I owe? I've paid for all my keeping a hundred times over. I *won't* bear it. No, I *won't!*" he said, clenching his hand with a fierce frown.

Eliza trembled, and was silent. She had never seen her husband in this mood before; and her gentle system of ethics seemed to bend like a reed in the surges of such passions.

"You know poor little Carlo, that you gave me," added George; "the creature has been about all the comfort that I've had. He has slept with me nights, and followed me around days, and kind o' looked at me as if he understood how I felt. Well, the other day I was just feeding him with a few old scraps I picked up by the kitchen door, and Mas'r came along, and said I was feeding him up at his expense, and that he couldn't afford to have every nigger keeping his dog, and ordered me to tie a stone to his neck and throw him in the pond."

"O, George, you didn't do it!"

"Do it? not I! but he did. Mas'r and Tom pelted the poor drowning creature with stones. Poor thing! he looked at me so mournful, as if he wondered why I didn't save him. I had to take a flogging because I wouldn't do it myself. I don't care. Mas'r will find out that I'm one that whipping won't tame. My day will come yet, if he don't look out."

"What are you going to do? O, George, don't do anything wicked; if you only trust in God, and try to do right, he'll deliver you."

"I ain't a Christian like you, Eliza; my heart's full of bitterness; I can't trust in God. Why does he let things be so?"

"O, George, we must have faith. Mistress says that when all things go wrong to us, we must believe that God is doing the very best."

"That's easy to say for people that are sitting on their sofas and riding in their carriages; but let 'em be where I am, I guess it would come some harder. I wish I could be good; but my heart burns, and can't be reconciled, anyhow. You couldn't, in my place—you can't now, if I tell you all I've got to say. You don't know the whole yet."

"What can be coming now?"

"Well, lately Mas'r has been saying that he was a fool to let me marry off the place; that he hates Mr. Shelby and all his tribe, because they are proud, and hold their heads up above him, and that I've got proud notions from you; and he says he won't let me come here anymore, and that I shall take a wife and settle down on his place. At first he only scolded and grumbled these things; but yesterday he told me that I should take Mina for a wife, and settle down in a cabin with her, or he would sell me down river."[1]

"Why—but you were married to *me*, by the minister, as much as if you'd been a white man!" said Eliza, simply.

"Don't you know a slave can't be married? There is no law in this country for that; I can't hold you for my wife, if he chooses to part us. That's why I wish I'd never seen you—why I wish I'd never been born; it would have been better for us both—it would have been better for this poor child if he had never been born. All this may happen to him yet!"

"O, but master is so kind!"

---

1 *down river* I.e., down the Mississippi. Conditions for enslaved people on the cotton and sugar plantations in the deep South were notoriously harsh and very often deadly.

"Yes, but who knows? he may die—and then he may be sold to nobody knows who. What pleasure is it that he is handsome, and smart, and bright? I tell you, Eliza, that a sword will pierce through your soul for every good and pleasant thing your child is or has; it will make him worth too much for you to keep!"

The words smote heavily on Eliza's heart; the vision of the trader came before her eyes, and, as if someone had struck her a deadly blow, she turned pale and gasped for breath. She looked nervously out on the verandah, where the boy, tired of the grave conversation, had retired, and where he was riding triumphantly up and down on Mrs. Shelby's walking-stick. She would have spoken to tell her husband her fears, but checked herself.

"No, no—he has enough to bear, poor fellow!" she thought. "No, I won't tell him; besides, it an't true; Missis never deceives us."

"So, Eliza, my girl," said the husband, mournfully, "bear up, now; and goodbye, for I'm going."

"Going, George! Going where?"

"To Canada," said he, straightening himself up; "and when I'm there, I'll buy you; that's all the hope that's left us. You have a kind master, that won't refuse to sell you. I'll buy you and the boy—God helping me, I will!"

"O, dreadful! if you should be taken?"

"I won't be taken, Eliza; I'll *die* first! I'll be free, or I'll die!"

"You won't kill yourself!"

"No need of that. They will kill me, fast enough; they never will get me down the river alive!"

"O, George, for my sake, do be careful! Don't do anything wicked; don't lay hands on yourself, or anybody else! You are tempted too much—too much; but don't—go you must—but go carefully, prudently; pray God to help you."

"Well, then, Eliza, hear my plan. Mas'r took it into his head to send me right by here, with a note to Mr. Symmes, that lives a mile past. I believe he expected I should come here to tell you what I have. It would please him, if he thought it would aggravate 'Shelby's folks,' as he calls 'em. I'm going home quite resigned, you understand, as if all was over. I've got some preparations made—and there are those that will help me; and, in the course of a week or so, I shall be among the missing, some day. Pray for me, Eliza; perhaps the good Lord will hear *you*."

"O, pray yourself, George, and go trusting in him; then you won't do anything wicked."

"Well now, *goodbye*," said George, holding Eliza's hands, and gazing into her eyes, without moving. They stood silent; then there were last words, and sobs, and bitter weeping—such parting as those may make whose hope to meet again is as the spider's web[1]—and the husband and wife were parted.

CHAPTER 4
AN EVENING IN UNCLE TOM'S CABIN

The cabin of Uncle Tom was a small log building, close adjoining to "the house," as the negro *par excellence* designates his master's dwelling. In front it had a neat garden-patch, where, every summer, strawberries, raspberries, and a variety of fruits and vegetables, flourished under careful tending. The whole front of it was covered by a large scarlet begonia and a native multiflora rose, which, entwisting and interlacing, left scarce a vestige of the rough logs to be seen. Here, also, in summer, various brilliant annuals, such as marigolds, petunias, four-o'clocks,[2] found an indulgent corner in which to unfold their splendors, and were the delight and pride of Aunt Chloe's heart.

Let us enter the dwelling. The evening meal at the house is over, and Aunt Chloe, who presided over its preparation as head cook, has left to inferior officers in the kitchen the business of clearing away and washing dishes, and come out into her own snug territories, to "get her ole man's supper"; therefore, doubt not that it is her you see by the fire, presiding with anxious interest over certain frizzling items in a stew-pan, and anon with grave consideration lifting the cover of a bake-kettle, from whence steam forth indubitable intimations of "something good." A round, black, shining face is hers, so glossy as to suggest the idea that she might have been washed over with white of eggs, like one of her own tea rusks.[3] Her whole plump

---

1 *whose hope ... spider's web*   See Job 8.13–14: "So are the paths of all that forget God; and the hypocrite's hope shall perish: Whose hope shall be cut off, and whose trust shall be a spider's web."

2 *four-o'clocks*   Common name for *Mirabilis jalapa*, a flower that generally opens around dusk.

3 *tea rusks*   Twice-baked biscuits, here presumably glazed with an egg wash before the second baking.

countenance beams with satisfaction and contentment from under her well-starched checked turban, bearing on it, however, if we must confess it, a little of that tinge of self-consciousness[1] which becomes the first cook of the neighborhood, as Aunt Chloe was universally held and acknowledged to be.

A cook she certainly was, in the very bone and centre of her soul. Not a chicken or turkey or duck in the barnyard but looked grave when they saw her approaching, and seemed evidently to be reflecting on their latter end; and certain it was that she was always meditating on trussing, stuffing and roasting, to a degree that was calculated to inspire terror in any reflecting fowl living. Her corn-cake, in all its varieties of hoe-cakes, dodgers, muffins, and other species too numerous to mention, was a sublime mystery to all less practiced compounders; and she would shake her fat sides with honest pride and merriment, as she would narrate the fruitless efforts that one and another of her compeers had made to attain to her elevation.

The arrival of company at the house, the arranging of dinners and suppers "in style," awoke all the energies of her soul; and no sight was more welcome to her than a pile of travelling trunks launched on the verandah, for then she foresaw fresh efforts and fresh triumphs.

Just at present, however, Aunt Chloe is looking into the bake-pan; in which congenial operation we shall leave her till we finish our picture of the cottage.

In one corner of it stood a bed, covered neatly with a snowy spread; and by the side of it was a piece of carpeting, of some considerable size. On this piece of carpeting Aunt Chloe took her stand, as being decidedly in the upper walks of life; and it and the bed by which it lay, and the whole corner, in fact, were treated with distinguished consideration, and made, so far as possible, sacred from the marauding inroads and desecrations of little folks. In fact, that corner was the *drawing-room* of the establishment. In the other corner was a bed of much humbler pretentions, and evidently designed for *use*. The wall over the fireplace was adorned with some very brilliant scriptural prints, and a portrait of General Washington, drawn and colored in a manner which would certainly have astonished that hero, if ever he had happened to meet with its like.

---

1   *self-consciousness*   I.e., self-esteem; confidence.

On a rough bench in the corner, a couple of woolly-headed boys, with glistening black eyes and fat shining cheeks, were busy in superintending the first walking operations of the baby, which, as is usually the case, consisted in getting up on its feet, balancing a moment, and then tumbling down—each successive failure being violently cheered, as something decidedly clever.

A table, somewhat rheumatic in its limbs,[1] was drawn out in front of the fire, and covered with a cloth, displaying cups and saucers of a decidedly brilliant pattern, with other symptoms of an approaching meal. At this table was seated Uncle Tom, Mr. Shelby's best hand, who, as he is to be the hero of our story, we must daguerreotype for our readers. He was a large, broad-chested, powerfully-made man, of a full glossy black, and a face whose truly African features were characterized by an expression of grave and steady good sense, united with much kindliness and benevolence. There was something about his whole air self-respecting and dignified, yet united with a confiding and humble simplicity.

He was very busily intent at this moment on a slate lying before him, on which he was carefully and slowly endeavoring to accomplish a copy of some letters, in which operation he was overlooked by young Mas'r George, a smart, bright boy of thirteen, who appeared fully to realize the dignity of his position as instructor.

"Not that way, Uncle Tom—not that way," said he, briskly, as Uncle Tom laboriously brought up the tail of his *g* the wrong side out; "that makes a *q*, you see."

"La sakes, now, does it?" said Uncle Tom, looking with a respectful, admiring air, as his young teacher flourishingly scrawled *q*'s and *g*'s innumerable for his edification; and then, taking the pencil in his big, heavy fingers, he patiently re-commenced.

"How easy white folks al' us does things!" said Aunt Chloe, pausing while she was greasing a griddle with a scrap of bacon on her fork, and regarding young Master George with pride. "The way he can write, now! and read, too! and then to come out here evenings and read his lessons to us—it's mighty interestin'!"

---

1   *rheumatic in its limbs*   Crooked or wobbly; the term "rheumatism" designates a class of disorders affecting the joints, such as arthritis.

"But, Aunt Chloe, I'm getting mighty hungry," said George. "Isn't that cake in the skillet almost done?"

"Mose¹ done, Mas'r George," said Aunt Chloe, lifting the lid and peeping in—"browning beautiful—a real lovely brown. Ah! let me alone for dat. Missis let Sally try to make some cake, t'other day, jes to *larn* her, she said, 'O, go way, Missis,' says I; 'it really hurts my feelin's, now, to see good vittles² spilt dat ar way! Cake ris all to one side—no shape at all; no more than my shoe—go way!'"

And with this final expression of contempt for Sally's greenness, Aunt Chloe whipped the cover off the bake-kettle, and disclosed to view a neatly-baked pound-cake, of which no city confectioner need to have been ashamed. This being evidently the central point of the entertainment, Aunt Chloe began now to bustle about earnestly in the supper department.

"Here you, Mose and Pete! get out de way, you niggers! Get away, Mericky, honey—mammy'll give her baby somefin, by and by. Now, Mas'r George, you jest take off dem books, and set down now with my old man, and I'll take up de sausages, and have de first griddle full of cakes on your plates in less dan no time."

"They wanted me to come to supper in the house," said George; "but I knew what was what too well for that, Aunt Chloe."

"So you did—so you did, honey," said Aunt Chloe, heaping the smoking batter-cakes on his plate; "you know'd your old aunty'd keep the best for you. O, let you alone for dat! Go way!" And, with that, aunty gave George a nudge with her finger, designed to be immensely facetious, and turned again to her griddle with great briskness.

"Now for the cake," said Mas'r George, when the activity of the griddle department had somewhat subsided; and, with that, the youngster flourished a large knife over the article in question.

"La bless you, Mas'r George!" said Aunt Chloe, with earnestness, catching his arm, "you wouldn't be for cuttin' it wid dat ar great heavy knife! Smash all down—spile all de pretty rise of it. Here, I've got a thin old knife, I keeps sharp a purpose. Dar now, see! comes apart light as a feather! Now eat away—you won't get anything to beat dat ar."

---

1 *Mose* Almost.
2 *vittles* Victuals; food.

"Tom Lincon says," said George, speaking with his mouth full, "that their Jinny is a better cook than you."

"Dem Lincons an't much count, no way!" said Aunt Chloe, contemptuously; "I mean, set alongside *our* folks. They's 'spectable folks enough in a kinder plain way; but, as to gettin' up anything in style, they don't begin to have a notion on 't. Set Mas'r Lincon, now, alongside Mas'r Shelby! Good Lor! and Missis Lincon—can she kinder sweep it into a room like my missis—so kinder splendid, yer know! O, go way! don't tell me nothin' of dem Lincons!"—and Aunt Chloe tossed her head as one who hoped she did know something of the world.

"Well, though, I've heard you say," said George, "that Jinny was a pretty fair cook."

"So I did," said Aunt Chloe, "I may say dat. Good, plain, common cookin', Jinny'll do—make a good pone[1] o' bread—bile her taters *far*[2]—her corn cakes isn't extra,[3] not extra now, Jinny's corn cakes isn't, but then they's *far*—but, Lor, come to de higher branches, and what *can* she do? Why, she makes pies—sartin she does; but what kinder crust? Can she make your real flecky paste,[4] as melts in your mouth, and lies all up like a puff? Now, I went over thar when Miss Mary was gwine to be married, and Jinny she jest showed me de weddin' pies. Jinny and I is good friends, ye know. I never said nothin'; but go long, Mas'r George! Why, I shouldn't sleep a wink for a week, if I had a batch of pies like dem ar. Why, dey wan't no 'count 't all."

"I suppose Jinny thought they were ever so nice," said George.

"Thought so! didn't she? Thar she was, showing 'em, as innocent—ye see, it's jest here, Jinny *don't know*. Lor, the family an't nothing! She can't be spected to know! 'Ta'nt no fault o' hern. Ah, Mas'r George, you doesn't know half your privileges in yer family and bringin' up!" Here Aunt Chloe sighed, and rolled up her eyes with emotion.

"I'm sure, Aunt Chloe, I understand all my pie and pudding privileges," said George. "Ask Tom Lincon if I don't crow over him, every time I meet him."

---

1 *pone* Small, usually cornmeal-based loaf of bread.
2 *bile her taters far* I.e., boil her potatoes fair.
3 *extra* I.e., of high quality.
4 *paste* Pastry.

Aunt Chloe sat back in her chair and indulged in a hearty guffaw of laughter at this witticism of young Mas'r's, laughing till the tears rolled down her black, shining cheeks, and varying the exercise with playfully slapping and poking Mas'r Georgey, and telling him to go way, and that he was a case—that he was fit to kill her, and that he sartin would kill her, one of these days; and, between each of these sanguinary predictions, going off into a laugh, each longer and stronger than the other, till George really began to think that he was a very dangerously witty fellow, and that it became him to be careful how he talked "as funny as he could."

"And so ye telled Tom, did ye? O, Lor! what young uns will be up ter! Ye crowed over Tom? O, Lord! Mas'r George, if ye wouldn't make a hornbug laugh!"

"Yes," said George, "I says to him, 'Tom, you ought to see some of Aunt Chloe's pies; they're the right sort,' says I."

"Pity, now, Tom couldn't," said Aunt Chloe, on whose benevolent heart the idea of Tom's benighted condition seemed to make a strong impression. "Ye oughter just ask him here to dinner, some o' these times, Mas'r George," she added; "it would look quite pretty of ye. Ye know, Mas'r George, ye oughtenter feel 'bove nobody, on 'count yer privileges, 'cause all our privileges is gi'n to us; we ought al'ays to 'member that," said Aunt Chloe, looking quite serious.

"Well, I mean to ask Tom here, some day next week," said George; "and you do your prettiest, Aunt Chloe, and we'll make him stare. Won't we make him eat so he won't get over it for a fortnight?"

"Yes, yes—sartin," said Aunt Chloe, delighted; "you'll see. Lor! to think of some of our dinners! Yer mind dat ar great chicken pie I made when we guv de dinner to General Knox? I and Missis, we come pretty near quarrelling about dat ar crust. What does get into ladies sometimes, I don't know; but, sometimes, when a body has de heaviest kind o' 'sponsibility on 'em, as ye may say, and is all kinder 'seris' and taken up, dey takes dat ar time to be hangin' round and kinder interferin'! Now, Missis, she wanted me to do dis way, and she wanted me to do dat way; and, finally, I got kinder sarcy, and, says I, 'Now, Missis, do jist look at dem beautiful white hands o' yourn, with long fingers, and all a sparkling with rings, like my white lilies when de dew's on 'em; and look at my great black stumpin hands. Now, don't ye think dat de Lord must have meant *me* to make de pie-crust, and you to stay in de parlor? Dar! I was jist so sarcy, Mas'r George."

"And what did mother say?" said George.

"Say?—why, she kinder larfed in her eyes—dem great handsome eyes o' hern; and, says she, 'Well, Aunt Chloe, I think you are about in the right on 't,' says she; and she went off in de parlor. She oughter cracked me over de head for bein' so sarcy; but dar's whar 'tis—I can't do nothin' with ladies in de kitchen!"

"Well, you made out well with that dinner,—I remember everybody said so," said George.

"Didn't I? And wan't I behind de dinin'-room door dat bery day? and didn't I see de General pass his plate three times for some more dat bery pie?—and, says he, 'You must have an uncommon cook, Mrs. Shelby.' Lor! I was fit to split myself.

"And de Gineral, he knows what cookin' is," said Aunt Chloe, drawing herself up with an air. "Bery nice man, de Gineral! He comes of one of de bery *fustest* families in Old Virginny! He knows what's what, now, as well as I do—de Gineral. Ye see, there's *pints* in all pies, Mas'r George; but tan't everybody knows what they is, or as orter be. But the Gineral, he knows; I knew by his 'marks he made. Yes, he knows what de pints is!"

By this time, Master George had arrived at that pass to which even a boy can come (under uncommon circumstances, when he really could not eat another morsel), and, therefore, he was at leisure to notice the pile of woolly heads and glistening eyes which were regarding their operations hungrily from the opposite corner.

"Here, you Mose, Pete," he said, breaking off liberal bits, and throwing it at them; "you want some, don't you? Come, Aunt Chloe, bake them some cakes."

And George and Tom moved to a comfortable seat in the chimney-corner, while Aunt Chloe, after baking a goodly pile of cakes, took her baby on her lap, and began alternately filling its mouth and her own, and distributing to Mose and Pete, who seemed rather to prefer eating theirs as they rolled about on the floor under the table, tickling each other, and occasionally pulling the baby's toes.

"O! go long, will ye?" said the mother, giving now and then a kick, in a kind of general way, under the table, when the movement became too obstreperous. "Can't ye be decent when white folks comes to see ye? Stop dat ar, now, will ye? Better mind yerselves, or I'll take ye down a button-hole lower, when Mas'r George is gone!"

What meaning was couched under this terrible threat, it is difficult to say; but certain it is that its awful indistinctness seemed to produce very little impression on the young sinners addressed.

"La, now!" said Uncle Tom, "they are so full of tickle all the while, they can't behave theirselves."

Here the boys emerged from under the table, and, with hands and faces well plastered with molasses, began a vigorous kissing of the baby.

"Get along wid ye!" said the mother, pushing away their woolly heads. "Ye'll all stick together, and never get clar, if ye do dat fashion. Go long to de spring and wash yerselves!" she said, seconding her exhortations by a slap, which resounded very formidably, but which seemed only to knock out so much more laugh from the young ones, as they tumbled precipitately over each other out of doors, where they fairly screamed with merriment.

"Did ye ever see such aggravating young uns?" said Aunt Chloe, rather complacently, as, producing an old towel, kept for such emergencies, she poured a little water out of the cracked tea-pot on it, and began rubbing off the molasses from the baby's face and hands; and, having polished her till she shone, she set her down in Tom's lap, while she busied herself in clearing away supper. The baby employed the intervals in pulling Tom's nose, scratching his face, and burying her fat hands in his woolly hair, which last operation seemed to afford her special content.

"Aint she a peart young un?" said Tom, holding her from him to take a full-length view; then, getting up, he set her on his broad shoulder, and began capering and dancing with her, while Mas'r George snapped at her with his pocket-handkerchief, and Mose and Pete, now returning again, roared after her like bears, till Aunt Chloe declared that they "fairly took her head off" with their noise. As, according to her own statement, this surgical operation was a matter of daily occurrence in the cabin, the declaration no whit abated the merriment, till everyone had roared and tumbled and danced themselves down to a state of composure.

"Well, now, I hopes you're done," said Aunt Chloe, who had been busy in pulling out a rude box of a trundle-bed; "and now, you Mose and you Pete, get into that; for we's goin' to have the meetin'."

"O mother, we don't wanter. We wants to sit up to meetin'—meetin's is so curis. We likes 'em."

"La, Aunt Chloe, shove it under, and let 'em sit up," said Mas'r George, decisively, giving a push to the rude machine.

Aunt Chloe, having thus saved appearances, seemed highly delighted to push the thing under, saying, as she did so, "Well, mebbe 't will do 'em some good."

The house now resolved itself into a committee of the whole, to consider the accommodations and arrangements for the meeting.

"What we's to do for cheers, now, *I* declar I don't know," said Aunt Chloe. As the meeting had been held at Uncle Tom's, weekly, for an indefinite length of time, without any more "cheers," there seemed some encouragement to hope that a way would be discovered at present.

"Old Uncle Peter sung both de legs out of dat oldest cheer, last week," suggested Mose.

"You go long! I'll boun' you pulled 'em out; some o' your shines," said Aunt Chloe.

"Well, it'll stand, if it only keeps jam up agin de wall!" said Mose.

"Den Uncle Peter mus'n't sit in it, cause he al'ays hitches when he gets a singing. He hitched pretty nigh across de room, t' other night," said Pete.

"Good Lor! get him in it, then," said Mose, "and den he'd begin, 'Come saints and sinners, hear me tell,' and den down he'd go,"—and Mose imitated precisely the nasal tones of the old man, tumbling on the floor, to illustrate the supposed catastrophe.

"Come now, be decent, can't ye?" said Aunt Chloe; "an't yer shamed?"

Mas'r George, however, joined the offender in the laugh, and declared decidedly that Mose was a "buster." So the maternal admonition seemed rather to fail of effect.

"Well, ole man," said Aunt Chloe, "you'll have to tote in them ar bar'ls."

"Mother's bar'ls is like dat ar widder's, Mas'r George was reading 'bout, in de good book,—dey never fails," said Mose, aside to Pete.

"I'm sure one on 'em caved in last week," said Pete, "and let 'em all down in de middle of de singin'; dat ar was failin', warnt it?"

During this aside between Mose and Pete, two empty casks had been rolled into the cabin, and being secured from rolling, by stones on each side, boards were laid across them, which arrangement, together with the turning down of certain tubs and pails, and the disposing of the rickety chairs, at last completed the preparation.

"Mas'r George is such a beautiful reader, now, I know he'll stay to read for us," said Aunt Chloe; "'pears like 't will be so much more interestin'."

George very readily consented, for your boy is always ready for anything that makes him of importance.

The room was soon filled with a motley assemblage, from the old gray-headed patriarch of eighty, to the young girl and lad of fifteen. A little harmless gossip ensued on various themes, such as where old Aunt Sally got her new red headkerchief, and how "Missis was a going to give Lizzy that spotted muslin gown, when she'd got her new berage made up"; and how Mas'r Shelby was thinking of buying a new sorel colt, that was going to prove an addition to the glories of the place. A few of the worshippers belonged to families hard by, who had got permission to attend, and who brought in various choice scraps of information, about the sayings and doings at the house and on the place, which circulated as freely as the same sort of small change does in higher circles.

After a while the singing commenced, to the evident delight of all present. Not even all the disadvantage of nasal intonation could prevent the effect of the naturally fine voices, in airs at once wild and spirited. The words were sometimes the well-known and common hymns sung in the churches about, and sometimes of a wilder, more indefinite character, picked up at camp-meetings.

The chorus of one of them, which ran as follows, was sung with great energy and unction:

Die on the field of battle,
Die on the field of battle,
  Glory in my soul.

Another special favorite had oft repeated the words—

O, I'm going to glory—won't you come along with me?
Don't you see the angels beck'ning, and a calling me away?
Don't you see the golden city and the everlasting day?

There were others, which made incessant mention of "Jordan's banks," and "Canaan's fields," and the "New Jerusalem"; for the negro mind, impassioned and imaginative, always attached itself to hymns and expressions of a vivid and pictorial nature; and, as they sung, some laughed, and some cried, and some clapped hands, or shook hands rejoicingly with each other, as if they had fairly gained the other side of the river.

Various exhortations, or relations of experience, followed, and intermingled with the singing. One old gray-headed woman, long past work, but much revered as a sort of chronicle of the past, rose, and leaning on her staff, said—

"Well, chil'en! Well, I'm mighty glad to hear ye all and see ye all once more, 'cause I don't know when I'll be gone to glory; but I've done got ready, chil'en; 'pears like I'd got my little bundle all tied up, and my bonnet on, jest a waitin' for the stage to come along and take me home; sometimes, in the night, I think I hear the wheels a rattlin', and I'm lookin' out all the time; now, you jest be ready too, for I tell ye all, chil'en," she said, striking her staff hard on the floor, "dat ar *glory* is a mighty thing! It's a mighty thing, chil'en,—you don'no nothing about it,—it's *wonderful*." And the old creature sat down, with streaming tears, as wholly overcome, while the whole circle struck up—

O Canaan, bright Canaan,
I'm bound for the land of Canaan.

Mas'r George, by request, read the last chapters of Revelation, often interrupted by such exclamations as "The *sakes* now!" "Only hear that!" "Jest think on 'it!" "Is all that a comin' sure enough?"

George, who was a bright boy, and well trained in religious things by his mother, finding himself an object of general admiration, threw in expositions of his own, from time to time, with a commendable seriousness and gravity, for which he was admired by the young and blessed by the old; and it was agreed, on all hands, that "a minister couldn't lay it off better than he did"; that "'twas reely 'mazin'!"

Uncle Tom was a sort of patriarch in religious matters, in the neighborhood. Having, naturally, an organization in which the *morale* was strongly predominant, together with a greater breadth and cultivation of mind than obtained among his companions, he was looked up to with great respect, as a sort of minister among them; and the simple, hearty, sincere style of his exhortations might have edified even better educated persons. But it was in prayer that he especially excelled. Nothing could exceed the touching simplicity, the child-like earnestness, of his prayer, enriched with the language of Scripture, which seemed so entirely to have wrought itself into his being, as to have become a part of himself, and to drop from his lips unconsciously; in the language of a pious old negro, he "prayed right up." And so much did his prayer always work on the devotional feelings of his audiences, that there seemed often a danger that it would be lost altogether in the abundance of the responses which broke out everywhere around him.

———

While this scene was passing in the cabin of the man, one quite otherwise passed in the halls of the master.

The trader and Mr. Shelby were seated together in the dining room afore-named, at a table covered with papers and writing utensils.

Mr. Shelby was busy in counting some bundles of bills, which, as they were counted, he pushed over to the trader, who counted them likewise.

"All fair," said the trader; "and now for signing these yer."

Mr. Shelby hastily drew the bills of sale towards him, and signed them, like a man that hurries over some disagreeable business, and then pushed them over with the money. Haley produced, from a well-worn valise, a parchment, which, after looking over it a moment, he handed to Mr. Shelby, who took it with a gesture of suppressed eagerness.

"Wal, now, the thing's *done!*" said the trader, getting up.

"It's *done!*" said Mr. Shelby, in a musing tone; and, fetching a long breath, he repeated, "*It's done!*"

"Yer don't seem to feel much pleased with it, 'pears to me," said the trader.

"Haley," said Mr. Shelby, "I hope you'll remember that you promised, on your honor, you wouldn't sell Tom, without knowing what sort of hands he's going into."

"Why, you've just done it, sir," said the trader.

"Circumstances, you well know, *obliged* me," said Shelby, haughtily.

"Wal, you know, they may 'blige *me*, too," said the trader. "Howsomever, I'll do the very best I can in getting' Tom a good berth; as to my treatin' on him bad, you needn't be a grain afeard. If there's anything that I thank the Lord for, it is that I'm never noways cruel."

After the expositions which the trader had previously given of his humane principles, Mr. Shelby did not feel particularly reassured by these declarations; but, as they were the best comfort the case admitted of, he allowed the trader to depart in silence, and betook himself to a solitary cigar.

Chapter 5
Showing the Feelings of Living Property on Changing Owners

Mr. and Mrs. Shelby had retired to their apartment for the night. He was lounging in a large easy-chair, looking over some letters that had come in the afternoon mail, and she was standing before her mirror, brushing out the complicated braids and curls in which Eliza had arranged her hair; for, noticing her pale cheeks and haggard eyes, she had excused her attendance that night, and ordered her to bed. The employment, naturally enough, suggested her conversation with the girl in the morning; and, turning to her husband, she said, carelessly,

"By the by, Arthur, who was that low-bred fellow that you lugged in to our dinner-table today?"

"Haley is his name," said Shelby, turning himself rather uneasily in his chair, and continuing with his eyes fixed on a letter.

"Haley! Who is he, and what may be his business here, pray?"

"Well, he's a man that I transacted some business with, last time I was at Natchez," said Mr. Shelby.

"And he presumed on it to make himself quite at home, and call and dine here, ay?"

"Why, I invited him; I had some accounts with him," said Shelby.

"Is he a negro-trader?" said Mrs. Shelby, noticing a certain embarrassment in her husband's manner.

"Why, my dear, what put that into your head?" said Shelby, looking up.

"Nothing—only Eliza came in here, after dinner, in a great worry, crying and taking on, and said you were talking with a trader, and that she heard him make an offer for her boy—the ridiculous little goose!"

"She did, hey?" said Mr. Shelby, returning to his paper, which he seemed for a few moments quite intent upon, not perceiving that he was holding it bottom upwards.

"It will have to come out," said he, mentally; "as well now as ever."

"I told Eliza," said Mrs. Shelby, as she continued brushing her hair, "that she was a little fool for her pains, and that you never had anything to do with that sort of persons. Of course, I knew you never meant to sell any of our people—least of all, to such a fellow."

"Well, Emily," said her husband, "so I have always felt and said; but the fact is that my business lies so that I cannot get on without. I shall have to sell some of my hands."

"To that creature? Impossible! Mr. Shelby, you cannot be serious."

"I'm sorry to say that I am," said Mr. Shelby. "I've agreed to sell Tom."

"What! our Tom? that good, faithful creature! been your faithful servant from a boy! O, Mr. Shelby! and you have promised him his freedom, too—you and I have spoken to him a hundred times of it. Well, I can believe anything now—I can believe *now* that you could sell little Harry, poor Eliza's only child!" said Mrs. Shelby, in a tone between grief and indignation.

"Well, since you must know all, it is so. I have agreed to sell Tom and Harry both; and I don't know why I am to be rated as if I were a monster for doing what everyone does every day."

"But why, of all others, choose these?" said Mrs. Shelby. "Why sell them, of all on the place, if you must sell at all?"

"Because they will bring the highest sum of any—that's why. I could choose another, if you say so. The fellow made me a high bid on Eliza, if that would suit you any better," said Mr. Shelby.

"The wretch!" said Mrs. Shelby, vehemently.

"Well, I didn't listen to it, a moment—out of regard to your feelings, I wouldn't—so give me some credit."

"My dear," said Mrs. Shelby, recollecting herself, "forgive me. I have been hasty. I was surprised, and entirely unprepared for this—but surely you will allow me to intercede for these poor creatures.

Tom is a noble-hearted, faithful fellow, if he is black. I do believe, Mr. Shelby, that if he were put to it, he would lay down his life for you."

"I know it, I dare say; but what's the use of all this? I can't help myself."

"Why not make a pecuniary sacrifice? I'm willing to bear my part of the inconvenience. O, Mr. Shelby, I have tried—tried most faithfully, as a Christian woman should—to do my duty to these poor, simple, dependent creatures. I have cared for them, instructed them, watched over them, and known all their little cares and joys, for years; and how can I ever hold up my head again among them if, for the sake of a little paltry gain, we sell such a faithful, excellent, confiding creature as poor Tom, and tear from him in a moment all we have taught him to love and value? I have taught them the duties of the family, of parent and child, and husband and wife; and how can I bear to have this open acknowledgement that we care for no tie, no duty, no relation, however sacred, compared with money? I have talked with Eliza about her boy—her duty to him as a Christian mother, to watch over him, pray for him, and bring him up in a Christian way; and now what can I say, if you tear him away, and sell him, soul and body, to a profane, unprincipled man, just to save a little money? I have told her that one soul is worth more than all the money in the world; and how will she believe me when she sees us turn round and sell her child? sell him, perhaps, to certain ruin of body and soul!"

"I'm sorry you feel so about it, Emily—indeed I am," said Mr. Shelby; "and I respect your feelings, too, though I don't pretend to share them to their full extent; but I tell you now, solemnly, it's of no use—I can't help myself. I didn't mean to tell you this, Emily; but, in plain words, there is no choice between selling these two and selling everything. Either they must go, or *all* must. Haley has come into possession of a mortgage, which, if I don't clear off with him directly, will take everything before it. I've raked, and scraped, and borrowed, and all but begged—and the price of these two was needed to make up the balance, and I had to give them up. Haley fancied the child; he agreed to settle the matter that way, and no other. I was in his power, and *had* to do it. If you feel so to have them sold, would it be any better to have *all* sold?"

Mrs. Shelby stood like one stricken. Finally, turning to her toilet, she rested her face in her hands, and gave a sort of groan.

"This is God's curse on slavery! a bitter, bitter, most accursed thing! a curse to the master and a curse to the slave! I was a fool to think I could make anything good out of such a deadly evil. It is a sin to hold a slave under laws like ours—I always felt it was—I always thought so when I was a girl—I thought so still more after I joined the church; but I thought I could gild it over—I thought, by kindness, and care, and instruction, I could make the condition of mine better than freedom—fool that I was!"

"Why, wife, you are getting to be an abolitionist, quite."

"Abolitionist! if they knew all I know about slavery, they *might* talk! We don't need them to tell us; you know I never thought that slavery was right—never felt willing to own slaves."

"Well, therein you differ from many wise and pious men," said Mr. Shelby. "You remember Mr. B.'s sermon, the other Sunday?"

"I don't want to hear such sermons; I never wish to hear Mr. B. in our church again. Ministers can't help the evil, perhaps—can't cure it, any more than we can—but defend it! it always went against my common sense. And I think you didn't think much of that sermon, either."

"Well," said Shelby, "I must say these ministers sometimes carry matters further than we poor sinners would exactly dare to do. We men of the world must wink pretty hard at various things, and get used to a deal that isn't the exact thing. But we don't quite fancy, when women and ministers come out broad and square, and go beyond us in matters of either modesty or morals, that's a fact. But now, my dear, I trust you see the necessity of the thing, and you see that I have done the very best that circumstances would allow."

"O yes, yes!" said Mrs. Shelby, hurriedly and abstractedly fingering her gold watch, "I haven't any jewelry of any amount," she added, thoughtfully; "but would not this watch do something? it was an expensive one, when it was bought. If I could only at least save Eliza's child, I would sacrifice anything I have."

"I'm sorry, very sorry, Emily," said Mr. Shelby, "I'm sorry this takes hold of you so; but it will do no good. The fact is, Emily, the thing's done; the bills of sale are already signed, and in Haley's hands; and you must be thankful it is no worse. That man has had it in his power to ruin us all—and now he is fairly off. If you knew the man as I do, you'd think that we had had a narrow escape."

"Is he so hard, then?"

"Why, not a cruel man, exactly, but a man of leather—a man alive to nothing but trade and profit—cool, and unhesitating, and unrelenting, as death and the grave. He'd sell his own mother at a good percentage—not wishing the old woman any harm, either."

"And this wretch owns that good, faithful Tom, and Eliza's child!"

"Well, my dear, the fact is that this goes rather hard with me; it's a thing I hate to think of. Haley wants to drive matters, and take possession tomorrow. I'm going to get out my horse bright and early, and be off. I can't see Tom, that's a fact; and you had better arrange a drive somewhere, and carry Eliza off. Let the thing be done when she is out of sight."

"No, no," said Mrs. Shelby; "I'll be in no sense accomplice or help in this cruel business. I'll go and see poor old Tom, God help him, in his distress! They shall see, at any rate, that their mistress can feel for and with them. As to Eliza, I dare not think about it. The Lord forgive us! What have we done, that this cruel necessity should come on us?"

There was one listener to this conversation whom Mr. and Mrs. Shelby little suspected.

Communicating with their apartment was a large closet, opening by a door into the outer passage. When Mrs. Shelby had dismissed Eliza for the night, her feverish and excited mind had suggested the idea of this closet; and she had hidden herself there, and, with her ear pressed close against the crack of the door, had not lost a word of the conversation.

When the voices died into silence, she rose and crept stealthily away. Pale, shivering, with rigid features and compressed lips, she looked an entirely altered being from the soft and timid creature she had been hitherto. She moved cautiously along the entry, paused one moment at her mistress' door, and raised her hands in mute appeal to Heaven, and then turned and glided into her own room. It was a quiet, neat apartment, on the same floor with her mistress. There was the pleasant sunny window, where she had often sat singing at her sewing; there a little case of books, and various little fancy articles, ranged by them, the gifts of Christmas holidays; there was her simple wardrobe in the closet and in the drawers: here was, in short, her home; and, on the whole, a happy one it had been to her. But there, on the bed, lay her slumbering boy, his long curls falling negligently around his unconscious face, his rosy mouth half open, his little fat hands thrown out over the bedclothes, and a smile spread like a sunbeam over his whole face.

"Poor boy! poor fellow!" said Eliza; "they have sold you! but your mother will save you yet!"

No tear dropped over that pillow; in such straits as these, the heart has no tears to give—it drops only blood, bleeding itself away in silence. She took a piece of paper and a pencil, and wrote, hastily,

"O, Missis! dear Missis! don't think me ungrateful—don't think hard of me, any way—I heard all you and master said tonight. I am going to try to save my boy—you will not blame me! God bless and reward you for all your kindness!"

Hastily folding and directing this, she went to a drawer and made up a little package of clothing for her boy, which she tied with a handkerchief firmly round her waist; and, so fond is a mother's remembrance, that, even in the terrors of that hour, she did not forget to put in the little package one or two of his favorite toys, reserving a gayly painted parrot to amuse him, when she should be called on to awaken him. It was some trouble to arouse the little sleeper; but, after some effort, he sat up, and was playing with his bird, while his mother was putting on her bonnet and shawl.

"Where are you going, mother?" said he, as she drew near the bed, with his little coat and cap.

His mother drew near, and looked so earnestly into his eyes, that he at once divined that something unusual was the matter.

"Hush, Harry," she said; "mustn't speak loud, or they will hear us. A wicked man was coming to take little Harry away from his mother, and carry him 'way off in the dark; but mother won't let him—she's going to put on her little boy's cap and coat, and run off with him, so the ugly man can't catch him."

Saying these words, she had tied and buttoned on the child's simple outfit, and, taking him in her arms, she whispered to him to be very still; and, opening a door in her room which led into the outer verandah, she glided noiselessly out.

It was a sparkling, frosty, starlight night, and the mother wrapped the shawl close round her child, as, perfectly quiet with vague terror, he clung round her neck.

Old Bruno, a great Newfoundland who slept at the end of the porch, rose, with a low groan, as she came near. She gently spoke his name, and the animal, an old pet and playmate of hers, instantly, wagging his tail, prepared to follow her, though apparently revolving much, in his simple dog's head, what such an indiscreet midnight promenade might mean. Some dim ideas of imprudence or impropriety in the measure seemed to embarrass him considerably; for he often stopped, as Eliza glided forward, and looked wistfully, first at her and then at the house, and then, as if reassured by reflection, he pattered along after her again. A few minutes brought them to the window of Uncle Tom's cottage, and Eliza, stopping, tapped lightly on the window-pane.

The prayer-meeting at Uncle Tom's had, in the order of hymn-singing, been protracted to a very late hour; and, as Uncle Tom had indulged himself in a few lengthy solos afterwards, the consequence was, that, although it was now between twelve and one o'clock, he and his worthy helpmeet were not yet asleep.

"Good Lord! what's that?" said Aunt Chloe, starting up and hastily drawing the curtain. "My sakes alive, if it an't Lizy! Get on your clothes, old man, quick! there's old Bruno, too, a pawin' round; what on airth! I'm gwine to open the door."

And, suiting the action to the word, the door flew open, and the light of the tallow candle, which Tom had hastily lighted, fell on the haggard face and dark, wild eyes of the fugitive.

"Lord bless you! I'm skeered to look at ye, Lizy! Are ye tuck[1] sick, or what's come over ye?"

"I'm running away—Uncle Tom and Aunt Chloe—carrying off my child—Master sold him!"

"Sold him?" echoed both, lifting up their hands in dismay.

"Yes, sold him!" said Eliza, firmly; "I crept into the closet by Mistress' door tonight, and I heard Master tell Missis that he had sold my Harry, and you, Uncle Tom, both, to a trader; and that he was going off this morning on his horse, and that the man was to take possession today."

Tom had stood, during this speech, with his hands raised, and his eyes dilated, like a man in a dream. Slowly and gradually, as its

---

1   *tuck*   Took; taken.

meaning came over him, he collapsed, rather than seated himself, on his old chair, and sunk his head down upon his knees.

"The good Lord have pity on us!" said Aunt Chloe. "O! it don't seem as if it was true! What has he done, that Mas'r should sell *him*?"

"He hasn't done anything—it isn't for that. Master don't want to sell; and Missis—she's always good. I heard her plead and beg for us; but he told her 'twas no use; that he was in this man's debt, and that this man had got the power over him; and that if he didn't pay him off clear, it would end in his having to sell the place and all the people, and move off. Yes, I heard him say there was no choice between selling these two and selling all, the man was driving him so hard. Master said he was sorry; but oh, Missis—you ought to have heard her talk! If she an't a Christian and an angel, there never was one. I'm a wicked girl to leave her so; but, then, I can't help it. She said, herself, one soul was worth more than the world; and this boy has a soul, and if I let him be carried off, who knows what'll become of it? It must be right: but, if it an't right, the Lord forgive me, for I can't help doing it!"

"Well, old man!" said Aunt Chloe, "why don't you go, too? Will you wait to be toted down river, where they kill niggers with hard work and starving? I'd a heap rather die than go there, any day! There's time for ye—be off with Lizy—you've got a pass to come and go any time.[1] Come, bustle up, and I'll get your things together."

Tom slowly raised his head, and looked sorrowfully but quietly around, and said,

"No, no—I an't going. Let Eliza go—it's her right! I wouldn't be the one to say no—'tant in *natur* for her to stay; but you heard what she said! If I must be sold, or all the people on the place, and everything go to rack, why, let me be sold. I s'pose I can b'ar it as well as any on 'em," he added, while something like a sob and a sigh shook his broad, rough chest convulsively. "Mas'r always found me on the spot—he always will. I never have broke trust, nor used my pass no ways contrary to my word, and I never will. It's better for me alone to go, than to break up the place and sell all. Mas'r an't to blame, Chloe, and he'll take care of you and the poor—"

Here he turned to the rough trundle-bed full of little woolly heads,

---

[1] *you've got ... any time* In order to travel on their own, enslaved persons often required written documents from their enslavers, granting them permission to do so.

and broke fairly down. He leaned over the back of the chair, and covered his face with his large hands. Sobs, heavy, hoarse and loud, shook the chair, and great tears fell through his fingers on the floor: just such tears, sir, as you dropped into the coffin where lay your first-born son; such tears, woman, as you shed when you heard the cries of your dying babe. For, sir, he was a man—and you are but another man. And, woman, though dressed in silk and jewels, you are but a woman, and, in life's great straits and mighty griefs, ye feel but one sorrow!

"And now," said Eliza, as she stood in the door, "I saw my husband only this afternoon, and I little knew then what was to come. They have pushed him to the very last standing-place, and he told me, today, that he was going to run away. Do try, if you can, to get word to him. Tell him how I went, and why I went; and tell him I'm going to try and find Canada. You must give my love to him, and tell him, if I never see him again,"—she turned away, and stood with her back to them for a moment, and then added, in a husky voice, "tell him to be as good as he can, and try and meet me in the kingdom of heaven."

"Call Bruno in there," she added. "Shut the door on him, poor beast! He mustn't go with me!"

A few last words and tears, a few simple adieus and blessings, and, clasping her wondering and affrighted child in her arms, she glided noiselessly away.

Chapter 7
The Mother's Struggle

It is impossible to conceive of a human creature more wholly desolate and forlorn than Eliza, when she turned her footsteps from Uncle Tom's cabin.

Her husband's suffering and dangers, and the danger of her child, all blended in her mind, with a confused and stunning sense of the risk she was running, in leaving the only home she had ever known, and cutting loose from the protection of a friend whom she loved and revered. Then there was the parting from every familiar object—the place where she had grown up, the trees under which she had played, the groves where she had walked many an evening in happier days, by the side of her young husband—everything, as it lay in the clear, frosty starlight, seemed to speak reproachfully to her, and ask her whither could she go from a home like that?

But stronger than all was maternal love, wrought into a paroxysm of frenzy by the near approach of a fearful danger. Her boy was old enough to have walked by her side, and, in an indifferent case, she would only have led him by the hand; but now the bare thought of putting him out of her arms made her shudder, and she strained him to her bosom with a convulsive grasp, as she went rapidly forward.

The frosty ground creaked beneath her feet, and she trembled at the sound; every quaking leaf and fluttering shadow sent the blood backward to her heart, and quickened her footsteps. She wondered within herself at the strength that seemed to be come upon her; for she felt the weight of her boy as if it had been a feather, and every flutter of fear seemed to increase the supernatural power that bore her on, while from her pale lips burst forth, in frequent ejaculations,[1] the prayer to a Friend above—"Lord, help! Lord, save me!"

If it were *your* Harry, mother, or your Willie, that were going to be torn from you by a brutal trader, tomorrow morning—if you had seen the man, and heard that the papers were signed and delivered, and you had only from twelve o'clock till morning to make good your escape—how fast could *you* walk? How many miles could you make in those few brief hours, with the darling at your bosom—the little sleepy head on your shoulder—the small, soft arms trustingly holding on to your neck?

For the child slept. At first, the novelty and alarm kept him waking; but his mother so hurriedly repressed every breath or sound, and so assured him that if he were only still she would certainly save him, that he clung quietly round her neck, only asking, as he found himself sinking to sleep,

"Mother, I don't need to keep awake, do I?"

"No, my darling; sleep, if you want to."

"But, mother, if I do get asleep, you won't let him get me?"

"No! so may God help me!" said his mother, with a paler cheek, and a brighter light in her large dark eyes.

"You're *sure*, an't you, mother?"

---

1 *ejaculations* Outbursts; exclamations.

"Yes, *sure!*" said the mother, in a voice that startled herself; for it seemed to her to come from a spirit within, that was no part of her; and the boy dropped his little weary head on her shoulder, and was soon asleep. How the touch of those warm arms, the gentle breathings that came in her neck, seemed to add fire and spirit to her movements! It seemed to her as if strength poured into her in electric streams, from every gentle touch and movement of the sleeping, confiding child. Sublime is the dominion of the mind over the body, that, for a time, can make flesh and nerve impregnable, and string the sinews like steel, so that the weak become so mighty.

The boundaries of the farm, the grove, the wood-lot, passed by her dizzily, as she walked on; and still she went, leaving one familiar object after another, slacking not, pausing not, till reddening daylight found her many a long mile from all traces of any familiar objects upon the open highway.

She had often been, with her mistress, to visit some connections, in the little village of T———, not far from the Ohio River, and knew the road well. To go thither, to escape across the Ohio River, were the first hurried outlines of her plan of escape; beyond that, she could only hope in God.

When horses and vehicles began to move along the highway, with that alert perception peculiar to a state of excitement, and which seems to be a sort of inspiration, she became aware that her headlong pace and distracted air might bring on her remark and suspicion. She therefore put the boy on the ground and, adjusting her dress and bonnet, she walked on at as rapid a pace as she thought consistent with the preservation of appearances. In her little bundle she had provided a store of cakes[1] and apples, which she used as expedients for quickening the speed of the child, rolling the apple some yards before them, when the boy would run with all his might after it; and this ruse, often repeated, carried them over many a half-mile.

After a while, they came to a thick patch of woodland, through which murmured a clear brook. As the child complained of hunger and thirst, she climbed over the fence with him; and, sitting down behind a large rock which concealed them from the road, she gave

---

1   *cakes*   Likely including leavened breads, corn cakes, and fruit cakes rather than confections.

him a breakfast out of her little package. The boy wondered and grieved that she could not eat; and when, putting his arms round her neck, he tried to wedge some of his cake into her mouth, it seemed to her that the rising in her throat would choke her.

"No, no, Harry darling! mother can't eat till you are safe! We must go on—on—till we come to the river!" And she hurried again into the road, and again constrained herself to walk regularly and composedly forward.

She was many miles past any neighborhood where she was personally known. If she should chance to meet any who knew her, she reflected that the well-known kindness of the family would be of itself a blind to suspicion, as making it an unlikely supposition that she could be a fugitive. As she was also so white as not to be known as of colored lineage, without a critical survey, and her child was white also, it was much easier for her to pass on unsuspected.

On this presumption, she stopped at noon at a neat farmhouse, to rest herself, and buy some dinner for her child and self; for, as the danger decreased with the distance, the supernatural tension of the nervous system lessened, and she found herself both weary and hungry.

The good woman, kindly and gossiping, seemed rather pleased than otherwise with having somebody come in to talk with; and accepted, without examination, Eliza's statement, that she "was going on a little piece, to spend a week with her friends,"—all which she hoped in her heart might prove strictly true.

An hour before sunset, she entered the village of T——, by the Ohio River, weary and foot-sore, but still strong in heart. Her first glance was at the river, which lay, like Jordan, between her and the Canaan[1] of liberty on the other side.

It was now early spring, and the river was swollen and turbulent; great cakes of floating ice were swinging heavily to and fro in the turbid waters. Owing to the peculiar form of the shore on the Kentucky side, the land bending far out into the water, the ice had been lodged and detained in great quantities, and the narrow channel which swept round the bend was full of ice, piled one cake over another, thus

---

1   *like Jordan ... Canaan* In the Old Testament, Canaan is a prosperous region west of the Jordan River that is promised by God to the Israelites after their liberation from slavery in Egypt. "Crossing Jordan" became a widespread metaphor for escaping from slavery.

forming a temporary barrier to the descending ice, which lodged, and formed a great, undulating raft, filling up the whole river, and extending almost to the Kentucky shore.

Eliza stood, for a moment, contemplating this unfavorable aspect of things, which she saw at once must prevent the usual ferry-boat from running, and then turned into a small public house[1] on the bank, to make a few inquiries.

The hostess, who was busy in various fizzing and stewing operations over the fire, preparatory to the evening meal, stopped, with a fork in her hand, as Eliza's sweet and plaintive voice arrested her.

"What is it?" she said.

"Isn't there any ferry or boat, that takes people over to B——, now?" she said.

"No, indeed!" said the woman; "the boats has stopped running."

Eliza's look of dismay and disappointment struck the woman, and she said, inquiringly,

"Maybe you're wanting to get over? anybody sick? Ye seem mighty anxious?"

"I've got a child that's very dangerous,"[2] said Eliza. "I never heard of it till last night, and I've walked quite a piece today, in hopes to get to the ferry."

"Well, now, that's onlucky," said the woman, whose motherly sympathies were much aroused; "I'm re'lly consarned for ye. Solomon!" she called, from the window, towards a small back building. A man, in leather apron and very dirty hands, appeared at the door.

"I say, Sol," said the woman, "is that ar man going to tote them bar'ls over tonight?"

"He said he should try, if 't was any way prudent," said the man.

"There's a man a piece down here, that's going over with some truck[3] this evening, if he durs' to; he'll be in here to supper tonight, so you'd better set down and wait. That's a sweet little fellow," added the woman, offering him a cake.

But the child, wholly exhausted, cried with weariness.

"Poor fellow! he isn't used to walking, and I've hurried him on so," said Eliza.

---

1   *public house*   Business providing food, drink, and often accommodation.
2   *dangerous*   I.e., dangerously ill.
3   *truck*   Goods for transport.

"Well, take him into this room," said the woman, opening into a small bedroom, where stood a comfortable bed. Eliza laid the weary boy upon it, and held his hands in hers till he was fast asleep. For her there was no rest. As a fire in her bones, the thought of the pursuer urged her on; and she gazed with longing eyes on the sullen, surging waters that lay between her and liberty.

Here we must take our leave of her for the present, to follow the course of her pursuers.

———

Though Mrs. Shelby had promised that the dinner should be hurried on table, yet it was soon seen, as the thing has often been seen before, that it required more than one to make a bargain. So, although the order was fairly given out in Haley's hearing, and carried to Aunt Chloe by at least half a dozen juvenile messengers, that dignitary only gave certain very gruff snorts, and tosses of her head, and went on with every operation in an unusually leisurely and circumstantial manner.

For some singular reason, an impression seemed to reign among the servants generally that Missis would not be particularly disobliged by delay; and it was wonderful what a number of counter accidents occurred constantly, to retard the course of things. One luckless wight[1] contrived to upset the gravy; and then gravy had to be got up *de novo*,[1] with due care and formality, Aunt Chloe watching and stirring with dogged precision, answering shortly, to all suggestions of haste, that she "warn't a going to have raw gravy on the table, to help nobody's catchings." One tumbled down with the water, and had to go to the spring for more; and another precipitated the butter into the path of events; and there was from time to time giggling news brought into the kitchen that "Mas'r Haley was mighty oneasy, and that he couldn't sit in his cheer no ways, but was a walkin' and stalkin' to the winders and through the porch."

"Sarves him right!" said Aunt Chloe, indignantly. "He'll get wus nor oneasy,[2] one of these days, if he don't mend his ways. *His* master'll be sending for him, and then see how he'll look!"

---

1   *wight* Creature; person;   *de novo* Latin: once again.
2   *wus nor oneasy* I.e., worse than uneasy.

"He'll go to torment, and no mistake," said little Jake.

"He desarves it!" said Aunt Chloe, grimly; "he's broke a many, many, many hearts—I tell ye all!" she said, stopping, with a fork uplifted in her hands; "it's like what Mas'r George reads in Ravelations—souls a callin' under the altar! and a callin' on the Lord for vengeance on sich! and by and by the Lord he'll hear 'em—so he will!"[1]

Aunt Chloe, who was much revered in the kitchen, was listened to with open mouth; and, the dinner being now fairly sent in, the whole kitchen was at leisure to gossip with her, and to listen to her remarks.

"Sich'll be burnt up forever, and no mistake; won't ther?" said Andy.

"I'd be glad to see it, I'll be boun'," said little Jake.

"Chil'en!" said a voice, that made them all start. It was Uncle Tom, who had come in, and stood listening to the conversation at the door.

"Chil'en!" he said, "I'm afeard you don't know what ye're sayin'. Forever is a *dre'ful* word, chil'en; it's awful to think on't. You oughten-ter wish that ar to any human crittur."

"We wouldn't to anybody but the soul-drivers,"[2] said Andy; "nobody can help wishing it to them, they's so awful wicked."

"Don't natur herself kinder cry out on 'em?" said Aunt Chloe. "Don't dey tear der suckin' baby right off his mother's breast, and sell him, and der little children as is crying and holding on by her clothes—don't dey pull 'em off and sells 'em? Don't dey tear wife and husband apart?" said Aunt Chloe, beginning to cry, "when it's jest takin' the very life on 'em? and all the while does they feel one bit—don't dey drink and smoke, and take it oncommon easy? Lor, if the devil don't get them, what's he good for?" And Aunt Chloe covered her face with her checked apron, and began to sob in good earnest.

---

1   *it's like ... he will!*   See Revelation 6.9–10, in which Christ opens the seven seals of a book, instigating the beginning of the Apocalypse: "And when he had opened the fifth seal, I saw under the altar the souls of them that were slain for the word of God, and for the testimony which they held: / And they cried with a loud voice, saying, How long, O Lord, holy and true, dost thou not judge and avenge our blood on them that dwell on the earth?"

2   *soul-drivers*   Phrase commonly used to refer either to slave traders or to plantation overseers.

"Pray for them that 'spitefully use you, the good book says,"[1] says Tom.

"Pray for 'em!" said Aunt Chloe; "Lor, it's too tough! I can't pray for 'em."

"It's natur, Chloe, and natur's strong," said Tom, "but the Lord's grace is stronger; besides, you oughter think what an awful state a poor crittur's soul's in that'll do them ar things—you oughter thank God that you an't *like* him, Chloe. I'm sure I'd rather be sold, ten thousand times over, than to have all that ar poor crittur's got to answer for."

"So'd I, a heap," said Jake. "Lor, *shouldn't* we cotch it, Andy?"

Andy shrugged his shoulders, and gave an acquiescent whistle.

"I'm glad Mas'r didn't go off this morning, as he looked to," said Tom; "that ar hurt me more than sellin', it did. Mebbe it might have been natural for him, but 't would have come desp't hard on me, as has known him from a baby; but I've seen Mas'r, and I begin ter feel sort o' reconciled to the Lord's will now. Mas'r couldn't help hisself; he did right, but I'm feared things will be kinder goin' to rack,[2] when I'm gone. Mas'r can't be spected to be a pryin' round everywhar, as I've done, a keepin' up all the ends. The boys all means well, but they's powerful car'less. That ar troubles me."

The bell here rang, and Tom was summoned to the parlor.

"Tom," said his master, kindly, "I want you to notice that I give this gentleman bonds to forfeit a thousand dollars if you are not on the spot when he wants you; he's going today to look after his other business, and you can have the day to yourself. Go anywhere you like, boy."

"Thank you, Mas'r," said Tom.

"And mind yerself," said the trader, "and don't come it over your master with any o' yer nigger tricks; for I'll take every cent out of him, if you an't thar. If he'd hear to me, he wouldn't trust any on ye—slippery as eels!"

---

1 *Pray for ... book says* See Matthew 5.44: "But I say unto you, Love your enemies, bless them that curse you, do good to them that hate you, and pray for them which despitefully use you, and persecute you," and Luke 6.28: "Bless them that curse you, and pray for them which despitefully use you."

2 *rack* Wreck.

"Mas'r," said Tom—and he stood very straight—"I was jist eight years old when ole Missis put you into my arms, and you wasn't a year old. 'Thar,' says she, 'Tom, that's to be *your* young Mas'r; take good care on him,' says she. And now I jist ask you, Mas'r, have I ever broke word to you, or gone contrary to you, 'specially since I was a Christian?"

Mr. Shelby was fairly overcome, and the tears rose to his eyes.

"My good boy," said he, "the Lord knows you say but the truth; and if I was able to help it, all the world shouldn't buy you."

"And sure as I am a Christian woman," said Mrs. Shelby, "you shall be redeemed as soon as I can any way bring together means. Sir," she said to Haley, "take good account of who you sell him to, and let me know."

"Lor, yes, for that matter," said the trader, "I may bring him up in a year, not much the wuss for wear, and trade him back."

"I'll trade with you then, and make it for your advantage," said Mrs. Shelby.

"Of course," said the trader, "all's equal with me; li'ves trade 'em up as down, so I does a good business. All I want is a livin', you know, ma'am; that's all any on us wants, I s'pose."

Mr. and Mrs. Shelby both felt annoyed and degraded by the familiar[1] impudence of the trader, and yet both saw the absolute necessity of putting a constraint on their feelings. The more hopelessly sordid and insensible he appeared, the greater became Mrs. Shelby's dread of his succeeding in recapturing Eliza and her child, and of course the greater her motive for detaining him by every female artifice. She therefore graciously smiled, assented, chatted familiarly, and did all she could to make time pass imperceptibly.

At two o'clock Sam and Andy[2] brought the horses up to the posts, apparently greatly refreshed and invigorated by the scamper of the morning.

Sam was there new oiled from dinner, with an abundance of zealous and ready officiousness. As Haley approached, he was boasting, in flourishing style, to Andy, of the evident and eminent success of the operation, now that he had "farly come to it."

---

1 *familiar* Inappropriately informal.

2 *Sam and Andy* Two other men enslaved by the Shelbys, commanded by Mr. Shelby to aid Haley in finding Eliza.

"Your master, I s'pose, don't keep no dogs," said Haley, thoughtfully, as he prepared to mount.

"Heaps on 'em," said Sam, triumphantly; "thar's Bruno—he's a roarer! and, besides that, 'bout every nigger of us keeps a pup of some natur or uther."

"Poh!" said Haley—and he said something else, too, with regard to the said dogs, at which Sam muttered,

"I don't see no use cussin' on 'em, no way."

"But your master don't keep no dogs (I pretty much know he don't) for trackin' out niggers."

Sam knew exactly what he meant, but he kept on a look of earnest and desperate simplicity.

"Our dogs all smells round considable sharp. I spect they's the kind, though they han't never had no practice. They's *far* dogs, though, at most anything, if you'd get 'em started. Here, Bruno," he called, whistling to the lumbering Newfoundland, who came pitching tumultuously toward them.

"You go hang!" said Haley, getting up. "Come, tumble up now."

Sam tumbled up accordingly, dexterously contriving to tickle Andy as he did so, which occasioned Andy to split out into a laugh, greatly to Haley's indignation, who made a cut at him with his riding-whip.

"I's 'stonished at yer, Andy," said Sam, with awful gravity. "This yer's a seris bisness, Andy. Yer mustn't be a makin' game. This yer an't no way to help Mas'r."

"I shall take the straight road to the river," said Haley, decidedly, after they had come to the boundaries of the estate. "I know the way of all of 'em—they makes tracks for the underground."[1]

"Sartin," said Sam, "dat's de idee. Mas'r Haley hits de thing right in de middle. Now, der's two roads to de river—de dirt road and der pike[2]—which Mas'r mean to take?"

Andy looked up innocently at Sam, surprised at hearing this new geographical fact, but instantly confirmed what he said, by a vehement reiteration.

"Cause," said Sam, "I'd rather be 'clined to 'magine that Lizy'd take de dirt road, bein' it's the least travelled."

---

1 *underground* The Underground Railroad, a secret traveling network (and network of safe-houses) by means of which many enslaved persons escaped to the North.

2 *pike* Paid road; highway.

Haley, notwithstanding that he was a very old bird, and naturally inclined to be suspicious of chaff,[1] was rather brought up by this view of the case.

"If yer warn't both on yer such cussed liars, now!" he said, contemplatively, as he pondered a moment.

The pensive, reflective tone in which this was spoken appeared to amuse Andy prodigiously, and he drew a little behind, and shook so as apparently to run a great risk of falling off his horse, while Sam's face was immovably composed into the most doleful gravity.

"Course," said Sam, "Mas'r can do as he'd ruther; go de straight road, if Mas'r thinks best—it's all one to us. Now, when I study 'pon it, I think de straight road de best, *decidedly*."

"She would naturally go a lonesome way," said Haley, thinking aloud, and not minding Sam's remark.

"Dar an't no sayin'," said Sam; "gals is pecular; they never does nothin' ye thinks they will; mose gen'lly the contrar. Gals is nat'lly made contrary; and so, if you thinks they've gone one road, it is sartin you'd better go t' other, and then you'll be sure to find 'em. Now, my private 'pinion is, Lizy took der dirt road; so I think we'd better take de straight one."

This profound generic view of the female sex did not seem to dispose Haley particularly to the straight road; and he announced decidedly that he should go the other, and asked Sam when they should come to it.

"A little piece ahead," said Sam, giving a wink to Andy with the eye which was on Andy's side of the head; and he added, gravely, "but I've studded on de matter, and I'm quite clar we ought not to go dat ar way. I nebber been over it no way. It's despit[2] lonesome, and we might lose our way—whar we'd come to, de Lord only knows."

"Nevertheless," said Haley, "I shall go that way."

"Now I think on't, I think I hearn 'em tell that dat ar road was all fenced up and down by der creek, and thar, an't it, Andy?"

Andy wasn't certain; he'd only "hearn tell" about that road, but never been over it. In short, he was strictly noncommittal.

---

1   *old bird … chaff* Allusion to the proverbial phrase "You cannot catch old birds with chaff," meaning that those who are old and wise are not easily deceived; *chaff* Empty grain husks.
2   *despit* Desperate.

Haley, accustomed to strike the balance of probabilities between lies of greater or lesser magnitude, thought that it lay in favor of the dirt road aforesaid. The mention of the thing he thought he perceived was involuntary on Sam's part at first, and his confused attempts to dissuade him he set down to a desperate lying on second thoughts, as being unwilling to implicate Eliza.

When, therefore, Sam indicated the road, Haley plunged briskly into it, followed by Sam and Andy.

Now, the road, in fact, was an old one, that had formerly been a thoroughfare to the river, but abandoned for many years after the laying of the new pike. It was open for about an hour's ride, and after that it was cut across by various farms and fences. Sam knew this fact perfectly well—indeed, the road had been so long closed up, that Andy had never heard of it. He therefore rode along with an air of dutiful submission, only groaning and vociferating occasionally that 't was "desp't rough, and bad for Jerry's[1] foot."

"Now, I jest give yer warning," said Haley, "I know yer; yer won't get me to turn off this yer road, with all yer fussin'—so you shet up!"

"Mas'r will go his own way!" said Sam, with rueful submission, at the same time winking most portentously to Andy, whose delight was now very near the explosive point.

Sam was in wonderful spirits—professed to keep a very brisk look-out—at one time exclaiming that he saw "a gal's bonnet" on the top of some distant eminence, or calling to Andy "if that thar wasn't 'Lizy' down in the hollow"; always making these exclamations in some rough or craggy part of the road, where the sudden quickening of speed was a special inconvenience to all parties concerned, and thus keeping Haley in a state of constant commotion.

After riding about an hour in this way, the whole party made a precipitate and tumultuous descent into a barnyard belonging to a large farming establishment. Not a soul was in sight, all the hands being employed in the fields; but, as the barn stood conspicuously and plainly square across the road, it was evident that their journey in that direction had reached a decided finale.

---

1 *Jerry* Andy's horse.

"Wan't dat ar what I telled Mas'r?" said Sam, with an air of injured innocence. "How does strange gentleman spect to know more about a country dan de natives born and raised?"

"You rascal!" said Haley, "you knew all about this."

"Didn't I tell yer I *know'd*, and yer wouldn't believe me? I telled Mas'r 't was all shet up, and fenced up, and I didn't spect we could get through—Andy heard me."

It was all too true to be disputed, and the unlucky man had to pocket his wrath with the best grace he was able, and all three faced to the right about, and took up their line of march for the highway.

In consequence of all the various delays, it was about three-quarters of an hour after Eliza had laid her child to sleep in the village tavern that the party came riding into the same place. Eliza was standing by the window, looking out in another direction, when Sam's quick eye caught a glimpse of her. Haley and Andy were two yards behind. At this crisis, Sam contrived to have his hat blown off, and uttered a loud and characteristic ejaculation, which startled her at once; she drew suddenly back; the whole train swept by the window, round to the front door.

A thousand lives seemed to be concentrated in that one moment to Eliza. Her room opened by a side door to the river. She caught her child, and sprang down the steps towards it. The trader caught a full glimpse of her, just as she was disappearing down the bank; and throwing himself from his horse, and calling loudly on Sam and Andy, he was after her like a hound after a deer. In that dizzy moment her feet to her scarce seemed to touch the ground, and a moment brought her to the water's edge. Right on behind they came; and, nerved with strength such as God gives only to the desperate, with one wild cry and flying leap, she vaulted sheer over the turbid current by the shore, on to the raft of ice beyond. It was a desperate leap—impossible to anything but madness and despair; and Haley, Sam, and Andy instinctively cried out, and lifted up their hands, as she did it.

The huge green fragment of ice on which she alighted pitched and creaked as her weight came on it, but she stayed there not a moment. With wild cries and desperate energy she leaped to another and still another cake; stumbling—leaping—slipping—springing upwards again! Her shoes are gone—her stockings cut from her feet—while blood marked every step; but she saw nothing, felt nothing, till dimly, as in a dream, she saw the Ohio side, and a man helping her up the bank.

"Yer a brave gal, now, whoever ye ar!" said the man, with an oath.

Eliza recognized the voice and face of a man who owned a farm not far from her old home.

"O, Mr. Symmes! save me—do save me—do hide me!" said Eliza.

"Why, what's this?" said the man. "Why, if 'tan't Shelby's gal!"

"My child! this boy! he'd sold him! There is his Mas'r," said she, pointing to the Kentucky shore. "O, Mr. Symmes, you've got a little boy!"

"So I have," said the man, as he roughly, but kindly, drew her up the steep bank. "Besides, you're a right brave gal. I like grit, wherever I see it."

When they had gained the top of the bank, the man paused.

"I'd be glad to do something for ye," said he; "but then there's nowhar I could take ye. The best I can do is to tell ye to go *thar*," said he, pointing to a large white house which stood by itself, off the main street of the village. "Go thar; they're kind folks. Thar's no kind o' danger but they'll help you—they're up to all that sort o' thing."

"The Lord bless you!" said Eliza, earnestly.

"No 'casion, no 'casion in the world," said the man. "What I've done's of no 'count."

"And, oh, surely, sir, you won't tell anyone!"

"Go to thunder, gal! What do you take a feller for? In course not," said the man. "Come, now, go along like a likely,[1] sensible gal, as you are. You've arnt your liberty, and you shall have it, for all me."

The woman folded her child to her bosom, and walked firmly and swiftly away. The man stood and looked after her.

"Shelby, now, mebbe won't think this yer the most neighborly thing in the world; but what's a feller to do? If he catches one of my gals in the same fix, he's welcome to pay back. Somehow I never could see no kind o' critter a strivin' and pantin', and trying to clar theirselves, with the dogs arter 'em, and go agin 'em. Besides, I don't see no kind of 'casion for me to be hunter and catcher for other folks, neither."

---

1 *likely* Term suggesting strength or capability, but also frequently physical attractiveness.

So spoke this poor, heathenish Kentuckian, who had not been instructed in his constitutional relations,[1] and consequently was betrayed into acting in a sort of Christianized manner, which, if he had been better situated and more enlightened, he would not have been left to do.

Haley had stood a perfectly amazed spectator of the scene, till Eliza had disappeared up the bank, when he turned a blank, inquiring look on Sam and Andy.

"That ar was a tolable fair stroke of business," said Sam.

"The gal's got seven devils in her, I believe!" said Haley. "How like a wildcat she jumped!"

"Wal, now," said Sam, scratching his head, "I hope Mas'r'll 'scuse us tryin' dat ar road. Don't think I feel spry enough for dat ar, no way!" and Sam gave a hoarse chuckle.

"*You* laugh!" said the trader, with a growl.

"Lord bless you, Mas'r, I couldn't help it, now," said Sam, giving way to the long pent-up delight of his soul. "She looked so curi's, a leapin' and springin'—ice a crackin'—and only to hear her—plump! ker chunk! ker splash! Spring! Lord! how she goes it!" and Sam and Andy laughed till the tears rolled down their cheeks.

"I'll make ye laugh t'other side yer mouths!" said the trader, laying about their heads with his riding-whip.

Both ducked, and ran shouting up the bank, and were on their horses before he was up.

"Good evening, Mas'r!" said Sam, with much gravity. "I berry much spect Missis be anxious 'bout Jerry. Mas'r Haley won't want us no longer. Missis wouldn't hear of our ridin' the critters over Lizy's bridge tonight"; and, with a facetious poke into Andy's ribs, he started off, followed by the latter, at full speed—their shouts of laughter coming faintly on the wind.

---

1   *constitutional relations*   The recently passed Fugitive Slave Act made it a federal crime to aid persons escaping from slavery, and placed increased pressures on ordinary citizens to aid in their capture.

CHAPTER 8
ELIZA'S ESCAPE[1]

Eliza made her desperate retreat across the river just in the dusk of twilight. The gray mist of evening, rising slowly from the river, enveloped her as she disappeared up the bank, and the swollen current and floundering masses of ice presented a hopeless barrier between her and her pursuer. Haley therefore slowly and discontentedly returned to the little tavern, to ponder further what was to be done. The woman opened to him the door of a little parlor, covered with a rag carpet, where stood a table with a very shining black oil-cloth, sundry lank, high-backed wood chairs, with some plaster images in resplendent colors on the mantel-shelf, above a very dimly-smoking grate; a long hard-wood settle[2] extended its uneasy length by the chimney, and here Haley sat him down to meditate on the instability of human hopes and happiness in general.

"What did I want with the little cuss, now," he said to himself, "that I should have got myself treed like a coon,[3] as I am, this yer way?" and Haley relieved himself by repeating over a not very select litany of imprecations[4] on himself, which, though there was the best possible reason to consider them as true, we shall, as a matter of taste, omit.

He was startled by the loud and dissonant voice of a man who was apparently dismounting at the door. He hurried to the window.

"By the land! if this yer an't the nearest, now, to what I've heard folks call Providence," said Haley. "I do b'lieve that ar's Tom Loker."

Haley hastened out. Standing by the bar, in the corner of the room, was a brawny, muscular man, full six feet in height, and broad in proportion. He was dressed in a coat of buffalo-skin, made with the hair outward, which gave him a shaggy and fierce appearance, perfectly in keeping with the whole air of his physiognomy.[5] In the head and

---

1   *ELIZA'S ESCAPE*   The 1852 edition of the novel does not include a chapter title here, though it appears as such in the Table of Contents.

2   *settle*   Bench.

3   *coon*   Extremely offensive term for a black person, derived from a slang word for "raccoon." (As seen a few paragraphs down, the term was also sometimes directed towards white persons with no derogatory intention.)

4   *imprecations*   Curses.

5   *physiognomy*   Facial appearance, especially as considered to indicate one's character.

face every organ and lineament expressive of brutal and unhesitating violence was in a state of the highest possible development.[1] Indeed, could our readers fancy a bulldog come unto man's estate, and walking about in a hat and coat, they would have no unapt idea of the general style and effect of his physique. He was accompanied by a travelling companion, in many respects an exact contrast to himself. He was short and slender, lithe and cat-like in his motions, and had a peering, mousing expression about his keen black eyes, with which every feature of his face seemed sharpened into sympathy; his thin, long nose ran out as if it was eager to bore into the nature of things in general; his sleek, thin, black hair was stuck eagerly forward, and all his motions and evolutions expressed a dry, cautious acuteness. The great big man poured out a big tumbler half full of raw spirits and gulped it down without a word. The little man stood tip-toe, and putting his head first to one side and then to the other, and snuffing considerably in the directions of the various bottles, ordered at last a mint julep, in a thin and quivering voice, and with an air of great circumspection. When poured out, he took it and looked at it with a sharp, complacent air, like a man who thinks he has done about the right thing, and hit the nail on the head, and proceeded to dispose of it in short and well-advised sips.

"Wal, now, who'd a thought this yer luck 'ad come to me? Why, Loker, how are ye?" said Haley, coming forward, and extending his hand to the big man.

"The devil!" was the civil reply. "What brought you here, Haley?"

The mousing man, who bore the name of Marks, instantly stopped his sipping, and, poking his head forward, looked shrewdly on the new acquaintance, as a cat sometimes looks at a moving dry leaf, or some other possible object of pursuit.

"I say, Tom, this yer's the luckiest thing in the world. I'm in a devil of a hobble, and you must help me out."

"Ugh? aw! like enough!" grunted his complacent acquaintance. "A body may be pretty sure of that, when *you're* glad to see 'em; something to be made off of 'em. What's the blow now?"

---

1   *every organ ... possible development*   Language evoking the popular pseudoscience of phrenology, which posited that the different aspects of one's personality are determined by the relative development of different "organs" in the brain, which can be seen in the shape of one's head.

"You've got a friend here?" said Haley, looking doubtfully at Marks; "partner, perhaps?"

"Yes, I have. Here, Marks! here's that ar feller that I was in with in Natchez."

"Shall be pleased with his acquaintance," said Marks, thrusting out a long, thin hand, like a raven's claw. "Mr. Haley, I believe?"

"The same, sir," said Haley. "And now, gentlemen, seein' as we've met so happily, I think I'll stand up to a small matter of a treat in this here parlor. So, now, old coon," said he to the man at the bar, "get us hot water, and sugar, and cigars, and plenty of the *real stuff*, and we'll have a blow-out."

Behold, then, the candles lighted, the fire stimulated to the burning point in the grate, and our three worthies seated round a table, well spread with all the accessories to good fellowship enumerated before.

Haley began a pathetic[1] recital of his peculiar troubles. Loker shut up his mouth, and listened to him with gruff and surly attention. Marks, who was anxiously and with much fidgeting compounding a tumbler of punch to his own peculiar taste, occasionally looked up from his employment, and, poking his sharp nose and chin almost into Haley's face, gave the most earnest heed to the whole narrative. The conclusion of it appeared to amuse him extremely, for he shook his shoulders and sides in silence, and perked up his thin lips with an air of great internal enjoyment.

"So, then, ye'r fairly sewed up, an't ye?" he said; "he! he! he! It's neatly done, too."

"This yer young-un business[2] makes lots of trouble in the trade," said Haley, dolefully.

"If we could get a breed of gals that didn't care, now, for their uns," said Marks; "tell ye, I think 't would be 'bout the greatest mod'rn improvement I knows on,"—and Marks patronized his joke by a quiet introductory sniggle.

"Jes so," said Haley; "I never couldn't see into it; young uns is heaps of trouble to 'em; one would think, now, they'd be glad to get clar on 'em; but they arn't. And the more trouble a young un is, and the more good for nothing, as a gen'l thing, the tighter they sticks to 'em."

---

1 *pathetic* I.e., arousing of pathos; emotionally affecting.
2 *young-un business* I.e., the business of trading in children.

"Wal, Mr. Haley," said Marks, "jest pass the hot water. Yes, sir; you say jest what I feel and all 'us have. Now, I bought a gal once, when I was in the trade—a tight, likely wench she was, too, and quite considerable smart—and she had a young un that was mis'able sickly; it had a crooked back, or something or other; and I jest gin 't away to a man that thought he'd take his chance raising on 't, being it didn't cost nothin'—never thought, yer know, of the gal's takin' on about it—but, Lord, yer oughter seen how she went on. Why, re'lly, she did seem to me to valley the child more 'cause 'twas sickly and cross, and plagued her; and she warn't making b'lieve, neither—cried about it, she did, and lopped round, as if she'd lost every friend she had. It re'lly was droll[1] to think on 't. Lord, there an't no end to women's notions."

"Wal, jest so with me," said Haley. "Last summer, down on Red River,[2] I got a gal traded off on me, with a likely lookin' child enough, and his eyes looked as bright as yourn; but, come to look, I found him stone blind. Fact—he was stone blind. Wal, ye see, I thought there warn't no harm in my jest passing him along, and not sayin' nothin'; and I'd got him nicely swapped off for a keg o' whiskey; but come to get him away from the gal, she was jest like a tiger. So 't was before we started, and I had n't got my gang chained up; so what should she do but ups on a cotton-bale, like a cat, ketches a knife from one of the deck hands, and, I tell ye, she made all fly for a minit, till she saw 'twan't no use; and she jest turns round, and pitches head first, young un and all, into the river—went down plump, and never ris."

"Bah!" said Tom Loker, who had listened to these stories with ill-repressed disgust—"shif'less,[3] both on ye! *my* gals don't cut up no such shines, I tell ye!"

"Indeed! how do you help it?" said Marks, briskly.

"Help it? why, I buys a gal, and if she's got a young un to be sold, I jest walks up and puts my fist to her face, and says, 'Look here, now, if you give me one word out of your head, I'll smash yer face in. I won't hear one word—not the beginning of a word.' I says to 'em, 'This yer young un's mine, and not yourn, and you've no kind o' business with it. I'm going to sell it, first chance; mind, you don't cut up none o'

---

1   *droll* Curious; funny.
2   *Red River* Major river in the South, flowing through Texas, Oklahoma, Arkansas, and Louisiana.
3   *shif'less* Shiftless; incompetent.

yer shines about it, or I'll make ye wish ye'd never been born.' I tell ye, they sees it an't no play, when I gets hold. I makes 'em as whist[1] as fishes; and if one on 'em begins and gives a yelp, why—" and Mr. Loker brought down his fist with a thump that fully explained the hiatus.

"That ar's what ye may call *emphasis*," said Marks, poking Haley in the side, and going into another small giggle. "An't Tom peculiar? he! he! he! I say, Tom, I s'pect you make 'em *understand*, for all niggers' heads is woolly. They don't never have no doubt o' your meaning, Tom. If you an't the devil, Tom, you's his twin brother, I'll say that for ye!"

Tom received the compliment with becoming modesty, and began to look as affable as was consistent, as John Bunyan says, "with his doggish nature."[2]

Haley, who had been imbibing very freely of the staple of the evening, began to feel a sensible elevation and enlargement of his moral faculties—a phenomenon not unusual with gentlemen of a serious and reflective turn, under similar circumstances.

"Wall, now, Tom," he said, "ye re'lly is too bad, as I al'ays have told ye; ye know, Tom, you and I used to talk over these yer matters down in Natchez, and I used to prove to ye that we made full as much, and was as well off for this yer world, by treatin' on 'em well, besides keepin' a better chance for comin' in the kingdom at last, when wust comes to wust, and that an't nothing else left to get, ye know."

"Boh!" said Tom, "*don't* I know? don't make me too sick with any yer stuff—my stomach is a leetle riled now"; and Tom drank half a glass of raw brandy.

"I say," said Haley, and leaning back in his chair and gesturing impressively, "I'll say this now, I al'ays meant to drive my trade so as to make money on 't, *fust and foremost*, as much as any man; but, then, trade an't everything, and money an't everything, 'cause we's all got souls. I don't care, now, who hears me say it—and I think a cussed sight on it—so I may as well come out with it. I b'lieve in religion, and one of these days, when I've got matters tight and snug,

---

1 *whist* Silent.

2 *as John Bunyan … nature* Reference to the second part of the widely read Christian allegorical novel *The Pilgrim's Progress* (1684) by John Bunyan, in which Satan is metaphorically presented as a violent and intimidating dog.

I calculates to tend to my soul and them ar matters; and so what's the use of doin' any more wickedness than's re'lly necessary? It don't seem to me it's 't all prudent."

"Tend to yer soul!" repeated Tom, contemptuously; "take a bright lookout to find a soul in you—save yourself any care on that score. If the devil sifts you through a hair sieve, he won't find one."

"Why, Tom, you're cross," said Haley; "why can't ye take it pleasant, now, when a feller's talking for your good?"

"Stop that ar jaw o' yourn, there," said Tom, gruffly. "I can stand most any talk o' yourn but your pious talk—that kills me right up. After all, what's the odds between me and you? 'Tan't that you care one bit more, or have a bit more feelin'—it's clean, sheer, dog meanness, wanting to cheat the devil and save your own skin; don't I see through it? And your 'gettin' religion,' as you call it, arter all, is too p'isin mean[1] for any crittur—run up a bill with the devil all your life, and then sneak out when pay time comes! Boh!"

"Come, come, gentlemen, I say; this isn't business," said Marks. "There's different ways, you know, of looking at all subjects. Mr. Haley is a very nice man, no doubt, and has his own conscience; and, Tom, you have your ways, and very good ones, too, Tom; but quarrelling, you know, won't answer no kind of purpose. Let's go to business. Now, Mr. Haley, what is it? you want us to undertake to catch this yer gal?"

"The gal's no matter of mine—she's Shelby's; it's only the boy. I was a fool for buying the monkey!"

"You're generally a fool!" said Tom, gruffly.

"Come, now, Loker, none of your huffs," said Marks, licking his lips; "you see, Mr. Haley's a puttin' us in a way of a good job, I reckon; just hold still—these yer arrangements is my forte. This yer gal, Mr. Haley, how is she? what is she?"

"Wal! white and handsome—well brought up. I'd a gin Shelby eight hundred or a thousand, and then made well on her."

"White and handsome—well brought up!" said Marks, his sharp eyes, nose and mouth, all alive with enterprise. "Look here, now, Loker, a beautiful opening. We'll do a business here on our own

---

1   *mean* Lowly or selfish.

account—we does the catchin'; the boy, of course, goes to Mr. Haley—we takes the gal to Orleans[1] to speculate on. An't it beautiful?"

Tom, whose great heavy mouth had stood ajar during this communication, now suddenly snapped it together, as a big dog closes on a piece of meat, and seemed to be digesting the idea at his leisure.

"Ye see," said Marks to Haley, stirring his punch as he did so, "ye see, we has justices convenient at all p'ints along shore, that does up any little jobs in our line quite reasonable.[2] Tom, he does the knockin' down and that ar; and I come in all dressed up—shining boots—everything first chop, when the swearin' 's to be done. You oughter see, now," said Marks, in a glow of professional pride, "how I can tone it off. One day, I'm Mr. Twickem, from New Orleans; 'nother day, I'm just come from my plantation on Pearl River,[3] where I works seven hundred niggers; then, again, I come out a distant relation of Henry Clay,[4] or some old cock in Kentuck. Talents is different, you know. Now, Tom's a roarer when there's any thumping or fighting to be done; but at lying he an't good, Tom an't—ye see it don't come natural to him; but, Lord, if thar's a feller in the country that can swear to anything and everything, and put in all the circumstances and flourishes with a longer face, and carry't through better'n I can, why, I'd like to see him, that's all! I b'lieve my heart, I could get along and snake through, even if justices were more particular than they is. Sometimes I rather wish they was more particular; 'twould be a heap more relishin' if they was—more fun, yer know."

Tom Loker, who, as we have made it appear, was a man of slow thoughts and movements, here interrupted Marks by bringing his heavy fist down on the table, so as to make all ring again. "*It'll do!*" he said.

"Lord bless ye, Tom, ye needn't break all the glasses!" said Marks; "save your fist for time o' need."

---

1   *Orleans*   I.e., New Orleans, a center of the domestic slave trade, and especially of the trade in young women for presumed sexual slavery.

2   *justices convenient ... quite reasonable*   I.e., corrupt legal officers willing to aid in the illicit trade of enslaved persons who have not been sold to the trader, or of free African Americans who have been kidnapped.

3   *Pearl River*   River forming part of the southern boundary between Mississippi and Louisiana.

4   *Henry Clay*   Famous Kentucky senator known for his key involvement in the Compromise of 1850 and associated legislation.

"But, gentlemen, an't I to come in for a share of the profits?"

"An't it enough we catch the boy for ye?" said Loker. "What do ye want?"

"Wal," said Haley, "if I gives you the job, it's worth something—say ten per cent on the profits, expenses paid."

"Now," said Loker, with a tremendous oath, and striking the table with his heavy fist, "don't I know *you*, Dan Haley? Don't you think to come it over me! Suppose Marks and I have taken up the catchin' trade, jest to 'commodate gentlemen like you, and get nothin' for ourselves? Not by a long chalk! we'll have the gal out and out, and you keep quiet, or, ye see, we'll have both—what's to hinder? Han't you show'd us the game? It's as free to us as you, I hope. If you or Shelby wants to chase us, look where the partridges was last year; if you find them or us, you're quite welcome."

"O, wal, certainly, jest let it go at that," said Haley, alarmed; "you catch the boy for the job; you allers did trade *far* with me, Tom, and was up to yer word."

"Ye know that," said Tom; "I don't pretend none of your snivelling ways, but I won't lie in my 'counts with the devil himself. What I ses I'll do, I will do—you know *that*, Dan Haley."

"Jes so, jes so—I said so, Tom," said Haley; "and if you'd only promise to have the boy for me in a week, at any point you'll name, that's all I want."

"But it an't all I want, by a long jump," said Tom. "Ye don't think I did business with you, down in Natchez, for nothing, Haley; I've learned to hold an eel, when I catch him. You've got to fork over fifty dollars, flat down, or this child don't start a peg. I know yer."

"Why, when you have a job in hand that may bring a clean profit of somewhere about a thousand or sixteen hundred, why, Tom, you're onreasonable," said Haley.

"Yes, and hasn't we business booked for five weeks to come—all we can do? And suppose we leaves all, and goes to bushwhacking round arter yer young un, and finally doesn't catch the gal—and gals allers is the devil *to* catch—what's then? would you pay us a cent—would you? I think I see you a doin' it—ugh! No, no; flap down your fifty. If we get the job, and it pays, I'll hand it back; if we don't, it's for our trouble—that's *far*, an't it, Marks?"

"Certainly, certainly," said Marks, with a conciliatory tone; "it's only a retaining fee, you see—he! he! he!—we lawyers, you know. Wal, we must all keep good-natured—keep easy, yer know. Tom'll have the boy for yer, anywhere ye'll name; won't ye, Tom?"

"If I find the young un, I'll bring him on to Cincinnati, and leave him at Granny Belcher's, on the landing," said Loker.

Marks had got from his pocket a greasy pocket-book, and taking a long paper from thence, he sat down, and fixing his keen black eyes on it, began mumbling over its contents: "Barnes—Shelby County—boy Jim, three hundred dollars for him, dead or alive.

"Edwards—Dick and Lucy—man and wife, six hundred dollars; wench Polly and two children—six hundred for her or her head.

"I'm jest a runnin' over our business, to see if we can take up this yer handily. Loker," he said, after a pause, "we must set Adams and Springer on the track of these yer; they've been booked some time."

"They'll charge too much," said Tom.

"I'll manage that ar; they's young in the business, and must spect to work cheap," said Marks, as he continued to read. "Ther's three on 'em easy cases, 'cause all you've got to do is to shoot 'em, or swear they is short; they couldn't, of course, charge much for that. Them other cases," he said, folding the paper, "will bear puttin' off a spell. So now let's come to the particulars. Now, Mr. Haley, you saw this yer gal when she landed?"

"To be sure—plain as I see you."

"And a man helpin' on her up the bank?" said Loker.

"To be sure, I did."

"Most likely," said Marks, "she's took in somewhere; but where, 's a question. Tom, what do you say?"

"We must cross the river tonight, no mistake," said Tom.

"But there's no boat about," said Marks. "The ice is running awfully, Tom; an't it dangerous?"

"Don'no nothin 'bout that—only it's got to be done," said Tom, decidedly.

"Dear me," said Marks, fidgeting, "it'll be—I say," he said, walking to the window, "it's dark as a wolf's mouth, and, Tom—"

"The long and short is, you're scared, Marks; but I can't help that—you've got to go. Suppose you want to lie by a day or two, till the gal's been carried on the underground line up to Sandusky[1] or so, before you start."

"O, no; I an't a grain afraid," said Marks, "only—"

"Only what?" said Tom.

"Well, about the boat. Yer see there an't any boat."

"I heard the woman say there was one coming along this evening, and that a man was going to cross over in it. Neck or nothing, we must go with him," said Tom.

"I s'pose you've got good dogs," said Haley.

"First rate," said Marks. "But what's the use? you han't got nothin' o' hers to smell on."

"Yes, I have," said Haley, triumphantly. "Here's her shawl she left on the bed in her hurry; she left her bonnet, too."

"That ar's lucky," said Loker; "fork over."

"Though the dogs might damage the gal, if they come on her unawars," said Haley.

"That ar's a consideration," said Marks. "Our dogs tore a feller half to pieces, once, down in Mobile,[2] 'fore we could get 'em off."

"Well, ye see, for this sort that's to be sold for their looks, that ar won't answer, ye see," said Haley.

"I do see," said Marks. "Besides, if she's got took in, 'tan't no go, neither. Dogs is no 'count in these yer up states where these critters gets carried; of course, ye can't get on their track. They only does down in plantations, where niggers, when they runs, has to do their own running, and don't get no help."

"Well," said Loker, who had just stepped out to the bar to make some inquiries, "they say the man's come with the boat; so, Marks—"

That worthy cast a rueful look at the comfortable quarters he was leaving, but slowly rose to obey. After exchanging a few words of further arrangement, Haley, with visible reluctance, handed over the fifty dollars to Tom, and the worthy trio separated for the night.

If any of our refined and Christian readers object to the society into which this scene introduces them, let us beg them to begin and conquer their prejudices in time. The catching business, we beg to remind them, is rising to the dignity of a lawful and patriotic profes-

---

1 *Sandusky* City in Ohio, not far from the Canadian border.
2 *Mobile* City in Alabama.

sion. If all the broad land between the Mississippi and the Pacific becomes one great market for bodies and souls, and human property retains the locomotive tendencies of this nineteenth century, the trader and catcher may yet be among our aristocracy.

———

While this scene was going on at the tavern, Sam and Andy, in a state of high felicitation, pursued their way home.

Sam was in the highest possible feather, and expressed his exultation by all sorts of supernatural howls and ejaculations, by diverse odd motions and contortions of his whole system. Sometimes he would sit backward, with his face to the horse's tail and sides, and then, with a whoop and a somerset,[1] come right side up in his place again, and, drawing on a grave face, begin to lecture Andy in high-sounding tones for laughing and playing the fool. Anon, slapping his sides with his arms, he would burst forth in peals of laughter, that made the old woods ring as they passed. With all these evolutions, he contrived to keep the horses up to the top of their speed, until, between ten and eleven, their heels resounded on the gravel at the end of the balcony. Mrs. Shelby flew to the railings.

"Is that you, Sam? Where are they?"

"Mas'r Haley's a-restin' at the tavern; he's drefful fatigued, Missis."

"And Eliza, Sam?"

"Wal, she's clar 'cross Jordan. As a body man say, in the land o' Canaan."

"Why, Sam, what *do* you mean?" said Mrs. Shelby, breathless, and almost faint, as the possible meaning of these words came over her.

"Wal, Missis, de Lord he presarves his own. Lizy's done gone over the river into 'Hio, as 'markably as if de Lord took her over in a charrit of fire and two hosses."[2]

Sam's vein of piety was always uncommonly fervent in his mistress' presence; and he made great capital of scriptural figures and images.

"Come up here, Sam," said Mr. Shelby, who had followed on to the verandah, "and tell your mistress what she wants. Come, come,

———

1 *somerset* Somersault.
2 *de Lord ... two hosses* See 2 Kings 2.11.

Emily," said he, passing his arm round her, "you are cold and all in a shiver; you allow yourself to feel too much."

"Feel too much! Am not I a woman[1]—a mother? Are we not both responsible to God for this poor girl? My God! lay not this sin to our charge."

"What sin, Emily? You see yourself that we have only done what we were obliged to."

"There's an awful feeling of guilt about it, though," said Mrs. Shelby. "I can't reason it away."

"Here, Andy, you nigger, be alive!" called Sam, under the verandah; "take these yer hosses to der barn; don't ye hear Mas'r a callin'?" and Sam soon appeared, palm-leaf in hand, at the parlor door.

"Now, Sam, tell us distinctly how the matter was," said Mr. Shelby. "Where is Eliza, if you know?"

"Wal, Mas'r, I saw her, with my own eyes, a crossin' on the floatin' ice. She crossed most 'markably; it wasn't no less nor a miracle; and I saw a man help her up the 'Hio side, and then she was lost in the dusk."

"Sam, I think this rather apocryphal[2]—this miracle. Crossing on floating ice isn't so easily done," said Mr. Shelby.

"Easy! couldn't nobody a done it, widout de Lord. Why, now," said Sam, "'twas jist dis yer way. Mas'r Haley, and me, and Andy, we comes up to de little tavern by the river, and I rides a leetle ahead—(I's so zealous to be a cotchin' Lizy, that I couldn't hold in, no way)—and when I comes by the tavern winder,[3] sure enough there she was, right in plain sight, and dey diggin' on behind. Wal, I loses off my hat, and sings out nuff to raise the dead. Course Lizy she hars,[4] and she dodges back, when Mas'r Haley he goes past the door; and then, I tell ye, she clared out de side door; she went down de river bank; Mas'r Haley he

---

1   *Am not I a woman*   Some scholars have suggested that this may be a reference to Sojourner Truth's famous speech (known as "Ar'n't I a Woman?"), a version of which was delivered at the Women's Rights Conference in Akron, Ohio, in 1851. This seems unlikely, however, since Truth's now-famous line was not included in the version of the speech published in 1851.

2   *apocryphal*   Of doubtful veracity. The term also refers to a number of ancient books considered part of the Old Testament by some Christian denominations, but which are considered non-canonical by most.

3   *winder*   Window.

4   *hars*   Hears.

seed her, and yelled out, and him, and me, and Andy, we took arter. Down she come to the river, and thar was the current running ten feet wide by the shore, and over t'other side ice a sawin' and a jiggling up and down, kinder as 'twere a great island. We come right behind her, and I thought my soul he'd got her sure enough—when she gin such a screech as I never hearn, and thar she was, clar over t'other side the current, on the ice, and then on she went, a screeching and a jumpin'—the ice went crack! c'wallop! cracking! chunk! and she a boundin' like a buck! Lord, the spring that ar gal's got in her an't common, I'm o' 'pinion."

Mrs. Shelby sat perfectly silent, pale with excitement, while Sam told his story.

"God be praised, she isn't dead!" she said; "but where is the poor child now?"

"De Lord will pervide," said Sam, rolling up his eyes piously. "As I've been a sayin', dis yer's a providence and no mistake, as Missis has allers been a instructin' on us. Thar's allers instruments ris up to do de Lord's will. Now, if 't hadn't been for me today, she'd a been took a dozen times. Warn't it I started off de hosses, dis yer mornin', and kept 'em chasin' till nigh dinner time? And didn't I car Mas'r Haley nigh five miles out of de road, dis evening, or else he'd a come up with Lizy as easy as a dog arter a coon. These yer's all providences."

"They are a kind of providences that you'll have to be pretty sparing of, Master Sam. I allow no such practices with gentlemen on my place," said Mr. Shelby, with as much sternness as he could command, under the circumstances.

Now, there is no more use in making believe be angry with a negro than with a child; both instinctively see the true state of the case, through all attempts to affect the contrary; and Sam was in no wise disheartened by this rebuke, though he assumed an air of doleful gravity, and stood with the corners of his mouth lowered in most penitential style.

"Mas'r's quite right—quite; it was ugly on me—there's no disputin' that ar; and of course Mas'r and Missis wouldn't encourage no such works. I'm sensible of dat ar; but a poor nigger like me's 'mazin' tempted to act ugly sometimes, when fellers will cut up such shines as dat ar Mas'r Haley; he an't no gen'l'man no way; anybody's been raised as I've been can't help a seein' dat ar."

"Well, Sam," said Mrs. Shelby, "as you appear to have a proper sense of your errors, you may go now and tell Aunt Chloe she may get you some of that cold ham that was left of dinner today. You and Andy must be hungry."

"Missis is a heap too good for us," said Sam, making his bow with alacrity, and departing.

It will be perceived, as has been before intimated, that Master Sam had a native talent that might, undoubtedly, have raised him to eminence in political life—a talent of making capital out of everything that turned up, to be invested for his own especial praise and glory; and having done up his piety and humility, as he trusted, to the satisfaction of the parlor, he clapped his palm-leaf on his head, with a sort of rakish, free-and-easy air, and proceeded to the dominions of Aunt Chloe, with the intention of flourishing largely in the kitchen.

"I'll speechify these yer niggers," said Sam to himself, "now I've got a chance. Lord, I'll reel it off to make 'em stare!"

It must be observed that one of Sam's especial delights had been to ride in attendance on his master to all kinds of political gatherings, where, roosted on some rail fence, or perched aloft in some tree, he would sit watching the orators, with the greatest apparent gusto, and then, descending among the various brethren of his own color, assembled on the same errand, he would edify and delight them with the most ludicrous burlesques and imitations, all delivered with the most imperturbable earnestness and solemnity; and though the auditors immediately about him were generally of his own color, it not unfrequently happened that they were fringed pretty deeply with those of a fairer complexion, who listened, laughing and winking, to Sam's great self-congratulation. In fact, Sam considered oratory as his vocation, and never let slip an opportunity of magnifying his office.[1]

Now, between Sam and Aunt Chloe there had existed, from ancient times, a sort of chronic feud, or rather a decided coolness; but, as Sam was meditating something in the provision department, as the necessary and obvious foundation of his operations, he determined, on the present occasion, to be eminently conciliatory; for he well knew that although "Missis' orders" would undoubtedly be followed to the letter, yet he should gain a considerable deal by enlisting the spirit also.

---

1   *office*   Role or position.

He therefore appeared before Aunt Chloe with a touchingly subdued, resigned expression, like one who has suffered immeasurable hardships in behalf of a persecuted fellow-creature—enlarged upon the fact that Missis had directed him to come to Aunt Chloe for whatever might be wanting to make up the balance in his solids and fluids—and thus unequivocally acknowledged her right and supremacy in the cooking department, and all thereto pertaining.

The thing took accordingly. No poor, simple, virtuous body was ever cajoled by the attentions of an electioneering politician with more ease than Aunt Chloe was won over by Master Sam's suavities; and if he had been the prodigal son[1] himself, he could not have been overwhelmed with more maternal bountifulness; and he soon found himself seated, happy and glorious, over a large tin pan, containing a sort of *olla podrida*[2] of all that had appeared on the table for two or three days past. Savory morsels of ham, golden blocks of corn-cake, fragments of pie of every conceivable mathematical figure, chicken wings, gizzards, and drumsticks, all appeared in picturesque confusion; and Sam, as monarch of all he surveyed, sat with his palm-leaf cocked rejoicingly to one side, and patronizing Andy at his right hand.

The kitchen was full of all his compeers, who had hurried and crowded in, from the various cabins, to hear the termination of the day's exploits. Now was Sam's hour of glory. The story of the day was rehearsed, with all kinds of ornament and varnishing which might be necessary to heighten its effect; for Sam, like some of our fashionable dilettanti,[3] never allowed a story to lose any of its gilding by passing through his hands. Roars of laughter attended the narration, and were taken up and prolonged by all the smaller fry,[4] who were lying, in any quantity, about on the floor, or perched in every corner. In the height of the uproar and laughter, Sam, however, preserved an immovable gravity, only from time to time rolling his eyes up, and giving his

---

1 *prodigal son* The parable of the prodigal (wasteful and extravagant) son, narrated in Luke 15.11–32, tells of a son who is welcomed lovingly back into his father's house despite having wasted his inheritance.

2 *olla podrida* Spanish stew made from a medley of available ingredients; by extension, any motley assortment of foods.

3 *dilettanti* Term generally referring to an amateur lover of the fine arts, here implying those who tell tales of their travels to artistic centers.

4 *fry* Children.

auditors diverse inexpressibly droll glances, without departing from the sententious elevation of his oratory.

"Yer see, fellow-countrymen," said Sam, elevating a turkey's leg, with energy, "yer see, now, what dis yer chile's up ter, for fendin' yer all—yes, all on yer. For him as tries to get one o' our people, is as good as tryin' to get all; yer see the principle's de same—dat ar's clar. And any one o' these yer drivers that comes smelling round arter any our people, why, he's got *me* in his way; *I'm* the feller he's got to set in with—I'm the feller for yer all to come to, bredren—I'll stand up for yer rights—I'll fend 'em to the last breath!"

"Why, but Sam, yer telled me, only this mornin', that you'd help this yer Mas'r to cotch Lizy; seems to me yer talk don't hang together," said Andy.

"I tell you now, Andy," said Sam, with awful superiority, "don't yer be a talkin' 'bout what yer don't know nothin' on; boys like you, Andy, means well, but they can't be spected to collusitate[1] the great principles of action."

Andy looked rebuked, particularly by the hard word collusitate, which most of the youngerly members of the company seemed to consider as a settler in the case, while Sam proceeded.

"Dat ar was *conscience*, Andy; when I thought of gwine arter Lizy, I railly spected Mas'r was sot dat way. When I found Missis was sot the contrar, dat ar was conscience *more yet*—cause fellers allers gets more by stickin' to Missis' side—so yer see I's persistent either way, and sticks up to conscience, and holds on to principles. Yes, *principles*," said Sam, giving an enthusiastic toss to a chicken's neck—"what's principles good for, if we isn't persistent, I wanter know? Thar, Andy, you may have dat ar bone—tan't picked quite clean."

Sam's audience hanging on his words with open mouth, he could not but proceed.

"Dis yer matter 'bout persistence, feller-niggers," said Sam, with the air of one entering into an abstruse subject, "dis yer 'sistency 's a thing what an't seed into very clar, by most anybody. Now, yer see, when a feller stands up for a thing one day and night, de contrar de next, folks ses (and nat'rally enough dey ses), why he an't persistent—hand me dat ar bit o' corn-cake, Andy. But let's look inter it.

---

[1] *collusitate* I.e., colligate; unite in common purpose.

I hope the gen'lmen and der fair sex will scuse my usin' an or'nary sort o' 'parison. Here! I'm a trying to get top o' der hay. Wal, I puts up my larder dis yer side; 'tan't no go; den, cause I don't try dere no more, but puts my larder right de contrar side, an't I persistent? I'm persistent in wantin' to get up which ary side my larder is; don't you see, all on yer?"

"It's the only thing ye ever was persistent in, Lord knows!" muttered Aunt Chloe, who was getting rather restive; the merriment of the evening being to her somewhat after the Scripture comparison— like "vinegar upon nitre."[1]

"Yes, indeed!" said Sam, rising, full of supper and glory, for a closing effort. "Yes, my feller-citizens and ladies of de other sex in general, I has principles—I'm proud to 'oon 'em—they's perquisite to dese yer times, and ter *all* times. I has principles, and I sticks to 'em like forty—jest anything that I thinks is principle, I goes in to 't; I wouldn't mind if dey burnt me 'live—I'd walk right up to de stake, I would, and say, here I comes to shed my last blood fur my principles, fur my country, fur de gen'l interests of s'ciety."

"Well," said Aunt Chloe, "one o' yer principles will have to be to get to bed some time tonight, and not be a keepin' everybody up till mornin'; now, every one of you young uns that don't want to be cracked, had better be scase, mighty sudden."

"Niggers! all on yer," said Sam, waving his palm-leaf with benignity, "I give yer my blessin'; go to bed now, and be good boys."

And, with this pathetic benediction, the assembly dispersed.

CHAPTER 9
In Which It Appears that a Senator Is but a Man

The light of the cheerful fire shone on the rug and carpet of a cozy parlor, and glittered on the sides of the teacups and well-brightened teapot, as Senator Bird was drawing off his boots, preparatory to inserting his feet in a pair of new handsome slippers, which his wife had been working for him while away on his senatorial tour. Mrs. Bird, looking the very picture of delight, was superintending

---

1 *like "vinegar upon nitre"* See Proverbs 25.20: "As he that taketh away a garment in cold weather, and as vinegar upon nitre, so is he that singeth songs to an heavy heart."

the arrangements of the table, ever and anon mingling admonitory remarks to a number of frolicsome juveniles, who were effervescing in all those modes of untold gambol and mischief that have astonished mothers ever since the flood.[1]

"Tom, let the doorknob alone—there's a man! Mary! Mary! don't pull the cat's tail—poor pussy! Jim, you mustn't climb on that table— no, no! You don't know, my dear, what a surprise it is to us all, to see you here tonight!" said she, at last, when she found a space to say something to her husband.

"Yes, yes, I thought I'd just make a run down, spend the night, and have a little comfort at home. I'm tired to death, and my head aches!"

Mrs. Bird cast a glance at a camphor-bottle,[2] which stood in the half-open closet, and appeared to meditate an approach to it, but her husband interposed.

"No, no, Mary, no doctoring! a cup of your good hot tea, and some of our good home living, is what I want. It's a tiresome business, this legislating!"

And the senator smiled, as if he rather liked the idea of considering himself a sacrifice to his country.

"Well," said his wife, after the business of the tea-table was getting rather slack, "and what have they been doing in the Senate?"

Now, it was a very unusual thing for gentle little Mrs. Bird ever to trouble her head with what was going on in the house of the state, very wisely considering that she had enough to do to mind her own. Mr. Bird, therefore, opened his eyes in surprise, and said,

"Not very much of importance."

"Well; but is it true that they have been passing a law forbidding people to give meat and drink to those poor colored folks that come along? I heard they were talking of some such law, but I didn't think any Christian legislature would pass it!"

"Why, Mary, you are getting to be a politician, all at once."

"No, nonsense! I wouldn't give a fip for all your politics, generally, but I think this is something downright cruel and unchristian. I hope, my dear, no such law has been passed."

---

1   *gambol* Playfulness; *ever since the flood* Reference to the great flood that God sends to destroy most life on Earth in Genesis 7; i.e., since the beginning of time.

2   *camphor-bottle* In the nineteenth century, camphor oil was used as a pain reliever.

"There has been a law passed forbidding people to help off the slaves that come over from Kentucky, my dear; so much of that thing has been done by these reckless Abolitionists, that our brethren in Kentucky are very strongly excited, and it seems necessary, and no more than Christian and kind, that something should be done by our state to quiet the excitement."

"And what is the law? It don't forbid us to shelter these poor creatures a night, does it, and to give 'em something comfortable to eat, and a few old clothes, and send them quietly about their business?"

"Why, yes, my dear; that would be aiding and abetting, you know."

Mrs. Bird was a timid, blushing little woman, of about four feet in height, and with mild blue eyes, and a peach-blow complexion, and the gentlest, sweetest voice in the world; as for courage, a moderate-sized cock-turkey had been known to put her to rout at the very first gobble, and a stout house-dog, of moderate capacity, would bring her into subjection merely by a show of his teeth. Her husband and children were her entire world, and in these she ruled more by entreaty and persuasion than by command or argument. There was only one thing that was capable of arousing her, and that provocation came in on the side of her unusually gentle and sympathetic nature; anything in the shape of cruelty would throw her into a passion, which was the more alarming and inexplicable in proportion to the general softness of her nature. Generally the most indulgent and easy to be entreated of all mothers, still her boys had a very reverent remembrance of a most vehement chastisement she once bestowed on them, because she found them leagued with several graceless boys of the neighborhood, stoning a defenceless kitten.

"I'll tell you what," Master Bill used to say, "I was scared that time. Mother came at me so that I thought she was crazy, and I was whipped and tumbled off to bed, without any supper, before I could get over wondering what had come about; and, after that, I heard mother crying outside the door, which made me feel worse than all the rest. I'll tell you what," he'd say, "we boys never stoned another kitten!"

On the present occasion, Mrs. Bird rose quickly, with very red cheeks, which quite improved her general appearance, and walked up to her husband, with quite a resolute air, and said, in a determined tone,

"Now, John, I want to know if you think such a law as that is right and Christian?"

"You won't shoot me, now, Mary, if I say I do!"

"I never could have thought it of you, John; you didn't vote for it?"

"Even so, my fair politician."

"You ought to be ashamed, John! Poor, homeless, houseless creatures! It's a shameful, wicked, abominable law, and I'll break it, for one, the first time I get a chance; and I hope I *shall* have a chance, I do! Things have got to a pretty pass, if a woman can't give a warm supper and a bed to poor, starving creatures, just because they are slaves, and have been abused and oppressed all their lives, poor things!"

"But, Mary, just listen to me. Your feelings are all quite right, dear, and interesting, and I love you for them; but, then, dear, we mustn't suffer our feelings to run away with our judgment; you must consider it's not a matter of private feeling—there are great public interests involved—there is such a state of public agitation rising, that we must put aside our private feelings."

"Now, John, I don't know anything about politics, but I can read my Bible; and there I see that I must feed the hungry, clothe the naked, and comfort the desolate;[1] and that Bible I mean to follow."

"But in cases where your doing so would involve a great public evil—"

"Obeying God never brings on public evils. I know it can't. It's always safest, all round, to *do as He* bids us."

"Now, listen to me, Mary, and I can state to you a very clear argument, to show—"

"O, nonsense, John! you can talk all night, but you wouldn't do it. I put it to you, John—would *you* now turn away a poor, shivering, hungry creature from your door, because he was a runaway? *Would* you, now?"

Now, if the truth must be told, our senator had the misfortune to be a man who had a particularly humane and accessible nature, and turning away anybody that was in trouble never had been his forte; and what was worse for him in this particular pinch of the argument was, that his wife knew it, and, of course, was making an assault on rather an indefensible point. So he had recourse to the usual means of gaining time for such cases made and provided; he said "ahem,"

---

1   *feed ... the desolate*   See Matthew 25.35–36: "For I was hungry, and ye gave me meat: I was thirsty, and ye gave me drink: I was a stranger, and ye took me in: Naked, and ye clothed me: I was sick, and ye visited me: I was in prison, and ye came unto me."

and coughed several times, took out his pocket-handkerchief, and began to wipe his glasses. Mrs. Bird, seeing the defenceless condition of the enemy's territory, had no more conscience than to push her advantage.

"I should like to see you doing that, John—I really should! Turning a woman out of doors in a snowstorm, for instance; or, maybe you'd take her up and put her in jail, wouldn't you? You would make a great hand at that!"

"Of course, it would be a very painful duty," began Mr. Bird, in a moderate tone.

"Duty, John! don't use that word! You know it isn't a duty—it can't be a duty! If folks want to keep their slaves from running away, let 'em treat 'em well—that's my doctrine. If I had slaves (as I hope I never shall have), I'd risk their wanting to run away from me, or you either, John. I tell you folks don't run away when they are happy; and when they do run, poor creatures! they suffer enough with cold and hunger and fear, without everybody's turning against them; and, law or no law, I never will, so help me God!"

"Mary! Mary! My dear, let me reason with you."

"I hate reasoning, John—especially reasoning on such subjects. There's a way you political folks have of coming round and round a plain right thing; and you don't believe in it yourselves, when it comes to practice. I know *you* well enough, John. You don't believe it's right any more than I do; and you wouldn't do it any sooner than I."

At this critical juncture, old Cudjoe, the black man-of-all-work, put his head in at the door, and wished "Missis would come into the kitchen"; and our senator, tolerably relieved, looked after his little wife with a whimsical mixture of amusement and vexation, and, seating himself in the armchair, began to read the papers.

After a moment, his wife's voice was heard at the door, in a quick, earnest tone—"John! John! I do wish you'd come here, a moment."

He laid down his paper, and went into the kitchen, and started, quite amazed at the sight that presented itself: A young and slender woman, with garments torn and frozen, with one shoe gone, and the stocking torn away from the cut and bleeding foot, was laid back in a deadly swoon upon two chairs. There was the impress of the despised race on her face, yet none could help feeling its mournful and pathetic[1] beauty, while its stony sharpness, its cold, fixed, deathly aspect, struck a solemn chill over him. He drew his breath short, and stood in silence. His wife, and their only colored domestic, old Aunt Dinah, were busily engaged in restorative measures; while old Cudjoe had got the boy on his knee, and was busy pulling off his shoes and stockings, and chafing his little cold feet.

"Sure, now, if she an't a sight to behold!" said old Dinah, compassionately; "'pears like 't was the heat that made her faint. She was tol'able peart[2] when she cum in, and asked if she couldn't warm herself here a spell; and I was just a askin' her where she cum from, and she fainted right down. Never done much hard work, guess, by the looks of her hands."

"Poor creature!" said Mrs. Bird, compassionately, as the woman slowly unclosed her large, dark eyes, and looked vacantly at her. Suddenly an expression of agony crossed her face, and she sprang up, saying, "O, my Harry! Have they got him?"

The boy, at this, jumped from Cudjoe's knee, and, running to her side, put up his arms. "O, he's here! he's here!" she exclaimed.

"O, ma'am!" said she, wildly, to Mrs. Bird, "do protect us! don't let them get him!"

"Nobody shall hurt you here, poor woman," said Mrs. Bird, encouragingly. "You are safe; don't be afraid."

"God bless you!" said the woman, covering her face and sobbing; while the little boy, seeing her crying, tried to get into her lap.

With many gentle and womanly offices,[3] which none knew better how to render than Mrs. Bird, the poor woman was, in time, rendered more calm. A temporary bed was provided for her on the settle, near the fire; and, after a short time, she fell into a heavy slumber, with the child, who seemed no less weary, soundly sleeping on her arm; for the mother resisted, with nervous anxiety, the kindest attempts to take him from her; and, even in sleep, her arm encircled him with an unrelaxing clasp, as if she could not even then be beguiled of her vigilant hold.

Mr. and Mrs. Bird had gone back to the parlor, where, strange as it may appear, no reference was made, on either side, to the preceding

---

1   *pathetic*   I.e., arousing a sense of pathos.
2   *peart*   Lively.
3   *offices*   Services.

conversation; but Mrs. Bird busied herself with her knitting work, and Mr. Bird pretended to be reading the paper.

"I wonder who and what she is!" said Mr. Bird, at last, as he laid it down.

"When she wakes up and feels a little rested, we will see," said Mrs. Bird.

"I say, wife!" said Mr. Bird, after musing in silence over his newspaper.

"Well, dear!"

"She couldn't wear one of your gowns, could she, by any letting down,[1] or such matter? She seems to be rather larger than you are."

A quite perceptible smile glimmered on Mrs. Bird's face, as she answered, "We'll see."

Another pause, and Mr. Bird again broke out,

"I say, wife!"

"Well! What now?"

"Why, there's that old bombasine[2] cloak, that you keep on purpose to put over me when I take my afternoon's nap; you might as well give her that—she needs clothes."

At this instant, Dinah looked in to say that the woman was awake, and wanted to see Missis.

Mr. and Mrs. Bird went into the kitchen, followed by the two eldest boys, the smaller fry having, by this time, been safely disposed of in bed.

The woman was now sitting up on the settle, by the fire. She was looking steadily into the blaze, with a calm, heartbroken expression, very different from her former agitated wildness.

"Did you want me?" said Mrs. Bird, in gentle tones. "I hope you feel better now, poor woman!"

A long-drawn, shivering sigh was the only answer; but she lifted her dark eyes, and fixed them on her with such a forlorn and imploring expression, that the tears came into the little woman's eyes.

"You needn't be afraid of anything; we are friends here, poor woman! Tell me where you came from, and what you want," said she.

"I came from Kentucky," said the woman.

---

1 *letting down* I.e., having the hems and seams altered so as to enlarge the garment.

2 *bombasine* Twill fabric combining silk or cotton with worsted wool.

"When?" said Mr. Bird, taking up the interrogatory.

"Tonight."

"How did you come?"

"I crossed on the ice."

"Crossed on the ice!" said everyone present.

"Yes," said the woman, slowly, "I did. God helping me, I crossed on the ice; for they were behind me—right behind—and there was no other way!"

"Law, Missis," said Cudjoe, "the ice is all in broken-up blocks, a swinging and a tetering up and down in the water!"

"I know it was—I know it!" said she, wildly; "but I did it! I wouldn't have thought I could—I didn't think I should get over, but I didn't care! I could but die, if I didn't. The Lord helped me; nobody knows how much the Lord can help 'em, till they try," said the woman, with a flashing eye.

"Were you a slave?" said Mr. Bird.

"Yes, sir; I belonged to a man in Kentucky."

"Was he unkind to you?"

"No, sir; he was a good master."

"And was your mistress unkind to you?"

"No, sir—no! my mistress was always good to me."

"What could induce you to leave a good home, then, and run away, and go through such dangers?"

The woman looked up at Mrs. Bird, with a keen, scrutinizing glance, and it did not escape her that she was dressed in deep mourning.

"Ma'am," she said, suddenly, "have you ever lost a child?"

The question was unexpected, and it was a thrust on a new wound; for it was only a month since a darling child of the family had been laid in the grave.

Mr. Bird turned around and walked to the window, and Mrs. Bird burst into tears; but, recovering her voice, she said,

"Why do you ask that? I have lost a little one."

"Then you will feel for me. I have lost two, one after another—left 'em buried there when I came away; and I had only this one left. I never slept a night without him; he was all I had. He was my comfort and pride, day and night; and, ma'am, they were going to take him away from me—to *sell* him—sell him down south, ma'am, to go all alone—a baby that had never been away from his mother in his life! I couldn't stand it, ma'am. I knew I never should be good for anything, if they did; and when I knew the papers were signed, and he was sold, I took him and came off in the night; and they chased me—the man that bought him, and some of Mas'r's folks—and they were coming down right behind me, and I heard 'em. I jumped right on to the ice; and how I got across, I don't know—but, first I knew, a man was helping me up the bank."

The woman did not sob nor weep. She had gone to a place where tears are dry; but everyone around her was, in some way characteristic of themselves, showing signs of hearty sympathy.

The two little boys, after a desperate rummaging in their pockets, in search of those pocket-handkerchiefs which mothers know are never to be found there, had thrown themselves disconsolately into the skirts of their mother's gown, where they were sobbing, and wiping their eyes and noses, to their hearts' content; Mrs. Bird had her face fairly hidden in her pocket-handkerchief; and old Dinah, with tears streaming down her black, honest face, was ejaculating, "Lord have mercy on us!" with all the fervor of a camp-meeting; while old Cudjoe, rubbing his eyes very hard with his cuffs, and making a most uncommon variety of wry faces, occasionally responded in the same key, with great fervor. Our senator was a statesman, and of course could not be expected to cry, like other mortals; and so he turned his back to the company, and looked out of the window, and seemed particularly busy in clearing his throat and wiping his spectacle-glasses, occasionally blowing his nose in a manner that was calculated to excite suspicion, had anyone been in a state to observe critically.

"How came you to tell me you had a kind master?" he suddenly exclaimed, gulping down very resolutely some kind of rising in his throat, and turning suddenly round upon the woman.

"Because he *was* a kind master; I'll say that of him, anyway—and my mistress was kind; but they couldn't help themselves. They were owing money; and there was some way, I can't tell how, that a man had a hold on them, and they were obliged to give him his will. I listened, and heard him telling mistress that, and she begging and pleading for me—and he told her he couldn't help himself, and that the papers were all drawn—and then it was I took him and left my home, and came away. I knew 't was no use of my trying to live, if they did it; for't 'pears like this child is all I have."

"Have you no husband?"

"Yes, but he belongs to another man. His master is real hard to him, and won't let him come to see me, hardly ever; and he's grown harder and harder upon us, and he threatens to sell him down south; it's like I'll never see *him* again!"

The quiet tone in which the woman pronounced these words might have led a superficial observer to think that she was entirely apathetic; but there was a calm, settled depth of anguish in her large, dark eye, that spoke of something far otherwise.

"And where do you mean to go, my poor woman?" said Mrs. Bird.

"To Canada, if I only knew where that was. Is it very far off, is Canada?" said she, looking up, with a simple, confiding air, to Mrs. Bird's face.

"Poor thing!" said Mrs. Bird, involuntarily.

"Is't a very great way off, think?" said the woman, earnestly.

"Much further than you think, poor child!" said Mrs. Bird; "but we will try to think what can be done for you. Here, Dinah, make her up a bed in your own room, close by the kitchen, and I'll think what to do for her in the morning. Meanwhile, never fear, poor woman; put your trust in God; he will protect you."

Mrs. Bird and her husband reentered the parlor. She sat down in her little rocking-chair before the fire, swaying thoughtfully to and fro. Mr. Bird strode up and down the room, grumbling to himself, "Pish! pshaw! confounded awkward business!" At length, striding up to his wife, he said.

"I say, wife, she'll have to get away from here, this very night. That fellow will be down on the scent bright and early tomorrow morning; if 't was only the woman, she could lie quiet till it was over; but that little chap can't be kept still by a troop of horse and foot,[1] I'll warrant me; he'll bring it all out, popping his head out of some window or door. A pretty kettle of fish it would be for me, too, to be caught with them both here, just now! No; they'll have to be got off tonight."

"Tonight! How is it possible? where to?"

---

1   *troop of horse and foot* I.e., an army.

"Well, I know pretty well where to," said the senator, beginning to put on his boots, with a reflective air; and, stopping when his leg was half in, he embraced his knee with both hands, and seemed to go off in deep meditation.

"It's a confounded awkward, ugly business," said he, at last, beginning to tug at his boot-straps again, "and that's a fact!" After one boot was fairly on, the senator sat with the other in his hand, profoundly studying the figure of the carpet. "It will have to be done, though, for aught I see—hang it all!" and he drew the other boot anxiously on, and looked out of the window.

Now, little Mrs. Bird was a discreet woman—a woman who never in her life said, "I told you so!" and, on the present occasion, though pretty well aware of the shape her husband's meditations were taking, she very prudently forbore to meddle with them, only sat very quietly in her chair, and looked quite ready to hear her liege lord's intentions, when he should think proper to utter them.

"You see," he said, "there's my old client, Van Trompe, has come over from Kentucky, and set all his slaves free; and he has bought a place seven miles up the creek, here, back in the woods, where nobody goes, unless they go on purpose; and it's a place that isn't found in a hurry. There she'd be safe enough; but the plague of the thing is, nobody could drive a carriage there tonight, but *me*."

"Why not? Cudjoe is an excellent driver."

"Ay, ay, but here it is. The creek has to be crossed twice; and the second crossing is quite dangerous, unless one knows it as I do. I have crossed it a hundred times on horseback, and know exactly the turns to take. And so, you see, there's no help for it. Cudjoe must put in the horses, as quietly as may be, about twelve o'clock, and I'll take her over; and then, to give color to the matter, he must carry me on to the next tavern, to take the stage for Columbus,[1] that comes by about three or four, and so it will look as if I had had the carriage only for that. I shall get into business bright and early in the morning. But I'm thinking I shall feel rather cheap there, after all that's been said and done; but, hang it, I can't help it!"

"Your heart is better than your head, in this case, John," said the wife, laying her little white hand on his. "Could I ever have loved you,

---

1   *stage* Stagecoach; *Columbus* Capital city of Ohio.

had I not known you better than you know yourself?" And the little woman looked so handsome, with the tears sparkling in her eyes, that the senator thought he must be a decidedly clever fellow, to get such a pretty creature into such a passionate admiration of him; and so, what could he do but walk off soberly, to see about the carriage. At the door, however, he stopped a moment, and then coming back, he said, with some hesitation,

"Mary, I don't know how you'd feel about it, but there's that drawer full of things—of—of—poor little Henry's." So saying, he turned quickly on his heel, and shut the door after him.

His wife opened the little bedroom door adjoining her room, and, taking the candle, set it down on the top of a bureau there; then from a small recess she took a key, and put it thoughtfully in the lock of a drawer, and made a sudden pause, while two boys, who, boy like, had followed close on her heels, stood looking, with silent, significant glances, at their mother. And oh! mother that reads this, has there never been in your house a drawer, or a closet, the opening of which has been to you like the opening again of a little grave? Ah! happy mother that you are, if it has not been so.

Mrs. Bird slowly opened the drawer. There were little coats of many a form and pattern, piles of aprons, and rows of small stockings; and even a pair of little shoes, worn and rubbed at the toes, were peeping from the folds of a paper. There was a toy horse and wagon, a top, a ball—memorials gathered with many a tear and many a heartbreak! She sat down by the drawer and, leaning her head on her hands over it, wept till the tears fell through her fingers into the drawer; then suddenly raising her head, she began, with nervous haste, selecting the plainest and most substantial articles, and gathering them into a bundle.

"Mamma," said one of the boys, gently touching her arm, "are you going to give away *those* things?"

"My dear boys," she said, softly and earnestly, "if our dear, loving little Henry looks down from heaven, he would be glad to have us do this. I could not find it in my heart to give them away to any common person—to anybody that was happy; but I give them to a mother more heartbroken and sorrowful than I am; and I hope God will send his blessings with them!"

There are in this world blessed souls whose sorrows all spring up into joys for others; whose earthly hopes, laid in the grave with many tears, are the seed from which spring healing flowers and balm for the desolate and the distressed. Among such was the delicate woman who sits there by the lamp, dropping slow tears, while she prepares the memorials of her own lost one for the outcast wanderer.

After a while, Mrs. Bird opened a wardrobe, and, taking from thence a plain, serviceable dress or two, she sat down busily to her work-table and, with needle, scissors, and thimble at hand, quietly commenced the "letting down" process which her husband had recommended, and continued busily at it till the old clock in the corner struck twelve, and she heard the low rattling of wheels at the door.

"Mary," said her husband, coming in, with his overcoat in his hand, "you must wake her up now; we must be off."

Mrs. Bird hastily deposited the various articles she had collected in a small plain trunk, and locking it, desired her husband to see it in the carriage, and then proceeded to call the woman. Soon, arrayed in a cloak, bonnet, and shawl, that had belonged to her benefactress, she appeared at the door with her child in her arms. Mr. Bird hurried her into the carriage, and Mrs. Bird pressed on after her to the carriage steps. Eliza leaned out of the carriage, and put out her hand—a hand as soft and beautiful as was given in return. She fixed her large, dark eyes, full of earnest meaning, on Mrs. Bird's face, and seemed going to speak. Her lips moved—she tried once or twice, but there was no sound—and pointing upward, with a look never to be forgotten, she fell back in the seat, and covered her face. The door was shut, and the carriage drove on.

What a situation, now, for a patriotic senator, that had been all the week before spurring up the legislature of his native state to pass more stringent resolutions against escaping fugitives, their harborers and abettors!

Our good senator in his native state had not been exceeded by any of his brethren at Washington in the sort of eloquence which has won for them immortal renown! How sublimely he had sat with his hands in his pockets, and scouted[1] all sentimental weakness of those who would put the welfare of a few miserable fugitives before great state interests!

---

1 *scouted* Scorned.

He was as bold as a lion about it, and "mightily convinced" not only himself, but everybody that heard him; but then his idea of a fugitive was only an idea of the letters that spell the word—or, at the most, the image of a little newspaper picture of a man with a stick and bundle, with "Ran away from the subscriber" under it. The magic of the real presence of distress—the imploring human eye, the frail, trembling human hand, the despairing appeal of helpless agony—these he had never tried. He had never thought that a fugitive might be a hapless mother, a defenceless child—like that one which was now wearing his lost boy's little well-known cap; and so, as our poor senator was not stone or steel—as he was a man, and a downright noble-hearted one, too—he was, as everybody must see, in a sad case for his patriotism. And you need not exult over him, good brother of the Southern States; for we have some inklings that many of you, under similar circumstances, would not do much better. We have reason to know, in Kentucky, as in Mississippi, are noble and generous hearts, to whom never was tale of suffering told in vain. Ah, good brother! is it fair for you to expect of us services which your own brave, honorable heart would not allow you to render, were you in our place?

Be that as it may, if our good senator was a political sinner, he was in a fair way to expiate it by his night's penance. There had been a long continuous period of rainy weather, and the soft, rich earth of Ohio, as everyone knows, is admirably suited to the manufacture of mud—and the road was an Ohio railroad of the good old times.

"And pray, what sort of a road may that be?" says some eastern traveller, who has been accustomed to connect no ideas with a railroad, but those of smoothness or speed.

Know, then, innocent eastern friend, that in benighted regions of the west, where the mud is of unfathomable and sublime depth, roads are made of round rough logs, arranged transversely side by side, and coated over in their pristine freshness with earth, turf, and whatsoever may come to hand, and then the rejoicing native calleth it a road, and straightway essayeth to ride thereupon. In process of time, the rains wash off all the turf and grass aforesaid, move the logs hither and thither, in picturesque positions, up, down and crosswise, with diverse chasms and ruts of black mud intervening.

Over such a road as this our senator went stumbling along, making moral reflections as continuously as under the circumstances could be expected, the carriage proceeding along much as follows—bump! bump! bump! slush! down in the mud!—the senator, woman and child, reversing their positions so suddenly as to come, without any very accurate adjustment, against the windows of the downhill side. Carriage sticks fast, while Cudjoe on the outside is heard making a great muster among the horses. After various ineffectual pullings and twitchings, just as the senator is losing all patience, the carriage suddenly rights itself with a bounce—two front wheels go down into another abyss, and senator, woman, and child, all tumble promiscuously on to the front seat—senator's hat is jammed over his eyes and nose quite unceremoniously, and he considers himself fairly extinguished—child cries, and Cudjoe on the outside delivers animated addresses to the horses, who are kicking, and floundering, and straining, under repeated cracks of the whip. Carriage springs up, with another bounce—down go the hind wheels—senator, woman, and child, fly over on to the back seat, his elbows encountering her bonnet, and both her feet being jammed into his hat, which flies off in the concussion. After a few moments the "slough" is passed, and the horses stop, panting—the senator finds his hat, the woman straightens her bonnet and hushes her child, and they brace themselves firmly for what is yet to come.

For a while only the continuous bump! bump! intermingled, just by way of variety, with diverse side plunges and compound shakes; and they begin to flatter themselves that they are not so badly off, after all. At last, with a square plunge, which puts all on to their feet and then down into their seats with incredible quickness, the carriage stops— and, after much outside commotion, Cudjoe appears at the door.

"Please, sir, it's powerful bad spot, this yer. I don't know how we's to get clar out. I'm a thinkin' we'll have to be a gettin' rails."[1]

The senator despairingly steps out, picking gingerly for some firm foothold; down goes one foot an immeasurable depth—he tries to pull it up, loses his balance, and tumbles over into the mud, and is fished out, in a very despairing condition, by Cudjoe.

---

[1]   *rails*   The boards from rail fences were sometimes removed to provide tracks to ease carriages through muddy terrain.

But we forbear, out of sympathy to our readers' bones. Western travellers, who have beguiled the midnight hour in the interesting process of pulling down rail fences, to pry their carriages out of mud holes, will have a respectful and mournful sympathy with our unfortunate hero. We beg them to drop a silent tear, and pass on.

It was full late in the night when the carriage emerged, dripping and bespattered, out of the creek, and stood at the door of a large farmhouse.

It took no inconsiderable perseverance to arouse the inmates; but at last the respectable proprietor appeared, and undid the door. He was a great, tall, bristling Orson[1] of a fellow, full six feet and some inches in his stockings, and arrayed in a red flannel hunting-shirt. A very heavy *mat* of sandy hair, in a decidedly tousled condition, and a beard of some days' growth, gave the worthy man an appearance, to say the least, not particularly prepossessing. He stood for a few minutes holding the candle aloft, and blinking on our travellers with a dismal and mystified expression that was truly ludicrous. It cost some effort of our senator to induce him to comprehend the case fully; and while he is doing his best at that, we shall give him a little introduction to our readers.

Honest old John Van Trompe was once quite a considerable land-holder and slave-owner in the State of Kentucky. Having "nothing of the bear about him but the skin,"[2] and being gifted by nature with a great, honest, just heart, quite equal to his gigantic frame, he had been for some years witnessing with repressed uneasiness the work-ings of a system equally bad for oppressor and oppressed. At last, one day, John's great heart had swelled altogether too big to wear his bonds any longer; so he just took his pocket-book out of his desk, and went over into Ohio, and bought a quarter of a township of good, rich land, made out free papers for all his people—men, women, and children—packed them up in wagons, and sent them off to settle down; and then honest John turned his face up the creek, and sat

---

1   *Orson* Bear-like; from the French word for bear, *ours*. The term also alludes to the fifteenth-century French story "Orson and Valentine," in which the lost son (Orson) of a king is abandoned in the woods and raised by a bear.

2   *nothing of … the skin* Oliver Goldsmith's description of Samuel Johnson, as quoted in James Boswell's *Life of Samuel Johnson* (1791): "Johnson, to be sure, has a roughness in his manner; but no man alive has a more tender heart. He has nothing of the bear but his skin."

quietly down on a snug, retired farm, to enjoy his conscience and his reflections.

"Are you the man that will shelter a poor woman and child from slave-catchers?" said the senator, explicitly.

"I rather think I am," said honest John, with some considerable emphasis.

"I thought so," said the senator.

"If there's anybody comes," said the good man, stretching his tall, muscular form upward, "why here I'm ready for him: and I've got seven sons, each six foot high, and they'll be ready for 'em. Give our respects to 'em," said John; "tell 'em it's no matter how soon they call—make no kinder difference to us," said John, running his fingers through the shock of hair that thatched his head, and bursting out into a great laugh.

Weary, jaded, and spiritless, Eliza dragged herself up to the door, with her child lying in a heavy sleep on her arm. The rough man held the candle to her face, and uttering a kind of compassionate grunt, opened the door of a small bedroom adjoining to the large kitchen where they were standing, and motioned her to go in. He took down a candle, and lighting it, set it upon the table, and then addressed himself to Eliza.

"Now, I say, gal, you needn't be a bit afeard, let who will come here. I'm up to all that sort o' thing," said he, pointing to two or three goodly rifles over the mantelpiece; "and most people that know me know that 't wouldn't be healthy to try to get anybody out o' my house when I'm agin it. So *now* you jist go to sleep now, as quiet as if yer mother was a rockin' ye," said he, as he shut the door.

"Why, this is an uncommon handsome un," he said to the senator. "Ah, well; handsome uns has the greatest cause to run, sometimes, if they has any kind o' feelin, such as decent women should. I know all about that."

The senator, in a few words, briefly explained Eliza's history.

"O! ou! aw! now, I want to know?" said the good man, pitifully; "sho! now sho! That's natur now, poor crittur! hunted down now like a deer—hunted down, jest for havin' natural feelin's, and doin' what no kind o' mother could help a doin'! I tell ye what, these yer things make me come the nighest to swearin', now, o' most anything," said honest John, as he wiped his eyes with the back of a great, freckled, yellow hand. "I tell yer what, stranger, it was years and years before I'd jine the church, 'cause the ministers round in our parts used to preach that the Bible went in for these ere cuttings up—and I couldn't be up to 'em with their Greek and Hebrew, and so I took up agin 'em, Bible and all. I never jined the church till I found a minister that was up to 'em all in Greek and all that, and he said right the contrary; and then I took right hold, and jined the church—I did now, fact," said John, who had been all this time uncorking some very frisky bottled cider, which at this juncture he presented.

"Ye'd better jest put up here, now, till daylight," said he, heartily, "and I'll call up the old woman, and have a bed got ready for you in no time."

"Thank you, my good friend," said the senator, "I must be along, to take the night stage for Columbus."

"Ah! well, then, if you must, I'll go a piece with you, and show you a cross road that will take you there better than the road you came on. That road's mighty bad."

John equipped himself, and, with a lantern in hand, was soon seen guiding the senator's carriage towards a road that ran down in a hollow, back of his dwelling. When they parted, the senator put into his hand a ten-dollar bill.

"It's for her," he said, briefly.

"Ay, ay," said John, with equal conciseness.

They shook hands, and parted.

Chapter 10
The Property Is Carried Off

The February morning looked gray and drizzling through the window of Uncle Tom's cabin. It looked on downcast faces, the images of mournful hearts. The little table stood out before the fire, covered with an ironing-cloth; a coarse but clean shirt or two, fresh from the iron, hung on the back of a chair by the fire, and Aunt Chloe had another spread out before her on the table. Carefully she rubbed and ironed every fold and every hem, with the most scrupulous exactness, every now and then raising her hand to her face to wipe off the tears that were coursing down her cheeks.

Tom sat by, with his Testament open on his knee, and his head leaning upon his hand—but neither spoke. It was yet early, and the children lay all asleep together in their little rude trundle-bed.

Tom, who had, to the full, the gentle, domestic heart, which, woe for them! has been a peculiar characteristic of his unhappy race, got up and walked silently to look at his children.

"It's the last time," he said.

Aunt Chloe did not answer, only rubbed away over and over on the coarse shirt, already as smooth as hands could make it; and finally setting her iron suddenly down with a despairing plunge, she sat down to the table, and "lifted up her voice and wept."[1]

"S'pose we must be resigned; but oh Lord! how ken I? If I know'd anything whar you's goin', or how they'd sarve you! Missis says she'll try and 'deem[2] ye, in a year or two; but Lor! nobody never comes up that goes down thar! They kills 'em! I've hearn 'em tell how dey works 'em up on dem ar plantations."

"There'll be the same God there, Chloe, that there is here."

"Well," said Aunt Chloe, "s'pose dere will; but de Lord lets drefful things happen, sometimes. I don't seem to get no comfort dat way."

"I'm in the Lord's hands," said Tom; "nothin' can go no furder than he lets it; and thar's *one* thing I can thank him for. It's *me* that's sold and going down, and not you nur the chil'en. Here you're safe; what comes will come only on me; and the Lord, he'll help me—I know he will."

Ah, brave, manly heart—smothering thine own sorrow, to comfort thy beloved ones! Tom spoke with a thick utterance, and with a bitter choking in his throat—but he spoke brave and strong.

"Let's think on our marcies!" he added, tremulously, as if he was quite sure he needed to think on them very hard indeed.

"Marcies!" said Aunt Chloe; "don't see no marcy in 't! 'tan't right! tan't right it should be so! Mas'r never ought ter left it so that ye *could* be took for his debts. Ye've arnt[3] him all he gets for ye, twice over. He owed ye yer freedom, and ought ter gin '*t* to yer years ago. Mebbe he can't help himself now, but I feel it's wrong. Nothing can't beat that

---

1   *lifted up … and wept*   Variations of this phrase are used numerous times throughout the Old Testament.
2   *'deem*   Redeem; re-purchase.
3   *arnt*   Earned.

ar out o' me. Sich a faithful crittur as ye've been—and allers sot his business *'fore* yer own every way—and reckoned on him more than yer own wife and chil'en! Them as sells heart's love and heart's blood, to get out thar scrapes, de Lord'll be up to *'em!*"

"Chloe! now, if ye love me, ye won't talk so, when perhaps jest the last time we'll ever have together! And I'll tell ye, Chloe, it goes agin me to hear one word agin Mas'r. Wan't he put in my arms a baby? it's natur I should think a heap of him. And he couldn't be spected to think so much of poor Tom. Mas'rs is used to havin' all these yer things done for *'em*, and nat'lly they don't think so much on *'t*. They can't be spected to, no way. Set him *'longside* of other Mas'rs—who's had the treatment and the livin' I've had? And he never would have let this yer come on me, if he could have seed it aforehand. I know he wouldn't."

"Wal, anyway, thar's wrong about it *somewhar*," said Aunt Chloe, in whom a stubborn sense of justice was a predominant trait; "I can't jest make out what *'t* is, but thar's wrong somewhar, I'm *clar* o' that."

"Yer ought ter look up to the Lord above—he's above all—thar don't a sparrow fall without him."[1]

"It don't seem to comfort me, but I spect it orter,"[2] said Aunt Chloe. "But dar's no use talkin'; I'll jes wet up de corn-cake, and get ye one good breakfast, *'cause* nobody knows when you'll get another."

In order to appreciate the sufferings of the negroes sold south, it must be remembered that all the instinctive affections of that race are peculiarly strong. Their local attachments are very abiding. They are not naturally daring and enterprising, but home-loving and affectionate. Add to this all the terrors with which ignorance invests the unknown, and add to this, again, that selling to the south is set before the negro from childhood as the last severity of punishment. The threat that terrifies more than whipping or torture of any kind is the threat of being sent down river. We have ourselves heard this feeling expressed by them, and seen the unaffected horror with which they will sit in their gossiping hours, and tell frightful stories of that "down river," which to them is

---

1   *thar don't ... without him*   See Matthew 10.29: "Are not two sparrows sold for a farthing? and one of them shall not fall on the ground without your Father."
2   *orter*   Ought to.

That undiscovered country, from whose bourn
No traveller returns.[1]

A missionary among the fugitives in Canada told us that many of the fugitives confessed themselves to have escaped from comparatively kind masters, and that they were induced to brave the perils of escape, in almost every case, by the desperate horror with which they regarded being sold south—a doom which was hanging either over themselves or their husbands, their wives or children. This nerves the African, naturally patient, timid and unenterprising, with heroic courage, and leads him to suffer hunger, cold, pain, the perils of the wilderness, and the more dread penalties of re-capture.

The simple morning meal now smoked on the table, for Mrs. Shelby had excused Aunt Chloe's attendance at the great house that morning. The poor soul had expended all her little energies on this farewell feast—had killed and dressed her choicest chicken, and prepared her corn-cake with scrupulous exactness, just to her husband's taste, and brought out certain mysterious jars on the mantelpiece, some preserves that were never produced except on extreme occasions.

"Lor, Pete," said Mose, triumphantly, "han't we got a buster of a breakfast!" at the same time catching at a fragment of the chicken.

Aunt Chloe gave him a sudden box on the ear. "Thar now! crowing over the last breakfast yer poor daddy's gwine to have to home!"

"O, Chloe!" said Tom, gently.

"Wal, I can't help it," said Aunt Chloe, hiding her face in her apron; "I's so tossed about, it makes me act ugly."

The boys stood quite still, looking first at their father and then at their mother, while the baby, climbing up her clothes, began an imperious, commanding cry.

"Thar!" said Aunt Chloe, wiping her eyes and taking up the baby; "now I's done, I hope—now do eat something. This yer's my nicest chicken. Thar, boys, ye shall have some, poor critturs! Yer mammy's been cross to yer."

The boys needed no second invitation, and went in with great zeal for the eatables; and it was well they did so, as otherwise there would have been very little performed to any purpose by the party.

---

1 *That undiscovered ... traveller returns* See Shakespeare's *Hamlet* 3.1.87–88.

"Now," said Aunt Chloe, bustling about after breakfast, "I must put up yer clothes. Jest like as not, he'll take 'em all away. I know thar ways—mean as dirt, they is! Wal, now, yer flannels for rhumatis is in this corner; so be carful, 'cause there won't nobody make ye no more. Then here's yer old shirts, and these yer is new ones. I toed off these yer stockings last night, and put de ball[1] in 'em to mend with. But Lor! who'll ever mend for ye?" and Aunt Chloe, again overcome, laid her head on the box side, and sobbed. "To think on 't! no critter to do for ye, sick or well! I don't railly think I ought ter be good now!"

The boys, having eaten everything there was on the breakfast table, began now to take some thought of the case; and, seeing their mother crying, and their father looking very sad, began to whimper and put their hands to their eyes. Uncle Tom had the baby on his knee, and was letting her enjoy herself to the utmost extent, scratching his face and pulling his hair, and occasionally breaking out into clamorous explosions of delight, evidently arising out of her own internal reflections.

"Ay, crow away, poor crittur!" said Aunt Chloe; "ye'll have to come to it, too! ye'll live to see yer husband sold, or mebbe be sold yerself; and these yer boys, they's to be sold, I s'pose, too, jest like as not, when dey gets good for somethin'; an't no use in niggers havin' nothin'!"

Here one of the boys called out, "Thar's Missis a-comin' in!"

"She can't do no good; what's she coming for?" said Aunt Chloe.

Mrs. Shelby entered. Aunt Chloe set a chair for her in a manner decidedly gruff and crusty. She did not seem to notice either the action or the manner. She looked pale and anxious.

"Tom," she said, "I come to—" and stopping suddenly, and regarding the silent group, she sat down in the chair, and, covering her face with her handkerchief, began to sob.

"Lor, now, Missis, don't—don't!" said Aunt Chloe, bursting out in her turn; and for a few moments they all wept in company. And in those tears they all shed together, the high and the lowly, melted away all the heart-burnings and anger of the oppressed. O, ye who visit the distressed, do ye know that everything your money can buy, given with a cold, averted face, is not worth one honest tear shed in real sympathy?

---

1   *ball*   Rounded tool used for darning the heels of socks.

"My good fellow," said Mrs. Shelby, "I can't give you anything to do you any good. If I give you money, it will only be taken from you. But I tell you solemnly, and before God, that I will keep trace of you, and bring you back as soon as I can command the money; and, till then, trust in God!"

Here the boys called out that Mas'r Haley was coming, and then an unceremonious kick pushed open the door. Haley stood there in very ill humor, having ridden hard the night before, and being not at all pacified by his ill success in re-capturing his prey.

"Come," said he, "ye nigger, ye'r ready? Servant, ma'am!" said he, taking off his hat, as he saw Mrs. Shelby.

Aunt Chloe shut and corded the box, and, getting up, looked gruffly on the trader, her tears seeming suddenly turned to sparks of fire.

Tom rose up meekly, to follow his new master, and raised up his heavy box on his shoulder. His wife took the baby in her arms to go with him to the wagon, and the children, still crying, trailed on behind.

Mrs. Shelby, walking up to the trader, detained him for a few moments, talking with him in an earnest manner; and while she was thus talking, the whole family party proceeded to a wagon, that stood ready harnessed at the door. A crowd of all the old and young hands on the place stood gathered around it, to bid farewell to their old associate. Tom had been looked up to, both as a head servant and a Christian teacher, by all the place, and there was much honest sympathy and grief about him, particularly among the women.

"Why, Chloe, you bar it better '*n* we do!" said one of the women, who had been weeping freely, noticing the gloomy calmness with which Aunt Chloe stood by the wagon.

"I's done *my* tears!" she said, looking grimly at the trader, who was coming up. "I does not feel to cry '*fore* dat ar old limb, no how!"

"Get in!" said Haley to Tom, as he strode through the crowd of servants, who looked at him with lowering brows.

Tom got in, and Haley, drawing out from under the wagon seat a heavy pair of shackles, made them fast around each ankle.

A smothered groan of indignation ran through the whole circle, and Mrs. Shelby spoke from the verandah—

"Mr. Haley, I assure you that precaution is entirely unnecessary."

"Do'n know, ma'am; I've lost one five hundred dollars from this yer place, and I can't afford to run no more risks."

"What else could she spect on him?" said Aunt Chloe, indignantly, while the two boys, who now seemed to comprehend at once their father's destiny, clung to her gown, sobbing and groaning vehemently.

"I'm sorry," said Tom, "that Mas'r George happened to be away."

George had gone to spend two or three days with a companion on a neighboring estate, and having departed early in the morning, before Tom's misfortune had been made public, had left without hearing of it.

"Give my love to Mas'r George," he said, earnestly.

Haley whipped up the horse, and, with a steady, mournful look, fixed to the last on the old place, Tom was whirled away.

Mr. Shelby at this time was not at home. He had sold Tom under the spur of a driving necessity, to get out of the power of a man whom he dreaded—and his first feeling, after the consummation of the bargain, had been that of relief. But his wife's expostulations awoke his half-slumbering regrets; and Tom's manly disinterestedness increased the unpleasantness of his feelings. It was in vain that he said to himself that he had a *right* to do it—that everybody did it—and that some did it without even the excuse of necessity; he could not satisfy his own feelings; and that he might not witness the unpleasant scenes of the consummation, he had gone on a short business tour up the country, hoping that all would be over before he returned.

Tom and Haley rattled on along the dusty road, whirling past every old familiar spot, until the bounds of the estate were fairly passed, and they found themselves out on the open pike.[1] After they had ridden about a mile, Haley suddenly drew up at the door of a blacksmith's shop, when, taking out with him a pair of handcuffs, he stepped into the shop, to have a little alteration in them.

"These yer's a little too small for his build," said Haley, showing the fetters, and pointing out to Tom.

"Lor! now, if thar an't Shelby's Tom. He han't sold him, now?" said the smith.

"Yes, he has," said Haley.

---

1 *pike* Turnpike; road.

"Now, ye don't! well, reely," said the smith, "who'd a thought it! Why, ye needn't go to fetterin' him up this yer way. He's the faithfullest, best crittur—"

"Yes, yes," said Haley; "but your good fellers are just the critturs to want ter run off. Them stupid ones, as doesn't care whar they go, and shifless, drunken ones, as don't care for nothin', they'll stick by, and like as not be rather pleased to be toted round; but these yer prime fellers, they hates it like sin. No way but to fetter 'em; got legs, they'll use 'em, no mistake."

"Well," said the smith, feeling among his tools, "them plantations down thar, stranger, an't jest the place a Kentuck nigger wants to go to; they dies thar tol'able fast, don't they?"

"Wal, yes, tol'able fast, ther dying is; what with the 'climating[1] and one thing and another, they dies so as to keep the market up pretty brisk," said Haley.

"Wal, now, a feller can't help thinkin' it's a mighty pity to have a nice, quiet, likely feller, as good un as Tom is, go down to be fairly ground up on one of them ar sugar plantations."

"Wal, he's got a fa'r chance. I promised to do well by him. I'll get him in house-servant in some good old family, and then, if he stands the fever and 'climating, he'll have a berth good as any nigger ought ter ask for."

"He leaves his wife and chil'en up here, s'pose?"

"Yes; but he'll get another thar. Lord, thar's women enough everywhar," said Haley.

Tom was sitting very mournfully on the outside of the shop while this conversation was going on. Suddenly he heard the quick, short click of a horse's hoof behind him; and, before he could fairly awake from his surprise, young Master George sprang into the wagon, threw his arms tumultuously round his neck, and was sobbing and scolding with energy.

"I declare, it's real mean! I don't care what they say, any of 'em! It's a nasty, mean shame! If I was a man, they shouldn't do it—they should not, so!" said George, with a kind of subdued howl.

"O! Mas'r George! this does me good!" said Tom. "I couldn't bar to go off without seein' ye! It does me real good, ye can't tell!" Here

---

1 'climating Acclimatizing.

Tom made some movement of his feet, and George's eye fell on the fetters.

"What a shame!" he exclaimed, lifting his hands. "I'll knock that old fellow down—I will!"

"No you won't, Mas'r George; and you must not talk so loud. It won't help me any, to anger him."

"Well, I won't, then, for your sake; but only to think of it—isn't it a shame? They never sent for me, nor sent me any word, and, if it hadn't been for Tom Lincon, I shouldn't have heard it. I tell you, I blew '*em* up well, all of '*em*, at home!"

"That ar wasn't right, I'm '*feard*, Mas'r George."

"Can't help it! I say it's a shame! Look here, Uncle Tom," said he, turning his back to the shop, and speaking in a mysterious tone, "*I've brought you my dollar!*"

"O! I couldn't think o' takin' on '*it*, Mas'r George, no ways in the world!" said Tom, quite moved.

"But you *shall* take it!" said George; "look here—I told Aunt Chloe I'd do it, and she advised me just to make a hole in it, and put a string through, so you could hang it round your neck, and keep it out of sight; else this mean scamp would take it away. I tell ye, Tom, I want to blow him up! it would do me good!"

"No, don't, Mas'r George, for it won't do *me* any good."

"Well, I won't, for your sake," said George, busily tying his dollar round Tom's neck; "but there, now, button your coat tight over it, and keep it, and remember, every time you see it, that I'll come down after you, and bring you back. Aunt Chloe and I have been talking about it. I told her not to fear; I'll see to it, and I'll tease father's life out, if he don't do it."

"O! Mas'r George, ye mustn't talk so '*bour* yer father!"

"Lor, Uncle Tom, I don't mean anything bad."

"And now, Mas'r George," said Tom, "ye must be a good boy; '*member* how many hearts is sot on ye. Al'ays keep close to yer mother. Don't be gettin' into any of them foolish ways boys has of gettin' too big to mind their mothers. Tell ye what, Mas'r George, the Lord gives good many things twice over; but he don't give ye a mother but once. Ye'll never see sich another woman, Mas'r George, if ye live to be a hundred years old. So, now, you hold on to her, and grow up, and be a comfort to her, thar's my own good boy—you will now, won't ye?"

"Yes, I will, Uncle Tom," said George, seriously.

"And be careful of yer speaking, Mas'r George. Young boys, when they comes to your age, is wilful, sometimes—it's natur they should be. But real gentlemen, such as I hopes you'll be, never lets fall no words that isn't *'spectful* to thar parents. Ye an't *'fended*, Mas'r George?"

"No, indeed, Uncle Tom; you always did give me good advice."

"I's older, ye know," said Tom, stroking the boy's fine, curly head with his large, strong hand, but speaking in a voice as tender as a woman's, "and I sees all that's bound up in you. O, Mas'r George, you has everything—l'arnin', privileges, readin', writin'—and you'll grow up to be a great, learned, good man, and all the people on the place and your mother and father'll be so proud on ye! Be a good Mas'r, like yer father; and be a Christian, like yer mother. *'Member* yer Creator in the days o' yer youth,[1] Mas'r George."

"I'll be *real* good, Uncle Tom, I tell you," said George. "I'm going to be a *first-rater*; and don't you be discouraged. I'll have you back to the place, yet. As I told Aunt Chloe this morning, I'll build your house all over, and you shall have a room for a parlor with a carpet on it, when I'm a man. O, you'll have good times yet!"

Haley now came to the door, with the handcuffs in his hands.

"Look here, now, Mister," said George, with an air of great superiority, as he got out, "I shall let father and mother know how you treat Uncle Tom!"

"You're welcome," said the trader.

"I should think you'd be ashamed to spend all your life buying men and women, and chaining them, like cattle! I should think you'd feel mean!" said George.

"So long as your grand folks wants to buy men and women, I'm as good as they is," said Haley; "'*tan't* any meaner sellin' on 'em, than '*tis* buyin'!"

"I'll never do either, when I'm a man," said George; "I'm ashamed, this day, that I'm a Kentuckian. I always was proud of it before"; and George sat very straight on his horse, and looked round with an air, as if he expected the state would be impressed with his opinion.

"Well, goodbye, Uncle Tom; keep a stiff upper lip," said George.

---

1 *'Member yer … youth* See Ecclesiastes 12.1: "Remember now thy Creator in the days of thy youth, while the evil days come not, nor the years draw nigh, when thou shalt say, I have no pleasure in them."

"Goodbye, Mas'r George," said Tom, looking fondly and admiringly at him. "God Almighty bless you! Ah! Kentucky han't got many like you!" he said, in the fulness of his heart, as the frank, boyish face was lost to his view. Away he went, and Tom looked, till the clatter of his horse's heels died away, the last sound or sight of his home. But over his heart there seemed to be a warm spot, where those young hands had placed that precious dollar. Tom put up his hand, and held it close to his heart.

"Now, I tell ye what, Tom," said Haley, as he came up to the wagon, and threw in the handcuffs, "I mean to start fa'r with ye, as I gen'ally do with my niggers; and I'll tell ye now, to begin with, you treat me fa'r, and I'll treat you fa'r; I an't never hard on my niggers. Calculates to do the best for 'em I can. Now, ye see, you'd better jest settle down comfortable, and not be tryin' no tricks; because nigger's tricks of all sorts I'm up to, and it's no use. If niggers is quiet, and don't try to get off, they has good times with me; and if they don't, why, it's thar fault, and not mine."

Tom assured Haley that he had no present intentions of running off. In fact, the exhortation seemed rather a superfluous one to a man with a great pair of iron fetters on his feet. But Mr. Haley had got in the habit of commencing his relations with his stock with little exhortations of this nature, calculated, as he deemed, to inspire cheerfulness and confidence, and prevent the necessity of any unpleasant scenes.

And here, for the present, we take our leave of Tom, to pursue the fortunes of other characters in our story.

Chapter II
In which Property Gets into an Improper State of Mind

It was late in a drizzly afternoon that a traveller alighted at the door of a small country hotel, in the village of N——, in Kentucky. In the barroom he found assembled quite a miscellaneous company, whom stress of weather had driven to harbor, and the place presented the usual scenery of such reunions. Great, tall, raw-boned Kentuckians, attired in hunting-shirts, and trailing their loose joints over a vast extent of territory, with the easy lounge peculiar to the race—rifles stacked away in the corner, shot-pouches, game-bags, hunting-dogs, and little negroes, all rolled together in the corners—were the characteristic features in the picture. At each end of the fireplace sat a long-legged gentleman, with his chair tipped back, his hat on his head, and the heels of his muddy boots reposing sublimely on the mantelpiece—a position, we will inform our readers, decidedly favorable to the turn of reflection incident to western taverns, where travellers exhibit a decided preference for this particular mode of elevating their understandings.

Mine host, who stood behind the bar, like most of his country-men, was great of stature, good-natured, and loose-jointed, with an enormous shock of hair on his head, and a great tall hat on the top of that.

In fact, everybody in the room bore on his head this characteristic emblem of man's sovereignty; whether it were felt hat, palm-leaf, greasy beaver, or fine new chapeau, there it reposed with true repub-lican independence. In truth, it appeared to be the characteristic mark of every individual. Some wore them tipped rakishly to one side—these were your men of humor, jolly, free-and-easy dogs; some had them jammed independently down over their noses—these were your hard characters, thorough men, who, when they wore their hats, *wanted* to wear them, and to wear them just as they had a mind to; there were those who had them set far over back—wide-awake[1] men, who wanted a clear prospect; while careless men, who did not know, or care, how their hats sat, had them shaking about in all directions. The various hats, in fact, were quite a Shakespearean study.

Diverse negroes, in very free-and-easy pantaloons, and with no redundancy in the shirt line,[2] were scuttling about, hither and thither, without bringing to pass any very particular results, except expressing a generic willingness to turn over everything in creation generally for the benefit of Mas'r and his guests. Add to this picture a jolly, crack-ing, rollicking fire, going rejoicingly up a great wide chimney—the outer door and every window being set wide open, and the calico window-curtain flopping and snapping in a good stiff breeze of damp raw air—and you have an idea of the jollities of a Kentucky tavern.

---

1   *wide-awake*   Reference to a style of man's hat known as the wideawake hat, with a broad brim and low crown.
2   *no redundancy in the shirt line*   I.e., shirtless.

Your Kentuckian of the present day is a good illustration of the doctrine of transmitted instincts and peculiarities. His fathers were mighty hunters—men who lived in the woods, and slept under the free, open heavens, with the stars to hold their candles; and their descendant to this day always acts as if the house were his camp—wears his hat at all hours, tumbles himself about, and puts his heels on the tops of chairs or mantelpieces, just as his father rolled on the green sward,[1] and put his upon trees and logs—keeps all the windows and doors open, winter and summer, that he may get air enough for his great lungs—calls everybody "stranger," with nonchalant bonhomie,[2] and is altogether the frankest, easiest, most jovial creature living.

Into such an assembly of the free and easy our traveller entered. He was a short, thick-set man, carefully dressed, with a round, good-natured countenance, and something rather fussy and particular in his appearance. He was very careful of his valise and umbrella, bringing them in with his own hands, and resisting, pertinaciously, all offers from the various servants to relieve him of them. He looked round the barroom with rather an anxious air, and, retreating with his valuables to the warmest corner, disposed them under his chair, sat down, and looked rather apprehensively up at the worthy whose heels illustrated the end of the mantelpiece, who was spitting from right to left, with a courage and energy rather alarming to gentlemen of weak nerves and particular habits.

"I say, stranger, how are ye?" said the aforesaid gentleman, firing an honorary salute of tobacco-juice in the direction of the new arrival.

"Well, I reckon," was the reply of the other, as he dodged, with some alarm, the threatening honor.

"Any news?" said the respondent, taking out a strip of tobacco and a large hunting-knife from his pocket.

"Not that I know of," said the man.

"Chaw?"[3] said the first speaker, handing the old gentleman a bit of his tobacco, with a decidedly brotherly air.

"No, thank ye—it don't agree with me," said the little man, edging off.

---

1   *sward*   Grassy field.
2   *bonhomie*   Camaraderie; friendliness.
3   *Chaw*   Chewing tobacco.

"Don't, eh?" said the other, easily, and stowing away the morsel in his own mouth, in order to keep up the supply of tobacco-juice, for the general benefit of society.

The old gentleman uniformly gave a little start whenever his long-sided brother fired in his direction; and this being observed by his companion, he very good-naturedly turned his artillery to another quarter, and proceeded to storm one of the fire-irons with a degree of military talent fully sufficient to take a city.

"What's that?" said the old gentleman, observing some of the company formed in a group around a large handbill.

"Nigger advertised!" said one of the company, briefly.

Mr. Wilson, for that was the old gentleman's name, rose up, and, after carefully adjusting his valise and umbrella, proceeded deliberately to take out his spectacles and fix them on his nose; and, this operation being performed, read as follows:

> Ran away from the subscriber, my mulatto boy, George. Said George six feet in height, a very light mulatto, brown curly hair; is very intelligent, speaks handsomely, can read and write; will probably try to pass for a white man; is deeply scarred on his back and shoulders; has been branded in his right hand with the letter H.
>
> I will give four hundred dollars for him alive, and the same sum for satisfactory proof that he has been killed.

The old gentleman read this advertisement from end to end, in a low voice, as if he were studying it.

The long-legged veteran, who had been besieging the fire-iron, as before related, now took down his cumbrous length, and rearing aloft his tall form, walked up to the advertisement, and very deliberately spit a full discharge of tobacco-juice on it.

"There's my mind upon that!" said he, briefly, and sat down again.

"Why, now, stranger, what's that for?" said mine host.

"I'd do it all the same to the writer of that ar paper, if he was here," said the long man, coolly resuming his old employment of cutting tobacco. "Any man that owns a boy like that, and can't find any better way o' treating on him, *deserves* to lose him. Such papers as these is a shame to Kentucky; that's my mind right out, if anybody wants to know!"

"Well, now, that's a fact," said mine host, as he made an entry in his book.

"I've got a gang of boys, sir," said the long man, resuming his attack on the fire-irons, "and I jest tells 'em—'Boys,' says I, 'run now! dig! put! jest when ye want to! I never shall come to look after you!' That's the way I keep mine. Let 'em know they are free to run any time, and it jest breaks up their wanting to. More 'n all, I've got free papers[1] for 'em all recorded, in case I gets keeled up any o' these times, and they knows it; and I tell ye, stranger, there an't a fellow in our parts gets more out of his niggers than I do. Why, my boys have been to Cincinnati, with five hundred dollars' worth of colts, and brought me back the money, all straight, time and agin. It stands to reason they should. Treat 'em like dogs, and you'll have dogs' works and dogs' actions. Treat 'em like men, and you'll have men's works." And the honest drover, in his warmth, endorsed this moral sentiment by firing a perfect *feu de joie*[2] at the fireplace.

"I think you're altogether right, friend," said Mr. Wilson; "and this boy described here *is* a fine fellow—no mistake about that. He worked for me some half-dozen years in my bagging factory, and he was my best hand, sir. He is an ingenious fellow, too: he invented a machine for the cleaning of hemp—a really valuable affair; it's gone into use in several factories. His master holds the patent of it."

"I'll warrant ye," said the drover, "holds it and makes money out of it, and then turns round and brands the boy in his right hand. If I had a fair chance, I'd mark him, I reckon, so that he'd carry it *one* while."

"These yer knowin' boys is allers aggravatin' and sarcy,"[3] said a coarse-looking fellow, from the other side of the room; "that's why they gets cut up and marked so. If they behaved themselves, they wouldn't."

"That is to say, the Lord made 'em men, and it's a hard squeeze getting 'em down into beasts," said the drover, dryly.

"Bright niggers isn't no kind of *'vantage* to their masters," continued the other, well intrenched, in a coarse, unconscious obtuseness, from the contempt of his opponent; "what's the use o' talents and

---

1 *free papers* Documents confirming a person's free status.
2 *feu de joie* French: literally, joyous fire; a celebratory rifle salute—though in this case, the reference is to spitting tobacco juice.
3 *sarcy* Saucy; insolent.

them things, if you can't get the use on 'em yourself? Why, all the use they make on 't is to get round you. I've had one or two of these fellers, and I jest sold 'em down river. I knew I'd got to lose 'em, first or last, if I didn't."

"Better send orders up to the Lord, to make you a set, and leave out their souls entirely," said the drover.

Here the conversation was interrupted by the approach of a small one-horse buggy to the inn. It had a genteel appearance, and a well-dressed, gentlemanly man sat on the seat, with a colored servant driving.

The whole party examined the new comer with the interest with which a set of loafers in a rainy day usually examine every new comer. He was very tall, with a dark, Spanish complexion, fine, expressive black eyes, and close-curling hair, also of a glossy blackness. His well-formed aquiline nose, straight thin lips, and the admirable contour of his finely-formed limbs, impressed the whole company instantly with the idea of something uncommon. He walked easily in among the company, and with a nod indicated to his waiter where to place his trunk, bowed to the company, and, with his hat in his hand, walked up leisurely to the bar, and gave his name as Henry Butler, Oaklands, Shelby County. Turning, with an indifferent air, he sauntered up to the advertisement, and read it over.

"Jim," he said to his man, "seems to me we met a boy something like this, up at Bernan's, didn't we?"

"Yes, Mas'r," said Jim, "only I an't sure about the hand."

"Well, I didn't look, of course," said the stranger, with a careless yawn. Then, walking up to the landlord, he desired him to furnish him with a private apartment, as he had some writing to do immediately.

The landlord was all obsequious, and a relay of about seven negroes, old and young, male and female, little and big, were soon whizzing about, like a covey of partridges, bustling, hurrying, treading on each other's toes, and tumbling over each other, in their zeal to get Mas'r's room ready, while he seated himself easily on a chair in the middle of the room, and entered into conversation with the man who sat next to him.

The manufacturer, Mr. Wilson, from the time of the entrance of the stranger, had regarded him with an air of disturbed and uneasy curiosity. He seemed to himself to have met and been acquainted with him somewhere, but he could not recollect. Every few moments, when the man spoke, or moved, or smiled, he would start and fix his eyes on him, and then suddenly withdraw them, as the bright, dark eyes met his with such unconcerned coolness. At last, a sudden recollection seemed to flash upon him, for he stared at the stranger with such an air of blank amazement and alarm, that he walked up to him.

"Mr. Wilson, I think," said he, in a tone of recognition, and extending his hand. "I beg your pardon, I didn't recollect you before. I see you remember me—Mr. Butler, of Oaklands, Shelby County."

"Ye—yes—yes, sir," said Mr. Wilson, like one speaking in a dream.

Just then a negro boy entered, and announced that Mas'r's room was ready.

"Jim, see to the trunks," said the gentleman, negligently; then addressing himself to Mr. Wilson, he added—"I should like to have a few moments' conversation with you on business, in my room, if you please."

Mr. Wilson followed him, as one who walks in his sleep; and they proceeded to a large upper chamber, where a new-made fire was crackling, and various servants flying about, putting finishing touches to the arrangements.

When all was done, and the servants departed, the young man deliberately locked the door, and putting the key in his pocket, faced about, and folding his arms on his bosom, looked Mr. Wilson full in the face.

"George!" said Mr. Wilson.

"Yes, George," said the young man.

"I couldn't have thought it!"

"I am pretty well disguised, I fancy," said the young man, with a smile. "A little walnut bark has made my yellow skin a genteel brown, and I've dyed my hair black; so you see I don't answer to the advertisement at all."

"O, George! but this is a dangerous game you are playing. I could not have advised you to it."

"I can do it on my own responsibility," said George, with the same proud smile.

We remark, *en passant*,[1] that George was, by his father's side, of white descent. His mother was one of those unfortunates of her race, marked out by personal beauty to be the slave of the passions of her possessor, and the mother of children who may never know a father. From one of the proudest families in Kentucky he had inherited a set of fine European features, and a high, indomitable spirit. From his mother he had received only a slight mulatto tinge, amply compensated by its accompanying rich, dark eye. A slight change in the tint of the skin and the color of his hair had metamorphosed him into the Spanish-looking fellow he then appeared; and as gracefulness of movement and gentlemanly manners had always been perfectly natural to him, he found no difficulty in playing the bold part he had adopted—that of a gentleman travelling with his domestic.

Mr. Wilson, a good-natured but extremely fidgety and cautious old gentleman, ambled up and down the room, appearing, as John Bunyan hath it, "much tumbled up and down in his mind,"[2] and divided between his wish to help George, and a certain confused notion of maintaining law and order: so, as he shambled about, he delivered himself as follows:

"Well, George, I s'pose you're running away—leaving your lawful master, George—(I don't wonder at it)—at the same time, I'm sorry, George—yes, decidedly—I think I must say that, George—it's my duty to tell you so."

"Why are you sorry, sir?" said George, calmly.

"Why, to see you, as it were, setting yourself in opposition to the laws of your country."

"*My* country!" said George, with a strong and bitter emphasis; "what country have I, but the grave—and I wish to God that I was laid there!"

"Why, George, no—no—it won't do; this way of talking is wicked—unscriptural. George, you've got a hard master—in fact, he is—well he conducts himself reprehensibly—I can't pretend to defend him. But you know how the angel commanded Hagar to return to

---

1   *en passant* French: in passing.
2   *much tumbled ... his mind* From *The Pilgrim's Progress* Part 2, Chapter 2.

her mistress, and submit herself under her hand; and the apostle sent back Onesimus to his master."[1]

"Don't quote Bible at me that way, Mr. Wilson," said George, with a flashing eye, "don't! for my wife is a Christian, and I mean to be, if ever I get to where I can; but to quote Bible to a fellow in my circumstances, is enough to make him give it up altogether. I appeal to God Almighty—I'm willing to go with the case to Him, and ask Him if I do wrong to seek my freedom."

"These feelings are quite natural, George," said the good-natured man, blowing his nose. "Yes they're natural, but it is my duty not to encourage 'em in you. Yes, my boy, I'm sorry for you, now; it's a bad case—very bad; but the apostle says, 'Let everyone abide in the condition in which he is called.'[2] We must all submit to the indications of Providence, George—don't you see?"

George stood with his head drawn back, his arms folded tightly over his broad breast, and a bitter smile curling his lips.

"I wonder, Mr. Wilson, if the Indians should come and take you a prisoner away from your wife and children, and want to keep you all your life hoeing corn for them, if you'd think it your duty to abide in the condition in which you were called. I rather think that you'd think the first stray horse you could find an indication of Providence—shouldn't you?"

The little old gentleman stared with both eyes at this illustration of the case; but, though not much of a reasoner, he had the sense in which some logicians on this particular subject do not excel—that of saying nothing, where nothing could be said. So, as he stood carefully stroking his umbrella, and folding and patting down all the creases in it, he proceeded on with his exhortations in a general way.

"You see, George, you know, now, I always have stood your friend; and whatever I've said, I've said for your good. Now, here, it seems to me, you're running an awful risk. You can't hope to carry it out. If

---

1   *the angel ... her mistress*   In the Book of Genesis, Hagar is the servant of Abraham's wife, Sarah. Having failed so far to bear Abraham any children, Sarah gives him Hagar, whom she then abuses jealously after Hagar becomes pregnant; Hagar flees the household in distress, but God commands her to return so as to bear Abraham his son, Ishmael;   *the apostle ... his master*   In the Epistle of Paul to Philemon (in the New Testament), Paul implores Philemon to welcome the formerly enslaved Onesimus, now converted to Christianity, back into his household as a brother rather than as a slave.

2   *Let everyone ... is called*   See 1 Corinthians 7.20.

you're taken, it will be worse with you than ever; they'll only abuse you, and half kill you, and sell you down river."

"Mr. Wilson, I know all this," said George. "I *do* run a risk, but—" he threw open his overcoat, and showed two pistols and a bowie-knife.[1] "There!" he said, "I'm ready for 'em! Down south I never *will* go. No! if it comes to that, I can earn myself at least six feet of free soil—the first and last I shall ever own in Kentucky!"

"Why, George, this state of mind is awful; it's getting really desperate, George. I'm concerned. Going to break the laws of your country!"

"My country again! Mr. Wilson, *you* have a country; but what country have *I*, or anyone like me, born of slave mothers? What laws are there for us? We don't make them—we don't consent to them— we have nothing to do with them; all they do for us is to crush us, and keep us down. Haven't I heard your Fourth-of-July speeches? Don't you tell us all, once a year, that governments derive their just power from the consent of the governed?[2] Can't a fellow *think*, that hears such things? Can't he put this and that together, and see what it comes to?"

Mr. Wilson's mind was one of those that may not unaptly be represented by a bale of cotton—downy, soft, benevolently fuzzy and confused. He really pitied George with all his heart, and had a sort of dim and cloudy perception of the style of feeling that agitated him; but he deemed it his duty to go on talking *good* to him, with infinite pertinacity.

"George, this is bad. I must tell you, you know, as a friend, you'd better not be meddling with such notions; they are bad, George, very bad, for boys in your condition—very"; and Mr. Wilson sat down to a table, and began nervously chewing the handle of his umbrella.

"See here, now, Mr. Wilson," said George, coming up and sitting himself determinately down in front of him; "look at me, now. Don't I sit before you, every way, just as much a man as you are? Look at my face—look at my hands—look at my body," and the young man drew himself up proudly; "why am I *not* a man, as much as anybody? Well, Mr. Wilson, hear what I can tell you. I had a father—one of your Kentucky gentlemen—who didn't think enough of me to keep

---

1 *bowie-knife* Short-handled fighting knife.

2 *governments derive ... the governed* Among the opening lines of the Declaration of Independence.

me from being sold with his dogs and horses, to satisfy the estate, when he died. I saw my mother put up at sheriff's sale, with her seven children. They were sold before her eyes, one by one, all to different masters; and I was the youngest. She came and kneeled down before old Mas'r, and begged him to buy her with me, that she might have at least one child with her; and he kicked her away with his heavy boot. I saw him do it; and the last that I heard was her moans and screams, when I was tied to his horse's neck, to be carried off to his place."

"Well, then?"

"My master traded with one of the men, and bought my oldest sister. She was a pious, good girl—a member of the Baptist church—and as handsome as my poor mother had been. She was well brought up, and had good manners. At first, I was glad she was bought, for I had one friend near me. I was soon sorry for it. Sir, I have stood at the door and heard her whipped, when it seemed as if every blow cut into my naked heart, and I couldn't do anything to help her; and she was whipped, sir, for wanting to live a decent Christian life,[1] such as your laws give no slave girl a right to live; and at last I saw her chained with a trader's gang, to be sent to market in Orleans—sent there for nothing else but that—and that's the last I know of her. Well, I grew up—long years and years—no father, no mother, no sister, not a living soul that cared for me more than a dog; nothing but whipping, scolding, starving. Why, sir, I've been so hungry that I have been glad to take the bones they threw to their dogs; and yet, when I was a little fellow, and laid awake whole nights and cried, it wasn't the hunger, it wasn't the whipping, I cried for. No, sir, it was for *my mother* and *my sisters*—it was because I hadn't a friend to love me on earth. I never knew what peace or comfort was. I never had a kind word spoken to me till I came to work in your factory. Mr. Wilson, you treated me well; you encouraged me to do well, and to learn to read and write, and to try to make something of myself; and God knows how grateful I am for it. Then, sir, I found my wife; you've seen her—you know how beautiful she is. When I found she loved me, when I married her, I scarcely could believe I was alive, I was so happy; and, sir, she is as good as she is beautiful. But now what? Why, now comes my

---

1 *for wanting ... Christian life* The implication here is that she refused to perform sexual services.

master, takes me right away from my work, and my friends, and all I like, and grinds me down into the very dirt! And why? Because, he says, I forgot who I was; he says, to teach me that I am only a nigger! After all, and last of all, he comes between me and my wife, and says I shall give her up, and live with another woman. And all this your laws give him power to do, in spite of God or man. Mr. Wilson, look at it! There isn't *one* of all these things, that have broken the hearts of my mother and my sister, and my wife and myself, but your laws allow, and give every man power to do, in Kentucky, and none can say to him nay! Do you call these the laws of *my* country? Sir, I haven't any country, any more than I have any father. But I'm going to have one. I don't want anything of *your* country, except to be let alone—to go peaceably out of it; and when I get to Canada, where the laws will own me and protect me, *that* shall be my country, and its laws I will obey. But if any man tries to stop me, let him take care, for I am desperate. I'll fight for my liberty to the last breath I breathe. You say your fathers did it; if it was right for them, it is right for me!"

This speech, delivered partly while sitting at the table, and partly walking up and down the room—delivered with tears, and flashing eyes, and despairing gestures—was altogether too much for the good-natured old body to whom it was addressed, who had pulled out a great yellow silk pocket-handkerchief, and was mopping up his face with great energy.

"Blast 'em all!" he suddenly broke out. "Haven't I always said so—the infernal old cusses! I hope I an't swearing, now. Well! go ahead, George, go ahead; but be careful, my boy; don't shoot anybody, George, unless—well—you'd *better* not shoot, I reckon; at least, I wouldn't *hit* anybody, you know. Where is your wife, George?" he added, as he nervously rose, and began walking the room.

"Gone, sir, gone, with her child in her arms, the Lord only knows where—gone after the north star; and when we ever meet, or whether we meet at all in this world, no creature can tell."

"Is it possible! astonishing! from such a kind family?"

"Kind families get in debt, and the laws of *our* country allow them to sell the child out of its mother's bosom to pay its master's debts," said George, bitterly.

"Well, well," said the honest old man, fumbling in his pocket: "I s'pose, perhaps, I an't following my judgment—hang it, I *won't* follow my judgment!" he added, suddenly; "so here, George," and, taking out a roll of bills from his pocket-book, he offered them to George.

"No, my kind, good sir!" said George, "you've done a great deal for me, and this might get you into trouble. I have money enough, I hope, to take me as far as I need it."

"No; but you must, George. Money is a great help everywhere; can't have too much, if you get it honestly. Take it—*do* take it, *now*—do, my boy!"

"On condition, sir, that I may repay it at some future time, I will," said George, taking up the money.

"And now, George, how long are you going to travel in this way? not long or far, I hope. It's well carried on, but too bold. And this black fellow—who is he?"

"A true fellow, who went to Canada more than a year ago. He heard, after he got there, that his master was so angry at him for going off that he had whipped his poor old mother; and he has come all the way back to comfort her, and get a chance to get her away."

"Has he got her?"

"Not yet; he has been hanging about the place, and found no chance yet. Meanwhile, he is going with me as far as Ohio, to put me among friends that helped him, and then he will come back after her."

"Dangerous, very dangerous!" said the old man.

George drew himself up, and smiled disdainfully.

The old gentleman eyed him from head to foot, with a sort of innocent wonder.

"George, something has brought you out wonderfully. You hold up your head, and speak and move like another man," said Mr. Wilson.

"Because I'm a *freeman*!" said George, proudly. "Yes, sir; I've said Mas'r for the last time to any man. *I'm free!*"

"Take care! You are not sure—you may be taken."

"All men are free and equal *in the grave*, if it comes to that, Mr. Wilson," said George.

"I'm perfectly dumb-foundered with your boldness!" said Mr. Wilson, "to come right here to the nearest tavern!"

"Mr. Wilson, it is *so* bold, and this tavern is so near, that they will never think of it; they will look for me on ahead, and you yourself wouldn't know me. Jim's master don't live in this county; he isn't known in these parts. Besides, he is given up; nobody is looking after him, and nobody will take me up from the advertisement, I think."

"But the mark in your hand?"

George drew off his glove, and showed a newly-healed scar in his hand.

"That is a parting proof of Mr. Harris' regard," he said, scornfully. "A fortnight ago, he took it into his head to give it to me, because he said he believed I should try to get away one of these days. Looks interesting, doesn't it?" he said, drawing his glove on again.

"I declare, my very blood runs cold when I think of it—your condition and your risks!" said Mr. Wilson.

"Mine has run cold a good many years, Mr. Wilson; at present, it's about up to the boiling point," said George.

"Well, my good sir," continued George, after a few moments' silence, "I saw you knew me; I thought I'd just have this talk with you, lest your surprised looks should bring me out. I leave early tomorrow morning, before daylight; by tomorrow night I hope to sleep safe in Ohio. I shall travel by daylight, stop at the best hotels, go to the dinner-tables with the lords of the land. So, goodbye, sir; if you hear that I'm taken, you may know that I'm dead!"

George stood up like a rock, and put out his hand with the air of a prince. The friendly little old man shook it heartily, and after a little shower of caution, he took his umbrella, and fumbled his way out of the room.

George stood thoughtfully looking at the door, as the old man closed it. A thought seemed to flash across his mind. He hastily stepped to it, and opening it, said,

"Mr. Wilson, one word more."

The old gentleman entered again, and George, as before, locked the door, and then stood for a few moments looking on the floor, irresolutely. At last, raising his head with a sudden effort—

"Mr. Wilson, you have shown yourself a Christian in your treatment of me—I want to ask one last deed of Christian kindness of you."

"Well, George."

"Well, sir—what you said was true. I *am* running a dreadful risk. There isn't, on earth, a living soul to care if I die," he added, drawing his breath hard, and speaking with a great effort, "I shall be kicked out and buried like a dog, and nobody'll think of it a day after—*only my poor wife!* Poor soul! she'll mourn and grieve; and if you'd only contrive, Mr. Wilson, to send this little pin to her. She gave it to me for a Christmas present, poor child! Give it to her, and tell her I loved her to the last. Will you? *Will* you?" he added, earnestly.

"Yes, certainly—poor fellow!" said the old gentleman, taking the pin, with watery eyes, and a melancholy quiver in his voice.

"Tell her one thing," said George; "it's my last wish, if she *can* get to Canada, to go there. No matter how kind her mistress is—no matter how much she loves her home; beg her not to go back—for slavery always ends in misery. Tell her to bring up our boy a free man, and then he won't suffer as I have. Tell her this, Mr. Wilson, will you?"

"Yes, George, I'll tell her; but I trust you won't die; take heart—you're a brave fellow. Trust in the Lord, George. I wish in my heart you were safe through, though—that's what I do."

"*Is* there a God to trust in?" said George, in such a tone of bitter despair as arrested the old gentleman's words. "O, I've seen things all my life that have made me feel that there can't be a God. You Christians don't know how these things look to us. There's a God for you, but is there any for us?"

"O, now, don't—don't, my boy!" said the old man, almost sobbing as he spoke; "don't feel so! There is—there is; clouds and darkness are around about him, but righteousness and judgment are the habitation of his throne.[1] There's a *God*, George—believe it; trust in Him, and I'm sure He'll help you. Everything will be set right—if not in this life, in another."

The real piety and benevolence of the simple old man invested him with a temporary dignity and authority, as he spoke. George stopped his distracted walk up and down the room, stood thoughtfully a moment, and then said, quietly,

"Thank you for saying that, my good friend; I'll *think of that.*"

---

1   *clouds and ... his throne*   See Psalm 97.2.

CHAPTER 12
SELECT INCIDENT OF LAWFUL TRADE

In Ramah there was a voice heard,—weeping, and lamentation, and great mourning; Rachel weeping for her children, and would not be comforted.[1]

Mr. Haley and Tom jogged onward in their wagon, each, for a time, absorbed in his own reflections. Now, the reflections of two men sitting side by side are a curious thing—seated on the same seat, having the same eyes, ears, hands and organs of all sorts, and having pass before their eyes the same objects—it is wonderful[2] what a variety we shall find in these same reflections!

As, for example, Mr. Haley: he thought first of Tom's length, and breadth, and height, and what he would sell for, if he was kept fat and in good case till he got him into market. He thought of how he should make out his gang; he thought of the respective market value of certain superstitious men and women and children who were to compose it, and other kindred topics of the business; then he thought of himself, and how humane he was, that whereas other men chained their "niggers" hand and foot both, he only put fetters on the feet, and left Tom the use of his hands, as long as he behaved well; and he sighed to think how ungrateful human nature was, so that there was even room to doubt whether Tom appreciated his mercies. He had been taken in so by "niggers" whom he had favored; but still he was astonished to consider how good-natured he yet remained!

As to Tom, he was thinking over some words of an unfashionable old book, which kept running through his head, again and again, as follows: "We have here no continuing city, but we seek one to come; wherefore God himself is not ashamed to be called our God; for he

---

1 *In Ramah ... be comforted* See Jeremiah 31.15–17: "Thus saith the Lord; A voice was heard in Ramah, lamentation, and bitter weeping; Rachel weeping for her children refused to be comforted for her children, because they were not. Thus saith the Lord; Refrain thy voice from weeping, and thine eyes from tears: for thy work shall be rewarded, saith the Lord; and they shall come again from the land of the enemy. And there is hope in thine end, saith the Lord, that thy children shall come again to their own border."

2 *wonderful* I.e., inducing a sense of wonder (not necessarily with a positive connotation).

hath prepared for us a city."[1] These words of an ancient volume, got up principally by "ignorant and unlearned men,"[2] have, through all time, kept up, somehow, a strange sort of power over the minds of poor, simple fellows, like Tom. They stir up the soul from its depths, and rouse, as with trumpet call, courage, energy, and enthusiasm, where before was only the blackness of despair.

Mr. Haley pulled out of his pocket sundry newspapers, and began looking over their advertisements with absorbed interest. He was not a remarkably fluent reader, and was in the habit of reading in a sort of recitative half-aloud, by way of calling in his ears to verify the deductions of his eyes. In this tone he slowly recited the following paragraph:

> Executor's Sale—Negroes! Agreeably to order of court, will be sold on Tuesday, February 20 before the Courthouse door, in the town of Washington, Kentucky, the following negroes: Hagar, aged 60; John, aged 30; Ben, aged 21; Saul, aged 25; Albert, aged 14. Sold for the benefit of the creditors and heirs of the estate of Jesse Blutchford, Esq.
>
> Samuel Morris,
> Thomas Flint,
> *Executors.*

"This yer I must look at," said he to Tom, for want of somebody else to talk to.

"Ye see, I'm going to get up a prime gang to take down with ye, Tom; it'll make it sociable and pleasant like—good company will, ye know. We must drive right to Washington first and foremost, and then I'll clap you into jail, while I does the business."

Tom received this agreeable intelligence quite meekly; simply wondering, in his own heart, how many of these doomed men had wives and children, and whether they would feel as he did about leaving them. It is to be confessed, too, that the naïve, off-hand information that he was

---

1   *We have ... a city*   See Hebrews 13.14: "For here have we no continuing city, but we seek one to come" and Hebrews 11.16: "But now they desire a better country, that is, an heavenly: wherefore God is not ashamed to be called their God: for he hath prepared for them a city."

2   *ignorant and unlearned men*   Acts 4.13: "Now when they saw the boldness of Peter and John, and perceived that they were unlearned and ignorant men, they marvelled; and they took knowledge of them, that they had been with Jesus." (Peter and John are both apostles credited with the authorship of books of the New Testament.)

to be thrown into jail by no means produced an agreeable impression on a poor fellow who had always prided himself on a strictly honest and upright course of life. Yes, Tom, we must confess it, was rather proud of his honesty, poor fellow—not having very much else to be proud of; if he had belonged to some of the higher walks of society, he, perhaps, would never have been reduced to such straits. However, the day wore on, and the evening saw Haley and Tom comfortably accommodated in Washington—the one in a tavern, and the other in a jail.

About eleven o'clock the next day, a mixed throng was gathered around the courthouse steps—smoking, chewing, spitting, swearing, and conversing, according to their respective tastes and turns—waiting for the auction to commence. The men and women to be sold sat in a group apart, talking in a low tone to each other. The woman who had been advertised by the name of Hagar was a regular African in feature and figure. She might have been sixty, but was older than that by hard work and disease, was partially blind, and somewhat crippled with rheumatism. By her side stood her only remaining son, Albert, a bright-looking little fellow of fourteen years. The boy was the only survivor of a large family, who had been successively sold away from her to a southern market. The mother held on to him with both her shaking hands, and eyed with intense trepidation everyone who walked up to examine him.

"Don't be feard, Aunt Hagar," said the oldest of the men, "I spoke to Mas'r Thomas 'bout it, and he thought he might manage to sell you in a lot both together."

"Dey needn't call me worn out yet," said she, lifting her shaking hands. "I can cook yet, and scrub, and scour—I'm wuth a buying, if I do come cheap; tell 'em dat ar—you *tell* 'em," she added, earnestly.

Haley here forced his way into the group, walked up to the old man, pulled his mouth open and looked in, felt of his teeth, made him stand and straighten himself, bend his back, and perform various evolutions to show his muscles; and then passed on to the next, and put him through the same trial. Walking up last to the boy, he felt of his arms, straightened his hands, and looked at his fingers, and made him jump, to show his agility.

"He an't gwine to be sold widout me!" said the old woman, with passionate eagerness; "he and I goes in a lot together; I's rail strong yet, Mas'r, and can do heaps o' work—heaps on it, Mas'r."

"On plantation?" said Haley, with a contemptuous glance. "Likely story!" and, as if satisfied with his examination, he walked out and looked, and stood with his hands in his pocket, his cigar in his mouth, and his hat cocked on one side, ready for action.

"What think of 'em?" said a man who had been following Haley's examination, as if to make up his own mind from it.

"Wal," said Haley, spitting, "I shall put in, I think, for the youngerly ones and the boy."

"They want to sell the boy and the old woman together," said the man.

"Find it a tight pull; why, she's an old rack o' bones—not worth her salt."

"You wouldn't, then?" said the man.

"Anybody'd be a fool 't would. She's half blind, crooked with rheumatis, and foolish to boot."

"Some buys up these yer old critturs, and ses there's a sight more wear in 'em than a body 'd think," said the man, reflectively.

"No go, 't all," said Haley; "wouldn't take her for a present—fact— I've *seen*, now."

"Wal, 't is kinder pity, now, not to buy her with her son—her heart seems so sot on him—s'pose they fling her in cheap."

"Them that's got money to spend that ar way, it's all well enough. I shall bid off on that ar boy for a plantation hand; wouldn't be bothered with her, no way—not if they'd give her to me," said Haley.

"She'll take on desp't,"[1] said the man.

"Nat'lly, she will," said the trader, coolly.

The conversation was here interrupted by a busy hum in the audience; and the auctioneer, a short, bustling, important fellow, elbowed his way into the crowd. The old woman drew in her breath, and caught instinctively at her son.

"Keep close to yer mammy, Albert—close—dey'll put us up togedder," she said.

"O, mammy, I'm feard they won't," said the boy.

"Dey must, child; I can't live, no ways, if they don't," said the old creature, vehemently.

---

1 *desp't* Desperate.

The stentorian tones of the auctioneer, calling out to clear the way, now announced that the sale was about to commence. A place was cleared, and the bidding began. The different men on the list were soon knocked off at prices which showed a pretty brisk demand in the market; two of them fell to Haley.

"Come, now, young un," said the auctioneer, giving the boy a touch with his hammer, "be up and show your springs, now."

"Put us two up togedder, togedder—do please, Mas'r," said the old woman, holding fast to her boy.

"Be off," said the man, gruffly, pushing her hands away; "you come last. Now, darkey, spring"; and, with the word, he pushed the boy toward the block, while a deep, heavy groan rose behind him. The boy paused, and looked back; but there was no time to stay, and, dashing the tears from his large, bright eyes, he was up in a moment.

His fine figure, alert limbs, and bright face, raised an instant competition, and half a dozen bids simultaneously met the ear of the auctioneer. Anxious, half-frightened, he looked from side to side, as he heard the clatter of contending bids—now here, now there—till the hammer fell. Haley had got him. He was pushed from the block toward his new master, but stopped one moment, and looked back, when his poor old mother, trembling in every limb, held out her shaking hands toward him.

"Buy me too, Mas'r, for de dear Lord's sake! buy me—I shall die if you don't!"

"You'll die if I do, that's the kink of it," said Haley, "no!" And he turned on his heel.

The bidding for the poor old creature was summary. The man who had addressed Haley, and who seemed not destitute of compassion, bought her for a trifle, and the spectators began to disperse.

The poor victims of the sale, who had been brought up in one place together for years, gathered round the despairing old mother, whose agony was pitiful to see.

"Couldn't dey leave me one? Mas'r allers said I should have one—he did," she repeated over and over, in heartbroken tones.

"Trust in the Lord, Aunt Hagar," said the oldest of the men, sorrowfully.

"What good will it do?" said she, sobbing passionately.

"Mother, mother—don't! don't!" said the boy. "They say you's got a good master."

"I don't care—I don't care. O, Albert! oh, my boy! you's my last baby. Lord, how ken I?"

"Come, take her off, can't some of ye?" said Haley, dryly; "don't do no good for her to go on that ar way."

The old men of the company, partly by persuasion and partly by force, loosed the poor creature's last despairing hold, and, as they led her off to her new master's wagon, strove to comfort her.

"Now!" said Haley, pushing his three purchases together, and producing a bundle of handcuffs, which he proceeded to put on their wrists; and fastening each handcuff to a long chain, he drove them before him to the jail.

A few days saw Haley, with his possessions, safely deposited on one of the Ohio boats. It was the commencement of his gang, to be augmented, as the boat moved on, by various other merchandise of the same kind, which he, or his agent, had stored for him in various points along shore.

The *La Belle Rivière*,[1] as brave and beautiful a boat as ever walked the waters of her namesake river, was floating gayly down the stream, under a brilliant sky, the stripes and stars of free America waving and fluttering overhead; the guards crowded with well-dressed ladies and gentlemen walking and enjoying the delightful day. All was full of life, buoyant and rejoicing—all but Haley's gang, who were stored, with other freight, on the lower deck, and who, somehow, did not seem to appreciate their various privileges, as they sat in a knot, talking to each other in low tones.

"Boys," said Haley, coming up, briskly, "I hope you keep up good heart, and are cheerful. Now, no sulks, ye see; keep stiff upper lip, boys; do well by me, and I'll do well by you."

The boys addressed responded the invariable "Yes, Mas'r," for ages the watchword of poor Africa; but it's to be owned they did not look particularly cheerful; they had their various little prejudices in favor of wives, mothers, sisters, and children, seen for the last time—and

---

1 *La Belle Rivière*   French: The Beautiful River.

though "they that wasted them required of them mirth,"[1] it was not instantly forthcoming.

"I've got a wife," spoke out the article enumerated as "John, aged thirty," and he laid his chained hand on Tom's knee—"and she don't know a word about this, poor girl!"

"Where does she live?" said Tom.

"In a tavern a piece down here," said John; "I wish, now, I *could* see her once more in this world," he added.

Poor John! It *was* rather natural; and the tears that fell, as he spoke, came as naturally as if he had been a white man. Tom drew a long breath from a sore heart, and tried, in his poor way, to comfort him.

And overhead, in the cabin, sat fathers and mothers, husbands and wives; and merry, dancing children moved round among them, like so many little butterflies, and everything was going on quite easy and comfortable.

"O, mamma," said a boy, who had just come up from below, "there's a negro trader on board, and he's brought four or five slaves down there."

"Poor creatures!" said the mother, in a tone between grief and indignation.

"What's that?" said another lady.

"Some poor slaves below," said the mother.

"And they've got chains on," said the boy.

"What a shame to our country that such sights are to be seen!" said another lady.

"O, there's a great deal to be said on both sides of the subject," said a genteel woman, who sat at her state-room door sewing, while her little girl and boy were playing round her. "I've been south, and I must say I think the negroes are better off than they would be to be free."

"In some respects, some of them are well off, I grant," said the lady to whose remark she had answered. "The most dreadful part of slavery, to my mind, is its outrages on the feelings and affections—the separating of families, for example."

---

1   *they that ... mirth*   See Psalm 137.3: "For there they that carried us away captive required of us a song; and they that wasted us required of us mirth, saying, Sing us one of the songs of Zion"—a line expressing the lamentations of the Jews who had been exiled from Judah and sentenced to captivity in Babylon.

"That *is* a bad thing, certainly," said the other lady, holding up a baby's dress she had just completed, and looking intently on its trimmings; "but then, I fancy, it don't occur often."

"O, it does," said the first lady, eagerly; "I've lived many years in Kentucky and Virginia both, and I've seen enough to make anyone's heart sick. Suppose, ma'am, your two children, there, should be taken from you, and sold?"

"We can't reason from our feelings to those of this class of persons," said the other lady, sorting out some worsteds[1] on her lap.

"Indeed, ma'am, you can know nothing of them, if you say so," answered the first lady, warmly. "I was born and brought up among them. I know they *do* feel, just as keenly—even more so, perhaps—as we do."

The lady said "Indeed!" yawned, and looked out the cabin window, and finally repeated, for a finale, the remark with which she had begun—"After all, I think they are better off than they would be to be free."

"It's undoubtedly the intention of Providence that the African race should be servants—kept in a low condition," said a grave-looking gentleman in black, a clergyman, seated by the cabin door. "'Cursed be Canaan; a servant of servants shall he be,' the scripture says."[2]

"I say, stranger, is that ar what that text means?" said a tall man, standing by.

"Undoubtedly. It pleased Providence, for some inscrutable reason, to doom the race to bondage, ages ago; and we must not set up our opinion against that."

"Well, then, we'll all go ahead and buy up niggers," said the man, "if that's the way of Providence—won't we, Squire?" said he, turning to Haley, who had been standing, with his hands in his pockets, by the stove, and intently listening to the conversation.

"Yes," continued the tall man, "we must all be resigned to the decrees of Providence. Niggers must be sold, and trucked round, and kept under; it's what they's made for. 'Pears like this yer view's quite refreshing, an't it, stranger?" said he to Haley.

---

1   *worsteds* Pieces of smooth woolen fabric.
2   *Cursed be ... scripture says* Noah's curse upon his grandson Canaan, taken by some Christian theologians to be the ancestor of all Africans, was often cited by proslavery Christians as constituting a biblical defense of slavery; see Genesis 9.21–27.

"I never thought on 't," said Haley. "I couldn't have said as much, myself; I ha'nt no larning. I took up the trade just to make a living; if 't an't right, I calculated to 'pent on 't in time, *ye* know."

"And now you'll save yerself the trouble, won't ye?" said the tall man. "See what 't is, now, to know scripture. If ye'd only studied yer Bible, like this yer good man, ye might have know'd it before, and saved ye a heap o' trouble. Ye could jist have said, 'Cussed be'—what's his name?—and 't would all have come right." And the stranger, who was no other than the honest drover whom we introduced to our readers in the Kentucky tavern,[1] sat down, and began smoking, with a curious smile on his long, dry face.

A tall, slender young man, with a face expressive of great feeling and intelligence, here broke in, and repeated the words, "'All things whatsoever ye would that men should do unto you, do ye even so unto them.'[2] I suppose," he added, "*that* is scripture, as much as 'Cursed be Canaan.'"

"Wal, it seems quite *as* plain a text, stranger," said John the drover, "to poor fellows like us, now"; and John smoked on like a volcano.

The young man paused, looked as if he was going to say more, when suddenly the boat stopped, and the company made the usual steamboat rush, to see where they were landing.

"Both them ar chaps parsons?" said John to one of the men, as they were going out.

The man nodded.

As the boat stopped, a black woman came running wildly up the plank, darted into the crowd, flew up to where the slave gang sat, and threw her arms round that unfortunate piece of merchandise before enumerated "John, aged thirty," and with sobs and tears bemoaned him as her husband.

But what needs tell the story, told too oft—every day told—of heartstrings rent[3] and broken—the weak broken and torn for the profit and convenience of the strong! It needs not to be told; every

---

1 *the honest drover ... Kentucky tavern* I.e., the slave driver introduced in Chapter 11 who, while clearly not opposed to slavery, is outspokenly contemptuous towards enslavers who treat those they enslave with cruelty.

2 *All things ... unto them* Line from Christ's Sermon on the Mount; see Matthew 7.12.

3 *rent* Torn.

day is telling it—telling it, too, in the ear of One who is not deaf, though he be long silent.

The young man who had spoken for the cause of humanity and God before stood with folded arms, looking on this scene. He turned, and Haley was standing at his side. "My friend," he said, speaking with thick utterance, "how can you, how dare you, carry on a trade like this? Look at those poor creatures! Here I am, rejoicing in my heart that I am going home to my wife and child; and the same bell which is a signal to carry me onward towards them will part this poor man and his wife forever. Depend upon it, God will bring you into judgment for this."

The trader turned away in silence.

"I say, now," said the drover, touching his elbow, "there's differences in parsons, an't there? 'Cussed be Canaan' don't seem to go down with this 'un, does it?"

Haley gave an uneasy growl.

"And that ar an't the worst on't," said John; "mabbe it won't go down with the Lord, neither, when ye come to settle with Him, one o' these days, as all on us must, I reckon."

Haley walked reflectively to the other end of the boat.

"If I make pretty handsomely on one or two next gangs," he thought, "I reckon I'll stop off this yer; it's really getting dangerous." And he took out his pocket-book, and began adding over his accounts—a process which many gentlemen besides Mr. Haley have found a specific[1] for an uneasy conscience.

The boat swept proudly away from the shore, and all went on merrily, as before. Men talked, and loafed, and read, and smoked. Women sewed, and children played, and the boat passed on her way.

One day, when she lay to for a while at a small town in Kentucky, Haley went up into the place on a little matter of business.

Tom, whose fetters did not prevent his taking a moderate circuit, had drawn near the side of the boat, and stood listlessly gazing over the railings. After a time, he saw the trader returning, with an alert step, in company with a colored woman, bearing in her arms a young child. She was dressed quite respectably, and a colored man followed her, bringing along a small trunk. The woman came cheerfully onward,

---

1 *specific* Remedy.

talking, as she came, with the man who bore her trunk, and so passed up the plank into the boat. The bell rung, the steamer whizzed, the engine groaned and coughed, and away swept the boat down the river.

The woman walked forward among the boxes and bales of the lower deck, and, sitting down, busied herself with chirruping to her baby.

Haley made a turn or two about the boat, and then, coming up, seated himself near her, and began saying something to her in an indifferent undertone.

Tom soon noticed a heavy cloud passing over the woman's brow; and that she answered rapidly, and with great vehemence.

"I don't believe it—I won't believe it!" he heard her say, "You're jist a foolin with me."

"If you won't believe it, look here!" said the man, drawing out a paper; "this yer's the bill of sale, and there's your master's name to it; and I paid down good solid cash for it, too, I can tell you—so, now!"

"I don't believe Mas'r would cheat me so; it can't be true!" said the woman, with increasing agitation.

"You can ask any of these men here, that can read writing. Here!" he said, to a man that was passing by, "jist read this yer, won't you! This yer gal won't believe me, when I tell her what 't is."

"Why, it's a bill of sale, signed by John Fosdick," said the man, "making over to you the girl Lucy and her child. It's all straight enough, for aught I see."

The woman's passionate exclamations collected a crowd around her, and the trader briefly explained to them the cause of the agitation.

"He told me that I was going down to Louisville,[1] to hire out as cook to the same tavern where my husband works—that's what Mas'r told me, his own self; and I can't believe he'd lie to me," said the woman.

"But he has sold you, my poor woman, there's no doubt about it," said a good-natured looking man, who had been examining the papers; "he has done it, and no mistake."

"Then it's no account talking," said the woman, suddenly growing quite calm; and, clasping her child tighter in her arms, she sat down on her box, turned her back round, and gazed listlessly into the river.

---

1   *Louisville*   Major city in Kentucky, along the Ohio River.

"Going to take it easy, after all!" said the trader. "Gal's got grit, I see."

The woman looked calm, as the boat went on; and a beautiful soft summer breeze passed like a compassionate spirit over her head—the gentle breeze, that never inquires whether the brow is dusky or fair that it fans. And she saw sunshine sparkling on the water, in golden ripples, and heard gay voices, full of ease and pleasure, talking around her everywhere; but her heart lay as if a great stone had fallen on it. Her baby raised himself up against her, and stroked her cheeks with his little hands; and, springing up and down, crowing and chatting, seemed determined to arouse her. She strained him suddenly and tightly in her arms, and slowly one tear after another fell on his wondering, unconscious face; and gradually she seemed, and little by little, to grow calmer, and busied herself with tending and nursing him.

The child, a boy of ten months, was uncommonly large and strong of his age, and very vigorous in his limbs. Never, for a moment, still, he kept his mother constantly busy in holding him, and guarding his springing activity.

"That's a fine chap!" said a man, suddenly stopping opposite to him, with his hands in his pockets. "How old is he?"

"Ten months and a half," said the mother.

The man whistled to the boy, and offered him part of a stick of candy, which he eagerly grabbed at, and very soon had it in a baby's general depository, to wit, his mouth.

"Rum[1] fellow!" said the man. "Knows what's what!" and he whistled, and walked on. When he had got to the other side of the boat, he came across Haley, who was smoking on top of a pile of boxes.

The stranger produced a match, and lighted a cigar, saying, as he did so,

"Decentish kind o' wench you 've got round there, stranger."

"Why, I reckon she *is* tol'able fair," said Haley, blowing the smoke out of his mouth.

"Taking her down south?" said the man.

Haley nodded, and smoked on.

"Plantation hand?" said the man.

---

1 *Rum* Good.

"Wal," said Haley, "I'm fillin' out an order for a plantation, and I think I shall put her in. They telled me she was a good cook; and they can use her for that, or set her at the cotton-picking. She's got the right fingers for that; I looked at 'em. Sell well, either way"; and Haley resumed his cigar.

"They won't want the young 'un on a plantation," said the man.

"I shall sell him, first chance I find," said Haley, lighting another cigar.

"S'pose you'd be selling him tol'able cheap," said the stranger, mounting the pile of boxes, and sitting down comfortably.

"Don't know 'bout that," said Haley; "he's a pretty smart young 'un—straight, fat, strong; flesh as hard as a brick!"

"Very true, but then there's all the bother and expense of raisin'."

"Nonsense!" said Haley; "they is raised as easy as any kind of critter there is going; they an't a bit more trouble than pups. This yer chap will be running all round, in a month."

"I've got a good place for raisin', and I thought of takin' in a little more stock," said the man. "One cook lost a young 'un last week—got drownded in a washtub, while she was a hangin' out clothes—and I reckon it would be well enough to set her to raisin' this yer."

Haley and the stranger smoked a while in silence, neither seeming willing to broach the test question of the interview. At last the man resumed:

"You wouldn't think of wantin' more than ten dollars for that ar chap, seeing you *must* get him off yer hand, anyhow?"

Haley shook his head, and spit impressively.

"That won't do, no ways," he said, and began his smoking again.

"Well, stranger, what will you take?"

"Well, now," said Haley, "I *could* raise that ar chap myself, or get him raised; he's oncommon likely and healthy, and he'd fetch a hundred dollars, six months hence; and, in a year or two, he'd bring two hundred, if I had him in the right spot; so I shan't take a cent less nor fifty for him now."

"O, stranger! that's rediculous, altogether," said the man.

"Fact!" said Haley, with a decisive nod of his head.

"I'll give thirty for him," said the stranger, "but not a cent more."

"Now, I'll tell ye what I will do," said Haley, spitting again, with renewed decision. "I'll split the difference, and say forty-five; and that's the most I will do."

"Well, agreed!" said the man, after an interval.

"Done!" said Haley. "Where do you land?"

"At Louisville," said the man.

"Louisville," said Haley. "Very fair, we get there about dusk. Chap will be asleep—all fair—get him off quietly, and no screaming—happens beautiful—I like to do everything quietly—I hates all kind of agitation and fluster." And so, after a transfer of certain bills had passed from the man's pocket-book to the trader's, he resumed his cigar.

It was a bright, tranquil evening when the boat stopped at the wharf at Louisville. The woman had been sitting with her baby in her arms, now wrapped in a heavy sleep. When she heard the name of the place called out, she hastily laid the child down in a little cradle formed by the hollow among the boxes, first carefully spreading under it her cloak; and then she sprung to the side of the boat, in hopes that, among the various hotel-waiters who thronged the wharf, she might see her husband. In this hope, she pressed forward to the front rails, and, stretching far over them, strained her eyes intently on the moving heads on the shore, and the crowd pressed in between her and the child.

"Now's your time," said Haley, taking the sleeping child up, and handing him to the stranger. "Don't wake him up, and set him to crying, now; it would make a devil of a fuss with the gal." The man took the bundle carefully, and was soon lost in the crowd that went up the wharf.

When the boat, creaking, and groaning, and puffing, had loosed from the wharf, and was beginning slowly to strain herself along, the woman returned to her old seat. The trader was sitting there—the child was gone!

"Why, why—where?" she began, in bewildered surprise.

"Lucy," said the trader, "your child's gone; you may as well know it first as last. You see, I know'd you couldn't take him down south; and I got a chance to sell him to a first-rate family, that'll raise him better than you can."

The trader had arrived at that stage of Christian and political perfection which has been recommended by some preachers and politicians of the north, lately, in which he had completely overcome every humane weakness and prejudice. His heart was exactly where yours, sir, and mine could be brought, with proper effort and cultivation. The wild look of anguish and utter despair that the woman cast on him might have disturbed one less practised; but he was used to it. He had seen that same look hundreds of times. You can get used to such things, too, my friend; and it is the great object of recent efforts to make our whole northern community used to them, for the glory of the Union. So the trader only regarded the mortal anguish which he saw working in those dark features, those clenched hands, and suffocating breathings, as necessary incidents of the trade, and merely calculated whether she was going to scream, and get up a commotion on the boat; for, like other supporters of our peculiar institution, he decidedly disliked agitation.

But the woman did not scream. The shot had passed too straight and direct through the heart, for cry or tear.

Dizzily she sat down. Her slack hands fell lifeless by her side. Her eyes looked straight forward, but she saw nothing. All the noise and hum of the boat, the groaning of the machinery, mingled dreamily to her bewildered ear; and the poor, dumb-stricken heart had neither cry nor tear to show for its utter misery. She was quite calm.

The trader, who, considering his advantages, was almost as humane as some of our politicians, seemed to feel called on to administer such consolation as the case admitted of.

"I know this yer comes kinder hard, at first, Lucy," said he; "but such a smart, sensible gal as you are, won't give way to it. You see it's *necessary*, and can't be helped!"

"O! don't, Mas'r, don't!" said the woman, with a voice like one that is smothering.

"You're a smart wench, Lucy," he persisted; "I mean to do well by ye, and get ye a nice place down river; and you'll soon get another husband—such a likely gal as you—"

"O! Mas'r, if you *only* won't talk to me now," said the woman, in a voice of such quick and living anguish that the trader felt that there was something at present in the case beyond his style of operation. He got up, and the woman turned away, and buried her head in her cloak.

The trader walked up and down for a time, and occasionally stopped and looked at her.

"Takes it hard, rather," he soliloquized, "but quiet, tho'; let her sweat a while; she'll come right, by and by!"

Tom had watched the whole transaction from first to last, and had a perfect understanding of its results. To him, it looked like something unutterably horrible and cruel, because, poor, ignorant black soul! he had not learned to generalize, and to take enlarged views. If he had only been instructed by certain ministers of Christianity, he might have thought better of it, and seen in it an everyday incident of a lawful trade; a trade which is the vital support of an institution which an American divine[1] tells us has "*no evils but such as are inseparable from any other relations in social and domestic life.*" But Tom, as we see, being a poor, ignorant fellow, whose reading had been confined entirely to the New Testament, could not comfort and solace himself with views like these. His very soul bled within him for what seemed to him the *wrongs* of the poor suffering thing that lay like a crushed reed on the boxes; the feeling, living, bleeding, yet immortal *thing*, which American state law coolly classes with the bundles, and bales, and boxes, among which she is lying.

Tom drew near, and tried to say something; but she only groaned. Honestly, and with tears running down his own cheeks, he spoke of a heart of love in the skies, of a pitying Jesus, and an eternal home; but the ear was deaf with anguish, and the palsied heart could not feel.

Night came on—night calm, unmoved, and glorious, shining down with her innumerable and solemn angel eyes, twinkling, beautiful, but silent. There was no speech nor language, no pitying voice or helping hand, from that distant sky. One after another, the voices of business or pleasure died away; all on the boat were sleeping, and the ripples at the prow were plainly heard. Tom stretched himself out on a box, and there, as he lay, he heard, ever and anon, a smothered sob or cry from the prostrate creature—"O! what shall I do? O Lord! O good Lord, do help me!" and so, ever and anon, until the murmur died away in silence.

---

1   [Stowe's note]   Dr. Joel Parker, of Philadelphia. [On 25 December 1846, Parker was quoted in the *Christian Observer* as having said, "What then are the evils inseparable from slavery? There is not one that is not equally inseparable from depraved human nature in other lawful relations." Parker later threatened Stowe with a libel suit for implying that his words were expressed in support of slavery.]

At midnight, Tom waked, with a sudden start. Something black passed quickly by him to the side of the boat; and he heard a splash in the water. No one else saw or heard anything. He raised his head—the woman's place was vacant! He got up, and sought about him in vain. The poor bleeding heart was still, at last, and the river rippled and dimpled just as brightly as if it had not closed above it.

Patience! patience! ye whose hearts swell indignant at wrongs like these. Not one throb of anguish, not one tear of the oppressed, is forgotten by the Man of Sorrows, the Lord of Glory. In his patient, generous bosom he bears the anguish of a world. Bear thou, like him, in patience, and labor in love; for sure as he is God, "the year of his redeemed *shall* come."[1]

The trader waked up bright and early, and came out to see to his live stock. It was now his turn to look about in perplexity,

"Where alive is that gal?" he said to Tom.

Tom, who had learned the wisdom of keeping counsel, did not feel called on to state his observations and suspicions, but said he did not know.

"She surely couldn't have got off in the night at any of the landings, for I was awake, and on the lookout, whenever the boat stopped. I never trust these yer things to other folks."

This speech was addressed to Tom quite confidentially, as if it was something that would be specially interesting to him. Tom made no answer.

The trader searched the boat from stem to stern, among boxes, bales and barrels, around the machinery, by the chimneys, in vain.

"Now, I say, Tom, be fair about this yer," he said, when, after a fruitless search, he came where Tom was standing. "You know something about it, now. Don't tell me—I know you do. I saw the gal stretched out here about ten o'clock, and ag'in at twelve, and ag'in between one and two; and then at four she was gone, and you was a sleeping right there all the time. Now, you know something—you can't help it."

---

1 *the year ... shall come* See Isaiah 63.4: "For the day of vengeance is in mine heart, and the year of my redemption is come."

"Well, Mas'r," said Tom, "towards morning something brushed by me, and I kinder half woke; and then I hearn a great splash, and then I clare woke up, and the gal was gone. That's all I know on 't."

The trader was not shocked nor amazed; because, as we said before, he was used to a great many things that you are not used to. Even the awful presence of Death struck no solemn chill upon him. He had seen Death many times—met him in the way of trade, and got acquainted with him—and he only thought of him as a hard customer, that embarrassed his property operations very unfairly; and so he only swore that the gal was a baggage, and that he was devilish unlucky, and that, if things went on in this way, he should not make a cent on the trip. In short, he seemed to consider himself an ill-used man, decidedly; but there was no help for it, as the woman had escaped into a state which *never will* give up a fugitive—not even at the demand of the whole glorious Union. The trader, therefore, sat discontentedly down, with his little account-book, and put down the missing body and soul under the head of *losses*!

"He's a shocking creature, isn't he—this trader? so unfeeling! It's dreadful, really!"

"O, but nobody thinks anything of these traders! They are universally despised—never received into any decent society."

But who, sir, makes the trader? Who is most to blame? The enlightened, cultivated, intelligent man, who supports the system of which the trader is the inevitable result, or the poor trader himself? You make the public sentiment that calls for his trade, that debauches and depraves him, till he feels no shame in it; and in what are you better than he?

Are you educated and he ignorant, you high and he low, you refined and he coarse, you talented and he simple?

In the day of a future Judgment, these very considerations may make it more tolerable for him than for you.

In concluding these little incidents of lawful trade, we must beg the world not to think that American legislators are entirely destitute of humanity, as might, perhaps, be unfairly inferred from the great efforts made in our national body to protect and perpetuate this species of traffic.

Who does not know how our great men are outdoing themselves, in declaiming against the *foreign* slave trade. There are a perfect host of Clarksons and Wilberforces[1] risen up among us on that subject, most edifying to hear and behold. Trading negroes from Africa, dear reader, is so horrid! It is not to be thought of! But trading them from Kentucky—that's quite another thing!

[During the voyage on *La Belle Rivière* with Haley, Tom rescues a white child named Eva St. Clare from drowning; out of gratefulness, and at Eva's request, her father Augustine St. Clare purchases Tom, and brings him home to their New Orleans estate. There, the reader also meets Augustine's unsympathetic wife, Marie St. Clare, and his cousin, Miss Ophelia, an abolitionist from the North who has come to stay with the family.]

CHAPTER 20

TOPSY

One morning, while Miss Ophelia was busy in some of her domestic cares, St. Clare's voice was heard, calling her at the foot of the stairs.

"Come down here, Cousin; I've something to show you."

"What is it?" said Miss Ophelia, coming down, with her sewing in her hand.

"I've made a purchase for your department—see here," said St. Clare; and, with the word, he pulled along a little negro girl, about eight or nine years of age.

She was one of the blackest of her race; and her round, shining eyes, glittering as glass beads, moved with quick and restless glances over everything in the room. Her mouth, half open with astonishment at the wonders of the new Mas'r's parlor, displayed a white and brilliant set of teeth. Her woolly hair was braided in sundry little tails, which stuck out in every direction. The expression of her face was an odd mixture of shrewdness and cunning, over which was oddly drawn, like a kind of veil, an expression of the most doleful gravity and solemnity. She was dressed in a single filthy, ragged garment, made of bagging; and stood with her hands demurely folded before

---

1 *Clarksons and Wilberforces* Thomas Clarkson (1760–1846) and William Wilberforce were English abolitionists who helped bring about the abolition of the Atlantic slave trade in 1807.

her. Altogether, there was something odd and goblin-like about her appearance—something, as Miss Ophelia afterwards said, "so heathenish," as to inspire that good lady with utter dismay; and turning to St. Clare, she said,

"Augustine, what in the world have you brought that thing here for?"

"For you to educate, to be sure, and train in the way she should go. I thought she was rather a funny specimen in the Jim Crow[1] line. Here, Topsy," he added, giving a whistle, as a man would to call the attention of a dog, "give us a song, now, and show us some of your dancing."

The black, glassy eyes glittered with a kind of wicked drollery, and the thing struck up, in a clear shrill voice, an odd negro melody, to which she kept time with her hands and feet, spinning round, clapping her hands, knocking her knees together, in a wild, fantastic sort of time, and producing in her throat all those odd guttural sounds which distinguish the native music of her race; and finally, turning a summerset[2] or two, and giving a prolonged closing note, as odd and unearthly as that of a steam-whistle, she came suddenly down on the carpet, and stood with her hands folded, and a most sanctimonious expression of meekness and solemnity over her face, only broken by the cunning glances which she shot askance from the corners of her eyes.

Miss Ophelia stood silent, perfectly paralyzed with amazement.

St. Clare, like a mischievous fellow as he was, appeared to enjoy her astonishment; and, addressing the child again, said,

"Topsy, this is your new mistress. I'm going to give you up to her; see now that you behave yourself."

"Yes, Mas'r," said Topsy, with sanctimonious gravity, her wicked eyes twinkling as she spoke.

"You're going to be good, Topsy, you understand," said St. Clare.

"O yes, Mas'r," said Topsy, with another twinkle, her hands still devoutly folded.

---

1   *Jim Crow* Comic character commonly depicted by blackface performers in minstrel shows; due to the popularity of such shows, "Jim Crow" was often used as a racist nickname for an enslaved person whose looks or mannerisms were perceived to be "entertaining" in some way.

2   *summerset* Somersault.

"Now, Augustine, what upon earth is this for?" said Miss Ophelia. "Your house is so full of these little plagues, now, that a body can't set down their foot without treading on 'em. I get up in the morning, and find one asleep behind the door, and see one black head poking out from under the table, one lying on the doormat—and they are mopping and mowing and grinning between all the railings, and tumbling over the kitchen floor! What on earth did you want to bring this one for?"

"For you to educate—didn't I tell you? You're always preaching about educating. I thought I would make you a present of a fresh-caught specimen, and let you try your hand on her, and bring her up in the way she should go."

"*I* don't want her, I am sure; I have more to do with 'em now than I want to."

"That's you Christians, all over! you'll get up a society, and get some poor missionary to spend all his days among just such heathen. But let me see one of you that would take one into your house with you, and take the labor of their conversion on yourselves! No; when it comes to that, they are dirty and disagreeable, and it's too much care, and so on."

"Augustine, you know I didn't think of it in that light," said Miss Ophelia, evidently softening. "Well, it might be a real missionary work," said she, looking rather more favorably on the child.

St. Clare had touched the right string. Miss Ophelia's conscientiousness was ever on the alert. "But," she added, "I really didn't see the need of buying this one; there are enough now, in your house, to take all my time and skill."

"Well, then, Cousin," said St. Clare, drawing her aside, "I ought to beg your pardon for my good-for-nothing speeches. You are so good, after all, that there's no sense in them. Why, the fact is, this concern belonged to a couple of drunken creatures that keep a low restaurant that I have to pass by every day, and I was tired of hearing her screaming, and them beating and swearing at her. She looked bright and funny, too, as if something might be made of her—so I bought her, and I'll give her to you. Try, now, and give her a good orthodox New England bringing up, and see what it'll make of her. You know I haven't any gift that way; but I'd like you to try."

"Well, I'll do what I can," said Miss Ophelia; and she approached her new subject very much as a person might be supposed to approach a black spider, supposing them to have benevolent designs toward it. "She's dreadfully dirty, and half naked," she said.

"Well, take her downstairs, and make some of them clean and clothe her up."

Miss Ophelia carried her to the kitchen regions.

"Don't see what Mas'r St. Clare wants of 'nother nigger!" said Dinah,[1] surveying the new arrival with no friendly air. "Won't have her around under *my* feet, I know!"

"Pah!" said Rosa and Jane,[2] with supreme disgust; "let her keep out of our way! What in the world Mas'r wanted another of these low niggers for, I can't see!"

"You go long! No more nigger dan you be, Miss Rosa," said Dinah, who felt this last remark a reflection on herself. "You seem to tink yourself white folks. You an't nerry one, black *nor* white. I'd like to be one or turrer."

Miss Ophelia saw that there was nobody in the camp that would undertake to oversee the cleansing and dressing of the new arrival; and so she was forced to do it herself, with some very ungracious and reluctant assistance from Jane.

It is not for ears polite to hear the particulars of the first toilet of a neglected, abused child. In fact, in this world, multitudes must live and die in a state that it would be too great a shock to the nerves of their fellow-mortals even to hear described. Miss Ophelia had a good, strong, practical deal of resolution; and she went through all the disgusting details with heroic thoroughness, though, it must be confessed, with no very gracious air—for endurance was the utmost to which her principles could bring her. When she saw, on the back and shoulders of the child, great welts and calloused spots, ineffaceable marks of the system under which she had grown up thus far, her heart became pitiful within her.

"See there!" said Jane, pointing to the marks, "don't that show she's a limb?[3] We'll have fine works with her, I reckon. I hate these nigger young uns! so disgusting! I wonder that Mas'r would buy her!"

---

1 *Dinah* The St. Clares' head cook.

2 *Rosa and Jane* Other housemaids enslaved by the St. Clares.

3 *limb* Mischievous person (derived from phrases such as "the devil's limb").

The "young un" alluded to heard all these comments with the subdued and doleful air which seemed habitual to her, only scanning, with a keen and furtive glance of her flickering eyes, the ornaments which Jane wore in her ears. When arrayed at last in a suit of decent and whole clothing, her hair cropped short to her head, Miss Ophelia, with some satisfaction, said she looked more Christian-like than she did, and in her own mind began to mature some plans for her instruction.

Sitting down before her, she began to question her.

"How old are you, Topsy?"

"Dunno, Missis," said the image, with a grin that showed all her teeth.

"Don't know how old you are? Didn't anybody ever tell you? Who was your mother?"

"Never had none!" said the child, with another grin.

"Never had any mother? What do you mean? Where were you born?"

"Never was born!" persisted Topsy, with another grin, that looked so goblin-like that, if Miss Ophelia had been at all nervous, she might have fancied that she had got hold of some sooty gnome from the land of Diablerie; but Miss Ophelia was not nervous, but plain and business-like, and she said, with some sternness,

"You mustn't answer me in that way, child; I'm not playing with you. Tell me where you were born, and who your father and mother were."

"Never was born," reiterated the creature, more emphatically; "never had no father nor mother, nor nothin'. I was raised by a speculator, with lots of others. Old Aunt Sue used to take car on us."

The child was evidently sincere; and Jane, breaking into a short laugh, said,

"Laws, Missis, there's heaps of 'em. Speculators buys 'em up cheap, when they's little, and gets 'em raised for market."

"How long have you lived with your master and mistress?"

"Dunno, Missis."

"Is it a year, or more, or less?"

"Dunno, Missis."

"Laws, Missis, those low negroes—they can't tell; they don't know anything about time," said Jane; "they don't know what a year is; they don't know their own ages."

"Have you ever heard anything about God, Topsy?"

The child looked bewildered, but grinned as usual.

"Do you know who made you?"

"Nobody, as I knows on," said the child, with a short laugh.

The idea appeared to amuse her considerably; for her eyes twinkled, and she added,

"I spect I grow'd. Don't think nobody never made me."

"Do you know how to sew?" said Miss Ophelia, who thought she would turn her inquiries to something more tangible.

"No, Missis."

"What can you do? What did you do for your master and mistress?"

"Fetch water, and wash dishes, and rub knives, and wait on folks."

"Were they good to you?"

"Spect they was," said the child, scanning Miss Ophelia cunningly.

Miss Ophelia rose from this encouraging colloquy; St. Clare was leaning over the back of her chair.

"You find virgin soil there, Cousin; put in your own ideas—you won't find many to pull up."

Miss Ophelia's ideas of education, like all her other ideas, were very set and definite, and of the kind that prevailed in New England a century ago, and which are still preserved in some very retired and unsophisticated parts, where there are no railroads. As nearly as could be expressed, they could be comprised in very few words: to teach them to mind when they were spoken to; to teach them the catechism,[1] sewing, and reading; and to whip them if they told lies. And though, of course, in the flood of light that is now poured on education, these are left far away in the rear, yet it is an undisputed fact that our grandmothers raised some tolerably fair men and women under this régime, as many of us can remember and testify. At all events, Miss Ophelia knew of nothing else to do; and, therefore, applied her mind to her heathen with the best diligence she could command.

The child was announced and considered in the family as Miss Ophelia's girl; and, as she was looked upon with no gracious eye in the kitchen, Miss Ophelia resolved to confine her sphere of operation and instruction chiefly to her own chamber. With a self-sacrifice

---

1   *catechism*   Book designed to test the orthodoxy of one's faith through a series of formal questions and answers, commonly taught to children.

which some of our readers will appreciate, she resolved, instead of comfortably making her own bed, sweeping and dusting her own chamber—which she had hitherto done, in utter scorn of all offers of help from the chambermaid of the establishment—to condemn herself to the martyrdom of instructing Topsy to perform these operations—ah, woe the day! Did any of our readers ever do the same, they will appreciate the amount of her self-sacrifice.

Miss Ophelia began with Topsy by taking her into her chamber, the first morning, and solemnly commencing a course of instruction in the art and mystery of bed-making.

Behold, then, Topsy, washed and shorn of all the little braided tails wherein her heart had delighted, arrayed in a clean gown, with well-starched apron, standing reverently before Miss Ophelia, with an expression of solemnity well befitting a funeral.

"Now, Topsy, I'm going to show you just how my bed is to be made. I am very particular about my bed. You must learn exactly how to do it."

"Yes, ma'am," says Topsy, with a deep sigh, and a face of woeful earnestness.

"Now, Topsy, look here; this is the hem of the sheet—this is the right side of the sheet, and this is the wrong; will you remember?"

"Yes, ma'am," says Topsy, with another sigh.

"Well, now, the under sheet you must bring over the bolster—so— and tuck it clear down under the mattress nice and smooth—so—do you see?"

"Yes, ma'am," said Topsy, with profound attention.

"But the upper sheet," said Miss Ophelia, "must be brought down in this way, and tucked under firm and smooth at the foot—so—the narrow hem at the foot."

"Yes, ma'am," said Topsy, as before—but we will add, what Miss Ophelia did not see, that, during the time when the good lady's back was turned, in the zeal of her manipulations, the young disciple had contrived to snatch a pair of gloves and a ribbon, which she had adroitly slipped into her sleeves, and stood with her hands dutifully folded, as before.

"Now, Topsy, let's see *you* do this," said Miss Ophelia, pulling off the clothes, and seating herself.

Topsy, with great gravity and adroitness, went through the exercise completely to Miss Ophelia's satisfaction; smoothing the sheets, patting out every wrinkle, and exhibiting, through the whole process, a gravity and seriousness with which her instructress was greatly edified. By an unlucky slip, however, a fluttering fragment of the ribbon hung out of one of her sleeves, just as she was finishing, and caught Miss Ophelia's attention. Instantly she pounced upon it. "What's this? You naughty, wicked child—you've been stealing this!"

The ribbon was pulled out of Topsy's own sleeve, yet was she not in the least disconcerted; she only looked at it with an air of the most surprised and unconscious innocence.

"Laws! why, that ar's Miss Feely's ribbon, an't it? How could it a got caught in my sleeve?"

"Topsy, you naughty girl, don't you tell me a lie—you stole that ribbon!"

"Missis, I declar for 't, I didn't—never seed it till dis yer blessed minnit."

"Topsy," said Miss Ophelia, "don't you know it's wicked to tell lies?"

"I never tells no lies, Miss Feely," said Topsy, with virtuous gravity; "it's jist the truth I've been a tellin now, and an't nothin else."

"Topsy, I shall have to whip you, if you tell lies so."

"Laws, Missis, if you's to whip all day, couldn't say no other way," said Topsy, beginning to blubber. "I never seed dat ar—it must a got caught in my sleeve. Miss Feeley must have left it on the bed, and it got caught in the clothes, and so got in my sleeve."

Miss Ophelia was so indignant at the barefaced lie, that she caught the child and shook her.

"Don't you tell me that again!"

The shake brought the gloves on to the floor, from the other sleeve.

"There, you!" said Miss Ophelia, "will you tell me now, you didn't steal the ribbon?"

Topsy now confessed to the gloves, but still persisted in denying the ribbon.

"Now, Topsy," said Miss Ophelia, "if you'll confess all about it, I won't whip you this time." Thus adjured, Topsy confessed to the ribbon and gloves, with woeful protestations of penitence.

"Well, now, tell me. I know you must have taken other things since you have been in the house, for I let you run about all day yesterday. Now, tell me if you took anything, and I shan't whip you."

"Laws, Missis! I took Miss Eva's red thing she wars on her neck."

"You did, you naughty child! Well, what else?"

"I took Rosa's yer-rings—them red ones."

"Go bring them to me this minute, both of 'em."

"Laws, Missis! I can't—they's burnt up!"

"Burnt up! what a story! Go get 'em, or I'll whip you."

Topsy, with loud protestations, and tears, and groans, declared that she *could* not. "They's burnt up—they was."

"What did you burn 'em for?" said Miss Ophelia.

"Cause I 's wicked—I is. I's mighty wicked, anyhow. I can't help it."

Just at this moment, Eva came innocently into the room, with the identical coral necklace on her neck.

"Why, Eva, where did you get your necklace?" said Miss Ophelia.

"Get it? Why, I've had it on all day," said Eva.

"Did you have it on yesterday?"

"Yes; and what is funny, Aunty, I had it on all night. I forgot to take it off when I went to bed."

Miss Ophelia looked perfectly bewildered; the more so, as Rosa, at that instant, came into the room, with a basket of newly-ironed linen poised on her head, and the coral ear-drops shaking in her ears!

"I'm sure I can't tell anything what to do with such a child!" she said, in despair. "What in the world did you tell me you took those things for, Topsy?"

"Why, Missis said I must 'fess; and I couldn't think of nothin' else to 'fess," said Topsy, rubbing her eyes.

"But, of course, I didn't want you to confess things you didn't do," said Miss Ophelia; "that's telling a lie, just as much as the other."

"Laws, now, is it?" said Topsy, with an air of innocent wonder.

"La, there an't any such thing as truth in that limb," said Rosa, looking indignantly at Topsy. "If I was Mas'r St. Clare, I'd whip her till the blood run. I would—I'd let her catch it!"

"No, no, Rosa," said Eva, with an air of command, which the child could assume at times; "you mustn't talk so, Rosa. I can't bear to hear it."

"La sakes! Miss Eva, you's so good, you don't know nothing how to get along with niggers. There's no way but to cut 'em well up, I tell ye."

"Rosa!" said Eva, "hush! Don't you say another word of that sort!" and the eye of the child flashed, and her cheek deepened its color.

Rosa was cowed in a moment.

"Miss Eva has got the St. Clare blood in her, that's plain. She can speak, for all the world, just like her papa," she said, as she passed out of the room.

Eva stood looking at Topsy.

There stood the two children, representatives of the two extremes of society. The fair, high-bred child, with her golden head, her deep eyes, her spiritual, noble brow, and prince-like movements; and her black, keen, subtle, cringing, yet acute neighbor. They stood the representatives of their races. The Saxon, born of ages of cultivation, command, education, physical and moral eminence; the Afric, born of ages of oppression, submission, ignorance, toil and vice!

Something, perhaps, of such thoughts struggled through Eva's mind. But a child's thoughts are rather dim, undefined instincts; and in Eva's noble nature many such were yearning and working, for which she had no power of utterance. When Miss Ophelia expatiated on Topsy's naughty, wicked conduct, the child looked perplexed and sorrowful, but said, sweetly,

"Poor Topsy, why need you steal? You're going to be taken good care of, now. I'm sure I'd rather give you anything of mine, than have you steal it."

It was the first word of kindness the child had ever heard in her life; and the sweet tone and manner struck strangely on the wild, rude[1] heart, and a sparkle of something like a tear shone in the keen, round, glittering eye; but it was followed by the short laugh and habitual grin. No! the ear that has never heard anything but abuse is strangely incredulous of anything so heavenly as kindness; and Topsy only thought Eva's speech something funny and inexplicable—she did not believe it.

But what was to be done with Topsy? Miss Ophelia found the case a puzzler; her rules for bringing up didn't seem to apply. She thought

---

1   *rude*   Crude; unrefined.

she would take time to think of it; and, by the way of gaining time, and in hopes of some indefinite moral virtues supposed to be inherent in dark closets, Miss Ophelia shut Topsy up in one till she had arranged her ideas further on the subject.

"I don't see," said Miss Ophelia to St. Clare, "how I'm going to manage that child, without whipping her."

"Well, whip her, then, to your heart's content; I'll give you full power to do what you like."

"Children always have to be whipped," said Miss Ophelia; "I never heard of bringing them up without."

"O, well, certainly," said St. Clare; "do as you think best. Only I'll make one suggestion: I've seen this child whipped with a poker, knocked down with the shovel or tongs, whichever came handiest, etc.; and, seeing that she is used to that style of operation, I think your whippings will have to be pretty energetic, to make much impression."

"What is to be done with her, then?" said Miss Ophelia.

"You have started a serious question," said St. Clare; "I wish you'd answer it. What is to be done with a human being that can be governed only by the lash—*that* fails—it's a very common state of things down here!"

"I'm sure I don't know; I never saw such a child as this."

"Such children are very common among us, and such men and women, too. How are they to be governed?" said St. Clare.

"I'm sure it's more than I can say," said Miss Ophelia.

"Or I either," said St. Clare. "The horrid cruelties and outrages that once and a while find their way into the papers—such cases as Prue's,[1] for example—what do they come from? In many cases, it is a gradual hardening process on both sides—the owner growing more and more cruel, as the servant more and more callous. Whipping and abuse are like laudanum; you have to double the dose as the sensibilities decline. I saw this very early when I became an owner; and I resolved never to begin, because I did not know when I should stop—and I

---

1 *Prue* A woman enslaved by a neighbor of the St. Clares, who later reveals her history to Tom. In years past, Prue had been repeatedly forced to bear children for her enslaver, only to have them sold at auction, and she had subsequently lost a newborn child to starvation after her enslavers prevented her from breastfeeding. Her enslaver eventually has her whipped to death.

resolved, at least, to protect my own moral nature. The consequence is, that my servants act like spoiled children; but I think that better than for us both to be brutalized together. You have talked a great deal about our responsibilities in educating, Cousin. I really wanted you to *try* with one child, who is a specimen of thousands among us."

"It is your system makes such children," said Miss Ophelia.

"I know it; but they are *made*—they exist—and what *is* to be done with them?"

"Well, I can't say I thank you for the experiment. But, then, as it appears to be a duty, I shall persevere and try, and do the best I can," said Miss Ophelia; and Miss Ophelia, after this, did labor, with a commendable degree of zeal and energy, on her new subject. She instituted regular hours and employments for her, and undertook to teach her to read and sew.

In the former art, the child was quick enough. She learned her letters as if by magic, and was very soon able to read plain reading; but the sewing was a more difficult matter. The creature was as lithe as a cat, and as active as a monkey, and the confinement of sewing was her abomination; so she broke her needles, threw them slyly out of the windows, or down in chinks of the walls; she tangled, broke, and dirtied her thread, or, with a sly movement, would throw a spool away altogether. Her motions were almost as quick as those of a practised conjurer, and her command of her face quite as great; and though Miss Ophelia could not help feeling that so many accidents could not possibly happen in succession, yet she could not, without a watchfulness which would leave her no time for anything else, detect her.

Topsy was soon a noted character in the establishment. Her talent for every species of drollery, grimace, and mimicry—for dancing, tumbling, climbing, singing, whistling, imitating every sound that hit her fancy—seemed inexhaustible. In her play-hours, she invariably had every child in the establishment at her heels, open-mouthed with admiration and wonder—not excepting Miss Eva, who appeared to be fascinated by her wild diablerie, as a dove is sometimes charmed by a glittering serpent. Miss Ophelia was uneasy that Eva should fancy Topsy's society so much, and implored St. Clare to forbid it.

"Poh! let the child alone," said St. Clare. "Topsy will do her good."

"But so depraved a child—are you not afraid she will teach her some mischief?"

"She can't teach her mischief; she might teach it to some children, but evil rolls off Eva's mind like dew off a cabbage-leaf—not a drop sinks in."

"Don't be too sure," said Miss Ophelia. "I know I'd never let a child of mine play with Topsy."

"Well, your children needn't," said St. Clare, "but mine may; if Eva could have been spoiled, it would have been done years ago."

Topsy was at first despised and contemned by the upper servants. They soon found reason to alter their opinion. It was very soon discovered that whoever cast an indignity on Topsy was sure to meet with some inconvenient accident shortly after; either a pair of earrings or some cherished trinket would be missing, or an article of dress would be suddenly found utterly ruined, or the person would stumble accidently into a pail of hot water, or a libation of dirty slop would unaccountably deluge them from above when in full gala dress; and on all these occasions, when investigation was made, there was nobody found to stand sponsor for the indignity. Topsy was cited, and had up before all the domestic judicatories, time and again; but always sustained her examinations with most edifying innocence and gravity of appearance. Nobody in the world ever doubted who did the things; but not a scrap of any direct evidence could be found to establish the suppositions, and Miss Ophelia was too just to feel at liberty to proceed to any lengths without it.

The mischiefs done were always so nicely timed, also, as further to shelter the aggressor. Thus, the times for revenge on Rosa and Jane, the two chamber maids, were always chosen in those seasons when (as not unfrequently happened) they were in disgrace with their mistress, when any complaint from them would of course meet with no sympathy. In short, Topsy soon made the household understand the propriety of letting her alone; and she was let alone, accordingly.

Topsy was smart and energetic in all manual operations, learning everything that was taught her with surprising quickness. With a few lessons, she had learned to do the proprieties of Miss Ophelia's chamber in a way with which even that particular lady could find no fault. Mortal hands could not lay spread smoother, adjust pillows more accurately, sweep and dust and arrange more perfectly, than Topsy, when she chose—but she didn't very often choose. If Miss Ophelia, after three or four days of careful patient supervision, was so sanguine as to suppose that Topsy had at last fallen into her way, could do without overlooking, and so go off and busy herself about something else, Topsy would hold a perfect carnival of confusion, for some one or two hours. Instead of making the bed, she would amuse herself with pulling off the pillow-cases, butting her woolly head among the pillows, till it would sometimes be grotesquely ornamented with feathers sticking out in various directions; she would climb the posts, and hang head downward from the tops; flourish the sheets and spreads all over the apartment; dress the bolster up in Miss Ophelia's night-clothes, and enact various scenic performances with that—singing and whistling, and making grimaces at herself in the looking-glass; in short, as Miss Ophelia phrased it, "raising Cain"[1] generally.

On one occasion, Miss Ophelia found Topsy with her very best scarlet India Canton crape[2] shawl wound round her head for a turban, going on with her rehearsals before the glass in great style—Miss Ophelia having, with carelessness most unheard-of in her, left the key for once in her drawer.

"Topsy!" she would say, when at the end of all patience, "what does make you act so?"

"Dunno, Missis—I spects cause I's so wicked!"

"I don't know anything what I shall do with you, Topsy."

"Law, Missis, you must whip me; my old Missis allers whipped me. I an't used to workin' unless I gets whipped."

"Why, Topsy, I don't want to whip you. You can do well, if you've a mind to; what is the reason you won't?"

"Laws, Missis, I's used to whippin'; I spects it's good for me."

Miss Ophelia tried the recipe, and Topsy invariably made a terrible commotion, screaming, groaning and imploring, though half an hour afterwards, when roosted on some projection of the balcony, and surrounded by a flock of admiring "young uns," she would express the utmost contempt of the whole affair.

"Law, Miss Feely whip! wouldn't kill a skeeter,[3] her whippins. Oughter see how old Mas'r made the flesh fly; old Mas'r know'd how!"

---

1   *raising Cain*   Causing commotion; the phrase refers to the biblical character Cain, who murdered his brother Abel.

2   *India Canton crape*   Type of thin, gauzy fabric.

3   *skeeter*   Mosquito.

Topsy always made great capital of her own sins and enormities, evidently considering them as something peculiarly distinguishing.

"Law, you niggers," she would say to some of her auditors, "does you know you's all sinners? Well, you is—everybody is. White folks is sinners too—Miss Feely says so; but I spects niggers is the biggest ones; but lor! ye an't any on ye up to me. I's so awful wicked there can't nobody do nothin' with me. I used to keep old Missis a swarin' at me half de time. I spects I's the wickedest critter in the world"; and Topsy would cut a summerset, and come up brisk and shining on to a higher perch, and evidently plume herself on the distinction.

Miss Ophelia busied herself very earnestly on Sundays, teaching Topsy the catechism. Topsy had an uncommon verbal memory, and committed with a fluency that greatly encouraged her instructress.

"What good do you expect it is going to do her?" said St. Clare.

"Why, it always has done children good. It's what children always have to learn, you know," said Miss Ophelia.

"Understand it or not," said St. Clare.

"O, children never understand it at the time; but, after they are grown up, it'll come to them."

"Mine hasn't come to me yet," said St. Clare, "though I'll bear testimony that you put it into me pretty thoroughly when I was a boy."

"Ah, you were always good at learning, Augustine. I used to have great hopes of you," said Miss Ophelia.

"Well, haven't you now?" said St. Clare.

"I wish you were as good as you were when you were a boy, Augustine."

"So do I, that's a fact, Cousin," said St. Clare. "Well, go ahead and catechize Topsy; maybe you'll make out something yet."

Topsy, who had stood like a black statue during this discussion, with hands decently folded, now, at a signal from Miss Ophelia, went on:

"Our first parents, being left to the freedom of their own will, fell from the state wherein they were created."

Topsy's eyes twinkled, and she looked inquiringly.

"What is it, Topsy?" said Miss Ophelia.

"Please, Missis, was dat ar state Kintuck?"

"What state, Topsy?"

"Dat state dey fell out of. I used to hear Mas'r tell how we came down from Kintuck."

St. Clare laughed.

"You'll have to give her a meaning, or she'll make one," said he. "There seems to be a theory of emigration suggested there."

"O! Augustine, be still," said Miss Ophelia; "how can I do anything, if you will be laughing?"

"Well, I won't disturb the exercises again, on my honor"; and St. Clare took his paper into the parlor, and sat down, till Topsy had finished her recitations. They were all very well, only that now and then she would oddly transpose some important words, and persist in the mistake, in spite of every effort to the contrary; and St. Clare, after all his promises of goodness, took a wicked pleasure in these mistakes, calling Topsy to him whenever he had a mind to amuse himself, and getting her to repeat the offending passages, in spite of Miss Ophelia's remonstrances.

"How do you think I can do anything with the child, if you will go on so, Augustine?" she would say.

"Well, it is too bad—I won't again; but I do like to hear the droll little image stumble over those big words!"

"But you confirm her in the wrong way."

"What's the odds? One word is as good as another to her."

"You wanted me to bring her up right; and you ought to remember she is a reasonable creature, and be careful of your influence over her."

"O, dismal! so I ought; but, as Topsy herself says, 'I's so wicked!'"

In very much this way Topsy's training proceeded, for a year or two—Miss Ophelia worrying herself, from day to day, with her, as a kind of chronic plague, to whose inflictions she became, in time, as accustomed, as persons sometimes do to the neuralgia or sick headache.

St. Clare took the same kind of amusement in the child that a man might in the tricks of a parrot or a pointer. Topsy, whenever her sins brought her into disgrace in other quarters, always took refuge behind his chair; and St. Clare, in one way or other, would make peace for her. From him she got many a stray picayune,[1] which she laid out in nuts and candies, and distributed, with careless generosity, to all the children in the family; for Topsy, to do her justice, was good-natured

---

1 *picayune* Spanish coin historically in use in Louisiana; by extension, any coin of small value.

and liberal, and only spiteful in self-defence. She is fairly introduced into our *corps de ballet*[1] and will figure, from time to time, in her turn, with other performers.

[Two years pass, during which period Tom is treated with relative kindness and develops an especially affectionate relationship with the pious young Eva. Chapter 26 picks up after Eva has grown seriously ill, and the family have moved to their summer residence on Lake Pontchartrain.]

CHAPTER 26
DEATH

Weep not for those whom the veil of the tomb,
In life's early morning, hath hid from our eyes.[2]

Eva's bedroom was a spacious apartment, which, like all the other rooms in the house, opened on to the broad verandah. The room communicated, on one side, with her father and mother's apartment; on the other, with that appropriated to Miss Ophelia. St. Clare had gratified his own eye and taste in furnishing this room in a style that had a peculiar keeping with the character of her for whom it was intended. The windows were hung with curtains of rose-colored and white muslin, the floor was spread with a matting which had been ordered in Paris, to a pattern of his own device, having round it a border of rose-buds and leaves, and a centrepiece with full-blown roses. The bedstead, chairs, and lounges were of bamboo, wrought in peculiarly graceful and fanciful patterns. Over the head of the bed was an alabaster bracket, on which a beautiful sculptured angel stood, with drooping wings, holding out a crown of myrtle-leaves. From this depended,[3] over the bed, light curtains of rose-colored gauze, striped with silver, supplying that protection from mosquitos which is an indispensable addition to all sleeping accommodation in that climate. The graceful bamboo lounges were amply supplied with cushions of rose-colored damask, while over them, depending from the hands of

---

1   *corps de ballet*   Group of dancers in a ballet who function as background and support for the main dancers.
2   *Weep not ... our eyes*   See "Weep Not for Those" by Irish poet Thomas Moore (1779–1852).
3   *depended*   Hung.

sculptured figures, were gauze curtains similar to those of the bed. A light, fanciful bamboo table stood in the middle of the room, where a Parian vase,[1] wrought in the shape of a white lily, with its buds, stood, ever filled with flowers. On this table lay Eva's books and little trinkets, with an elegantly wrought alabaster writing-stand, which her father had supplied to her when he saw her trying to improve herself in writing. There was a fireplace in the room, and on the marble mantle above stood a beautifully wrought statuette of Jesus receiving little children, and on either side marble vases, for which it was Tom's pride and delight to offer bouquets every morning. Two or three exquisite paintings of children, in various attitudes,[2] embellished the wall. In short, the eye could turn nowhere without meeting images of childhood, of beauty, and of peace. Those little eyes never opened, in the morning light, without falling on something which suggested to the heart soothing and beautiful thoughts.

The deceitful strength which had buoyed Eva up for a little while was fast passing away; seldom and more seldom her light footstep was heard in the verandah, and oftener and oftener she was found reclined on a little lounge by the open window, her large, deep eyes fixed on the rising and falling waters of the lake.

It was towards the middle of the afternoon, as she was so reclining—her Bible half open, her little transparent fingers lying listlessly between the leaves—suddenly she heard her mother's voice, in sharp tones, in the verandah.

"What now, you baggage! what new piece of mischief! You've been picking the flowers, hey?" and Eva heard the sound of a smart slap.

"Law, Missis! they's for Miss Eva," she heard a voice say, which she knew belonged to Topsy.

"Miss Eva! A pretty excuse! you suppose she wants *your* flowers, you good-for-nothing nigger! Get along off with you!"

In a moment, Eva was off from her lounge, and in the verandah.

"O, don't, mother! I should like the flowers; do give them to me; I want them!"

"Why, Eva, your room is full now."

"I can't have too many," said Eva. "Topsy, do bring them here."

---

1   *Parian vase*   Vase made of a type of bisque porcelain, designed to imitate carved marble.
2   *attitudes*   Poses.

Topsy, who had stood sullenly, holding down her head, now came up and offered her flowers. She did it with a look of hesitation and bashfulness, quite unlike the eldrich[1] boldness and brightness which was usual with her.

"It's a beautiful bouquet!" said Eva, looking at it.

It was rather a singular one, a brilliant scarlet geranium, and one single white japonica,[2] with its glossy leaves. It was tied up with an evident eye to the contrast of color, and the arrangement of every leaf had carefully been studied.

Topsy looked pleased, as Eva said, "Topsy, you arrange flowers very prettily. Here," she said, "is this vase I haven't any flowers for. I wish you'd arrange something every day for it."

"Well, that's odd!" said Marie. "What in the world do you want that for?"

"Never mind, mamma; you'd as lief[3] as not Topsy should do it— had you not?"

"Of course, anything you please, dear! Topsy, you hear your young mistress; see that you mind."

Topsy made a short courtesy, and looked down; and, as she turned away, Eva saw a tear roll down her dark cheek.

"You see, mamma, I knew poor Topsy wanted to do something for me," said Eva to her mother.

"O, nonsense! it's only because she likes to do mischief. She knows she mustn't pick flowers—so she does it; that's all there is to it. But, if you fancy to have her pluck them, so be it."

"Mamma, I think Topsy is different from what she used to be; she's trying to be a good girl."

"She'll have to try a good while before *she* gets to be good," said Marie, with a careless laugh.

"Well, you know, mamma, poor Topsy! everything has always been against her."

"Not since she's been here, I'm sure. If she hasn't been talked to, and preached to, and every earthly thing done that anybody could

---

1 *eldrich* Odd, or spooky.

2 *japonica* Likely *camellia japonica*, an east Asian plant widely grown in the American South and bearing large, ornate flowers.

3 *lief* Happily.

do—and she's just so ugly, and always will be; you can't make anything of the creature!"

"But, mamma, it's so different to be brought up as I've been, with so many friends, so many things to make me good and happy; and to be brought up as she's been, all the time, till she came here!"

"Most likely," said Marie, yawning, "dear me, how hot it is!"

"Mamma, you believe, don't you, that Topsy could become an angel, as well as any of us, if she were a Christian?"

"Topsy! what a ridiculous idea! Nobody but you would ever think of it. I suppose she could, though."

"But, mamma, isn't God her father, as much as ours? Isn't Jesus her Saviour?"

"Well, that may be. I suppose God made everybody," said Marie. "Where is my smelling bottle?"[1]

"It's such a pity—oh! *such* a pity!" said Eva, looking out on the distant lake, and speaking half to herself.

"What's a pity?" said Marie.

"Why, that anyone, who could be a bright angel, and live with angels, should go all down, down, down, and nobody help them! oh, dear!"

"Well, we can't help it; it's no use worrying, Eva! I don't know what's to be done; we ought to be thankful for our own advantages."

"I hardly can be," said Eva, "I'm so sorry to think of poor folks that haven't any."

"That's odd enough," said Marie; "I'm sure my religion makes me thankful for my advantages."

"Mamma," said Eva, "I want to have some of my hair cut off—a good deal of it."

"What for?" said Marie.

"Mamma, I want to give some away to my friends, while I am able to give it to them myself. Won't you ask aunty to come and cut it for me?"

Marie raised her voice, and called Miss Ophelia, from the other room.

---

[1] *smelling bottle* I.e., bottle of smelling salts, a compound used to enliven people when feeling faint.

The child half rose from her pillow as she came in, and, shaking down her long golden-brown curls, said, rather playfully, "Come, aunty, shear the sheep!"

"What's that?" said St. Clare, who just then entered with some fruit he had been out to get for her.

"Papa, I just want aunty to cut off some of my hair; there's too much of it, and it makes my head hot. Besides, I want to give some of it away."

Miss Ophelia came, with her scissors.

"Take care—don't spoil the looks of it!" said her father; "cut underneath, where it won't show. Eva's curls are my pride."

"O, papa!" said Eva, sadly.

"Yes, and I want them kept handsome against the time I take you up to your uncle's plantation, to see Cousin Henrique," said St. Clare, in a gay tone.

"I shall never go there, papa; I am going to a better country. O, do believe me! Don't you see, papa, that I get weaker, every day?"

"Why do you insist that I shall believe such a cruel thing, Eva?" said her father.

"Only because it is *true*, papa: and, if you will believe it now, perhaps you will get to feel about it as I do."

St. Clare closed his lips, and stood gloomily eying the long, beautiful curls which, as they were separated from the child's head, were laid, one by one, in her lap. She raised them up, looked earnestly at them, twined them around her thin fingers, and looked, from time to time, anxiously at her father.

"It's just what I've been foreboding!" said Marie; "it's just what has been preying on my health, from day to day, bringing me downward to the grave, though nobody regards it. I have seen this, long. St. Clare, you will see, after a while, that I was right."

"Which will afford you great consolation, no doubt!" said St. Clare, in a dry, bitter tone.

Marie lay back on a lounge, and covered her face with her cambric handkerchief.

Eva's clear blue eye looked earnestly from one to the other. It was the calm, comprehending gaze of a soul half loosed from its earthly bonds; it was evident she saw, felt, and appreciated, the difference between the two.

She beckoned with her hand to her father. He came, and sat down by her.

"Papa, my strength fades away every day, and I know I must go. There are some things I want to say and do—that I ought to do; and you are so unwilling to have me speak a word on this subject. But it must come; there's no putting it off. Do be willing I should speak now!"

"My child, I *am* willing!" said St. Clare, covering his eyes with one hand, and holding up Eva's hand with the other.

"Then, I want to see all our people together. I have some things I *must* say to them," said Eva.

"*Well,*" said St. Clare, in a tone of dry endurance.

Miss Ophelia dispatched a messenger, and soon the whole of the servants were convened in the room.

Eva lay back on her pillows; her hair hanging loosely about her face, her crimson cheeks contrasting painfully with the intense whiteness of her complexion and the thin contour of her limbs and features, and her large, soul-like eyes fixed earnestly on everyone.

The servants were struck with a sudden emotion. The spiritual face, the long locks of hair cut off and lying by her, her father's averted face, and Marie's sobs, struck at once upon the feelings of a sensitive and impressible race; and, as they came in, they looked one on another, sighed, and shook their heads. There was a deep silence, like that of a funeral.

Eva raised herself, and looked long and earnestly round at every-one. All looked sad and apprehensive. Many of the women hid their faces in their aprons.

"I sent for you all, my dear friends," said Eva, "because I love you. I love you all; and I have something to say to you, which I want you always to remember. I am going to leave you. In a few more weeks, you will see me no more—"

Here the child was interrupted by bursts of groans, sobs, and lam-entations, which broke from all present, and in which her slender voice was lost entirely. She waited a moment, and then, speaking in a tone that checked the sobs of all, she said,

"If you love me, you must not interrupt me so. Listen to what I say. I want to speak to you about your souls. . . . . . Many of you, I am afraid, are very careless. You are thinking only about this world. I want you to remember that there is a beautiful world, where Jesus is. I am going there, and you can go there. It is for you, as much as me. But, if you want to go there, you must not live idle, careless, thoughtless lives. You must be Christians. You must remember that each one of you can become angels, and be angels forever. . . . . If you want to be Christians, Jesus will help you. You must pray to him; you must read—"

The child checked herself, looked piteously at them, and said, sorrowfully,

"O, dear! you *can't* read[1]—poor souls!" and she hid her face in the pillow and sobbed, while many a smothered sob from those she was addressing, who were kneeling on the floor, aroused her.

"Never mind," she said, raising her face and smiling brightly through her tears, "I have prayed for you; and I know Jesus will help you, even if you can't read. Try all to do the best you can; pray every day; ask Him to help you, and get the Bible read to you whenever you can; and I think I shall see you all·in heaven."

"Amen," was the murmured response from the lips of Tom and Mammy, and some of the elder ones, who belonged to the Methodist church. The younger and more thoughtless ones, for the time completely overcome, were sobbing, with their heads bowed upon their knees.

"I know," said Eva, "you all love me."

"Yes; oh, yes! indeed we do! Lord bless her!" was the involuntary answer of all.

"Yes, I know you do! There isn't one of you that hasn't always been very kind to me; and I want to give you something that, when you look at, you shall always remember me. I'm going to give all of you a curl of my hair; and, when you look at it, think that I loved you and am gone to heaven, and that I want to see you all there."

It is impossible to describe the scene, as, with tears and sobs, they gathered round the little creature, and took from her hands what seemed to them a last mark of her love. They fell on their knees; they sobbed, and prayed, and kissed the hem of her garment; and the elder ones poured forth words of endearment, mingled in prayers and blessings, after the manner of their susceptible race.

---

1   *you can't read*   Unlike Kentucky—but like most other slave states—Louisiana had strict legislation against teaching enslaved people to read or write.

As each one took their gift, Miss Ophelia, who was apprehensive for the effect of all this excitement on her little patient, signed to each one to pass out of the apartment.

At last, all were gone but Tom and Mammy.

"Here, Uncle Tom," said Eva, "is a beautiful one for you. O, I am so happy, Uncle Tom, to think I shall see you in heaven—for I'm sure I shall; and Mammy—dear, good, kind Mammy!" she said, fondly throwing her arms round her old nurse—"I know you'll be there, too."

"O Miss Eva, don't see how I can live without ye, no how!" said the faithful creature. "'Pears like it's just taking everything off the place to oncet!"[1] And Mammy gave way to a passion of grief.

Miss Ophelia pushed her and Tom gently from the apartment, and thought they were all gone; but, as she turned, Topsy was standing there.

"Where did you start up from?" she said, suddenly.

"I was here," said Topsy, wiping the tears from her eyes. "O, Miss Eva, I've been a bad girl; but won't you give *me* one, too?"

"Yes, poor Topsy! to be sure, I will. There—every time you look at that, think that I love you, and wanted you to be a good girl!"

"O, Miss Eva, I *is* tryin!" said Topsy, earnestly; "but, Lor, it's so hard to be good! 'Pears like I an't used to it, no ways!"

"Jesus knows it, Topsy; he is sorry for you; he will help you."

Topsy, with her eyes hid in her apron, was silently passed from the apartment by Miss Ophelia; but, as she went, she hid the precious curl in her bosom.

All being gone, Miss Ophelia shut the door. That worthy lady had wiped away many tears of her own, during the scene; but concern for the consequence of such an excitement to her young charge was uppermost in her mind.

St. Clare had been sitting, during the whole time, with his hand shading his eyes, in the same attitude. When they were all gone, he sat so still.

"Papa!" said Eva, gently, laying her hand on his.

He gave a sudden start and shiver; but made no answer.

"Dear papa!" said Eva.

---

1   *to oncet*   At once.

"I *cannot*," said St. Clare, rising, "I *cannot* have it so! The Almighty hath dealt *very bitterly* with me!"[1] and St. Clare pronounced these words with a bitter emphasis, indeed.

"Augustine! has not God a right to do what he will with his own?" said Miss Ophelia.

"Perhaps so; but that doesn't make it any easier to bear," said he, with a dry, hard, tearless manner, as he turned away.

"Papa, you break my heart!" said Eva, rising and throwing herself into his arms; "you must not feel so!" and the child sobbed and wept with a violence which alarmed them all, and turned her father's thoughts at once to another channel.

"There, Eva—there, dearest! Hush! hush! I was wrong; I was wicked. I will feel anyway, do anyway—only don't distress yourself; don't sob so. I will be resigned; I was wicked to speak as I did."

Eva soon lay like a wearied dove in her father's arms; and he, bending over her, soothed her by every tender word he could think of.

Marie rose and threw herself out of the apartment into her own, when she fell into violent hysterics.

"You didn't give me a curl, Eva," said her father, smiling sadly.

"They are all yours, papa," said she, smiling—"yours and mamma's; and you must give dear aunty as many as she wants. I only gave them to our poor people myself, because you know, papa, they might be forgotten when I am gone, and because I hoped it might help them remember. . . . . You are a Christian, are you not, papa?" said Eva, doubtfully.

"Why do you ask me?"

"I don't know. You are so good, I don't see how you can help it."

"What is being a Christian, Eva?"

"Loving Christ most of all," said Eva.

"Do you, Eva?"

"Certainly I do."

"You never saw him," said St. Clare.

"That makes no difference," said Eva. "I believe him, and in a few days I shall *see* him"; and the young face grew fervent, radiant with joy.

---

1 *The Almighty ... with me!* See Ruth 1.20.

St. Clare said no more. It was a feeling which he had seen before in his mother; but no chord within vibrated to it.

Eva, after this, declined rapidly; there was no more any doubt of the event; the fondest hope could not be blinded. Her beautiful room was avowedly a sick room; and Miss Ophelia day and night performed the duties of a nurse—and never did her friends appreciate her value more than in that capacity. With so well-trained a hand and eye, such perfect adroitness and practice in every art which could promote neatness and comfort, and keep out of sight every disagreeable incident of sickness—with such a perfect sense of time, such a clear, untroubled head, such exact accuracy in remembering every prescription and direction of the doctors—she was everything to him. They who had shrugged their shoulders at her little peculiarities and setnesses, so unlike the careless freedom of southern manners, acknowledged that now she was the exact person that was wanted.

Uncle Tom was much in Eva's room. The child suffered much from nervous restlessness, and it was a relief to her to be carried; and it was Tom's greatest delight to carry her little frail form in his arms, resting on a pillow, now up and down her room, now out into the verandah; and when the fresh sea-breezes blew from the lake—and the child felt freshest in the morning—he would sometimes walk with her under the orange-trees in the garden, or, sitting down in some of their old seats, sing to her their favorite old hymns.

Her father often did the same thing; but his frame was slighter, and when he was weary, Eva would say to him,

"O, papa, let Tom take me. Poor fellow! it pleases him; and you know it's all he can do now, and he wants to do something!"

"So do I, Eva!" said her father.

"Well, papa, you can do everything, and are everything to me. You read to me—you sit up nights—and Tom has only this one thing, and his singing; and I know, too, he does it easier than you can. He carries me so strong!"

The desire to do something was not confined to Tom. Every servant in the establishment showed the same feeling, and in their way did what they could.

Poor Mammy's heart yearned towards her darling; but she found no opportunity, night or day, as Marie declared that the state of her mind[1] was such, it was impossible for her to rest; and, of course, it was against her principles to let anyone else rest. Twenty times in a night, Mammy would be roused to rub her feet, to bathe her head, to find her pocket-handkerchief, to see what the noise was in Eva's room, to let down a curtain because it was too light, or to put it up because it was too dark; and, in the daytime, when she longed to have some share in the nursing of her pet, Marie seemed unusually ingenious in keeping her busy anywhere and everywhere all over the house, or about her own person; so that stolen interviews and momentary glimpses were all she could obtain.

"I feel it my duty to be particularly careful of myself, now," she would say, "feeble as I am, and with the whole care and nursing of that dear child upon me."

"Indeed, my dear," said St. Clare, "I thought our cousin relieved you of that."

"You talk like a man, St. Clare—just as if a mother *could* be relieved of the care of a child in that state; but, then, it's all alike—no one ever knows what I feel! I can't throw things off, as you do."

St. Clare smiled. You must excuse him, he couldn't help it—for St. Clare could smile yet. For so bright and placid was the farewell voyage of the little spirit—by such sweet and fragrant breezes was the small bark[2] borne towards the heavenly shores—that it was impossible to realize that it was death that was approaching. The child felt no pain—only a tranquil, soft weakness, daily and almost insensibly increasing; and she was so beautiful, so loving, so trustful, so happy, that one could not resist the soothing influence of that air of innocence and peace which seemed to breathe around her. St. Clare found a strange calm coming over him. It was not hope—that was impossible; it was not resignation; it was only a calm resting in the present, which seemed so beautiful that he wished to think of no future. It was like that hush of spirit which we feel amid the bright, mild woods of autumn, when the bright hectic flush is on the trees, and the last lingering flowers by the brook; and we joy in it all the more, because we know that soon it will all pass away.

---

1   *the state of her mind*   Marie suffers from a variety of physical and mental ailments that are strongly implied by the narrator to be of her own invention; her enslaved handmaid, Mammy, is forced to abandon her own children in order to attend to Marie day and night.
2   *bark*   Boat.

The friend who knew most of Eva's own imaginings and foreshadowings was her faithful bearer, Tom. To him she said what she would not disturb her father by saying. To him she imparted those mysterious intimations which the soul feels, as the cords begin to unbind, ere it leaves its clay[1] forever.

Tom, at last, would not sleep in his room, but lay all night in the outer verandah, ready to rouse at every call.

"Uncle Tom, what alive[2] have you taken to sleeping anywhere and everywhere, like a dog, for?" said Miss Ophelia. "I thought you was one of the orderly sort, that liked to lie in bed in a Christian way."

"I do, Miss Feely," said Tom, mysteriously. "I do, but now—"

"Well, what now?"

"We mustn't speak loud; Mas'r St. Clare won't hear on't; but Miss Feely, you know there must be somebody watchin' for the bridegroom."

"What do you mean, Tom?"

"You know it says in Scripture, 'At midnight there was a great cry made. Behold, the bridegroom cometh.'[3] That's what I'm spectin now, every night, Miss Feely—and I couldn't sleep out o' hearin, no ways."

"Why, Uncle Tom, what makes you think so?"

"Miss Eva, she talks to me. The Lord, he sends his messenger in the soul. I must be thar, Miss Feely; for when that ar blessed child goes into the kingdom, they'll open the door so wide, we'll all get a look in at the glory, Miss Feely."

"Uncle Tom, did Miss Eva say she felt more unwell than usual tonight?"

"No; but she told me, this morning, she was coming nearer—thar's them that tells it to the child, Miss Feely. It's the angels—'it's the trumpet sound afore the break o' day,'"[4] said Tom, quoting from a favorite hymn.

This dialogue passed between Miss Ophelia and Tom, between ten and eleven, one evening, after her arrangements had all been made

---

1 *clay* Earthly body.

2 *what alive* I.e., why on earth.

3 *the bridegroom cometh* See Matthew 25.1: "Then shall the kingdom of heaven be likened unto ten virgins, which took their lamps, and went forth to meet the bridegroom."

4 *it's the ... o' day* Line from "The Wings of the Morning," a hymn commonly sung in camp meetings. The line is taken from Psalm 139.9.

for the night, when, on going to bolt her outer door, she found Tom stretched along by it, in the outer verandah.

She was not nervous or impressible; but the solemn, heartfelt manner struck her. Eva had been unusually bright and cheerful, that afternoon, and had sat raised in her bed, and looked over all her little trinkets and precious things, and designated the friends to whom she would have them given; and her manner was more animated, and her voice more natural, than they had known it for weeks. Her father had been in, in the evening, and had said that Eva appeared more like her former self than ever she had done since her sickness; and when he kissed her for the night, he said to Miss Ophelia, "Cousin, we may keep her with us, after all; she is certainly better"; and he had retired with a lighter heart in his bosom than he had had there for weeks.

But at midnight—strange, mystic hour!—when the veil between the frail present and the eternal future grows thin—then came the messenger!

There was a sound in that chamber, first of one who stepped quickly. It was Miss Ophelia, who had resolved to sit up all night with her little charge, and who, at the turn of the night, had discerned what experienced nurses significantly call "a change." The outer door was quickly opened, and Tom, who was watching outside, was on the alert, in a moment.

"Go for the doctor, Tom! lose not a moment," said Miss Ophelia; and, stepping across the room, she rapped at St. Clare's door.

"Cousin," she said, "I wish you would come."

Those words fell on his heart like clods upon a coffin. Why did they? He was up and in the room in an instant, and bending over Eva, who still slept.

What was it he saw that made his heart stand still? Why was no word spoken between the two? Thou canst say, who hast seen that same expression on the face dearest to thee; that look indescribable, hopeless, unmistakable, that says to thee that thy beloved is no longer thine.

On the face of the child, however, there was no ghastly imprint— only a high and almost sublime expression—the overshadowing presence of spiritual natures, the dawning of immortal life in that childish soul.

They stood there so still, gazing upon her, that even the ticking of the watch seemed too loud. In a few moments, Tom returned, with the doctor. He entered, gave one look, and stood silent as the rest.

"When did this change take place?" said he, in a low whisper, to Miss Ophelia.

"About the turn of the night," was the reply.

Marie, roused by the entrance of the doctor, appeared, hurriedly, from the next room.

"Augustine! Cousin! O! what!" she hurriedly began.

"Hush!" said St. Clare, hoarsely; "*she is dying!*"

Mammy heard the words, and flew to awaken the servants. The house was soon roused—lights were seen, footsteps heard, anxious faces thronged the verandah, and looked tearfully through the glass doors; but St. Clare heard and said nothing—he saw only *that look* on the face of the little sleeper.

"O, if she would only wake, and speak once more!" he said; and, stooping over her, he spoke in her ear, "Eva, darling!"

The large blue eyes unclosed—a smile passed over her face; she tried to raise her head, and to speak.

"Do you know me, Eva?"

"Dear papa," said the child, with a last effort, throwing her arms about his neck. In a moment they dropped again; and, as St. Clare raised his head, he saw a spasm of mortal agony pass over the face— she struggled for breath, and threw up her little hands.

"O, God, this is dreadful!" he said, turning away in agony, and wringing Tom's hand, scarce conscious what he was doing. "O, Tom, my boy, it is killing me!"

Tom had his master's hands between his own; and, with tears streaming down his dark cheeks, looked up for help where he had always been used to look.

"Pray that this may be cut short!" said St. Clare, "this wrings my heart."

"O, bless the Lord! it's over—it's over, dear Master!" said Tom; "look at her."

The child lay panting on her pillows, as one exhausted—the large clear eyes rolled up and fixed. Ah, what said those eyes, that spoke so much of heaven? Earth was past, and earthly pain; but so solemn, so mysterious, was the triumphant brightness of that face, that it checked even the sobs of sorrow. They pressed around her, in breathless stillness.

"Eva," said St. Clare, gently.

She did not hear.

"O, Eva, tell us what you see! What is it?" said her father.

A bright, a glorious smile passed over her face, and she said, brokenly, "O! love, joy, peace!" gave one sigh, and passed from death unto life!

"Farewell, beloved child! the bright, eternal doors have closed after thee; we shall see thy sweet face no more. O, woe for them who watched thy entrance into heaven, when they shall wake and find only the cold gray sky of daily life, and thou gone forever!"

[Following Eva's death, several characters embrace Christianity, including Augustine, who resolves to eventually free those whom he enslaves. His plans fail, however, upon his death in a tavern fight, leading his wife to take control of the estate. Marie sells Tom to Simon Legree, an exceedingly cruel planter in rural Louisiana who takes a particular dislike to Tom because of his religious convictions. Tom is purchased alongside Emmeline, a young woman whom Legree clearly intends to force into sexual slavery, and at the plantation he meets the older Cassy, who suffered the same fate under Legree previously. With Tom's help, Emmeline and Cassy resolve to flee the plantation.]

CHAPTER 40
THE MARTYR

Deem not the just by Heaven forgot!
 Though life its common gifts deny—
Though, with a crushed and bleeding heart,
 And spurned of man, he goes to die!
For God hath marked each sorrowing day,
 And numbered every bitter tear;
And heaven's long years of bliss shall pay
 For all his children suffer here.[1]   BRYANT

---

1 *Deem not ... suffer here*   See "Blessed Are They that Mourn" (1832) by American poet and supporter of abolition William Cullen Bryant (1794–1878). The first line of this passage actually reads, "Nor let the good man's trust depart."

The longest way must have its close—the gloomiest night will wear on to a morning. An eternal, inexorable lapse of moments is ever hurrying the day of the evil to an eternal night, and the night of the just to an eternal day. We have walked with our humble friend thus far in the valley of slavery; first through flowery fields of ease and indulgence, then through heartbreaking separations from all that man holds dear. Again, we have waited with him in a sunny island, where generous hands concealed his chains with flowers; and, lastly, we have followed him when the last ray of earthly hope went out in night, and seen how, in the blackness of earthly darkness, the firmament of the unseen has blazed with stars of new and significant lustre.

The morning-star now stands over the tops of the mountains, and gales and breezes, not of earth, show that the gates of day are unclosing.

The escape of Cassy and Emmeline irritated the before surly temper of Legree to the last degree; and his fury, as was to be expected, fell upon the defenceless head of Tom. When he hurriedly announced the tidings among his hands, there was a sudden light in Tom's eye, a sudden upraising of his hands, that did not escape him. He saw that he did not join the muster of the pursuers. He thought of forcing him to do it; but, having had, of old, experience of his inflexibility when commanded to take part in any deed of inhumanity, he would not, in his hurry, stop to enter into any conflict with him.

Tom, therefore, remained behind, with a few who had learned of him to pray, and offered up prayers for the escape of the fugitives.

When Legree returned, baffled and disappointed, all the long-working hatred of his soul towards his slave began to gather in a deadly and desperate form. Had not this man braved him—steadily, powerfully, resistlessly—ever since he bought him? Was there not a spirit in him which, silent as it was, burned on him like the fires of perdition?

"I *hate* him!" said Legree, that night, as he sat up in his bed; "I *hate* him! And isn't he mine? Can't I do what I like with him? Who's to hinder, I wonder?" And Legree clenched his fist, and shook it, as if he had something in his hands that he could rend in pieces.

But, then, Tom was a faithful, valuable servant; and, although Legree hated him the more for that, yet the consideration was still somewhat of a restraint to him.

The next morning, he determined to say nothing, as yet; to assemble a party, from some neighboring plantations, with dogs and guns; to surround the swamp, and go about the hunt systematically. If it succeeded, well and good; if not, he would summon Tom before him, and—his teeth clenched and his blood boiled—*then* he would break that fellow down, or—there was a dire inward whisper, to which his soul assented.

Ye say that the *interest* of the master is a sufficient safeguard for the slave. In the fury of man's mad will, he will wittingly, and with open eye, sell his own soul to the devil to gain his ends; and will he be more careful of his neighbor's body?

"Well," said Cassy, the next day, from the garret, as she reconnoitred through the knothole, "the hunt's going to begin again, today!"

Three or four mounted horsemen were curvetting[1] about on the space front of the house; and one or two leashes of strange dogs were struggling with the negroes who held them, baying and barking at each other.

The men are, two of them, overseers of plantations in the vicinity; and others were some of Legree's associates at the tavern-bar of a neighboring city, who had come for the interest of the sport. A more hard-favored set, perhaps, could not be imagined. Legree was serving brandy, profusely, round among them, as also among the negroes, who had been detailed from the various plantations for this service; for it was an object to make every service of this kind, among the negroes, as much of a holiday as possible.

Cassy placed her ear at the knothole; and, as the morning air blew directly towards the house, she could overhear a good deal of the conversation. A grave sneer overcast the dark, severe gravity of her face, as she listened, and heard them divide out the ground, discuss the rival merits of the dogs, give orders about firing, and the treatment of each, in case of capture.

Cassy drew back; and, clasping her hands, looked upward, and said, "O, great Almighty God! we are *all* sinners; but what have *we* done, more than all the rest of the world, that we should be treated so?"

There was a terrible earnestness in her face and voice, as she spoke.

---

1   *curvetting*   Leaping or frolicking.

"If it wasn't for *you*, child," she said, looking at Emmeline, "I'd *go* out to them; and I'd thank any one of them that *would* shoot me down; for what use will freedom be to me? Can it give me back my children, or make me what I used to be?"[1]

Emmeline, in her childlike simplicity, was half afraid of the dark moods of Cassy. She looked perplexed, but made no answer. She only took her hand, with a gentle, caressing movement.

"Don't!" said Cassy, trying to draw it away; "you'll get me to loving you; and I never mean to love anything, again!"

"Poor Cassy!" said Emmeline, "don't feel so! If the Lord gives us liberty, perhaps he'll give you back your daughter; at any rate, I'll be like a daughter to you. I know I'll never see my poor old mother again! I shall love you, Cassy, whether you love me or not!"

The gentle, childlike spirit conquered. Cassy sat down by her, put her arm round her neck, stroked her soft, brown hair; and Emmeline then wondered at the beauty of her magnificent eyes, now soft with tears.

"O, Em!" said Cassy, "I've hungered for my children, and thirsted for them, and my eyes fail with longing for them! Here! here!" she said, striking her breast, "it's all desolate, all empty! If God would give me back my children, then I could pray."

"You must trust him, Cassy," said Emmeline; "he is our Father!"

"His wrath is upon us," said Cassy; "he has turned away in anger."

"No, Cassy! He will be good to us! Let us hope in Him," said Emmeline—"I always have had hope."

———

The hunt was long, animated, and thorough, but unsuccessful; and, with grave, ironic exultation, Cassy looked down on Legree as, weary and dispirited, he alighted from his horse.

"Now, Quimbo," said Legree, as he stretched himself down in the sitting room, "you jest go and walk that Tom up here, right away! The old cuss is at the bottom of this yer whole matter; and I'll have it out of his old black hide, or I'll know the reason why!"

---

1   *Can it ... to be?*   Cassy was separated from her own children when she was purchased by Legree; she eventually became pregnant by him, and subsequently killed the child rather than have it suffer under slavery as well.

Sambo and Quimbo both, though hating each other, were joined in one mind by a no less cordial hatred of Tom. Legree had told them, at first, that he had bought him for a general overseer, in his absence; and this had begun an ill will, on their part, which had increased, in their debased and servile natures, as they saw him becoming obnoxious to their master's displeasure. Quimbo, therefore, departed, with a will, to execute his orders.

Tom heard the message with a forewarning heart; for he knew all the plan of the fugitives' escape, and the place of their present concealment; he knew the deadly character of the man he had to deal with, and his despotic power. But he felt strong in God to meet death, rather than betray the helpless.

He sat his basket down by the row, and, looking up, said, "Into thy hands I commend my spirit! Thou hast redeemed me, oh Lord God of truth!"[1] and then quietly yielded himself to the rough, brutal grasp with which Quimbo seized him.

"Ay, ay!" said the giant, as he dragged him along; "ye'll cotch it, now! I'll boun' Mas'r's back 's up *high*! No sneaking out, now! Tell ye, ye'll get it, and no mistake! See how ye'll look, now, helpin' Mas'r's niggers to run away! See what ye'll get!"

The savage words none of them reached that ear! A higher voice there was saying, "Fear not them that kill the body, and, after that, have no more that they can do."[2] Nerve and bone of that poor man's body vibrated to those words, as if touched by the finger of God; and he felt the strength of a thousand souls in one. As he passed along, the trees and bushes, the huts of his servitude, the whole scene of his degradation, seemed to whirl by him as the landscape by the rushing car. His soul throbbed—his home was in sight—and the hour of release seemed at hand.

"Well, Tom!" said Legree, walking up, and seizing him grimly by the collar of his coat, and speaking through his teeth, in a paroxysm of determined rage, "do you know I've made up my mind to kill you?"

"It's very likely, Mas'r," said Tom, calmly.

---

1   *Into thy hands ... truth!* See Luke 23.46, the last words of Christ on the cross: "And when Jesus had cried with a loud voice, he said, Father, into thy hands I commend my spirit: and having said thus, he gave up the ghost."

2   *Fear not ... can do* See Matthew 10.28: "And fear not them which kill the body, but are not able to kill the soul: but rather fear him which is able to destroy both soul and body in hell."

"I *have*," said Legree, with grim, terrible calmness, "*done—just—that—thing*, Tom, unless you'll tell me what you know about these yer gals!"

Tom stood silent.

"D'ye hear?" said Legree, stamping, with a roar like that of an incensed lion. "Speak!"

"*I han't got nothing to tell, Mas'r*," said Tom, with a slow, firm, deliberate utterance.

"Do you dare to tell me, ye old black Christian, ye don't *know?*" said Legree.

Tom was silent.

"Speak!" thundered Legree, striking him furiously. "Do you know anything?"

"I know, Mas'r; but I can't tell anything. *I can die!*"

Legree drew in a long breath; and, suppressing his rage, took Tom by the arm, and, approaching his face almost to his, said, in a terrible voice, "Hark 'e, Tom! Ye think, 'cause I've let you off before, I don't mean what I say; but, this time, I've *made up my mind*, and counted the cost. You've always stood it out agin' me: now, I'll *conquer ye, or kill ye!* one or t' other. I'll count every drop of blood there is in you, and take 'em, one by one, till ye give up!"

Tom looked up to his master, and answered, "Mas'r, if you was sick, or in trouble, or dying, and I could save ye, I'd *give* ye my heart's blood; and, if taking every drop of blood in this poor old body would save your precious soul, I'd give 'em freely, as the Lord gave his for me. O, Mas'r! don't bring this great sin on your soul! It will hurt you more than 't will me! Do the worst you can, my troubles 'll be over soon; but, if ye don't repent, yours won't *never* end!"

Like a strange snatch of heavenly music, heard in the lull of a tempest, this burst of feeling made a moment's blank pause. Legree stood aghast, and looked at Tom; and there was such a silence, that the tick of the old clock could be heard, measuring, with silent touch, the last moments of mercy and probation to that hardened heart.

It was but a moment. There was one hesitating pause—one irresolute, relenting thrill—and the spirit of evil came back, with sevenfold vehemence; and Legree, foaming with rage, smote his victim to the ground.

Scenes of blood and cruelty are shocking to our ear and heart. What man has nerve to do, man has not nerve to hear. What brother-man and brother-Christian must suffer, cannot be told us, even in our secret chamber, it so harrows up the soul! And yet, oh my country! these things are done under the shadow of thy laws! O, Christ! thy church sees them, almost in silence!

But, of old, there was One whose suffering changed an instrument of torture, degradation and shame, into a symbol of glory, honor, and immortal life;[1] and, where His spirit is, neither degrading stripes, nor blood, nor insults, can make the Christian's last struggle less than glorious.

Was he alone, that long night, whose brave, loving spirit was bearing up, in that old shed, against buffeting and brutal stripes?

Nay! There stood by him One—seen by him alone—"like unto the Son of God."[2]

The tempter[3] stood by him, too—blinded by furious, despotic will—every moment pressing him to shun that agony by the betrayal of the innocent. But the brave, true heart was firm on the Eternal Rock.[4] Like his Master, he knew that, if he saved others, himself he could not save; nor could utmost extremity wring from him words, save of prayer and holy trust.

"He's most gone, Mas'r," said Sambo, touched, in spite of himself, by the patience of his victim.

"Pay away, till he gives up! Give it to him! give it to him!" shouted Legree. "I'll take every drop of blood he has, unless he confesses!"

Tom opened his eyes, and looked upon his master. "Ye poor miserable critter!" he said, "there an't no more ye can do! I forgive ye,[5] with all my soul!" and he fainted entirely away.

---

1 *One whose ... immortal life* Reference to Christ's sacrifice on the cross.
2 *One ... of God* I.e., God. See Hebrews 7.3: "Without father, without mother, without descent, having neither beginning of days, nor end of life; but made like unto the Son of God; abideth a priest continually."
3 *tempter* Satan.
4 *Eternal Rock* The "Rock of Ages" is a common metaphor for Christ, as well as the name of a popular Christian hymn.
5 *I forgive ye* Words spoken by Christ at the beginning of his crucifixion; see Luke 23.34: "Then said Jesus, Father, forgive them; for they know not what they do. And they parted his raiment, and cast lots."

"I b'lieve, my soul, he's done for, finally," said Legree, stepping forward, to look at him. "Yes, he is! Well, his mouth's shut up, at last—that's one comfort!"

Yes, Legree; but who shall shut up that voice in thy soul? that soul, past repentance, past prayer, past hope, in whom the fire that never shall be quenched is already burning!

Yet Tom was not quite gone. His wondrous words and pious prayers had struck upon the hearts of the imbruted blacks, who had been the instruments of cruelty upon him; and, the instant Legree withdrew, they took him down, and, in their ignorance, sought to call him back to life—as if *that* were any favor to him.

"Sartin, we's been doin' a drefful wicked thing!" said Sambo; "hopes Mas'r 'll have to 'count for it, and not we."

They washed his wounds—they provided a rude[1] bed of some refuse cotton for him to lie down on; and one of them, stealing up to the house, begged a drink of brandy of Legree, pretending that he was tired, and wanted it for himself. He brought it back, and poured it down Tom's throat.

"O, Tom!" said Quimbo, "we's been awful wicked to ye!"

"I forgive ye, with all my heart!" said Tom, faintly.

"O, Tom! do tell us who is *Jesus*, anyhow?" said Sambo; "Jesus, that's been a standin' by you so, all this night! Who is he?"

The word roused the failing, fainting spirit. He poured forth a few energetic sentences of that wondrous One—his life, his death, his everlasting presence, and power to save.

They wept—both the two savage men.

"Why didn't I never hear this before?" said Sambo; "but I do believe! I can't help it! Lord Jesus, have mercy on us!"

"Poor critters!" said Tom, "I'd be willing to bar' all I have, if it'll only bring ye to Christ! O, Lord! give me these two more souls, I pray!"

That prayer was answered!

---

1   *rude* Crude; rustic.

CHAPTER 41
THE YOUNG MASTER

Two days after, a young man drove a light wagon up through the avenue of china trees,[1] and, throwing the reins hastily on the horses' neck, sprang out and inquired for the owner of the place.

It was George Shelby; and, to show how he came to be there, we must go back in our story.

The letter of Miss Ophelia to Mrs. Shelby[2] had, by some unfortunate accident, been detained, for a month or two, at some remote post-office, before it reached its destination; and, of course, before it was received, Tom was already lost to view among the distant swamps of the Red River.

Mrs. Shelby read the intelligence with the deepest concern; but any immediate action upon it was an impossibility. She was then in attendance on the sickbed of her husband, who lay delirious in the crisis of a fever. Master George Shelby, who, in the interval, had changed from a boy to a tall young man, was her constant and faithful assistant, and her only reliance in superintending his father's affairs. Miss Ophelia had taken the precaution to send them the name of the lawyer who did business for the St. Clares; and the most that, in the emergency, could be done, was to address a letter of inquiry to him. The sudden death of Mr. Shelby a few days after brought, of course, an absorbing pressure of other interests, for a season.

Mr. Shelby showed his confidence in his wife's ability, by appointing her sole executrix upon his estates; and thus immediately a large and complicated amount of business was brought upon her hands.

Mrs. Shelby, with characteristic energy, applied herself to the work of straightening the entangled web of affairs; and she and George were for some time occupied with collecting and examining accounts, selling property and settling debts; for Mrs. Shelby was determined that everything should be brought into tangible and recognizable shape,

---

1   *china trees*   Native to southeast Asia and Australia, the *Melia azedarach* is naturalized in the Southern United States and known for its long clusters of purple flowers and ornamental yellow fruit.

2   *The letter … Mrs. Shelby*   Before Tom's sale, and after unsuccessfully pleading with Marie St. Clare to grant Tom his freedom, Miss Ophelia had sent a letter to Mrs. Shelby, in the hopes that she could send funds for his purchase.

let the consequences to her prove what they might. In the meantime they received a letter from the lawyer to whom Miss Ophelia had referred them, saying that he knew nothing of the matter; that the man was sold at a public auction, and that, beyond receiving the money, he knew nothing of the affair.

Neither George nor Mrs. Shelby could be easy at this result; and, accordingly, some six months after, the latter,[1] having business for his mother down the river, resolved to visit New Orleans in person and push his inquiries, in hopes of discovering Tom's whereabouts, and restoring him.

After some months of unsuccessful search, by the merest accident, George fell in with a man in New Orleans who happened to be possessed of the desired information; and with his money in his pocket, our hero took steamboat for Red River, resolving to find out and re-purchase his old friend.

He was soon introduced into the house, where he found Legree in the sitting room.

Legree received the stranger with a kind of surly hospitality.

"I understand," said the young man, "that you bought, in New Orleans, a boy, named Tom. He used to be on my father's place, and I came to see if I couldn't buy him back."

Legree's brow grew dark, and he broke out, passionately: "Yes, I did buy such a fellow—and a h—l of a bargain I had of it, too! The most rebellious, saucy, impudent dog! Set up my niggers to run away; got off two gals, worth eight hundred or a thousand dollars apiece. He owned to that, and, when I bid him tell me where they was, he up and said he knew, but he wouldn't tell; and stood to it, though I gave him the cussedest flogging I ever gave nigger yet. I b'lieve he's trying to die; but I don't know as he'll make it out."

"Where is he?" said George, impetuously. "Let me see him." The cheeks of the young man were crimson, and his eyes flashed fire; but he prudently said nothing, as yet.

"He's in dat ar shed," said a little fellow, who stood holding George's horse.

Legree kicked the boy, and swore at him; but George, without saying another word, turned and strode to the spot.

---

1   *the latter* A slip: Stowe clearly intends "the former."

Tom had been lying two days since the fatal night; not suffering, for every nerve of suffering was blunted and destroyed. He lay, for the most part, in a quiet stupor; for the laws of a powerful and well-knit frame would not at once release the imprisoned spirit. By stealth, there had been there, in the darkness of the night, poor desolated creatures, who stole from their scanty hours' rest, that they might repay to him some of those ministrations of love in which he had always been so abundant. Truly, those poor disciples had little to give—only the cup of cold water;[1] but it was given with full hearts.

Tears had fallen on that honest, insensible face—tears of late repentance in the poor, ignorant heathen, whom his dying love and patience had awakened to repentance, and bitter prayers, breathed over him to a late-found Saviour, of whom they scarce knew more than the name, but whom the yearning ignorant heart of man never implores in vain.

Cassy, who had glided out of her place of concealment, and, by over-hearing, learned the sacrifice that had been made for her and Emmeline, had been there, the night before, defying the danger of detection; and, moved by the few last words which the affectionate soul had yet strength to breathe, the long winter of despair, the ice of years, had given way, and the dark, despairing woman had wept and prayed.

When George entered the shed, he felt his head giddy[2] and his heart sick.

"Is it possible—is it possible?" said he, kneeling down by him. "Uncle Tom, my poor, poor old friend!"

Something in the voice penetrated to the ear of the dying. He moved his head gently, smiled, and said,

Jesus can make a dying-bed
Feel soft as downy pillows are.[3]

Tears which did honor to his manly heart fell from the young man's eyes as he bent over his poor friend.

---

1   *the cup of cold water*   See Matthew 10.42: "And whosoever shall give to drink unto one of these little ones a cup of cold water only in the name of a disciple, verily I say unto you, he shall in no wise lose his reward."

2   *giddy*   Dizzy.

3   *Jesus can … pillows are*   See "Hymn 31" by popular hymnodist Isaac Watts (1674–1748). In the nineteenth century, these lines were often used as gravestone epitaphs.

"O, dear Uncle Tom! do wake—do speak once more! Look up! Here's Mas'r George—your own little Mas'r George. Don't you know me?"

"Mas'r George!" said Tom, opening his eyes, and speaking in a feeble voice; "Mas'r George!" He looked bewildered.

Slowly the idea seemed to fill his soul; and the vacant eye became fixed and brightened, the whole face lighted up, the hard hands clasped, and tears ran down the cheeks.

"Bless the Lord! it is—it is—it's all I wanted! They haven't forgot me. It warms my soul; it does my old heart good! Now I shall die content! Bless the Lord, oh my soul!"

"You shan't die! you *mustn't* die, nor think of it! I've come to buy you, and take you home," said George, with impetuous vehemence.

"O, Mas'r George, ye're too late. The Lord's bought me, and is going to take me home—and I long to go. Heaven is better than Kintuck."

"O, don't die! It'll kill me! It'll break my heart to think what you've suffered—and lying in this old shed, here! Poor, poor fellow!"

"Don't call me poor fellow!" said Tom, solemnly. "I *have* been poor fellow; but that's all past and gone, now. I'm right in the door, going into glory! O, Mas'r George! *Heaven has come!* I've got the victory! The Lord Jesus has given it to me! Glory be to His name!"

George was awestruck at the force, the vehemence, the power, with which these broken sentences were uttered. He sat gazing in silence.

Tom grasped his hand, and continued, "Ye mustn't, now, tell Chloe, poor soul! how ye found me—'t would be so drefful to her. Only tell her ye found me going into glory; and that I couldn't stay for no one. And tell her the Lord's stood by me everywhere and al'ays, and made everything light and easy. And oh, the poor chil'en, and the baby! my old heart's been most broke for 'em, time and agin! Tell 'em all to follow me—follow me! Give my love to Mas'r, and dear good Missis, and everybody in the place! Ye don't know! 'Pears like I loves 'em all! I loves every creatur', everywhar! it's nothing *but* love! O, Mas'r George! what a thing 't is to be a Christian!"

At this moment, Legree sauntered up to the door of the shed, looked in, with a dogged air of affected carelessness, and turned away.

"The old satan!" said George, in his indignation. "It's a comfort to think the devil will pay *him* for this, some of these days!"

"O, don't! oh, ye mustn't!" said Tom, grasping his hand; "he's a poor mis'able critter! it's awful to think on 't! O, if he only could repent, the Lord would forgive him now; but I'm 'feared he never will!"

"I hope he won't!" said George; "I never want to see *him* in heaven!"

"Hush, Mas'r George! it worries me! Don't feel so! He an't done me no real harm—only opened the gate of the kingdom for me; that's all!"

At this moment, the sudden flush of strength which the joy of meeting his young master had infused into the dying man gave way. A sudden sinking fell upon him; he closed his eyes; and that mysterious and sublime change passed over his face, that told the approach of other worlds.

He began to draw his breath with long, deep inspirations; and his broad chest rose and fell, heavily. The expression of his face was that of a conqueror.

"Who—who—who shall separate us from the love of Christ?"[1] he said, in a voice that contended with mortal weakness; and, with a smile, he fell asleep.

George sat fixed with solemn awe. It seemed to him that the place was holy; and, as he closed the lifeless eyes, and rose up from the dead, only one thought possessed him—that expressed by his simple old friend—"What a thing it is to be a Christian!"

He turned: Legree was standing, sullenly, behind him.

Something in that dying scene had checked the natural fierceness of youthful passion. The presence of the man was simply loathsome to George; and he felt only an impulse to get away from him, with as few words as possible.

Fixing his keen dark eyes on Legree, he simply said, pointing to the dead, "You have got all you ever can of him. What shall I pay you for the body? I will take it away, and bury it decently."

"I don't sell dead niggers," said Legree, doggedly. "You are welcome to bury him where and when you like."

"Boys," said George, in an authoritative tone, to two or three negroes, who were looking at the body, "help me lift him up, and carry him to my wagon; and get me a spade."

---

1   *Who ... love of Christ?*   See Romans 8.35: "Who shall separate us from the love of Christ? shall tribulation, or distress, or persecution, or famine, or nakedness, or peril, or sword?"

One of them ran for a spade; the other two assisted George to carry the body to the wagon.

George neither spoke to nor looked at Legree, who did not countermand his orders, but stood, whistling, with an air of forced unconcern. He sulkily followed them to where the wagon stood at the door. George spread his cloak in the wagon, and had the body carefully disposed of in it—moving the seat, so as to give it room. Then he turned, fixed his eyes on Legree, and said, with forced composure, "I have not, as yet, said to you what I think of this most atrocious affair; this is not the time and place. But, sir, this innocent blood shall have justice. I will proclaim this murder.[1] I will go to the very first magistrate, and expose you."

"Do!" said Legree, snapping his fingers, scornfully. "I'd like to see you doing it. Where you going to get witnesses? how you going to prove it? Come, now!"

George saw, at once, the force of this defiance. There was not a white person on the place; and, in all southern courts, the testimony of colored blood is nothing. He felt, at that moment, as if he could have rent the heavens with his heart's indignant cry for justice; but in vain.

"After all, what a fuss, for a dead nigger!" said Legree.

The word was as a spark to a powder magazine.[2] Prudence was never a cardinal virtue of the Kentucky boy. George turned, and, with one indignant blow, knocked Legree flat upon his face; and, as he stood over him, blazing with wrath and defiance, he would have formed no bad personification of his great namesake triumphing over the dragon.[3]

Some men, however, are decidedly bettered by being knocked down. If a man lays them fairly flat in the dust, they seem immediately

---

1   *I will ... murder* As in other slave states, it was illegal in Louisiana to kill an enslaved person, or to punish an enslaved person with excessive cruelty. However, such crimes were almost never prosecuted, and offenders were if convicted punished only with modest fines; only a tiny number of instances have been recorded where slaveowners received the maximum punishment for murder. Furthermore, the testimony of another enslaved person or a free African American was not accepted in courts.

2   *powder magazine* Storehouse of gunpowder.

3   *his great namesake ... dragon* Reference to the legend of Saint George (c. 275–303), the Patron Saint of England, who is said to have slain a dragon that tyrannized a village, demanding human sacrifices.

to conceive a respect for him; and Legree was one of this sort. As he rose, therefore, and brushed the dust from his clothes, he eyed the slowly retreating wagon with some evident consideration; nor did he open his mouth till it was out of sight.

Beyond the boundaries of the plantation, George had noticed a dry, sandy knoll, shaded by a few trees: there they made the grave.

"Shall we take off the cloak, Mas'r?" said the negroes, when the grave was ready.

"No, no—bury it with him! It's all I can give you, now, poor Tom, and you shall have it."

They laid him in; and the men shovelled away, silently. They banked it up, and laid green turf over it.

"You may go, boys," said George, slipping a quarter into the hand of each. They lingered about, however.

"If young Mas'r would please buy us—" said one.

"We'd serve him so faithful!" said the other.

"Hard times here, Mas'r!" said the first. "Do, Mas'r, buy us, please!"

"I can't! I can't!" said George, with difficulty, motioning them off; "it's impossible!"

The poor fellows looked dejected, and walked off in silence.

"Witness, eternal God!" said George, kneeling on the grave of his poor friend; "oh, witness, that, from this hour, I will do *what one man can* to drive out this curse of slavery from my land!"

There is no monument to mark the last resting-place of our friend. He needs none! His Lord knows where he lies, and will raise him up, immortal, to appear with him when he shall appear in his glory.

Pity him not! Such a life and death is not for pity! Not in the riches of omnipotence is the chief glory of God; but in self-denying, suffering love! And blessed are the men whom he calls to fellowship with him, bearing their cross after him with patience. Of such it is written, "Blessed are they that mourn, for they shall be comforted."[1]

[The story of George, Eliza, and Harry is concluded in the novel's final chapters. The family is reunited, and they successfully make their way to Canada, where they live in peace for several years. Over time, however, George Harris finds himself uncomfortable with his position in

---

[1] *Blessed are ... be comforted* See Matthew 5.4, from Jesus' Sermon on the Mount.

a predominantly white community and yearning to connect with his African ancestry. The Harrises ultimately make their way to Liberia, an American colony in west Africa founded by whites as a settlement for free blacks.]

CHAPTER 45
CONCLUDING REMARKS[1]

The writer has often been inquired of, by correspondents from different parts of the country, whether this narrative is a true one; and to these inquiries she will give one general answer.

The separate incidents that compose the narrative are, to a very great extent, authentic, occurring, many of them, either under her own observation, or that of her personal friends. She or her friends have observed characters the counterpart of almost all that are here introduced; and many of the sayings are word for word as heard herself, or reported to her.

The personal appearance of Eliza, the character ascribed to her, are sketches drawn from life. The incorruptible fidelity, piety and honesty, of Uncle Tom, had more than one development, to her personal knowledge. Some of the most deeply tragic and romantic, some of the most terrible incidents, have also their parallel in reality. The incident of the mother's crossing the Ohio River on the ice is a well-known fact. The story of "old Prue," in the second volume, was an incident that fell under the personal observation of a brother of the writer,[2] then collecting-clerk to a large mercantile house in New Orleans. From the same source was derived the character of the planter Legree. Of him her brother thus wrote, speaking of visiting his plantation, on a collecting tour: "He actually made me feel of his fist, which was like a blacksmith's hammer, or a nodule of iron, telling me that it was 'calloused with knocking down niggers.' When I left the plantation, I drew a long breath, and felt as if I had escaped from an ogre's den."

---

1 This final chapter was written for the book publication of *Uncle Tom's Cabin*, following its serialization in *The National Era*.

2 *a brother of the writer* Charles Beecher (1815–1900), who wrote to his family about his experiences and observations while traveling around New Orleans as part of his work for a cotton commission warehouse.

That the tragical fate of Tom, also, has too many times had its parallel, there are living witnesses, all over our land, to testify. Let it be remembered that in all southern states it is a principle of jurisprudence that no person of colored lineage can testify in a suit against a white, and it will be easy to see that such a case may occur, wherever there is a man whose passions outweigh his interests, and a slave who has manhood or principle enough to resist his will. There is, actually, nothing to protect the slave's life, but the *character* of the master. Facts too shocking to be contemplated occasionally force their way to the public ear, and the comment that one often hears made on them is more shocking than the thing itself. It is said, "Very likely such cases may now and then occur, but they are no sample of general practice." If the laws of New England were so arranged that a master could *now and then* torture an apprentice to death, without a possibility of being brought to justice, would it be received with equal composure? Would it be said, "These cases are rare, and no samples of general practice"? This injustice is an *inherent* one in the slave system—it cannot exist without it.

The public and shameless sale of beautiful mulatto and quadroon girls has acquired a notoriety, from the incidents following the capture of the *Pearl*.[1] We extract the following from the speech of Hon. Horace Mann,[2] one of the legal counsel for the defendants in that case. He says: "In that company of seventy-six persons, who attempted, in 1848, to escape from the District of Columbia in the schooner *Pearl*, and whose officers I assisted in defending, there were several young and healthy girls, who had those peculiar attractions of form and feature which connoisseurs prize so highly. Elizabeth Russel was one of them. She immediately fell into the slave-trader's fangs, and was doomed for the New Orleans market. The hearts of those that saw her were touched with pity for her fate. They offered eighteen hundred dollars to redeem her; and some there were who offered to give, that would not have much left after the gift; but the

---

1 *the incidents ... the Pearl* In April 1848, seventy-six enslaved persons living in Washington, D.C. attempted to escape to the free state of New Jersey aboard the schooner *The Pearl*, in a plot orchestrated by a group of white and African American abolitionists. The endeavor was largely unsuccessful, with most of the escapees subsequently sold into the Deep South; six individuals, however, had their freedom purchased with funds raised by the Beecher family.

2 *Horace Mann* Massachusetts politician and educational reformer (1796–1859).

fiend of a slave-trader was inexorable. She was dispatched to New Orleans; but, when about halfway there, God had mercy on her, and smote her with death. There were two girls named Edmundson in the same company. When about to be sent to the same market, an older sister went to the shambles,[1] to plead with the wretch who owned them, for the love of God, to spare his victims. He bantered her, telling what fine dresses and fine furniture they would have. 'Yes,' she said, 'that may do very well in this life, but what will become of them in the next?' They too were sent to New Orleans; but were afterwards redeemed, at an enormous ransom, and brought back." Is it not plain, from this, that the histories of Emmeline and Cassy may have many counterparts?

Justice, too, obliges the author to state that the fairness of mind and generosity attributed to St. Clare are not without a parallel, as the following anecdote will show. A few years since, a young southern gentleman was in Cincinnati with a favorite servant, who had been his personal attendant from a boy. The young man took advantage of this opportunity to secure his own freedom, and fled to the protection of a Quaker[2] who was quite noted in affairs of this kind. The owner was exceedingly indignant. He had always treated the slave with such indulgence, and his confidence in his affection was such, that he believed he must have been practised upon[3] to induce him to revolt from him. He visited the Quaker in high anger; but, being possessed of uncommon candor and fairness, was soon quieted by his arguments and representations. It was a side of the subject which he never had heard—never had thought on; and he immediately told the Quaker that if his slave would, to his own face, say that it was his desire to be free, he would liberate him. An interview was forthwith procured, and Nathan was asked by his young master whether he had ever had any reason to complain of his treatment, in any respect.

"No, Mas'r," said Nathan; "you've always been good to me."

"Well, then, why do you want to leave me?"

"Mas'r may die, and then who get me? I'd rather be a free man."

After some deliberation, the young master replied, "Nathan, in your place, I think I should feel very much so, myself. You are free."

---

1   *shambles*   Place of carnage or misery; literally, a slaughterhouse.
2   *a Quaker*   Many Quakers were ardent abolitionists.
3   *practised upon*   Deceived.

He immediately made him out free papers; deposited a sum of money in the hands of the Quaker, to be judiciously used in assisting him to start in life, and left a very sensible and kind letter of advice to the young man. That letter was for some time in the writer's hands.

The author hopes she has done justice to that nobility, generosity, and humanity, which in many cases characterize individuals at the South. Such instances save us from utter despair of our kind. But, she asks any person who knows the world, are such characters *common* anywhere?

For many years of her life, the author avoided all reading upon or allusion to the subject of slavery, considering it as too painful to be inquired into, and one which advancing light and civilization would certainly live down. But, since the legislative act of 1850, when she heard, with perfect surprise and consternation, Christian and humane people actually recommending the remanding escaped fugitives into slavery, as a duty binding on good citizens—when she heard, on all hands, from kind, compassionate and estimable people, in the free states of the North, deliberations and discussions as to what Christian duty could be on this head—she could only think, These men and Christians cannot know what slavery is; if they did, such a question could never be open for discussion. And from this arose a desire to exhibit it in a *living dramatic reality*. She has endeavored to show it fairly, in its best and its worst phases. In its *best* aspect, she has, per-haps, been successful; but, oh! who shall say what yet remains untold in that valley and shadow of death,[1] that lies the other side?

To you, generous, noble-minded men and women, of the South— you, whose virtue, and magnanimity, and purity of character, are the greater for the severer trial it has encountered—to you is her appeal. Have you not, in your own secret souls, in your own private con-versings, felt that there are woes and evils, in this accursed system, far beyond what are here shadowed, or can be shadowed? Can it be otherwise? Is *man* ever a creature to be trusted with wholly irrespon-sible power? And does not the slave system, by denying the slave all legal right of testimony, make every individual owner an irresponsible despot? Can anybody fail to make the inference what the practical

---

1   *that valley ... of death* See Psalm 23.4, as well as Bunyan's *The Pilgrim's Progress*, in which the protagonist must traverse the Valley of the Shadow of Death on his way to the Celestial City.

result will be? If there is, as we admit, a public sentiment among you, men of honor, justice and humanity, is there not also another kind of public sentiment among the ruffian, the brutal and debased? And cannot the ruffian, the brutal, the debased, by slave law, own just as many slaves as the best and purest? Are the honorable, the just, the high-minded and compassionate, the majority anywhere in this world? The slave trade is now, by American law, considered as piracy. But a slave trade as systematic as ever was carried on on the coast of Africa, is an inevitable attendant and result of American slavery.[1] And its heartbreak and its horrors, *can* they be told?

The writer has given only a faint shadow, a dim picture, of the anguish and despair that are, at this very moment, riving thousands of hearts, shattering thousands of families, and driving a helpless and sensitive race to frenzy and despair. There are those living who know the mothers whom this accursed traffic has driven to the murder of their children; and themselves seeking in death a shelter from woes more dreaded than death. Nothing of tragedy can be written, can be spoken, can be conceived, that equals the frightful reality of scenes daily and hourly acting on our shores, beneath the shadow of American law, and the shadow of the cross of Christ.

And now, men and women of America, is this a thing to be trifled with, apologized for, and passed over in silence? Farmers of Massachusetts, of New Hampshire, of Vermont, of Connecticut, who read this book by the blaze of your winter-evening fire—strong-hearted, generous sailors and ship-owners of Maine—is this a thing for you to countenance and encourage? Brave and generous men of New York, farmers of rich and joyous Ohio, and ye of the wide prairie states—answer, is this a thing for you to protect and countenance? And you, mothers of America—you who have learned, by the cradles of your own children, to love and feel for all mankind—by the sacred love you bear your child; by your joy in his beautiful, spotless infancy; by the motherly pity and tenderness with which you guide his growing years; by the anxieties of his education; by the prayers you breathe for his soul's eternal good—I beseech you, pity the mother who has all

---

1   *a slave trade ... slavery* I.e., the domestic or internal slave trade, which only strengthened after the abolition of the international slave trade, and meant that enslaved women were even more likely to be forced to bear children for their owners in order to sustain the trade.

your affections, and not one legal right to protect, guide, or educate, the child of her bosom! By the sick hour of your child; by those dying eyes, which you can never forget; by those last cries, that wrung your heart when you could neither help nor save; by the desolation of that empty cradle, that silent nursery—I beseech you, pity those mothers that are constantly made childless by the American slave trade! And say, mothers of America, is this a thing to be defended, sympathized with, passed over in silence?

Do you say that the people of the free states have nothing to do with it, and can do nothing? Would to God this were true! But it is not true. The people of the free states have defended, encouraged, and participated; and are more guilty for it, before God, than the South, in that they have *not* the apology of education or custom.

If the mothers of the free states had all felt as they should, in times past, the sons of the free states would not have been the holders, and, proverbially, the hardest masters of slaves; the sons of the free states would not have connived at the extension of slavery in our national body; the sons of the free states would not, as they do, trade the souls and bodies of men as an equivalent to money, in their mercantile dealings. There are multitudes of slaves temporarily owned, and sold again, by merchants in northern cities; and shall the whole guilt or obloquy of slavery fall only on the South?

Northern men, northern mothers, northern Christians, have something more to do than denounce their brethren at the South; they have to look to the evil among themselves.

But, what can any individual do? Of that, every individual can judge. There is one thing that every individual can do—they can see to it that *they feel right.* An atmosphere of sympathetic influence encircles every human being; and the man or woman who *feels* strongly, healthily and justly, on the great interests of humanity, is a constant benefactor to the human race. See, then, to your sympathies in this matter! Are they in harmony with the sympathies of Christ? or are they swayed and perverted by the sophistries of worldly policy?

Christian men and women of the North! still further, you have another power; you can *pray!* Do you believe in prayer? or has it become an indistinct apostolic[1] tradition? You pray for the heathen

---

1   *apostolic*   Of the time of the apostles; i.e., ancient.

abroad; pray also for the heathen at home. And pray for those distressed Christians whose whole chance of religious improvement is an accident of trade and sale; from whom any adherence to the morals of Christianity is, in many cases, an impossibility, unless they have given them, from above, the courage and grace of martyrdom.

But, still more. On the shores of our free states are emerging the poor, shattered, broken remnants of families—men and women, escaped, by miraculous providences, from the surges of slavery—feeble in knowledge, and, in many cases, infirm in moral constitution, from a system which confounds and confuses every principle of Christianity and morality. They come to seek a refuge among you; they come to seek education, knowledge, Christianity.

What do you owe to these poor unfortunates, oh Christians? Does not every American Christian owe to the African race some effort at reparation for the wrongs that the American nation has brought upon them? Shall the doors of churches and schoolhouses be shut upon them? Shall states arise and shake them out? Shall the church of Christ hear in silence the taunt that is thrown at them, and shrink away from the helpless hand that they stretch out; and, by her silence, encourage the cruelty that would chase them from our borders? If it must be so, it will be a mournful spectacle. If it must be so, the country will have reason to tremble, when it remembers that the fate of nations is in the hands of One who is very pitiful, and of tender compassion.

Do you say, "We don't want them here; let them go to Africa"?

That the providence of God has provided a refuge in Africa[1] is, indeed, a great and noticeable fact; but that is no reason why the church of Christ should throw off that responsibility to this outcast race which her profession demands of her.

To fill up Liberia with an ignorant, inexperienced, half-barbarized race, just escaped from the chains of slavery, would be only to prolong,

---

1 *a refuge in Africa* Stowe alludes to Liberia, which was established as a colony for freed African Americans in 1822 by the (white-led) American Colonization Society. Stowe, like many white abolitionists, supported colonization early in her career, though the movement was intensely controversial, especially amongst African Americans; perhaps most damningly, a number of the Society's original members were slaveowners who hoped that by encouraging free African Americans to leave the United States they could protect the institution of slavery from their influence. Stowe eventually renounced her support of colonization.

for ages, the period of struggle and conflict which attends the inception of new enterprises. Let the church of the north receive these poor sufferers in the spirit of Christ; receive them to the educating advantages of Christian republican society and schools, until they have attained to somewhat of a moral and intellectual maturity, and then assist them in their passage to those shores, where they may put in practice the lessons they have learned in America.

There is a body of men at the north, comparatively small, who have been doing this; and, as the result, this country has already seen examples of men, formerly slaves, who have rapidly acquired property, reputation, and education. Talent has been developed, which, considering the circumstances, is certainly remarkable; and, for moral traits of honesty, kindness, tenderness of feeling—for heroic efforts and self-denials, endured for the ransom of brethren and friends yet in slavery—they have been remarkable to a degree that, considering the influence under which they were born, is surprising.

The writer has lived, for many years, on the frontier-line of slave states, and has had great opportunities of observation among those who formerly were slaves. They have been in her family as servants; and, in default of any other school to receive them, she has, in many cases, had them instructed in a family school, with her own children. She has also the testimony of missionaries, among the fugitives in Canada, in coincidence with her own experience; and her deductions, with regard to the capabilities of the race, are encouraging in the highest degree.

The first desire of the emancipated slave, generally, is for *education*. There is nothing that they are not willing to give or do to have their children instructed; and, so far as the writer has observed herself, or taken the testimony of teachers among them, they are remarkably intelligent and quick to learn. The results of schools, founded for them by benevolent individuals in Cincinnati, fully establish this.

The author gives the following statement of facts, on the authority of Professor C.E. Stowe, then of Lane Seminary, Ohio, with regard to emancipated slaves, now resident in Cincinnati;[1] given to show the

---

1   *The author ... Cincinnati* When Stowe moved to Maine in 1850, her husband Calvin Ellis Stowe (1802–86) was still teaching at Lane Theological Seminary in Cincinnati, which enabled him to gather these accounts.

capability of the race, even without any very particular assistance or encouragement.

The initial letters alone are given. They are all residents of Cincinnati.

"B——. Furniture maker; twenty years in the city; worth ten thousand dollars, all his own earnings; a Baptist.

"C——. Full black; stolen from Africa; sold in New Orleans; been free fifteen years; paid for himself six hundred dollars; a farmer; owns several farms in Indiana; Presbyterian; probably worth fifteen or twenty thousand dollars, all earned by himself.

"K——. Full black; dealer in real estate; worth thirty thousand dollars; about forty years old; free six years; paid eighteen hundred dollars for his family; member of the Baptist church; received a legacy from his master, which he has taken good care of, and increased.

"G——. Full black; coal dealer; about thirty years old; worth eighteen thousand dollars; paid for himself twice, being once defrauded to the amount of sixteen hundred dollars; made all his money by his own efforts—much of it while a slave, hiring his time of his master, and doing business for himself; a fine, gentlemanly fellow.

"W——. Three-fourths black; barber and waiter; from Kentucky; nineteen years free; paid for self and family over three thousand dollars; deacon in the Baptist church.

"G.D——. Three-fourths black; white-washer; from Kentucky; nine years free; paid fifteen hundred dollars for self and family; recently died, aged sixty; worth six thousand dollars."

Professor Stowe says, "With all these, except G——, I have been, for some years, personally acquainted, and make my statements from my own knowledge."

The writer well remembers an aged colored woman who was employed as a washerwoman in her father's family. The daughter of this woman married a slave. She was a remarkably active and capable young woman, and, by her industry and thrift, and the most persevering self-denial, raised nine hundred dollars for her husband's freedom, which she paid, as she raised it, into the hands of his master. She yet wanted[1] a hundred dollars of the price, when he died. She never recovered any of the money.

---

1 *wanted* Lacked.

These are but few facts, among multitudes which might be adduced, to show the self-denial, energy, patience, and honesty, which the slave has exhibited in a state of freedom.

And let it be remembered that these individuals have thus bravely succeeded in conquering for themselves comparative wealth and social position, in the face of every disadvantage and discouragement. The colored man, by the law of Ohio, cannot be a voter,[1] and, till within a few years, was even denied the right of testimony in legal suits with the white. Nor are these instances confined to the State of Ohio. In all states of the Union we see men, but yesterday burst from the shackles of slavery, who, by a self-educating force, which cannot be too much admired, have risen to highly respectable stations in society. Pennington, among clergymen, Douglas and Ward,[2] among editors, are well known instances.

If this persecuted race, with every discouragement and disadvantage, have done thus much, how much more they might do, if the Christian church would act towards them in the spirit of her Lord!

This is an age of the world when nations are trembling and convulsed. A mighty influence is abroad, surging and heaving the world, as with an earthquake. And is America safe? Every nation that carries in its bosom great and unredressed injustice has in it the elements of this last convulsion.

For what is this mighty influence thus rousing in all nations and languages those groanings that cannot be uttered, for man's freedom and equality?

O, Church of Christ, read the signs of the times![3] Is not this power

---

1   *The colored man ... voter*   By the 1850s, black men were legally allowed to vote in state and municipal elections in Maine, Massachusetts, Rhode Island, New Hampshire, Vermont, and, to a very limited degree, Wisconsin. Numerous other states had allowed some degree of black (male) suffrage at certain points following the American Revolution, but in all these states the right was later rescinded. Even where black men could legally vote, harsh discrimination and violence often prevented them from exercising their supposed right.

2   *Pennington ... Ward*   Stowe lists three men who escaped from slavery in Maryland to become well-known public figures: James William Charles Pennington (1809–71), a prominent pastor and publisher; Frederick Douglass (1817–95), a renowned abolitionist author, orator, and newspaper editor; and Samuel Ringgold Ward (1817–66), a newspaper editor and schoolteacher.

3   *O ... the times!*   See Matthew 16.3: "And in the morning, It will be foul weather today: for the sky is red and lowering. O ye hypocrites, ye can discern the face of the sky; but can ye not discern the signs of the times?"

the spirit of Him whose kingdom is yet to come, and whose will to be done on earth as it is in heaven?

But who may abide the day of his appearing? "For that day shall burn as an oven: and he shall appear as a swift witness against those that oppress the hireling in his wages, the widow and the fatherless, and that *turn aside the stranger in his right*: and he shall break in pieces the oppressor."[1]

Are not these dread words for a nation bearing in her bosom so mighty an injustice? Christians! every time that you pray that the kingdom of Christ may come, can you forget that prophecy associates, in dread fellowship, the *day of vengeance* with the year of his redeemed?

A day of grace is yet held out to us. Both North and South have been guilty before God; and the *Christian church* has a heavy account to answer. Not by combining together to protect injustice and cruelty, and making a common capital of sin, is this Union to be saved—but by repentance, justice and mercy; for, not surer is the eternal law by which the millstone sinks[2] in the ocean, than that stronger law, by which injustice and cruelty shall bring on nations the wrath of Almighty God!

—1852

---

1 *For that day ... oppressor* See Malachi 4.1: "For, behold, the day cometh, that shall burn as an oven; and all the proud, yea, and all that do wickedly, shall be stubble: and the day that cometh shall burn them up, saith the Lord of hosts, that it shall leave them neither root nor branch."

2 *the millstone sinks* See Matthew 18.6: "But whoso shall offend one of these little ones which believe in me, it were better for him that a millstone were hanged about his neck, and that he were drowned in the depth of the sea"; Luke 17.2: "It were better for him that a millstone were hanged about his neck, and he cast into the sea, than that he should offend one of these little ones"; and Revelation 18.21: "And a mighty angel took up a stone like a great millstone, and cast it into the sea, saying, Thus with violence shall that great city Babylon be thrown down, and shall be found no more at all."

In Context

American Slavery: Contemporary Accounts

from Theodore Dwight Weld, Angelina Grimké Weld, and Sarah Grimké, *American Slavery as It Is: Testimony of a Thousand Witnesses* (1839)

A compendious, impassioned compilation of firsthand testimony about slavery, *American Slavery as It Is* influenced the development of the American abolitionist movement more than quite possibly any other single work. The degree of the book's importance can be measured by the fact that its primary rival for the title of most influential abolitionist work, *Uncle Tom's Cabin*, relied heavily on it. The book was co-authored by Theodore Dwight Weld (1803–95), a prominent abolitionist during the movement's formative years in the 1830s and 40s, and the Grimké sisters, Angelina (1805–79) and Sarah (1792–1873), antislavery activists originally from South Carolina (Angelina Grimké was also Weld's wife). Weld and the Grimkés put together the book largely from numerous direct descriptions of, or examples of, slavery's brutality, most of them written by observers in the slave states and especially by enslavers themselves; newspaper advertisements offering rewards for fugitive enslaved people were a particularly useful resource. (The book emphasized the accounts of enslavers over those of enslaved people, because, as its authors put it, "That [enslavers] should utter falsehoods, for the sake of proclaiming their own infamy, is not probable.") The book's impact thus derived not just from its array of factual evidence about what slavery was actually like, but specifically from the way in which it derived this evidence in large part from enslavers' own words. Stowe references the work frequently in *A Key to Uncle Tom's Cabin* (1853), her compendium of documents proving the veracity of her own fictionalized portrait of slavery.

It is assumed by slaveholders that "public opinion" at the ... South[1] so frowns on cruelty to the slaves, that *fear of disgrace* would restrain from the infliction of it, were there no other consideration.

Now, that this is sheer fiction is shown by the fact that the newspapers in the slaveholding states teem with advertisements for runaway slaves, in which the masters and mistresses describe their men and women as having been "branded with a hot iron," on their "cheeks," "jaws," "breasts," "arms," "legs," and "thighs"; also as "scarred," "very much scarred," "cut up," "marked," etc. "with the whip," also with "iron collars on," "chains," "bars of iron," "fetters," "bells," "horns,"[2] "shackles," etc. They also describe them as having been wounded by "buckshot," "rifle-balls," etc. fired at them by their "owners," and others when in pursuit; also, as having "notches" cut in their ears, the tops or bottoms of their ears "cut off," or "slit," or "one ear cut off," or "both ears cut off," etc. etc. The masters and mistresses who thus advertise their runaway slaves coolly sign their names to their advertisements, giving the street and number of their residences, if in cities, their post office address, etc. if in the country; thus making public proclamation as widely as possible that *they* "brand," "scar," "gash," "cut up," etc. the flesh of their slaves; load them with irons, cut off their ears, etc.; they speak of these things with the utmost *sang froid*,[3] not seeming to think it possible that any one will esteem them at all the less because of these outrages upon their slaves; further, these advertisements swarm in many of the largest and most widely circulated political and commercial papers that are published in the slave states. The editors of those papers constitute the main body of the literati of the slave states; they move in the highest circle of society, are among the "popular" men in the community, and *as a class*, are more influential than any other; yet these editors publish these advertisements with iron indifference. So far from proclaiming

---

1   *at the South*   I.e., in the South.
2   *bells, horns*   Enslaved people—especially those who had previously attempted to escape— were sometimes forced to wear metal collars with bells attached, often known as a "bell and horns," to prevent further escape attempts. Moses Roper's *Narrative of the Adventures and Escape of Moses Roper, from American Slavery* (1838) described the use of "iron horns, with bells, attached to the back of the slave's neck," calling such implements (which could be several feet in height) an "instrument of torture."
3   *sang froid*   French: cold blood.

to such felons, homicides, and murderers, that they will not be their bloodhounds, to hunt down the innocent and mutilated victims who have escaped from their torture, they freely furnish them with every facility,[1] become their accomplices and share their spoils; and instead of outraging "public opinion" by doing it, they are the men after its own heart, its organs, its representatives, its *self.*

To show that the "public opinion" of the slave states towards the slaves is absolutely *diabolical,* we will insert a few, out of a multitude, of similar advertisements from a variety of southern papers now before us.

The North Carolina Standard, of July 18, 1838, contains the following:

"TWENTY DOLLARS REWARD. Ran away from the subscriber, a negro woman and two children; the woman is tall and black, and *a few days before she went off,* I burnt her with a hot iron on the left side of her face; I tried to make the letter M, *and she kept a cloth over her head and face and a fly bonnet on her head so as to cover the burn;* her children are both boys, the oldest is in his seventh year; he is a *mulatto*[2] and has blue eyes; the youngest is black and is in his fifth year. The woman's name is Betty, commonly called Bet.

MICAJAH RICKS.

Nash County, July 7, 1838."

Hear the wretch tell his story, with as much indifference as if he were describing the cutting of his initials in the bark of a tree.

"I burnt her with a hot iron on the left side of her face," "I tried to make the letter M," and this he says in a newspaper, and puts his name to it, and the editor of the paper, who is also its proprietor, publishes it for him and pockets his fee. ...

J.P. Ashford advertises as follows in the "Natchez Courier," August 24, 1838.

"Ran away, a negro girl called Mary, has a small scar over her eye, a *good many teeth missing,* the letter A. *is branded on her cheek and forehead."*

---

1 *facility* Opportunity, accommodation.

2 *mulatto* Term, now universally regarded as offensive, that was widely used in the nineteenth century to classify individuals of mixed racial background—typically, someone with one white parent and one parent of African descent.

A.B. Metcalf thus advertises a woman in the same paper, June 15, 1838.

"Ran away, Mary, a black woman, has a *scar* on her back and right arm near the shoulder, *caused by a rifle ball.*"

John Henderson, in the "Grand Gulf Advertiser," August 29, 1838, advertises Betsey.

"Ran away, a black woman Betsey, has an *iron bar on her right leg.*"

Robert Nicoll, whose residence is in Mobile, in Dauphin street, between Emmanuel and Conception streets, thus advertises a woman in the "Mobile Commercial Advertiser."

"TEN DOLLARS REWARD will be given for my negro woman Liby. The said Liby is about 30 years old, and VERY MUCH SCARRED ABOUT THE NECK AND EARS, occasioned by whipping, had on a handkerchief tied round her ears, as she COMMONLY wears it to HIDE THE SCARS."

To show that slaveholding brutality now is the same that it was the eighth of a century ago, we publish the following advertisement from the "Charleston (S.C.) Courier," of 1825.

"TWENTY DOLLARS REWARD—Ran away from the subscriber, on the 14th instant,[1] a negro girl named Molly.

"The said girl was sold by Messrs. Wm. Payne & Sons, as the property of an estate of a Mr. Gearrall, and purchased by a Mr. Moses, and sold by him to a Thomas Prisley, of Edgefield District, of whom I bought her on the 17th of April, 1819. She is 16 or 17 years of age, slim made, LATELY BRANDED ON THE LEFT CHEEK, THUS, R, and a piece taken off of her ear on the same side; the same letter on the inside of both her legs.

ABNER ROSS, Fairfield District."

But instead of filling pages with similar advertisements, illustrating the horrible brutality of slaveholders towards their slaves, the reader is referred to the preceding pages of this work, to the scores of advertisements written by slaveholders, printed by slaveholders, published by slaveholders, in newspapers edited by slaveholders, and patronized by slaveholders; advertisements describing not only men and boys, but women, aged and middle-aged, matrons and girls of tender years, their necks chafed with iron collars with prongs, their limbs

---

1   *instant*   Anglicization of the Latin "instante mense," meaning "[of] this month."

galled with iron rings, and chains, and bars of iron, iron hobbles and shackles, all parts of their persons scarred with the lash, and branded with hot irons, and torn with rifle bullets, pistol balls and buck shot, and gashed with knives, their eyes out, their ears cut off, their teeth drawn out, and their bones broken. He is referred also to the cool and shocking indifference with which these slaveholders, "gentlemen" and "ladies," Reverends, and Honorables, and Excellencies, write and print, and publish and pay, and take money for, and read and circulate, and sanction, such infernal barbarity. Let the reader ponder all this, and then lay it to heart, that this is that "public opinion" of the slaveholders which protects their slaves from all injury, and is an effectual guarantee of personal security. ...

But we are not yet quite ready to dismiss this protector, "Public Opinion." To illustrate the hardened brutality with which slaveholders regard their slaves, the shameless and apparently unconscious indecency with which they speak of their female slaves, examine their persons, and describe them, under their own signatures, in newspapers, hand-bills, etc. just as they would describe the marks of cattle and swine, on all parts of their bodies; we will make a few extracts from southern papers. Reader, as we proceed to these extracts, remember our motto—"True humanity consists *not* in a squeamish ear."

Mr. P. Abdie, of New Orleans, advertises in the New Orleans Bee, of January 29, 1838, for one of his female slaves, as follows;

"Ran away, the negro wench[1] named Betsey, aged about 22 years, handsome-faced, and good countenance; having the marks of the whip behind her neck, and several others on her rump. The above reward ($10) will be given to whoever will bring that wench to P. Abdie." ...

Mr. William Robinson, Georgetown, District of Columbia, advertised for his slave in the National Intelligencer, of Washington City, Oct. 2, 1837, as follows:

"Eloped from my residence a young negress, 22 years old, of a chesnut, or brown color. She has a very singular mark—this mark, to the best of my recollection, covers a part of her *breasts*,

---

1   *wench*   In American usage, this word, a now-derogatory term for a female servant, was exclusively applied to black women.

body, and *limbs*; and when her neck and arms are uncovered, is very perceptible; she has been frequently seen east and south of the Capitol Square, and is harbored by ill-disposed persons, of every complexion, for her services."

Mr. John C. Beasley, near Huntsville, Alabama, thus advertises a young girl of eighteen, in the Huntsville Democrat, of August 1st, 1837. "Ran away Maria, about 18 years old, *very far advanced with child.*" He then offers a reward to any one who will commit this young girl, in this condition, *to jail.* ...

The above are a few specimens of the gross[1] details, in describing the persons of females, of all ages, and the marks upon all parts of their bodies; proving incontestably, that slaveholders are in the habit not only of stripping their female slaves of their clothing, and inflicting punishment upon their "shrinking flesh,"[2] but of subjecting their naked persons to the most minute and revolting inspection, and then of publishing to the world the results of their examination, as well as the scars left by their own inflictions upon them, their length, size, and exact position on the body; and all this without impairing in the least, the standing in the community of the shameless wretches who thus proclaim their own abominations. That such things should not at all affect the standing of such persons in society, is certainly no marvel: how could they affect it, when the same communities enact laws *requiring* their own legal officers to inspect minutely the persons and bodily marks of all slaves taken up as runaways, and to publish in the newspapers a particular description of all such marks and peculiarities of their persons, their size, appearance, position on the body, etc. Yea, verily, when the "public opinion" of the community, in the solemn form of law, commands jailors, sheriffs, captains of police, etc. to divest of their clothing aged matrons and young girls, minutely examine their naked persons, and publish the results of their examination—who can marvel, that the same "public opinion" should tolerate the slaveholders themselves, in doing the same things to their own

---

1   *gross*   Repulsively immoral or uncivilized.
2   *shrinking flesh*   See the abolitionist poet John Greenleaf Whittier's "Stanzas," later retitled "Expostulation" (1834): "What, ho!—*our* countrymen in chains! / The whip on woman's shrinking flesh!"

property, which they have appointed legal officers to do as their proxies.[1] ...

---

1 [Authors' note]   As a sample of these laws, we give the following extract from one of the laws of Maryland, where slaveholding "public opinion" exists in its mildest form.

"It shall be the duty of the sheriffs of the several counties of this state, upon any runaway servant or slave being committed to his custody, to cause the same to be advertised, etc. and to make particular and minute descriptions of the *person and bodily marks* of such runaway." –*Laws of Maryland of* 1802, Chap. 96, Sec. 1 and 2.

That the sheriffs, jailors, etc. do not neglect this part of their official "duty" is plain from the minute description which they give in the advertisements of marks upon all parts of the persons of females, as well as males; and also from the occasional declaration "no scars discoverable on any part," or "no marks discoverable *about* her"; which last is taken from an advertisement in the Milledgeville (Geo.) Journal, June 26, 1838, signed "T.S. Densler, Jailor."

from *The Narratives of Fugitive Slaves in Canada* (1856)

The only collection ever compiled of first-hand interviews of black people who had escaped slavery by taking the Underground Railroad to Canada, *The Narratives of Fugitive Slaves in Canada* was published in 1856 by the Massachusetts abolitionist Benjamin Drew (1812–1903). The book—the full title of which is *A North-Side View of Slavery. The Refugee: or the Narratives of Fugitive Slaves in Canada*—was partially a response to *A South-Side View of Slavery* (1855), a book by Drew's fellow white Massachusetts writer Nehemiah Adams that described the supposed moral and religious benefits that enslavement conferred on African Americans and criticized the abolition movement's ostensible radicalism. In order to rebut Adams's arguments, Drew traveled widely in Canada West (the present-day Canadian province of Ontario), interviewing some of the thousands of escapees from slavery who had settled there and recording their accounts of their lives in slavery, their journeys to freedom, and their experiences in Canada.

WILLIAM JOHNSON

I look upon slavery as I do upon a deadly poison. The slaves are not contented nor happy in their lot. Neither on the farm where I was in Virginia, nor in the neighborhood were the slaves satisfied. The man I belonged to did not give us enough to eat. My feet were frostbitten on my way North, but I would rather have died on the way than to go back.

It would not do to stop at all about our work—if the people should try to get a little rest, there would be a cracking spell amongst them.[1] I have had to go through a great deal of affliction; I have been compelled to work when I was sick. I used to have rheumatism,[2] and could not always do so much work as those who were well—then I would sometimes be whipped. I have never seen a runaway that wanted to go back—I have never heard of one.

I knew a very smart young man—he was a fellow-servant of mine, who had recently professed religion[3]—who was tied up by a quick-

---

1   *there would ... amongst them*   I.e., they would be beaten severely.
2   *rheumatism*   Term for a class of disorders affecting the joints, such as arthritis.
3   *professed religion*   Publicly embraced Christianity.

tempered overseer, and whipped terribly. He died not long after, and the people there believed it was because of the whipping. Some of the slaves told the owner, but he did not discharge the overseer. He will have to meet it at the day of judgment.

I had grown up quite large, before I thought anything about liberty. The fear of being sold South[1] had more influence in inducing me to leave than any other thing. Master used to say, that if we didn't suit him, he would put us in his pocket quick—meaning he would sell us. He never gave me a great coat[2] in his life—he said he knew he ought to do it, but that he couldn't get ahead far enough. His son had a child by a colored woman, and he would have sold it—his own grandchild—if the other folks hadn't opposed it.

I have found good friends in Canada, but have been able to do no work on account of my frozen feet—I lost two toes from my right foot. My determination is to go to work as soon as I am able. I have been about among the colored people in St. Catharines[3] considerably, and have found them industrious and frugal. No person has offered me any liquor since I have been here: I have seen no colored person use it. I have been trying to learn to read since I came here, and I know a great many fugitives who are trying to learn.

Harriet Tubman[4]

I grew up like a neglected weed—ignorant of liberty, having no experience of it. Then I was not happy or contented: every time I saw a

---

1   *The fear ... South*   Conditions for enslaved people in the Deep South, where most large-scale cotton cultivation took place, were generally much worse than in the more northerly slave states; consequently, enslaved people in "Upper South" states such as Virginia greatly feared being sold to new enslavers in the Deep South.

2   *great coat*   Long, warm overcoat.

3   *St. Catharines*   Town in what is now the Canadian province of Ontario, not far from the U.S. border, that became a center of abolitionist activity and a place of refuge and settlement for enslaved people who took the Underground Railroad to Canada. By the mid-1850s, about 800 black people lived there, out of a total population of approximately 6,000.

4   *Harriet Tubman*   African American abolitionist and activist (c. 1822–1913) who was one of the most famous "conductors" on the Underground Railroad. After herself escaping from slavery in Maryland in 1849, she guided first her family and then numerous other enslaved people to freedom, for which she became known as "Moses." Tubman lived in St. Catharines from 1851 to 1858.

Harriet Tubman as she appeared during the Civil War, in which she served as a scout and spy for the U.S. Army. Tubman guided federal troops on an 1863 raid on plantations along the Combahee River in South Carolina, an action in which more than 750 enslaved people were freed. This image was printed as a frontispiece to *Scenes in the Life of Harriet Tubman* (1869).

HARRIET TUBMAN.

white man, I was afraid of being carried away. I had two sisters carried away in a chain-gang—one of them left two children. We were always uneasy. Now I've been free, I know what a dreadful condition slavery is. I have seen hundreds of escaped slaves, but I never saw one who was willing to go back and be a slave. I have no opportunity to see my friends in my native land. We would rather stay in our native land, if we could be as free there as we are here. I think slavery is the next thing to hell. If a person would send another into bondage, he would, it appears to me, be bad enough to send him into hell, if he could.

Mrs. Christopher Hamilton

I left Mississippi about fourteen years ago. I was raised a house servant, and was well used,[1] but I saw and heard a great deal of the cruelty of slavery. I saw more than I wanted to—I never want to see so much again. The slaveholders say their slaves are better off than if they were free, and that they prefer slavery to freedom. I do not, and never saw one that wished to go back. It would be a hard trial to make me a slave again. I had rather live in Canada, on one potato a day,

---

1 *well used* I.e., well treated.

than to live in the South with all the wealth they have got. I am now my own mistress, and need not work when I am sick. I can do my own thinkings, without having any one to think for me—to tell me when to come, what to do, and to sell me when they get ready. I wish I could have my relatives here. I might say a great deal more against slavery—nothing for it.

The people who raised me failed; they borrowed money and mortgaged me. I went to live with people whose ways did not suit me, and I thought it best to come to Canada, and live as I pleased.

BEN BLACKBURN

I was born in Maysville, Ky. I got here last Tuesday evening, and spent the Fourth of July in Canada. I felt as big and free as any man could feel, and I worked part of the day for my own benefit: I guess my master's time is out. Seventeen came away in the same gang that I did.

LYDIA ADAMS

[Mrs. A. lives in a very comfortable log-house on the road from Windsor to the Refugees' Home.[1]]

I am seventy or eighty years old. I was from Fairfax County, old Virginia. I was married and had three children when I left there for Wood County, where I lived twenty years: thence to Missouri, removing with my master's family. One by one they sent four of my children away from me, and sent them to the South: and four of my grandchildren all to the South but one. My oldest son, Daniel—then Sarah—all gone. "It's no use to cry about it," said one of the young women, "she's got to go." That's what she said when Esther went away. Esther's husband is here now, almost crazy about her: they took her and sold her away from him. They were all Methodist people—great Methodists—all belonged to the church. My master died—he left

---

1   *on the road ... Refugees' Home* In 1851, the Refugee Home Society, an international Canadian–American abolitionist organization, founded a settlement for fugitive enslaved people twenty miles from Windsor, a Canadian city directly across the U.S.–Canada border from Detroit, Michigan.

no testimony whether he was willing to go or not. ... I have been in Canada about one year, and like it as far as I have seen.

I've been wanting to be free ever since I was a little child. I said to them I didn't believe God ever meant me to be a slave, if my skin was black—at any rate not all my lifetime: why not have it as in old times, seven years' servants?[1] Master would say, "No, you were made to wait on white people: what was niggers[2] made for? Why, just to wait on us all."

I am afraid the slaveholders will go to a bad place—I am really afraid they will. I don't think any slaveholder can get to the kingdom.[3]

David Grier

I was born free in Maryland—was stolen and sold in Kentucky, when between eight and nine years old. In Kentucky I was set free by will,[4] and as they were trying to break the will up, some of my claimant's friends persuaded me to come off to Ohio. From Ohio, I came here on account of the oppressive laws demanding security for good behavior[5]—I was a stranger and could not give it. I had to leave my family in Kentucky.

I came in 1831. I have cleared land on lease for five or six years, then have to leave it, and go into the bush again. I worked so about thirteen years. I could do no better, and the white people, I believe, took advantage of it to get the land cleared. This has kept me poor. I guess I have cleared not short of seventy or eighty acres, and got no benefit. I have now six acres cleared.

---

1   *why not ... servants*   Reference to the practice of indentured servitude, widespread during the early colonial period, according to which the indentured person was obliged to perform unpaid labor for a fixed period of time—usually four to seven years—after which they would be free.

2   *niggers*   By the nineteenth century, as the context here suggests, "the n-word" (today universally acknowledged to be an utterly unacceptable expression of racism) had achieved its current, emphatically pejorative meaning in white American vernacular.

3   *the kingdom*   The kingdom of God—i.e., heaven.

4   *by will*   I.e., according to the written will of his enslaver after his enslaver's death.

5   *the oppressive ... good behavior*   Ohio's so-called "Black Laws," passed in 1807 in order to discourage African American migration to the state, required, among other things, that black residents find at least two people who would guarantee a surety of five hundred dollars—an amount of money designed to be prohibitively expensive—for their good behavior.

Runaway Advertisements

For nearly two centuries, advertisements for fugitive enslaved people—posted either by enslavers offering rewards for their return or by authorities announcing their capture—were an extremely common feature of American newspapers. Such advertisements began to appear almost as soon as the first newspapers were founded in the American colonies, and they continued to be printed—as the final example below indicates—even after the official abolition of slavery, as the so-called "Black Codes" (bodies of law introduced immediately after the Civil War in many Southern states that imposed numerous restrictions on the freedom of emancipated African Americans, including labor requirements) attempted to perpetuate legal African American servitude in a different form. The examples of runaway advertisements from the early and mid-nineteenth century included here provide insight into how enslavers thought about their "property"; they also offer small but valuable windows into the lives of enslaved people who may otherwise have left no trace in the historical record.

from the *Raleigh Register and North Carolina Weekly Advertiser* (19 May 1820)

RUNAWAY NEGROES

On the 10th of this month I bought at a Sheriff's sale, a stout black negro woman by the name of Sooky, considerably advanced in years, and her female child, called Olive, about four years old. They were sold as the property of Samuel G. Briggs, of Raleigh. They formerly belonged to a Miss Hart, who lived in Mr. Briggs's family, and were, as I understand, brought from Northampton County. They were at my house in the night after the sale, and apparently contented, but in the morning were missing. Whether they have attempted to make their way to Northampton; or whether they are harbored in or about Raleigh; or what has become of them, I am at a loss to conjecture.

Any useful information on this subject will be thankfully received; and I will give a reward of ten dollars to any person who will deliver the negroes to me, together with a suitable reward for any services beyond my present expectation.

HENRY POTTER.
Raleigh, May 18, 1820.

from the *Mobile Commercial Register* (2 June 1826)

NOTICE.

COMMITTED to the Jail of Mobile County, on the 23d of January last, a Negro Man, named GUY, five feet, eight inches high, with a scar on his right cheek, & also a small scar on the right side of his nose. Appears to be 35 years of age, says he came from Monticello, in Mississippi, to this place, and professes to be free. If he is not taken out in the time prescribed by law, he will be sold to pay jail fees.

James P. Bates,
Sheriff.

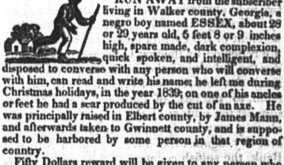

$100 Reward.

RUN AWAY from the subscriber living in Walker county, Georgia, a negro boy named ESSEX, about 28 or 29 years old, 5 feet 8 or 9 inches high, spare made, dark complexion, quick spoken, and intelligent, and disposed to converse with any person who will converse with him, can read and write his name; he left me during Christmas holidays, in the year 1839; on one of his ancles or feet he had a scar produced by the cut of an axe. He was principally raised in Elbert county, by James Mann, and afterwards taken to Gwinnett county, and is supposed to be harbored by some person in that region of country.

Fifty Dollars reward will be given to any person who will deliver said boy to me, or lodge him in some jail so that I get him, and Fifty Dollars more for the thief or harborer with sufficient testomony to convict him.

JAMES GORDEN.
Lafayette, Walker co., Ga., May 20, 1841.   50–4t
☞ The Southern Whig, Athens, will give the above four insertions, and forward their account to me.
J. G.

Runaway advertisement from the *Milledgeville Federal Union*, 8 June 1841.

from the *Milledgeville Federal Union* (1 November 1853)

$400 Reward.

RAN AWAY or stolen from my negro mart in Columbus,[1] in December last, TWO NEGRO MEN, one named Simon, the other named John, both carpenters. Simon is a yellow[2] copper-colored man, about forty years old, middling height, stout built, he has a scar in one corner of his mouth cut with a knife; since his departure he has been seen lurking about Mr. Bowin's in Coweta County, where he has a wife. He was purchased of E.C. Bowin in the neighborhood of Griffin; he may be in that section, or he may be in Carroll County. John is a mulatto about 45 or 50 years of age, middling height, stout built, in a previous runaway scrape he tried to pass himself off as a Frenchman, he can talk French a little. A few days previous to his leaving he received a severe scar on his forehead in a fight with a negro. I presume the scar is still to be seen; he is considerably gray, perhaps half gray, the black hairs are very black. It is not likely that he will acknowledge himself a slave. When he was apprehended before, he claimed to be a free Frenchman, and threatened to prosecute the party that took him for unlawfully detaining him. They were on the point of releasing him, when he was recognized by a carpenter that he had worked for. The above reward will be given for the delivery of the two negroes if stolen with sufficient proof to convict the thief, or ONE HUNDRED DOLLARS for either of the negroes, if delivered to me by the fifteenth of November next, or FIFTY DOLLARS, if delivered any time after the 15th of November or placed in any jail so that I can get them.

H.H. LOWE.

.

---

1   *negro mart* I.e., establishment of a trader and seller of enslaved people; *Columbus* City in western Georgia. Milledgeville, where this newspaper was published, was at the time the Georgia state capital.

2   *yellow* Term, now considered offensive except in African American usage, for a (usually mixed-race) African American with light brown skin.

from *The Daily Picayune* (26 March 1854)

TWENTY-FIVE DOLLARS REWARD—For the apprehension of the griffe[1] woman JOSEPHINE, about 34 years of age, of medium height, some teeth missing, and rather polite or modest. She formerly lived at Algiers,[2] and was until recently owned by Mr. J.C. Wilson at the Balize,[3] where she has a daughter about 16 years of age, of whom she appears to be very fond.

She left on Friday last, 18th inst.,[4] about 2 o'clock P.M., was dressed ordinarily, had no shoes on and appeared to be intoxicated.

The above reward will be paid by
MAJOR HARBIN, 169 Gravier street,
or at No. 30 Poydras street.

from the *Greensborough Patriot* (29 November 1867)

Runaway—GEORGE WASHINGTON, a negro boy aged about 15 years who was indentured to the undersigned by the Assistant Superintendent of the Freedmen's Bureau[5] on the 25th day of September, 1865, has absconded from my service and employment, without any just cause or provocation. This is to forewarn all persons against harboring or employing the said indentured boy, as in such cases the law will be rigidly enforced against those so employing or harboring the said George. And for the apprehension and return of him to me in Greensboro[6] a reasonable reward will be paid.

JAMES F. PEARCE.

---

1 *griffe*   Term for a person with three-quarters black and one-quarter white ancestry. Like all such nineteenth-century terms classifying people in terms of their racial background, it is today considered archaic and offensive.

2 *Algiers*   Neighborhood in New Orleans, Louisiana, the second-oldest neighborhood in the city.

3 *the Balize*   La Balize, Louisiana, a community at the mouth of the Mississippi River; it was abandoned in 1860 after being destroyed by a hurricane.

4 *inst.*   Abbreviation of Latin "instante mense," meaning "[of] this month."

5 *Freedmen's Bureau*   U.S. government agency established after the Civil War to provide essential services to formerly enslaved people ("freedmen"), including food, medical care, education, locating and communicating with family members, and employment.

6 *Greensboro*   Town in North Carolina.

Uncle Tom's Cabin and the Public

William Lloyd Garrison, *The Liberator* (26 March 1852)

William Lloyd Garrison (1805–79) was among the most vocal and influential white abolitionists of the nineteenth century. His newspaper, *The Liberator*, often featured reviews of abolitionist literature.

In the execution of her very familiar task, Mrs. Stowe has displayed rare descriptive powers, a familiar acquaintance with slavery under its best and its worst phases, uncommon moral and philosophical acumen, great facility of thought and expression, feelings and emotions of the strongest character. Intimate as we have been, for a score[1] of years, with the features and operations of the slave system, and often as we have listened to the recitals of its horrors from the lips of the poor hunted fugitives, we confess to the frequent moistening of our eyes, and the making of our heart grow liquid as water, and the trembling of every nerve within us, in the perusal of the incidents and scenes so vividly depicted in her pages. The effect of such a work upon all intelligent and humane minds coming in contact with it, and especially upon the rising generation in its plastic[2] condition, to awaken the strongest compassion for the oppressed and the utmost abhorrence of the system which grinds them to the dust, cannot be estimated: it must be prodigious, and therefore eminently serviceable in the tremendous conflict now waged for the immediate and entire suppression of slavery on the American soil.

The appalling liabilities which constantly impend over such slaves as have "kind and indulgent masters" are thrillingly illustrated in various personal narratives; especially in that of "Uncle Tom," over whose fate every reader will drop the scalding tear, and for whose character the highest reverence will be felt. No insult, no outrage, no suffering, could ruffle the Christlike meekness of his spirit, or shake the steadfastness of his faith. Towards his merciless oppressors he cherished no animosity, and breathed nothing of retaliation. Like his Lord and

---

1 *a score* Twenty.
2 *plastic* Malleable; able to be changed.

Master, he was willing to be "led as a lamb to slaughter,"[1] returning blessing for cursing, and anxious only for the salvation of his enemies. His character is sketched with great power and rare religious perception. It triumphantly exemplifies the nature, tendency, and results of CHRISTIAN NON-RESISTANCE.[2] We are curious to know whether Mrs. Stowe is a believer in the duty of non-resistance for the white man, under all possible outrage and peril, as well as for the black man; whether she is for self-defense on her own part, or that of her husband and friends or country, in case of malignant assault, or whether she impartially disarms all mankind in the name of Christ, be the danger or the suffering what it may. We are curious to know this, because our opinion of her, as a religious teacher, would be greatly strengthened or lessened as the inquiry might terminate. That all the slaves of the South ought, "if smitten on one cheek, to turn the other also"[3]—to repudiate all carnal weapons, shed no blood, "be obedient to their masters,"[4] wait for a peaceful deliverance, and abstain from any insurrectionary movements—is everywhere taken for granted, because the VICTIMS ARE BLACK. *They* cannot be animated by a Christian spirit and yet return blow for blow, or conspire for the destruction of their oppressors. *They* are required by the Bible to put away all wrath, to submit to every conceivable outrage without resistance, to suffer with Christ if they would reign with him. None of *their* advocates may seek to inspire *them* to imitate the example of the Greeks, the Poles, the Hungarians, our Revolutionary sires;[5] for such teaching would evince a most unchristian and bloodthirsty disposition. For *them* there is no hope of heaven unless *they* give the most literal interpretations to the

---

1   *led as ... to slaughter*   See Isaiah 53.6; while this phrase originally appears in the Hebrew Bible, or Old Testament, and refers to a Jewish servant, it was later interpreted by many Christians as being relevant to the story of Christ's execution.

2   *CHRISTIAN NON-RESISTANCE*   Garrison, as a Quaker, was strongly in favor of nonviolent resistance.

3   *if smitten ... other also*   In his Sermon on the Mount, Matthew 5.39, Christ instructs his followers to "resist not evil: but whosoever shall smite thee on thy right cheek, turn to him the other also."

4   *be obedient ... masters*   Various biblical passages exhort faithful servants to be obedient to their "masters," including Ephesians 6.5 and Titus 2.9.

5   *the Greeks, the Poles, the Hungarians*   All three of these nations had experienced democratic revolutions earlier in the nineteenth century;   *our Revolutionary sires*   I.e., the leaders of the American Revolution.

non-resisting injunctions contained in the Sermon on the Mount, touching the treatment of enemies. It is for *them*, though despoiled of all their rights and deprived of all protection, to "threaten not, but to commit the keeping of their souls to God in well-doing, as unto a faithful Creator."[1]

Nothing can be plainer than that such conduct is obligatory upon *them*; and when, through the operations of divine grace, they are enabled to manifest a spirit like this, it is acknowledged to be worthy of great commendation, as in the case of "Uncle Tom." But, for those whose skin is of a different complexion, the case is materially altered. When they are spit upon and buffeted, outraged and oppressed, talk not then of a non-resisting Saviour—it is fanaticism! Talk not of overcoming evil with good—it is madness! Talk not of peacefully submitting to chains and stripes[2]—it is base servility! Talk not of servants being obedient to their masters—let the blood of the tyrants flow! How can this be explained or reconciled? Is there one law of submission and non-resistance for the black man, and another law of rebellion and conflict for the white man? When it is the whites who are trodden in the dust, does Christ justify them in taking up arms to vindicate their rights? And when it is the blacks who are thus treated, does Christ require them to be patient, harmless, long-suffering, and forgiving? And are there two Christs?

The work, towards its conclusion, contains some objectionable sentiments respecting African colonization, which we regret to see.[3]

---

1 *threaten not ... faithful Creator* See 1 Peter 4.19: "Wherefore let them that suffer according to the will of God commit the keeping of their souls to him in well doing, as unto a faithful Creator."

2 *stripes* Wounds from being whipped.

3 *The work ... to see* Chapter 43 shows the Harris family, who have been settled peacefully in Canada for several years, emigrating to the colony of Liberia in West Africa. Liberia had been founded earlier in the nineteenth century by wealthy white Americans, many of whom were slaveowners, as a colony for free African Americans. Though colonization was initially supported by many white abolitionists, it was soon acknowledged by more radical abolitionists as a racist plan that would work only to set back the cause of black liberation—and it never had the support of most African Americans.

from William J. Wilson ["Ethiop"], *Uncle Tom's Cabin!*," *Frederick Douglass' Paper* (17 June 1852)

William J. Wilson (b. 1818) was a Brooklyn-based teacher, abolitionist, and anti-colonizationist, and a regular correspondent of *Frederick Douglass' Paper*, the newspaper run by African American abolitionist Frederick Douglass. He regularly wrote articles under the pen name "Ethiop," referencing the rhetorical tradition of associating all people of African ancestry with Ethiopia. Today, Wilson is remembered especially for his "Afric-American Picture Gallery" (1859), a series of articles describing an imaginary art gallery of black history.

Uncle Tom's Cabin is all the topic here, aside from the vulgar theme of politics; which (though surface-broad penetrates no deeper) is at present well nigh being eclipsed by its greater rival, my *Uncle Tom's Cabin*, since its entry into Gotham.[1]

Mrs. Beecher Stowe has deserved well of her country, in thus bringing *Uncle Tom's Cabin*, and all its associations, from the sunny *South*, into these *Northern regions*, and placing it upon the *Northern track*, and sending it thence round the land. This species of abolitionism finds its way into quarters here, hitherto so faced over with the adamant[2] of pro-slavery politics, unionism, churchism, and every other shade of "*ism*" hammered out, and welded on by his *satanic majesty* and faithful subjects, for the last half century, that it completely staggers belief and puts credulity wholly at fault. Shopkeepers that heretofore exposed for sale but fancy articles for Southern gentry, ponderous volumes for the benefit of Southern slavery, Webster speeches and other dough-faced[3] articles for Southern benefits; or, exhibited in their windows Zip Coon, or Jim Crow,[4] with his naked toes kicking out the panes, for general amusement, profit and loyalty to the Southern God; I say that these very shopkeepers are now

---

1   *Gotham*   Common nickname for New York City.

2   *adamant*   Extremely hard and impenetrable substance.

3   *Webster*   New England lawyer and politician Daniel Webster (1782–1852), a renowned orator but also notoriously tolerant of slavery;   *dough-faced*   In the nineteenth century, "doughface" was a common pejorative for Northern politicians seen as overly eager to appease the South.

4   *Zip Coon, or Jim Crow*   Two popular characters of blackface minstrelsy; "coon" is also an extremely derogatory term for a black person.

proud to illume these very windows through the windows of my *Uncle Tom's Cabin*; while good *Old Aunt Chloe* peeps out just to see what the matter is. May she continue to look out until every Uncle Tom is restored to his God-*given rights*—his full manhood—till every vestige of justice is done him.

The truth is, this species of literature will soon assume its wanted place here, which is one of high eminence, and it may yet be regretted should its march be in an inverted order; the blacks (who by position ought to be the more faithful delineators of oppression, and the keenest searchers after justice, that she fully does her office-work) being found in the REAR instead of being found, not merely in the FRONT rank, but in the very LEAD. Of one thing, however, be assured, there is something in the heart of this community of *politicians, demagogues,* and *robed priests,* and is growing, and will, if they do not mend their ways, and change their teaching, in its giant-strength, eject them from society, and consign them to their proper place—*Oblivion.*

from Charles Sumner, U.S. Senate Speech on his Motion to repeal the fugitive Slave Bill (as reprinted in the *Anti-Slavery Bugle,* Lisbon, Ohio) (18 September 1852)

Massachusetts lawyer and politician Charles Sumner (1811–72) was among the most vocal antislavery members of the Senate in the 1850s. He is perhaps most famous for an antislavery speech given in Senate on 20 May 1856, in retaliation for which he was brutally attacked and nearly killed by South Carolina politician Preston Brooks two days later.

It is a sorry fact that the "mercantile interest," in its unpardonable selfishness, ... sought to baffle Wilberforce's great effort for the abolition of the African slave trade;[1] and that, by a sordid

---

1   *Wilberforce's great ... slave trade*   Reference to renowned British politician and abolitionist William Wilberforce (1759–1833), whose efforts in Parliament helped lead to the abolition of the Atlantic slave trade in 1807 and the abolition of slavery in most British colonies in 1833.

compromise, at the formation of our Constitution,[1] it exempted the same detested, heaven-defying traffic from American judgement. And now representatives of this "interest," forgetful that commerce is the child of Freedom, join in hunting the slave. But the great heart of the people recoils from this enactment. It palpitates for the fugitive, and rejoices in his escape. Sir, I am telling you facts. The literature of the age is all on his side. The songs, more potent than laws, are for him. The poets, with voices of melody, are for Freedom. Who could sing for Slavery? They who make the permanent opinion of the country, who mould our youth, whose words, dripped into the soul, are the germs of character, supplicate for the slave. And now, sir, behold a new and heavenly ally—a woman, inspired by Christian genius, enters the lists, like another Joan of Arc,[2] and with marvellous power sweeps the chords of the popular heart. Now melting to tears, and now inspiring to rage, her work everywhere touches the conscience and makes the slave hunter more hateful. In a brief period, nearly 100,000 copies of *Uncle Tom's Cabin* have been already circulated. But this extraordinary and sudden success—surpassing all other instances in the records of literature—cannot be regarded merely as the triumph of genius. Higher far than this, it is the testament of the people, by an unprecedented act, against the Fugitive Slave Bill.

from anonymous, "Uncle Tom's Cabin," *The New York Observer* (21 October 1852)

... *Uncle Tom's Cabin* is a fiction in every sense of the word. It is not only untrue, but it is untruthful. It conveys erroneous impressions, it introduces false conclusions. It is not, as it purports to be, a picture of slavery as it is. All of the two hundred thousand

---

1   *a sordid … our Constitution*   Two "compromises" between the Northern and Southern states were arranged at the formation of the U.S. Constitution in 1787. One was that Congress would not have the power to outlaw the Atlantic Slave Trade until 1808. The other was the "Three-Fifths Compromise," which stipulated that three-fifths of the number of enslaved people in a given state would be counted towards its total population, a compromise that favored slaveholding states—where enslaved people formed a substantial portion of the population—in matters of taxation and legislative representation.

2   *Joan of Arc*   Jeanne D'Arc (1412–31), a young peasant who was persuaded by divine visions to take part in the Hundred Years' War. Her leadership led the French to several victories over English forces, and helped revive the French people's investment in the conflict.

Englishmen, and no small number of the one hundred thousand Americans, who now have it in their hands, are duped men. It is not one individual alone against whom Mrs. Stowe has borne false witness; she has slandered hundreds of thousand of her own countrymen. She has done it by attaching to them as slaveholders, in the eyes of the world, the guilt of the abuses of an institution, of which they are absolutely guiltless. Her story is so devised as to present slavery in three dark aspects—first, the *cruel treatment* of the slaves, second, *the separation of families*, and third, their *want*[1] *of religious instruction*.

To show the first she causes a reward to be offered for the recovery of a runaway slave "dead or alive," when it has been decided over and over again in Southern courts that "a slave who is merely flying away cannot be killed." She puts such language as this into the mouth of one of her speakers: "The master who goes furthest and does the worst only uses within limits the power that the law gives him,"[2] when in fact the Civil Code of the very State where it is represented the language was uttered—Louisiana—declares that:

"The slave is entirely subject to the will of his master, who may correct and chastise him, though not with unusual rigor, nor so as to maim or mutilate him, or to expose him to the danger of loss of life, or to cause his death," and provides for a compulsory sale,

"When the master shall be convicted of cruel treatment of his slaves, and the judge shall deem proper to pronounce, besides the penalty established for such cases, that the slave can be sold at public auction, in order to place him out of the reach of the power which his master has abused." ...

So too in reference to the separation of children from their parents. A considerable part of the plot is made to hinge upon the selling in Louisiana of the child Eliza "eight or nine years old" away from her mother, when had its inventor looked in the statute book of Louisiana she would have found the following language:

"Every person is expressly prohibited from selling separately from their mothers, the children who shall not have attained the full age of ten years." ...

---

1   *want*   Lack.
2   *The master ... gives him*   Words spoken by St. Clare in discussion with Miss Ophelia in Chapter 19.

The peculiar falsity of this whole book consists in making exceptional or impossible cases the representatives of the system. By the same process which she has used it would not be difficult to frame a fatal argument against the relation of husband and wife, or of parent and child, or of guardian and ward, for thousands of wives and children and wards have been maltreated and even murdered. It is wrong, unpardonably wrong, to impute to any relation of life those enormities which spring only out of the worst depravity of human nature. A ridiculous extravagant spirit of generalization pervades this fiction from beginning to end. The Uncle Tom of the authoress is a perfect angel, and her blacks generally are half-angels; her Simon Legree is a perfect demon, and her whites generally are half-demons. She has quite a peculiar spite against the clergy; and, of the many she introduces at different times into the scenes, all save an insignificant exception are Pharisees[1] or hypocrites. One who would know nothing of the United States and its people except by what he might gather from this book, would judge that it was some region just on the confines of the infernal world. We do not say that Mrs. Stowe was actuated by wrong motives in the preparation of this work, but we do say that she has done a wrong which no ignorance can excuse and no penance can expiate.

from Louisa S. McCord, "Uncle Tom's Cabin," *Southern Quarterly Review* (January 1853)

McCord (1810–79) was a well-known poet and political writer from South Carolina. She was staunchly proslavery and pro-white supremacy, and a vocal opponent as well of other social reform movements such as women's suffrage. A short excerpt from her long review of *Uncle Tom's Cabin* appears below.

Mrs. Stowe herself has, evidently most unintentionally, shown that however her theories and her fanaticism may lead her opinions, instinct, even in her mind, is endeavoring to point her right. Everywhere in her book is the mulatto represented as the man superior to, and suffering in, his position. She has been obliged, wher-

---

1   *Pharisees*   Hypocritical Christians; Christians only in form and not in spirit.

ever she has introduced her fugitives into the hearts of white families, and *fraternized* them with their white protectors, to represent these fugitives as white, with the slightest possible negro tint. Even *she* has not dared to represent the negro in those scenes where she has boldly introduced the mulatto. Even she would not have dared to paint a pretty little Quakeress[1] liberator snatching up a negro bantling[2] and covering it with kisses, and putting the mother into her own bed, and "snugly tucking her in," as she does by the white mulattoes whom she introduces. Even in *her*, the instinct of race is too strong. She dares not so belie her nature. She takes the mulatto as an approach to the white man, gives scope enough to her fancy to make him a thorough white, and then goes ahead with her romance. The real unfortunate being throughout her work is the mulatto. The negro, except where her imagination has manufactured for him such brutes of masters as are difficult to conceive, seems well enough suited to his position. It is the mulatto whom she represents as homeless and hopeless; and we confess that, in fact, although far below her horrible imaginings, his position is a painful one. Nature, who has suited her every creation to its destined end, seems to disavow him as a monstrous formation which her hand disowns. Raised in intellect and capacity above the black, yet incapable of ranking with the white, he is of no class and no caste. His happiest position is probably in the slave States, where he quietly passes over a life which, we thank God, seems like all other monstrous creations, not capable of continuous transmission. This mongrel breed is a most painful feature, arising from the juxtaposition of creatures so differing in nature as the white man and the negro; but it is a feature which, so far from being the result of slavery, is rather checked by it. The same unhappy being must occasionally exist, wherever the two peoples are brought in contact, and much more frequently where abolition license prevails, than under the rules and restraints of slavery. ...

We thought we had done; but one point more we must glance upon. Mrs. Stowe, in spite of experience, in spite of science, determines that the negro is intellectually the white man's equal. She "has

---

1   *Quakeress* Female Quaker, or member of the Religious Society of Friends. Quakers were extremely prominent in the abolitionist movement, and play a prominent role in *Uncle Tom's Cabin* in aiding the Harrises escape to freedom.
2   *bantling* Infant (often somewhat derogatory, like "brat").

lived on the frontiers of a slave State," "she has the testimony of missionaries," etc., and "her deductions, with regard to the capabilities of the race, are encouraging in the highest degree." Bravo! Mrs. Stowe! Your deductions are bold things, and override sense and reason with wonderful facility. Perhaps they would become a little more amenable to ordinary reasoning, if, instead of living "on the frontiers of a slave State," you should see fit to carry your experience, not theoretically, but practically, into the heart of one; or still better, perhaps, avoiding the contaminating system, to explore at once the negro nature in its negro home, and behold in native majesty the undegraded negro nature. In native and in naked majesty, the lords of the wild might probably suggest more appreciable arguments, for difference of race, than any to which Mrs. Stowe has chosen to hearken. The negro alone has, of all races of men, remained entirely without all shadow of civilization.[1]

from George Sand, "George Sand and Uncle Tom," *The National Era* (27 January 1853)

> "George Sand" was the pen name of Amantine Lucile Aurore Dupin (1804–76), one of the most well-known French novelists of the nineteenth century and an active proponent of a variety of liberal social and political causes. Her review of *La Cabine de l'Oncle Tom* was first translated into English for *The New York Evening Post*; the excerpt below is taken from *The National Era*, the Washington paper in which *Uncle Tom's Cabin* was first serialized.

The most popular female novelist of France has written an elaborate criticism of the romance[2] of Mrs. Beecher Stowe. It appeared in the Paris *Presse* of the 20th of December, a few days after the close of Mr. Piatt's translation of the work. Our readers will of course feel a vivid curiosity to know what such an authority can say of such

---

1   [McCord's note] We speak, of course, of the *real* negro, and not of the African. All Africans are no more negroes, than all fish are flying-fish. The real woolly-headed and thick-lipped negro is as distinct from many African races as he is from the Saxon. And when Mrs. Stowe tells us that "Tom looked respectable enough to be Bishop of Carthage, as men of colour were in other ages," either she chooses to forget that all men of colour are not negroes, or she is lamentably ignorant of the facts to which she refers.

2   *romance* I.e., novel. The terms "novel" and "romance" were used interchangeably by some writers well into the nineteenth century.

a work, and we mean to gratify it by rendering the criticism into English.—*N. Y. Eve. Post.*

Uncle Tom's Cabin

To speak of a book on the morrow of its appearance (says Madame Sand), and in the very journal in which it has been published, is contrary to custom; but in the present case, this is a disinterested homage, since the immense success which the book has acquired acquits one of any motive of attempting to aid its circulation. It is already in all hands—in all journals. Editions of all sizes have appeared, and everybody devours it, and covers it with tears. No one who can read is permitted to go without reading it; and the only regret is that there are so many among us who cannot read—the Helots[1] of misery, the slaves of ignorance—for whom politics has not yet solved the problem of bread for the soul and bread for the body. ...

If the best praise that can be given to an author is to love him, the truest that can be shown his book, is to love its faults. We cannot pass these in silence, we cannot elude the discussion of them, but we need not trouble ourselves about them, while others rally us for weeping over the simple narratives of the victims described. The defects of Mrs. Stowe's book exist only in respect to certain conventions of art, which are not absolute. If the judges, treating it as a mere bit of bookmaking, find parts that are tedious, repetitions, unskilfulness, let them take care, when they try to confirm their judgments by selecting some chance chapter, that their eyes are dry! They will remind themselves of that Ohio Senator, who argued with his little wife that he was right in voting for the Fugitive Slave Law, and yet took off two fugitives himself in his carriage in the depth of the night, getting out into the mud up to his middle often, to help push on the wheels.[2] This charming episode paints in the most admirable manner the situation of the greater part of men, placed between custom, prejudice, and their own hearts, otherwise, more naive and generous than their institutions and manners.

This is the history, both touching and ludicrous, of a great number of independent critics. Whether the question be a social or literary

---

1   *Helots*   Class of people between the enslaved and the citizenry in ancient Spartan society.
2   *that Ohio Senator ... wheels*   Reference to the character of Mr. Bird in *Uncle Tom's Cabin*, Chapter 9.

one, those who pretend to judge it coldly, and at the point of view of the abstract law, are often surprised into the deepest emotions, and sometimes conquered, without being willing to confess it. I am always charmed with the anecdote of Voltaire, who, wishing to hold the fables of Lafontaine¹ up to contempt, took the book, and said— "listen! you shall see—take the first we come to!" He read it. "Ah! that's passable—but here's another, quite stupid!" He read the second, and found it very pretty. A third quite disarmed him; but reading on to find a bad one, he threw down the book, exclaiming, with ingenious spite, "It's only a hotch-potch of masterpieces." Great minds may be bilious² and vindictive, but when they reflect, it is impossible for them to be unjust or insensible. '

This work, badly constructed according to the laws of modern romances as they are accepted in France, inspires everybody, and triumphs over all criticism in every discussion raised in the family circle. For it is essentially a domestic and family book, with its long dialogues, its minute details, and its portraits, so carefully studied. Mothers, young persons, children, and servants, read and comprehend it; and men, even superior men, cannot disdain it—we do not say, because its finer qualities redeem its defects, but because of these very pretended defects.

In France, we combated for a long while the prolixities of exposition in Walter Scott.³ We next cried out against these of Balzac;⁴ but on consideration, it was seen that in paintings of manners and characters, there was never too much when every stroke of the pencil was in its place, and concurred in the general effect. Sobriety and rapidity are eminent qualities; but we should learn to like all methods that are good, and which bear the sign of a wise and instinctive mastery.

Mrs. Stowe is all instinct, and for that reason she appears at first not to have talent. No talent! What is talent? Nothing, doubtless, compared to genius! But has she genius? I do not know that she has

---

1 *Voltaire* French Enlightenment philosopher and novelist (1694–1778); *Lafontaine* Jean de La Fontaine (1621–95), French poet best known for his collection of European fables.

2 *bilious* Ill-tempered.

3 *prolixities* Overly verbose writings; *Walter Scott* Popular Scottish poet and novelist (1771–1832), known for his colorful and romantic depictions of Scottish Highland life.

4 *Balzac* Honoré de Balzac (1799–1850), popular French novelist, known for his detailed portraits of French society.

talent, as it is understood in the world of letters, but she has the genius which humanity has the most need of—the genius of good! This is not to be a man of letters, but do you know what it is? It is to be a saint—nothing more. Yes, a saint! Three times holy is the soul which loves, blesses, and consoles martyrs! Pure, penetrating, and profound, is the spirit which sounds the depths of human nature! Great, generous, and vast the heart, which embraces in its pity, in its love, in its respect, a race sunken in blood and mire, under the scourges of cruel men, and the maledictions of the impious.

It is well for us that it is so; it is well that we feel, in spite of ourselves, that genius is the heart, that power is faith, that finally, success is sympathy, since this book quite overturns us, chokes the throat, melts the spirits, and fills us with a strange sentiment of tenderness and admiration for the figure of a poor negro, lacerated with blows, stretched in the dust, and exhaling, in a coach-house, his last breath to God.

In respect to art, moreover, there is but one rule, one law, which is to show and to move. Where do we find creations more complete, types more living, situations more touching and more original, than in Uncle Tom? The sweet relations of the slave with the child of his master,[1] exhibit a condition of things unknown amongst us—the protest of the master himself against slavery endures the whole phase of his life,[2] when his soul belongs to God alone. Society absorbs him then, law expels deity, and interest deposes conscience. Arriving at manhood the child ceases to be a man, he becomes a master, and God goes out of his heart.

What experienced hand has ever traced a type more striking and attractive than St. Clare—that refined, noble, loving, generous nature, but too soft and indifferent to be great? Is he not man in general, man with his fine innate qualities, his good impulses, and his deplorable carelessness—the charming master, who loves and is loved, who thinks, who reasons, but who never concludes or acts?

---

1 *The sweet ... his master* Uncle Tom's affectionate friendship with the angelic daughter of his owners, Eva.

2 *the protest ... his life* Augustine St. Clare, Tom's enslaver in Louisiana, is deeply uncomfortable with the institution of slavery and determines, after Eva's death, to free those whom he enslaves although he dies before he can accomplish it.

He expends in a day the treasures of indulgence, of reason, of justice, and of goodness; he dies without having saved. His precious life is all resumed in a word—aspiration and regret. He could not will. Alas! there are not a few such among the best and strongest of men.

The life and death of a child, the life and death of a negro, is the whole of this book. That child and that negro are two saints for Heaven. The friendship which unites them, their respect for each other, is the whole love and passion of the drama. I do not know any other genius than that of sanctity, which could have spread over such a situation, a charm so powerful, and sustained.

Children are the true heroes of Mrs. Stowe. Her soul, the most maternal that ever was, has conceived all the little beings in the very light of Heaven (*rayon de la grace*[1]). George Shelby, little Harry, the cousin of Eva, the baby of the little wife of the Senator, and Topsy,[2] the poor, devilish, and excellent Topsy, those that are seen, and those that are not seen in this romance, but of which only three words are spoken by their desolate mothers—are a world of little white and black angels, in which every woman recognises the object of her love, the source of her joys and her tears. In taking form in the mind of Mrs. Stowe, these children, without ceasing to be children, taken also ideal proportions, and come to interest us more than all the personages in love romances.

The women, too, are designed with the hand of a master—not only the mothers, who are sublime, but those who are not mothers, either in heart or in face, and whose infirmities are treated with indulgence or rigor. By the side of the methodical miss Ophelia, who learns that duty is nothing without affection, Marie St. Clare[3] is a portrait of frightful fidelity. One trembles to think that she exists—this American lioness; that she is everywhere; that each of us has seen her; for slaves are not wanting to her to make her reveal herself as a torturer in the midst of her vapors and tremblings of the nerve.

Saints have also their claw; it is that of the lion; it respects human

---

1   *rayon de la grace*   French: ray of grace.
2   *Topsy*   Child purchased by Augustine as a charity case for his abolitionist cousin Miss Ophelia to educate; Topsy had an exceedingly cruel upbringing and is portrayed as being naïve and unruly as a result.
3   *Marie St. Clare*   Following Augustine's sudden death, his unfeeling wife Marie sells Tom to a cruel plantation owner, despite the fact that Augustine had promised Tom his freedom.

flesh; but it fastens upon the conscience. A little warm indignation, a little terrible mockery, is not unbecoming Mrs. Harriet Beecher Stowe, the woman so gentle, so humane, so religious, so full of evangelical unction. Yes, she is a woman of great goodness, but not what we derisively call "a very good woman"; she is a strong, courageous heart, which, in blessing the unhappy, in caressing the faithful, aiding the irresolute, attracting the weak, does not fear to spit the hardened sinners, that she may show their deformity to the world.

from George Frederick Holmes, "A Key to Uncle Tom's Cabin," *Southern Literary Messenger* (June 1853)

The excerpt below is from an eight-page review of Stowe's *A Key to Uncle Tom's Cabin* (1853); Holmes had already contributed to the December 1852 issue of the *Southern Literary Messenger* a ten-page review condemning *Uncle Tom's Cabin* itself. That initial review had barely touched on gender issues, however; Holmes returned to the subject of *Uncle Tom's Cabin* in his review of *A Key* in order to focus on that aspect of Stowe's novel.

Before touching on the Key, ... we have a preliminary remark to introduce, which may seem foreign to our immediate subject, but is most intimately combined with it as explaining and perpetuating the agitation which Mrs. Stowe has been able to excite. It is a horrible thought that a woman should write or a lady read such productions as those by which her celebrity has been acquired. Are scenes of licence and impurity, and ideas of loathsome depravity and habitual prostitution to be made the cherished topics of the female pen, and the familiar staple of domestic consideration...? Is the mind of woman to be tainted, seduced, contaminated, and her heart disenchanted of its native purity of sentiment, by the unblushing perusal, the free discussion, and the frequent meditation of such thinly veiled pictures of corruption? Can a lady of stainless mind read such works without a blush of confusion, or a man think of their being habitually read by ladies without shame and repugnance? It is sufficiently disgraceful that a woman should be an instrument in disseminating the vile stream of contagion; but it is intolerable that Southern women should defile themselves by bringing the putrid waters to their lips.

If they will drink of them in secret, let them repent in secret, and not make vices unknown to the pure and upright of their sex the subject of daily thought and conversation. [Even if] every accusation brought by Mrs. Stowe [were] perfectly true, ... the pollution of such literature to the mind and heart of woman is not less—but perhaps even more to be apprehended. ... If Mrs. Stowe will chronicle or imagine the incidents of debauchery, let us hope that women—and especially Southern women—will not be found poring over her pages. The Gospels according to Fanny Wright, and George Sand, the fashionable favour extended to the licentious novels of the French school, and the woman's rights Conventions, which have rendered the late years infamous, have unsexed in great measure the female mind, and shattered the template of feminine delicacy and moral graces; and the result is before us in these dirty insinuations of Mrs. Stowe. ...

from anonymous, *The North American Review* (October 1853)

The enthusiastic reception of Mrs. Stowe's novel is the result of various causes. One is the merit of the book itself. It is, unquestionably, a work of genius. It has defects of conception and style, exhibits a want of artistic skill, is often tame and inadequate in description, and is tinctured with methodistic cant;[1] but, with all its blemishes—thought, imagination, feeling, high moral and religious sentiment, and dramatic power shine in every page. It has the capital excellence of exciting the interest of the reader; this never stops or falters from the beginning to the end. The characters are drawn with spirit and truth. St. Clare is a person of talents and education, high-minded, generous, and impulsive; the influences of his position and circumstances on his character are well developed. Ophelia is an admirable picture of a conscientious, practical, kind-hearted, energetic New England woman. St. Clare's wife is well imagined, but somewhat overdrawn. The Shelbys are worthy, amiable, commonplace people, soberly and truly sketched. Legree is a monster, and is

---

1   *methodistic* I.e., relating to the Methodist faith. Here the term seems to be used more generally to refer to beliefs or values associated with any branch of Christianity based in Calvinism; Stowe's family were Congregationalists;   *cant*   Pretentious or insincere language.

painted in strong colors; but the picture wants[1] truth and minuteness of detail to bring out the conception, for no woman's hand could properly describe him. The pencil that drew Front de Boeuf, Dirk Hatteraick, and William de la Marck[2] would have made him start from the canvas. We fear he is not exaggerated. There are many such at the North and South; only, in the North, we do not give them so much power, and they sometimes, when not saved by the "ingenuity of counsel," or an executive pardon, or the sympathy of a jury, or the lenity of an elected judge, meet their reward in the dungeon or on the gallows. Eva and Tom are dreams; the one is a saint, the other an angel. But dreams are founded on realities, and "we are all such stuff as dreams are made of."[3] These characters are both exaggerated; but to color and idealize is the privilege of romance,[4] provided the picture does not overstep the modesty of nature or contradict nature. There are no Evas or Uncle Toms, but there are some who possess, in a lower degree, their respective virtues. Many a home has been blessed by the presence, and darkened by the departure, of a child, whose early intelligence seemed inspired, and whose purity, sweetness, and love were too delicate to mingle with the coarse passions of the world—and many an old family servant in the South is distinguished for probity, fidelity, truthfulness, and religious feeling, and, slave though he be, is the object of respect and attachment.

But whatever may be the literary merits of Uncle Tom, they do not account for its success. It exhibits by no means the highest order of genius or skill. It is not to be named in comparison with the novels of Scott or Dickens;[5] and in regard to variety of knowledge, eloquence, imaginative power, and spirited delineations of life and character, manners and events, it is inferior even to those of Bulwer, or Currer

---

1 *wants* Lacks.

2 *Front de Boeuf... de la Marck* Rugged, villainous characters created by highly respected Scottish author Sir Walter Scott and depicted, respectively, in his novels *Ivanhoe* (1819), *Guy Mannering* (1815), and *Quentin Durward* (1823); de la Marck was based on the historical adventurer William I de la Marck (1446–85).

3 *we are ... made of* See Shakespeare's *The Tempest* 4.1.174.

4 *romance* Here suggesting a type of prose fiction characterized by sensational events and exaggerated, idealized characters.

5 *Dickens* English novelist Charles Dickens (1812–70).

Bell, or Hawthorne.[1] Yet none of these have been read and talked of, for months together, by Europe and America, or have sensibly influenced a great moral movement, or have disturbed whole communities by the dread of a social revolution. It is true that, were Uncle Tom not well written, it would not have produced these effects; but the result is so disproportioned to its merit as a work of art, that we must look to other causes. The book has one idea and purpose to which it is wholly devoted. Its sole object is to reveal to the world the nature of American slavery, and thus to promote the cause of abolition.

Now this subject of slavery is one in which the world, or at least the reading and thinking part of it, which has become a very large part, just now takes a very lively interest. In Europe, the dream of political liberty, in the sense of the French Revolutionary school, has vanished. It has been discovered, after repeated and most disastrous experiments, that it means the absolute power of the mob and its demagogues; that equality means plunder, and fraternity, massacre. The people of France have discovered, by bitter experience, that there, at least, democracy is inconsistent with freedom, property, and civilization; and they have acquiesced quietly and cheerfully in a strong government, supported and guided by the public opinion of the rich and educated, and surrounded by bayonets to protect property and order, and keep the dangerous classes in subjection.[2]

Disenchanted on the subject of political liberty, disgusted with Kossuth, and Mazzini, and Louis Blanc,[3] tired and out of humor

---

1   *Bulwer*   Edward Bulwer-Lytton (1803–73), popular English writer known for his sensational novels;   *Currer Bell*   Pseudonym of celebrated English novelist Charlotte Brontë (1816–55);   *Hawthorne*   Respected American novelist Nathaniel Hawthorne (1804–64).

2   *In Europe ... in subjection*   The reference in this paragraph is to the wave of democratic uprisings that took place in various European nations, beginning with France, in 1848. France itself had experienced numerous democratic revolutions since the French Revolution of 1789, and the writer may also have in mind the Reign of Terror, a period in the early 1790s when the revolutionary fervor in France rose to an extreme level, leading to mass imprisonments and executions without trial. Though the 1848 revolutions were largely unsuccessful in terms of concrete political change, popular support for their democratic, nationalistic, and pro-working-class aims remained substantial in Europe and the Americas, and this culture of revolution contributed to the popularity of *Uncle Tom's Cabin* among Europeans.

3   *Kossuth*   Hungarian politician Lajos Kossuth (1802–94), who served as *de facto* Governor-President of Hungary from 1848 to 1849, during a brief period of independence before the Austro-Hungarian Empire regained control of Hungary;   *Mazzini*   Italian politician Giuseppe Mazzini (1805–72), an advocate of Italian unification and various other liberal reforms, who served as Triumvir of the short-lived Roman Republic in 1849;   *Louis*

with Poles and Hungarians, with French Revolutions, Chartist movements, and Irish rebellions,[1] which have ended in nothing but sound and fury, because destitute of truth and reason, adequate cause, virtuous motive, or definite purpose; their sympathies have found an object in the condition of the negro slave. Political liberty, in the democratic sense, they have found a delusion; but personal liberty is quite another thing. They can understand why it is dangerous to the security of society to give political power to the ignorant and reckless mob; but they cannot understand why it is necessary for any community to deprive a portion of its people of all civil rights whatever, and reduce them to the condition of property. They see a great, prosperous, and civilized democracy, advancing with rapid strides to the position of a formidable power, rivalling them not only in wealth but in refinement, boasting of liberty, advocating liberty, openly and avowedly giving countenance and support to every revolutionary movement among their discontented classes—yet all the while, holding four millions of its own people in abject slavery, and defending with warrant and defiance its right so to hold them. This strange inconsistency provokes comment and discussion. The subject is not a new one in Europe; late events have revived it there. Constant intercourse with us has brought it closer to their minds and feelings. They see in it an incongruity—a contradiction to the advanced culture, the enlightened intelligence, of the age, a stain and blemish on the common humanity and civilization of the world. They have got rid of it themselves; personal slavery with them is matter of history. It lies behind them, among the barbarisms of the past. They regard it as a wrong and an evil which ought not to exist, and which, therefore, the good, the wise, and the gifted should endeavor to remove by those means which have dispelled so much moral evil from the world—by truth and reason, by argument and persuasion, by the keen arrows of invective and scorn. Mixed with

---

Blanc French socialist politician (1811–82), who served as a member of the short-lived French provisional government in 1848.

1 *Poles* Reference to the Greater Poland Uprising of 1848; *Chartist movements* In the Britain, Chartism was a mid-nineteenth-century political movement led by members of the working class, which sought a number of social and political reforms (including extending suffrage to all adult men); *Irish rebellions* Numerous rebellions against English rule over Ireland had taken place; the Young Ireland rebellion of 1848 was the most recent.

these sentiments, there is, doubtless, something of national jealousy and fear, something of dislike to republican government, and of triumph at being able to point to such a blot on its mantle. But these feelings only add to the excitement of the subject, and prepare the public mind of Europe to receive, with the greater eagerness and interest, the animated pictures, the heart-stirring scenes, the passionate appeals of Uncle Tom.

With us, the subject is of far deeper concern. It comes home closely and immediately to our firesides and altars, to our honor and prosperity, to our peace and union. On it hang the issues of life and death. It is not an abstract question, to be discussed with philosophic serenity in the seclusion of libraries and drawing rooms; but it involves property and security, sectional power and party power, and sweeps into its vortex the passions which disturb the repose of society and shake the stability of empires. The country has just passed through a painful and perilous crisis growing out of this question, which yet did not decide it.[1] It still hangs like a dark cloud over the horizon of the future. The public mind, like the sea after a storm, heaves and swells with ominous agitation, and parties are mustering their forces to renew the contest. It is a question about which many are alarmed, many more are strongly excited, and none are indifferent. Viewed simply as a moral question, affecting individual conduct and the condition of millions of human beings, it is one of deep and serious interest; but involving, as it necessarily does, a vast amount of property, and connected, as it has become, with party strife and sectional rivalry, moderation, fairness, and reason in the treatment of it are not to be expected. A work like Uncle Tom, coming at such a moment, so admirably suited to the common mind, teaching, not by abstract reasoning addressed to the intellect, but by actual scenes and events affecting the imagination and the feelings, written, too, with so much power and beauty, is eagerly seized on by one party as a valuable auxiliary, and indignantly resented by the other as a new attack. It becomes at once the topic of animated criticism and discussion, and the result is—it is read by all.

---

1   *The country ... decide it*   The Compromise of 1850 brought temporary peace, but arguably made war more likely in the longer term.

from Mary Chesnut, *Diary*, 1861–62

Mary Boykin Miller Chesnut (1823–86) was born into one prominent South Carolina planter family and married into another. During the Civil War, her husband, James Chesnut Jr. (1815–85), became a general in the Confederate Army and served as an aide to Confederate President Jefferson Davis; as a result, the Chesnuts moved in the highest circles of the Confederacy. Mary chronicled her wartime experiences in a diary she kept throughout the war. She heavily revised this diary in the 1880s with the aim of publishing it but died before she could accomplish this goal. An extensively edited and abridged version of the work appeared in 1905 under the title *A Diary from Dixie*, and the novelist Ben Ames Williams published a longer version, reworked for readability, in 1949. These two publications won Chesnut widespread admiration for the novelistic skill with which she depicted the war's events and personalities, as she perceived them. Not until an authoritative scholarly edition of Chesnut's diary was published in 1981, however, did much of her original wartime writing appear in print.

The selections presented below provide a sense of how white Southern women of Chesnut's class viewed *Uncle Tom's Cabin* and its subject matter. In her 27 August 1861 entry, Chesnut includes her record of a conversation she had had on this topic with one or more other women who express decided views on the topic of white Southern men acting like Simon Legree (in other words, forcing enslaved women to have sex with them). Chesnut's 13 March 1862 entry, written entirely in her own voice, records her reactions after having re-read *Uncle Tom's Cabin*.

August 27, 1861

"I hate slavery. I hate a man who...—You say there are no more fallen women on a plantation than in London in proportion to numbers. But what do you say to this—to a magnate who runs a hideous black harem, with its consequences, under the same roof with his lovely white wife and his beautiful and accomplished daughters? He holds his head high and poses as the model of all human virtues to these poor women whom God and the laws have given him. From the height of his awful majesty he scolds and thunders at them as if he never did wrong in his life. Fancy such a man finding his daughter reading *Don Juan*.[1] 'You with that immoral book!' he would say, and then he would order her out of his sight. You see Mrs. Stowe did not hit the sorest spot. She makes Legree a bachelor." ...

"Oh, I know half a Legree—a man said to be as cruel as Legree, but the other half of him did not correspond. He was a man of polished manners, and the best husband and father and member of the church in the world."

"Can that be so?"

"Yes, I know it. Exceptional case, that sort of thing, always. And I knew the dissolute half of Legree well. He was high and mighty, but the kindest creature to his slaves. And the unfortunate results of his bad ways were not sold, had not to jump over ice-blocks. They were kept in full view, and provided for handsomely in his will."

"The wife and daughters in the might of their purity and innocence are supposed never to dream of what is as plain before their eyes as the sunlight, and they play their parts of unsuspecting angels to the letter. They profess to adore the father as the model of all saintly goodness."

"Well, yes; if he is rich he is the fountain from whence all blessings flow."

"The one I have in my eye—my half of Legree, the dissolute half—was so furious in temper and thundered his wrath so at the poor women, they were glad to let him do as he pleased in peace if they could only escape his everlasting fault-finding, and noisy bluster, making everybody so uncomfortable."

"Now—now, do you know any woman of this generation who would stand that sort of thing? No, never, not for one moment. The make-believe angels were of the last century. We know, and we won't have it."

"The condition of women is improving, it seems."

"Women are brought up not to judge their fathers or their husbands. They take them as the Lord provides and are thankful."

---

1   *Don Juan*   Long poem (1819–24) by George Gordon, Lord Byron, in which the amorous adventures of Don Juan are recounted.

Read *Uncle Tom's Cabin* again. These negro women have a chance here that women have nowhere else. They can redeem themselves—the "impropers"[1] can. They can marry decently, and nothing is remembered against these colored ladies. It is not a nice[2] topic, but Mrs. Stowe revels in it. How delightfully Pharisaic[3] a feeling it must be to rise superior and fancy [that] we are so degraded as to defend and like to live with such degraded creatures around us—such men as Legree and his women. The best way to take negroes to your heart is to get as far away from them as possible. As far as I can see, Southern women do all that missionaries could do to prevent and alleviate evils. The social evil[4] has not been suppressed in old England or in New England, in London or in Boston. People in those places expect more virtue from a plantation African than they can insure in practise among themselves with all their own high moral surroundings—light, education, training, and support. Lady Mary Montagu[5] says, "Only men and women at last." "Male and female, created he them," says the Bible. There are cruel, graceful, beautiful mothers of angelic Evas North as well as South, I dare say. The Northern men and women who came here were always hardest, for they expected an African to work and behave as a white man. We do not.

I have often thought from observation truly that perfect beauty hardens the heart, and as to grace, what so graceful as a cat, a tigress, or a panther? Much love, admiration, worship hardens an idol's heart. It becomes utterly callous and selfish. It expects to receive all and to give nothing. It even likes the excitement of seeing people

---

1   *impropers*   I.e., enslaved women who have "behaved improperly" when forced by their enslavers into sexual liaisons.

2   *nice*   Delicate, decent; fit for polite discussion.

3   *Pharisaic*   Reference to the Pharisees, a Jewish sect whose members are portrayed in the Bible as hypocrites.

4   *The social evil*   I.e., prostitution. It was common practice among Southern whites to equate the behavior of enslaved women (who had been forced by their enslavers to have sex) with the behavior of prostitutes (who sold sexual services).

5   *Lady Mary Montagu*   English aristocrat (1689–1762) who traveled to the Ottoman Empire with her ambassador husband and wrote a series of famous letters about her experiences and observations, especially on the lives of Turkish women.

suffer. I speak now of what I have watched with horror and amaze-ment.

Topsys I have known, but none that were beaten or ill-used. Evas are mostly in the heaven of Mrs. Stowe's imagination. People can't love things dirty, ugly, and repulsive, simply because they ought to do so, but they can be good to them at a distance; that's easy. You see, I can not rise very high; I can only judge by what I see.

Advertisement ("An Edition for the Million"), *New England Farmer* (25 December 1852)

Advertisement, *Hartford Courant* (12 August 1852)

The following advertisement from the Connecticut *Hartford Courant* describes one of the many novels published in the 1850s that aimed to provide a favorable portrait of slavery in contrast to that presented in *Uncle Tom's Cabin*—a genre that came to be known as the "anti-Tom" novel.

"LIGHT, MORE LIGHT STILL!"
A BOOK FOR THE TIMES!

Now ready and contains 500 12mo pages, beautifully illustrated with original designs, and neatly bound, price $1.50, entitled—

LIFE AT THE SOUTH;
—OR—
"UNCLE TOM'S CABIN" AS IT IS;
Being Narratives, Scenes and Incidents in the real "Life of the Lowly."
BY W.L.G. SMITH, ESQ.

The object of the author is to represent the condition of the slave in his rude but comfortable cabin, his daily occupations and pastimes, the relations between master and slave, the mistaken impulses and misconceived views of the Northern Philanthropist, &c. &c., and to represent the passions and sentiments in their natural forms, as the same are displayed in the humblest lot in society, thus showing that, in the case of the slave at least, contentment bestows more happiness than freedom; and at the same time to represent, AS IT IS, a class of people, viz.: the Planter, to whom justice has seldom been done, and whose character as exhibited in everyday life, is well calculated to win the amiable judgment of the world.

The "Anti-Tom" Novel

from Caroline Lee Hentz, *The Planter's Northern Bride* (1854)

Born in Massachusetts, Caroline Lee Hentz (1800–56) moved to the South in 1826, when her husband took up a faculty position at the University of North Carolina. She spent most of the rest of her life in various Southern states. A prolific writer of novels, short stories, poetry, and drama, Hentz is best known today for *The Planter's Northern Bride*, a novel she wrote in response to the massive success of *Uncle Tom's Cabin*. The book—one of a spate of so-called "anti-Tom novels" that sought to contest Stowe's depiction of slavery's brutalities—chronicles the changing views of Eulalia, the daughter of a New England abolitionist who comes to abandon her father's beliefs after she marries a Southern plantation owner named Moreland and witnesses what the novel characterizes as the contentment and devotion of the people Moreland enslaves. (Ironically, early in her time in the South, Hentz had mentored George Moses Horton, an enslaved North Carolinian poet whose work advocates openly for release from slavery.) The book was well received, including in the North; the New York *Mirror* wrote, "We have seldom been more charmed by the perusal of a novel," adding that "It cannot be read without a moistening of the eyes, a softening of the heart, and a mitigation of sectional and most unchristian prejudices."

Hentz's agenda with the novel is clearly summarized in the novel's preface, excerpted below.

from PREFACE

It was the intention of the author to have given this book to the world during the course of the past season, but unforeseen occurrences have prevented the accomplishment of her purpose. She no longer regrets the delay, as she believes it will meet a more cordial reception at the present time.

When individual or public feeling is too highly wrought on any subject, there must inevitably follow a reaction, and reason, recovering from the effects of transient inebriation, is ready to assert its original sovereignty.

Not in the spirit of egotism, do we repeat what was said in the preface of a former work, that we were born at the North, and though destiny has removed us far from our native scenes, we cherish for them a sacred regard, an undying attachment. It cannot therefore be supposed that we are actuated by hostility or prejudice, in endeavouring to represent the unhappy consequences of that intolerant and fanatical spirit, whose fatal influence we so deeply deplore.

We believe that there are a host of noble, liberal minds, of warm, generous, candid hearts, at the North, that will bear us out in our views of Southern character, and that feel with us that our *national* honour is tarnished, when a portion of our country is held up to public disgrace and foreign insult, by those, too, whom every feeling of patriotism should lead to defend it from ignominy and shield it from dishonour. The hope that they will appreciate and do justice to our motives, has imparted enthusiasm to our feelings, and energy to our will, in the prosecution of our literary labour.

When we have seen the dark and horrible pictures drawn of slavery and exhibited to a gazing world, we have wondered if we were one of those favoured individuals to whom the fair side of life is ever turned, or whether we were created with a moral blindness, incapable of distinguishing its lights and shadows. One thing is certain, and if we were on judicial oath we would repeat it, that during our residence in the South, we have never *witnessed* one scene of cruelty or oppression, never beheld a chain or a manacle, or the infliction of a punishment more severe than parental authority would be justified in applying to filial disobedience or transgression. This is not owing to our being placed in a limited sphere of observation, for we have seen and studied domestic, social, and plantation life, in Carolina, Alabama, Georgia, and Florida. We have been admitted into close and familiar communion with numerous families in each of these States, not merely as a passing visitor, but as an indwelling guest,[1] and we have never been pained by an inhuman exercise of authority, or a wanton abuse of power.

---

1   *indwelling guest*   In Christian writing, this phrase is commonly used to refer to the Holy Spirit's abiding presence in each Christian believer.

On the contrary, we have been touched and gratified by the exhibition of affectionate kindness and care on one side, and loyal and devoted attachment on the other. We have been especially struck with the cheerfulness and contentment of the slaves, and their usually elastic[1] and buoyant spirits. From the abundant opportunities we have had of judging, we give it as our honest belief, that the negroes of the South are the happiest *labouring class* on the face of the globe; even subtracting from their portion of enjoyment all that can truly be said of their trials and sufferings. The fugitives who fly to the Northern States are no proof against the truth of this statement. They have most of them been made disaffected by the influence of others—tempted by promises which are seldom fulfilled. Even in the garden of Eden, the seeds of discontent and rebellion were sown; surely we need not wonder that they sometimes take root in the beautiful groves of the South.

In the large cities we have heard of families who were cruel to their slaves, as well as unnaturally severe in the discipline of their children. (Are there no similar instances at the North?) But the indignant feeling which any known instance of inhumanity calls forth at the South, proves that they are not of common occurrence.

We have conversed a great deal with the coloured people, feeling the deepest interest in learning their own views of their peculiar situation,[2] and we have almost invariably been delighted and affected[3] by their humble devotion to their master's family, their child-like, affectionate reliance on their care and protection, and above all, with their genuine cheerfulness and contentment.

This very morning, since commencing these remarks, our sympathies have been strongly moved by the simple eloquence of a negro woman in speaking of her former master and mistress, who have been dead for many years.

"Oh!" said she, her eyes swimming with tears, and her voice choking with emotion, "I loved my master and mistress like my own soul.

---

1   *elastic* Easily uplifted.

2   *peculiar situation* The adjective "peculiar," when used in the context of slavery, carried a specific meaning in the United States at this point in history. Southern enslavers often referred to slavery as "our peculiar institution," in the sense of an institution that was specific only to them; this euphemism came to be used by abolitionists as well, though with them it was used ironically.

3   *affected* Moved.

If I could have died in their stead, I would gladly done it. I would have gone into the grave and brought them up, if the Lord had let me do it. Oh! they were so good—so kind. All on us black folks would 'ave laid down our lives for 'em at any minute."

"Then you were happy?" we said; "you did not sigh to be free?"

"No, mistress, that I didn't. I was too well off for that. I wouldn't have left my master and mistress for all the freedom in the world. I'd left my own father and mother first. I loved 'em better than I done them. I loved their children too. Every one of 'em has been babies in my arms—and I loved 'em a heap better than I done my own, I want to stay with 'em as long as I live, and I know they will take care of me when I get too old to work."

These are her own words. We have not sought this simple instance of faithful and enduring love. It came to us as if in corroboration of our previous remarks, and we could not help recording it. ...

Many of the circumstances we have recorded in these pages are founded on truth. The plot of the insurrection, the manner in which it was instigated and detected[1] ... are literally true.

If any one should think the affection manifested by the slaves of Moreland for their master is too highly coloured, we would refer them to the sketch of Thomas Jefferson's arrival at Monticello on his return from Paris, after an absence of five years. It is from the pen of his daughter, and no one will doubt its authenticity.

"The negroes discovered the approach of the carriage as soon as it reached Shadwell, and such a scene I never witnessed in my life. They collected in crowds around it, and almost drew it up the mountain by hand. The shouting, etc., had been sufficiently obstreperous before, but the moment the carriage arrived on the top it reached the climax. When the door of the carriage was opened, they received him in their arms and bore him into the house, crowding around, kissing his hands and feet, some blubbering and crying, others laughing. It appeared impossible to satisfy their eyes, or their anxiety to touch, and even to kiss the very earth that bore him. These were the first ebullitions[2] of joy for his return, after a long absence, which they would of course

---

1   *The plot ... detected* Part of the plot of *The Planter's Northern Bride* concerns Eulalia's discovery of a conspiracy by local abolitionists to foment an uprising of enslaved people and murder Eulalia and Moreland, which is successfully thwarted.

2   *ebullitions* Boilings-over, outbursts.

feel; but it is perhaps not out of place to add here, that they were at all times very devoted in their attachment to their master. They believed him to be one of the greatest, and they knew him to be one of the best of men, and kindest of masters. They spoke to him freely, and applied confidingly to him in all their difficulties and distresses; and he watched over them in sickness and health; interested himself in all their concerns; advising them, and showing esteem and confidence in the good, and indulgence to all."[1]

We can add nothing to this simple, pathetic[2] description. Monticello is hallowed ground, and the testimony that proceeds from its venerated retreat should be listened to with respect and confidence. The same accents might be heard from Mount Vernon's august shades,[3] where the grave of Washington has been bedewed by the tears of the grateful African.[4]

But we have done.

If we fail to accomplish the purpose for which we have written, we shall at least have the consolation of knowing that our motives are disinterested,[5] and our aim patriotic and true.

Should no Northern heart respond to our earnest appeal, we trust the voice of the South will answer to our own, not in a faint, cold, dying echo, but in a full, spontaneous strain, whose reverberations shall reach to the green hills and granite cliffs of New England's "rock-bound coast."[6]

CAROLINE LEE HENTZ.

---

1 *The negroes ... to all* This description by Thomas Jefferson's daughter, Martha Jefferson Randolph, of Jefferson's return to Monticello in December 1789 was first published by the Virginian politician, historian, and writer George Tucker in his *Life of Thomas Jefferson* (1837), the first comprehensive biography of Jefferson.

2 *pathetic* I.e., eliciting pathos; moving.

3 *Mount Vernon* George Washington's plantation estate on the banks of the Potomac River in Virginia, which he owned from 1761 until his death in 1799 and where he is buried; *august shades* Revered or exalted spirits.

4 *grave ... African* George Washington enslaved African Americans throughout his life, but—unlike most of the other slaveholding founders of the United States—he emancipated all enslaved people he owned in his will. By the 1850s, both pro- and antislavery factions were claiming Washington's legacy to support their own positions.

5 *disinterested* Not self-interested; unbiased.

6 *rock-bound coast* See the first two lines of English poet Felicia Hemans's "The Landing of the Pilgrim Fathers in New England" (1825): "The breaking waves dashed high / On a stern and rock-bound coast."

Martin Delany and Frederick Douglass Debate Harriet Beecher Stowe

The prominent abolitionist, orator, and newspaper editor Frederick Douglass, who had escaped slavery in Maryland in 1838, was among the most vocal African American supporters of *Uncle Tom's Cabin* and of Stowe herself—though he and Stowe by no means agreed on everything concerning abolition. His newspaper *Frederick Douglass' Paper* published countless reviews, articles, and poems dealing with the novel in the years following its publication. Among the number of black activists who were openly wary regarding the merits of *Uncle Tom's Cabin*—and of Stowe's new position as an apparent representative of the abolitionist movement—was Douglass's former colleague, journalist and physician Martin R. Delany. In spring 1853, *Frederick Douglass' Paper* featured an epistolary exchange between the two men, in which Delany vehemently argued against allowing a white woman—whose novel had been heavily influenced by the slave narratives of black authors—to be so readily accepted as the spokesperson of black rights and liberation. Selections from that correspondence are included below.

Pittsburgh, March 20, 1853

Frederick Douglass, Esq: Dear Sir: I notice in your paper of March 4th, an article in which you speak of having paid a visit to Mrs. H. E. B. Stowe, for the purpose, as you say, of consulting her, "as to some method which should contribute successfully, and permanently, to the improvement and elevation of the free people of color in the United States."[1] Also, in the number of March 18th, in an article by a writer over the initials of "P.C.S." in reference to the same subject, he concludes by saying, "I await with much interest the suggestions of Mrs. Stowe in this matter."

Now I simply wish to say that we have always fallen into great

---

1   *your paper ... United States*   Delany refers to the article published in *Frederick Douglass' Paper* as "A Day and Night in 'Uncle Tom's Cabin,'" in which Douglass reflects on a visit paid to Stowe's home in Massachusetts.

errors in efforts of this kind, going to others than the *intelligent* and *experienced* among *ourselves*, and in all due respect and deference to Mrs. Stowe, I beg leave to say that she *knows nothing about us*, "the Free Colored people of the United States," neither does any other white person—and, consequently, can contrive no successful scheme for our elevation; it must be done by ourselves. I am aware, that I differ with many in thus expressing myself, but I cannot help it; though I stand alone, and offend my best friends, so help me God! in a matter of such moment and importance, I will express my opinion. Why, in God's name, don't the leaders among our people make suggestions, and *consult* the most competent among *their own* brethren concerning our elevation? This they do not do; and I have not known one, whose province it was to do so, to go ten miles for such a purpose. We shall never effect anything until this is done.

I accord with the suggestions of H.O. Wagoner[1] for a National Council or Consultation of our people, provided *intelligence, maturity*, and *experience*, in matters among them, could be so gathered together; other than this, would be a mere mockery—like the Convention of 1848,[2] a coming together of rivals, to test their success for the "biggest offices." As God lives, I will never, knowingly, lend my aid to any such work, while our brethren groan in vassalage[3] and bondage, and I and mine under oppression and degradation, such as we now suffer.

I would not give the counsel of one dozen *intelligent colored* freemen of the *right stamp*, for that of all the white and unsuitable colored persons in the land. But something must be done, and that speedily.

The so-called free states, by their acts,[4] are now virtually saying to the South, "you *shall not* emancipate; your blacks *must be slaves*, and should they come North, there is no refuge for them." I shall not be surprised to see, at no distant day, a solemn Convention called

---

1 *H.O. Wagoner* Abolitionist Henry O. Wagoner (1816–1901), a frequent correspondent of Douglass's, who had proposed such a National Council in *Frederick Douglass' Paper* for 18 March 1853.

2 *Convention of 1848* I.e., the Colored National Convention held in Cleveland, Ohio on September 6, attended by both Douglass and Delany.

3 *vassalage* Subordination.

4 *their acts* Delany refers to the federal Fugitive Slave Act (1850), and various related state laws, which required Northerners to aid in the capture and re-enslavement of individuals found (or suspected) to have escaped slavery.

by the whites in the North, to deliberate on the propriety of changing the whole policy to that of slave states. This will be the remedy
to prevent dissolution; *and it will come, mark that!* anything on the
part of the American people to *save* their *Union.* Mark me—the non-
slaveholding states *will become slave states.*

Yours for God and Humanity.
M.R. DELANY

[1 April 1853]

REMARKS—That colored men would agree among themselves to do
something for the efficient and permanent aid of themselves and their
race, "is a consummation devoutly to be wished";[1] but until they do, it
is neither wise nor graceful for them, or for any one of them to throw
cold water upon plans and efforts made for that purpose by others.
To scornfully reject all aid from our white friends, and to denounce
them as unworthy of our confidence, looks high and mighty enough
on paper; but unless the back ground is filled up with facts dem-
onstrating our independence and self-sustaining power, of what use
is such display of self-consequence? Brother DELANY has worked
long and hard—he has written vigorously, and spoken eloquently to
colored people—beseeching them, in the name of liberty, and all the
dearest interests of humanity, to unite their energies, and to increase
their activities in the work of their own elevation; yet where has his
voice been heeded? and where is the practical result? Echo answers,
where? Is not the field open? Why, then, should any man object to the
efforts of Mrs. Stowe, or anyone else, who is moved to do anything
on our behalf? The assertion that Mrs. Stowe "knows nothing about
us," shows that Bro. DELANY knows nothing about Mrs. Stowe, for
he certainly would not so violate his moral, or common sense if he
did. When Brother DELANY will submit any plan for benefitting the
colored people, or will candidly criticise any plan already submitted,
he will be heard with pleasure. But we expect no plan from him. He
has written a book—and we may say that it is, in many respects,

---

1   *is a consummation ... be wished*   See Shakespeare's *Hamlet* 3.1.72–73.

an excellent book—on the condition, character, and destiny of the colored people,[1] but it leaves us just where it finds us, without chart or compass, and in more doubt and perplexity than before we read it. Brother Delany is one of our strong men; and we are therefore all the more grieved, that at a moment when all our energies should be united in giving effect to the benevolent designs of our friends, his voice should be uplifted to strike a jarring note, or to awaken a feeling of distrust.

In respect to a national convention, we are for it—and will not only go "ten miles," but a thousand, if need be, to attend it. Away, therefore, with all unworthy flings on that score.—ED.[2]

PITTSBURGH, April 15th, 1853

... It is now certain, that the Rev. JOSIAH HENSON, of Dawn, Canada West, is the real *Uncle Tom*, the Christian hero, in Mrs. Stowe's far-famed book of "Uncle Tom's Cabin."[3] Mr. Henson is well known to both you and I, and what is said of him in Mrs. S.'s "Key," as far as we are acquainted with the man, and even the opinion we might form of him from our knowledge of his character, we know, or at least believe, to be true to the letter.

Now, what I simply wish to suggest to you, is this: Since Mrs. Stowe and Messrs. Jewett & Co.,[4] Publishers have realized so great an amount of money from the sale of a work founded upon this good old man, whose *living testimony* has to be brought to sustain this great book—and believing that the publishers have realized *five dollars* to the authoress' *one*—would it be expecting too much to suggest, that they—the *publishers*—present Father Henson—for by that name we all know him—with at least *five thous*—now, I won't name any

---

1   *a book ... colored people*   Douglass refers to Delany's *The Condition, Elevation, Emigration, and Destiny of the Colored People of the United States, Politically Considered* (1852).

2   *ED.*   Presumably "Editor;" i.e., Douglass.

3   *Rev. JOSIAH HENSON ... Uncle Tom's Cabin*   Josiah Henson (1789–1883) escaped slavery and fled to Canada in 1830, becoming a prominent black leader and abolitionist. His autobiography *The Life of Josiah Henson* (1849) was widely believed to have inspired Stowe's novel—a rumor which Stowe herself confirmed in 1853 in her *A Key to Uncle Tom's Cabin*, in which she defended the factual basis for her depictions of southern slavery.

4   *Messrs. Jewett & Co.*   Boston-based publishers of *Uncle Tom's Cabin*.

particular sum—but a portion of the profits? I do not know what you may think about it; but it strikes me that this would be but just and right.

I have always thought that George and Eliza were Mr. Henry Bibb and his first wife, with the character of Mr. Lewis Hayden, his wife Harriet and little son, who also effected their escape from Kentucky, under the auspices of Delia Webster, and that martyr philanthropist, Calvin Fairbanks, now incarcerated in a Kentucky State's prison dungeon.[1] I say the *person* of Bibb with the *character* of Hayden; because, in personal appearance of stature and color, as well as circumstances, Bibb answers precisely to George; while he stood quietly by, as he tells us in his own great narrative[2]—and it is a *great book*—with a hoe in his hand, begging his master to desist, while he *stripped his wife's clothes off (!!!)* and lacerated her flesh, until the blood flowed in pools at her feet! To the contrary, had this been Hayden—who, by the way, is not like Bibb nearly *white*, but *black*—he would have buried the hoe deep in the master's skull, laying him lifeless at his feet.

I am of the opinion that Mrs. Stowe has draughted[3] largely on all of the best fugitive slave narratives—at least on Douglass's, Brown's, Bibb's, and perhaps Clark's,[4] as well as the living household of old Father Henson; but of this I am not competent to judge, not having as yet *read* "Uncle Tom's Cabin," *my wife* having *told* me the most I know about it. But these draughts on your narratives, clothed in Mrs. Stowe's own language, only make her work the more valuable, as it is the more *truthful.*

The "negro language," attributed to Uncle Tom by the authoress, makes the character more natural for a slave; but I would barely state,

---

1 *Mr. Henry Bibb ... prison dungeon* Abolitionist Henry Bibb (1815–54) was born into slavery in Kentucky and fled to Canada; Lewis (1811–89) and Harriet Hayden (1816–93) also escaped slavery in Kentucky, aided by Underground Railroad operators Delia Webster (1817–1904) and Calvin Fairbank (1816–98). Webster and Fairbank both faced imprisonment for their activities, Webster for only two months, and Fairbank for a total of nineteen years over various periods.

2 *his own great narrative* Bibb's *Narrative of the Life and Adventures of Henry Bibb* (1849).

3 *draughted* Drawn upon; taken inspiration from.

4 *Douglass's ... Clark's* I.e.: Frederick Douglass's *Narrative of the Life of Frederick Douglass* (1845); William Wells Brown's *Narrative of William W. Brown* (1847); and Lewis G. Clarke's *Narrative of the Sufferings of Lewis Clarke* (1845).

that Father Josiah Henson makes use of as good language, as any one in a thousand Americans.

The probability is, that either to make the story the more affecting, or to conceal the facts of the old man's still being alive, Mrs. Stowe closed his earthly career in New Orleans; but a fact which the publishers may not know: *Father Henson is still a slave* by the laws of the United States—a fugitive slave in Canada. It may be but justice to him to say that I have neither seen nor heard directly or indirectly from Father Henson since September, 1851—then, I was in Toronto, Canada.

The person of Father Henson will increase the valuation of Mrs. Stowe's work very much in England, as he is well known, and highly respected there. His son, Josiah Henson, Jr., is still in England, having accompanied his father there in the winter of 1850.

I may perhaps have made freer use of your and the other names herein mentioned, than what was altogether consonant with your feelings; but I didn't ask you—that's all. Yours for God and Humanity,

M. R. DELANY

PITTSBURGH, April 18th, 1853

FREDERICK DOUGLASS, ESQ: DEAR SIR: ... In saying in my letter of the 22nd of March, that "Mrs. Stowe knows nothing about us—'the *Free* Colored People of the United States'—neither does any white person," I admit the expression to be ironical, and not intended to be taken in its literal sense; but I meant to be understood in so saying, that they know nothing, comparatively, about us, to the intelligent, reflecting, general observers among the Free Colored People of the North. And while I readily admit that I "know nothing about Mrs. Stowe," I desire very much to *learn* something of her; and as I could not expect it of Mrs. Stowe, to do so, were she in the country at present,[1] I may at least ask it of brother Douglass, and hope that he will neither consider it derogatory to Mrs. Stowe's position nor

---

1   *were she ... at present*   Stowe was at this time undertaking a promotional tour of England and continental Europe.

attainments, to give me the required information concerning her. I go beyond the mere point of asking it as a favor; I demand it as a right—from you I mean—as I am an interested party, and however humble, may put such reasonable questions to the other party—looking upon you, in this case, as the attorney of said party—as may be necessary to the pending proceedings.

First, then, *assertion*; is not Mrs. Stowe a *Colonizationist?*[1] having so avowed, or at least subscribed to, and recommended their principles in her great work of Uncle Tom.

Secondly; although Mrs. Stowe has ably, eloquently and pathetically[2] portrayed some of the sufferings of the slave, is it any evidence that she has any sympathy for his thrice-morally crucified, semi-free brethren anywhere, or of the *African race* at all; when in the same world-renowned and widely circulated work, she sneers at Haiti—the only truly free and independent civilized black nation as such, or colored if you please, on the face of the earth—at the same time holding up the little dependent colonization settlement of Liberia in high estimation? I must be permitted to draw my own conclusions, when I say that I can see no other cause for this singular discrepancy in Mrs. Stowe's interest in the colored race, than that one is independent of, and the other subservient to, white men's power.[3]

You will certainly not consider this idea *farfetched*, because it is true American policy; and I do not think it strange, even of Mrs. Stowe, for following in a path so conspicuous, as almost to become the principal public highway. At least, no one will dispute its being a *well-trodden path*. ...

Lastly; the Industrial Institution in contemplation by Mrs. Stowe, for the tuition of colored youth, proposed, as I understand it, the

---

1 *is not ... Colonizationist* Throughout the early- to mid-1800s, a number of movements—especially that led by the American Colonization Society, which founded Liberia—arose in the United States, encouraging free blacks to leave the country and colonize Africa. Those who supported such movements claimed that free blacks would have better opportunities abroad than in the United States. Stowe portrays emigration to Liberia positively in *Uncle Tom's Cabin*, though her thoughts on the issue changed over the years, and she eventually renounced colonization (partly as a result of her correspondence with Douglass).

2 *pathetically* Evoking pathos; affectingly.

3 *one is independent ... white men's power* Haiti had declared its independence from France following the black-led Haitian Revolution (1791–1804), while Liberia had declared its own independence from the United States in 1847—but the U.S. did not recognize either country's independence until 1862.

entire employment of white instructors. This I strongly object to, as having a tendency to engender in our youth a higher degree of respect and confidence for white persons than for those of their own color; and creates the impression that colored persons are incapable of teaching, and only suited to *subordinate* positions. I have observed carefully, in all of my travels in our country—in all the schools that I visited—colored schools I mean—that in those taught in whole or part by colored persons, the pupils were always the most respectful towards me, and the less menial in their general bearing. I do not object to white teachers in part; but I do say that wherever competent colored teachers could be obtained for any of the departments, they should be employed. Self-respect begets *due* obedience to others; and obedience is the first step to *self-government* among any people. Certainly, this should be an essential part of the training of our people, separated in interests as we have been, in this country. All the rude and abominable ideas that exist among us, in *preferences for color*, have been engendered *from the whites*, and in God's name, I ask them to do nothing more to increase this absurdity.

Another consideration, is, that all of the pecuniary advantages arising from this position go into the pockets of white men and women, thereby depriving colored persons, so far, of this livelihood. This is the same old song sung over again,

"Dimes and dollars—dollars and dimes."

And I will say, without the fear of offence, that nothing that has as yet been gotten up by our friends, for the assistance of the colored people of the United States, has even been of any pecuniary benefit to them. Our white friends take care of *that* part. There are, to my knowledge, two exceptions to this allegation—Douglass' printing establishment, and the "Alleghany Institute";[1] the one having a colored man at the head, and in the other, the assistant being a colored man. ...

Let me say another thing, brother Douglass; that is, that no enterprize, institution, or anything else, should be commenced *for us*, or our general benefit, without *first consulting us*. By this I mean consulting the various communities of the colored people in the United

---

1 *Alleghany Institute* College, later called Avery College after its white founder Charles Avery (1784–1858), offering higher education to African Americans; John Peck (1802–75), a black abolitionist, was among the school's board of trustees.

States, by such a correspondence as should make public the measure, and solicit their general interests and coincidence. In this way, the intelligence and desires of the whole people would be elicited, and an intelligent understanding of their real desires obtained. Other than this, is treating us as slaves, and presupposing us all to be ignorant, and incapable of knowing our own *wants*. Many of the measures of our friends have failed from this very cause; and I am fearful that many more will fail.

In conclusion, brother Douglass, let me say, that I am the last person among us who would wilfully "strike a jarring note, or awaken a feeling of distrust," uncalled for; and although you may pronounce it "unwise, ungraceful, and sounding high and mighty on paper"; as much high respect as an humble simple-minded person should have for them, and as much honored as I should feel in having such names enrolled as our benefactors—associated with our degraded position in society; believe me when I tell you, that I speak it as a son, a brother, a husband and a father; I speak it from the consciousness of oppressed humanity, outraged manhood, of a degraded husband and disabled father; I speak it from the recesses of a wounded bleeding heart—in the name of my wife and children, who look to me for protection, as the joint partner of our humble fireside; I say, if this great fund and aid are to be sent here to foster and aid the schemes of the American Colonization Society, as I say to you—I say with reverence, and an humbleness of feeling, becoming my position, with a bowed-down head, that the benevolent, great and good, the Duchess of Sutherland, Mr. Gurney, their graces the Earl of Shaftesbury and the Earl of Carlisle; had far better retain their money in the Charity Fund of Stafford House,[1] or any other place, than to send it to the United States for any such unhallowed purposes! No person will be more gratified, nor will more readily join in commendation, than I, of any good measure attempted to be carried out by Mrs. Stowe, if the contrary of her colonization principles be disproved. I will not accept *chains* from a king, any sooner than from a peasant; and never shall,

---

1   *Duchess of Sutherland … Stafford House*   The London home of Harriet Elizabeth Georgiana Sutherland-Leveson-Gower (1806–68) was the meeting place of many English abolitionists and other social activists, including Quaker philanthropist Joseph John Gurney (1788–1847), Anthony Ashley-Cooper, Earl of Shaftesbury (1801–85), and George Howard, Earl of Carlisle (1802–64).

willingly, submit to any measures for my own degradation. I am in hopes, brother Douglass, as every one else will understand my true position.

Yours for God and down-trodden Humanity,

M. R. DELANY

[6 May 1853]

The Letter of M. R. Delany [Published on the page preceding Delany's final letter.]

This letter is premature, unfair, uncalled for, and, withal, needlessly long; but, happily it needs not a long reply.

Can brother Delany be the writer of it?—It lacks his generous spirit. The letter is premature, because it attacks a plan, the details of which are yet undefined. It is unfair, because it imputes designs (and replies to them) which have never been declared. It is uncalled for, because there is nothing in the position of Mrs. Stowe which should awaken against her a single suspicion of unfriendliness towards the free colored people of the United States; but, on the contrary, there is much in it to inspire confidence in her friendship.

The information for which brother Delany asks concerning Mrs. Stowe, he has given himself. He says *she* is a colonizationist; and we ask, what if she is?—names do not frighten us. A little while ago, brother Delany was a colonizationist. If we do not misremember, in his book[1] he declared in favor of colonizing the eastern coast of Africa. Yet, we never suspected his friendliness to the colored people; nor should we feel called upon to oppose any plan he might submit, for the benefit of the colored people, on that account. We recognize friends wherever we find them.

Whoever will bring a straw's weight of influence to break the chains of our brother bondmen, or whisper one word of encouragement and

---

1 *his book* I.e., *The Condition, Elevation, Emigration, and Destiny of the Colored People of the United States, Politically Considered* (1852).

sympathy to our proscribed race in the North, shall be welcomed by us to that philanthropic field of labor. We shall not, therefore, allow the sentiments put in the brief letter of GEORGE HARRIS, at the close of *Uncle Tom's Cabin*,[1] to vitiate forever Mrs. Stowe's power to do us good. Who doubts that Mrs. Stowe is more of an abolitionist now than when she wrote that chapter?—We believe that lady to be but at the beginning of her labors for the colored people of this country.

Brother Delany says, nothing should be done for us, or commenced for us, without "consulting us." Where will he find "*us*" to consult with? Through what organization, or what channel could such consulting be carried on? Does he mean by consulting "*us*" that nothing is to be done for the improvement of the colored people in general, without consulting each colored man in the country whether it shall be done? *How many*, in this case, constitute "*us*"? Evidently brother Delany is a little unreasonable here.

Four years ago, a proposition was made, through the columns of *The North Star*,[2] for the formation of a "*National League*," and a constitution for said League was drawn up, fully setting forth a plan for united, intelligent and effective co-operation on the part of the free colored people of the United States—a body capable of being "*consulted*." The colored people, in their wisdom, or in their indifference, gave the scheme little or no encouragement—and it failed. Now, we happen to know that such an organization as was then proposed, was enquired for, and sought for by Mrs. Harriet Beecher Stowe; she wished, most of all, to hear from such a body *what could* be done for the *free colored people* of the United States? But there was no such body to answer.

The fact is, brother Delany, we are a disunited and scattered people, and very much of the responsibility of this disunion must fall upon such colored men as yourself and the writer of this. We want more confidence in each other, as a race—more self-forgetfulness, and less disposition to find fault with well-meant efforts for our benefit. Mr. Delany knows that, at this moment, he could call a respectable Convention of the free colored people of the Northern States. Why don't

---

1   *brief letter … Uncle Tom's Cabin*   At the end of the novel, the formerly enslaved George Harris emigrates to Liberia, and sends back a letter explaining and justifying his decision.

2   *The North Star*   Douglass's previous newspaper, which evolved into *Frederick Douglass' Paper* in 1851.

he issue his call? and he knows, too, that, were we to issue such a call, it would instantly be regarded as an effort to promote the interests of our *paper*. This consideration, and a willingness on our part to occupy an obscure position in such a movement, has led us to refrain from issuing a call. *The Voice of the Fugitive*, we observe, has suggested the holding, in New York, of a "World's Convention" during the "World's Fair."[1] A better proposition, we think, would be to hold in that city a "National Convention" of the colored people. Will not friend Delany draw up a call for such a Convention, and send it to us for publication?

But to return. Brother Delany asks, if we should allow *"anybody"* to undertake measures for our elevation? YES, we answer—anybody, even a slaveholder. Why not? Then says brother Delany, why not accept the measures of "Gurley and Pinney"?[2] We answer, simply because *their measures* do not commend themselves to our judgment. That is all. If "Gurley and Pinney" would establish an industrial college, where colored young men could learn useful trades, with a view to their becoming useful men and respectable citizens of the United States, we should applaud them and co-operate with them.

We don't object to Colonizations because they express a lively interest in the civilization and Christianization of Africa; nor because they desire the prosperity of Liberia; but it is because, like brother Delany, they have not sufficient faith in the people of the United States to believe that the black man can ever get justice at their hands on American soil. It is because they have systematically, and almost universally, sought to spread their hopelessness among the free colored people themselves; and thereby rendered them, if not contented with, at least resigned to the degradation which they have been taught to believe must be perpetual and immutable, while they remain where they are. It is because, having denied the possibility of our elevation here, they have sought to make good this denial, by encouraging the enactment of laws subjecting us to the most flagrant outrages,

---

1   *The Voice of the Fugitive*   Antislavery newspaper founded by Henry Bibb in Canada in 1851;   *World's Fair*   The Exhibition of the Industry of All Nations was held in New York in 1853.

2   *Gurley and Pinney*   Ralph Randolph Gurley (1797–1872) and John Brooke Pinney (1806–82), ministers in the Presbyterian Church and prominent members of the American Colonization Society.

and stripping us of all the safeguards necessary to the security of our liberty, persons and property. We say all this of the American Colonization Society; but we are *far* from saying this of many who speak and wish well to Liberia. As to the imputation that all the pecuniary profit arising out of the industrial scheme will probably pass into the pockets of the whites, it will be quite time enough to denounce such a purpose when such a purpose is avowed. But we have already dwelt too long on a letter which perhaps carried its own answer with it.

Visualizing *Uncle Tom's Cabin* in the Nineteenth Century

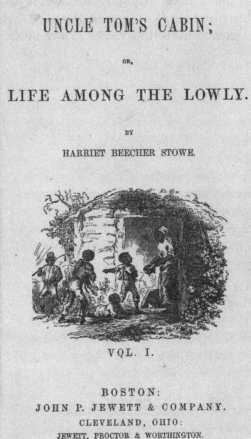

Frontispiece of the first edition of *Uncle Tom's Cabin*, which featured seven illustrations by Boston-based engraver Hammatt Billings (1818–74). Billings was already known for his work on the illustrated magazine *Gleason's Pictorial*, and in 1850 had redesigned the iconic masthead for the influential abolitionist newspaper *The Liberator*.

Hammatt Billings, *Little Eva Reading the Bible to Uncle Tom in the Arbor*, 1852. Billings's illustrations of the friendship between Eva and Uncle Tom were extremely influential and formed the basis for countless later visualizations of the novel.

Louisa Corbaux, *Eva and Topsy*, 1852. Colored lithograph.

UNCLE

TOM'S CABIN.

BY

HARRIET BEECHER STOWE.

WITH

Twenty-seven Illustrations on Wood

BY

GEORGE CRUIKSHANK, ESQ.

EVA AND TOPSY.

LONDON:

JOHN CASSELL, LUDGATE HILL.

1852.

Frontispiece to the 1852 London edition, illustrated by George Cruikshank. Earlier in his career, Cruikshank (1792–1878) was best known as a caricaturist, his cartoons often targeting the royal family, contemporary fashions, and political ideologies on either side of the spectrum; interestingly, many of his cartoons targeted the abolitionist movement in particular, and were highly racist. He turned increasingly to book illustration in the 1830s, providing illustrations for several novels by Charles Dickens. The London edition featured twenty-seven engravings designed by Cruikshank.

George Cruikshank, *Eliza Crosses the Ohio on the Floating Ice*, 1852.

George Cruikshank, *Topsy with Miss Ophelia's Wardrobe*, 1852.

White actor Caroline Howard in blackface as the character of Topsy in the 1852 stage adaptation of *Uncle Tom's Cabin*, written by George Aiken. The play was produced by Caroline's father, George C. Howard, who himself starred as George Harris; other members of the Howard family also acted in the play.

For Christmas 1852, Jewett and Co. commissioned a second edition of *Uncle Tom's Cabin*, a lavishly illustrated "gift book" featuring over one hundred new images by Hammatt Billings. One of the last images in the edition is this one depicting a crowd of freed people reaching towards the African continent. The narrative of George and Eliza Harris in the novel concludes with them emigrating to Liberia, a colony that had been established by white politicians expressly for freed African Americans. The first edition of *Uncle Tom's Cabin* had sold for around $1.50; the Christmas edition sold for $15.

Advertisement for the 1881 stage play *Jay Rial's Ideal Uncle Tom's Cabin.* Eliza's dramatic escape over the Ohio was among the most popular scenes for stage adaptations of the novel, which often featured live bloodhounds—even though Eliza is not pursued by dogs in this scene in the original novel.

From the Publisher

A name never says it all, but the word "Broadview" expresses a good deal of the philosophy behind our company. We are open to a broad range of academic approaches and political viewpoints. We pay attention to the broad impact book publishing and book printing has in the wider world; for some years now we have used 100% recycled paper for most titles. Our publishing program is internationally oriented and broad-ranging. Our individual titles often appeal to a broad readership too; many are of interest as much to general readers as to academics and students.

Founded in 1985, Broadview remains a fully independent company owned by its shareholders—not an imprint or subsidiary of a larger multinational.

To order our books or obtain up-to-date information, please visit broadviewpress.com.

broadview press
www.broadviewpress.com

This book is made of paper from well-managed FSC® - certified forests, recycled materials, and other controlled sources.